Apocalypse Drift

by

Joe Nobody

Edited by:
E. T. Ivester
Contributors:
D. Hall
D. Allen
www.holdingyourground.com

Other Books by Joe Nobody:

- Holding Your Ground: Preparing for Defense if it All Falls Apart
- The TEOTWAWKI Tuxedo: Formal Survival Attire
- Without Rule of Law: Advanced Skill to Help You Survive
- The Home Schooled Shootist – Training to fight with a carbine
- Holding Their Own: A Story of Survival
- Holding Their Own II: The Independents
- Holding Their Own III: Pedestals of Ash

From the Author

While this is a work of fiction, references to monetary policy, US federal budgets, the money supply, and general economics are accurate to the best of my knowledge. As I started researching this work, my intent was merely to provide a believable backdrop for a post-Apocalyptic novel, as well as a plausible resolution. As I delved deeper into the subject matter of federal revenue sources, budgeting, the Federal Reserve System and tax collections, I was forced to take the subject matter seriously.

Henry Ford is credited with saying, "It is well that the people of the nation do not understand our banking and monetary system, for if they did, I believe there would be a revolution before tomorrow morning." After my research, I think he was spot on.

After months of extensive investigation, I have yet to find a single explanation why the solutions postulated in this book wouldn't benefit our country today. The math is real. The numbers are real. Of course, you, the reader will be the final judge regarding the efficacy of the suggested resolution.

Joe Nobody

Prologue

Virginia Countryside
November 2016

The vast majority of leaves had fallen early this year, covering the forest floor with uneven ripples of burnt orange and soiled brown. Bare limbs and branches exposed the Virginia sky, now a bleached, cobalt gray, peppered with low rolling clouds – formations that a vivid imagination might paint as the ribs of some giant, heavenly beast. The steely sky and hibernating forest outside closely mimicked the uninviting atmosphere inside the van. Colorless, cold and practically devoid of sound, two men sat in silence, keeping vigil.

The minivan was about as dirt plain and common as it could be. Other than the darker-than-usual tint on the side panels of glass, there was nothing significant or noteworthy about the vehicle. It was like millions of such cars driven every day by families all across America. Even the color had been carefully selected – paint that appeared gold, or perhaps brown, maybe even tan in different light. The nondescript transport would be difficult for any witness to describe, let alone pinpoint an identifying characteristic.

Of Asian descent, the sentinels were in their mid-twenties and in excellent physical condition. Both wore custom-tailored suit jackets, complete with hand-sewn pleats to accommodate the holstered pistols beneath. Each man wore tight calfskin gloves that hadn't been removed since leaving their hotel room that morning. This was a precaution born purely of habit, since neither man's fingerprints were stored in any database, foreign or domestic. Both wanted to keep it that way, and besides, the gloves provided minimal warmth against the colder than normal November dusk.

The tone of a cell phone disturbed the calm. The prepaid, featureless unit had been purchased at a drugstore less than three hours ago with cash. The driver glanced at the device and pressed the green button, immediately moving the speaker to his ear.

"Five minutes," a male voice said in Mandarin.

The driver hit the red button, ending the call and then nodded at his passenger.

Precisely four minutes later, the van started. Making sure the headlights were switched off, the driver pulled the shift lever and slowly rolled down the abandoned, gravel lane where they were lurking.

A short distance in front of them laid the crest of a rise. Four hundred meters further and down a gradual slope, a blacktop county road wound its way through the remote countryside. The driver stopped the van just as the pavement came into view.

Right on time, the roadway below was illuminated by the glow of headlights, soon followed by a passing white Honda sedan. A few seconds later, the van pulled onto the asphalt, allowing for a suitable expanse of time and distance.

Hugging the shadows, the van tailed the white car. The operators knew exactly where the vehicle was going, who was driving, and why it was heading to the remote farmhouse. In fact, they knew practically everything about the young lady who steered the compact car through the rural countryside. Their purpose tonight was to add one remaining piece of critical information to her extensive dossier.

~  ~

Susan Wilkes zipped around the curves a little faster than normal. The traffic from Fairfax had been atrocious, and she detested arriving at the farm after the sun set. Lee would join her later, having the longer journey from Alexandria.

The thought of Lee's inevitable grumbling about traffic gridlock actually put a smile on her lips. When she reached the country house, she would heat water and set out the makings for tea. A steaming cup of ginseng brew would serve to mellow both of them after the hectic workweek and stressful commute to escape the city. The twenty-something computer specialist could barely believe her luck. She felt a sense of optimism that Lee might be Mr. Right. Until recently, Susie's dates had been with Mr. Right Now.

Maneuvering through the next curve, she recalled the first time Lee invited her to this retreat. Even though they had been dating for several weeks, she was cautious in accepting his offer. She couldn't help but hope that ultimately Lee and she would share a more permanent commitment. Was it too early for the two of them to spend a romantic weekend alone?

Initially, she'd considered it odd that such a metropolitan guy needed to "get away from it all and enjoy the fresh air of the countryside." It seemed unusual that such an experienced, well-traveled representative of a major Chinese trade organization would choose a rural property for a weekend sanctuary. His confessed love of horses was the clincher, the shy admission being both boyish and romantic. Growing up, Susie had always been fascinated by all things equestrian. Now she'd found someone who rekindled those childhood dreams. The wistful expression on her face betrayed her realization, *"A guy like that doesn't come along every day."*

Susie hoped that a relationship based on their shared interests would overcome Lee's traditional expectations of her.

She understood Lee's perspective was based on the incongruence between her progressive spirit and her physical appearance. "You're a paradox," he once told her. "You look and move like the most beautiful Chinese girl I've ever seen, yet you act, think and speak like an American."

"I'm an American," she had responded in her best country accent. "One hundred percent born and bred. If you're looking for one of those subservient Asian girls, you're barking up the wrong tree, cowboy."

Susie's mother escaped China as a teenage girl in 1989. Her grandparents were political dissidents, and the Catholic Church had smuggled the family out of the country. A short time later, The United States granted asylum to the refugees.

Susie's father was an American who met and fell in love with her mother in a college freshman English course. The two waited until after graduation to exchange vows, their first child debuting about a year later. With almond-shaped, mocha eyes and silky dark tresses, there was no doubt of Susan Li Wilkes' ancestry. Her mother's contribution to the gene pool dominated the girl's physical features, her slight build, and creamy skin indicative of generations of striking oriental women. Her father wasn't completely left out of her DNA sequence - Sue's strong-willed streak of independence being attributed to his influence.

Growing up in the suburbs of the nation's capital, Susie populated her slight expanse of urban sprawl with three rescued pups, a tabby cat, and two hamsters. Remembering an elementary school field trip to a working farm, she could still picture the beautiful horses that were the highlight of the outing. Then there had been Maryon, a college roommate whose family owned a stable. Sue smiled broadly, thinking about that summer spent riding and caring for the steeds. It had been hard, sweaty work, but she had loved every minute of it.

A stop sign made her focus on the here and now. After passing through the intersection, she wondered why she had ignored the interest since. "Life," she said to herself, "Life came rolling along and didn't leave time. Graduation...career...no time left to think about horses."

A short distance from the farm, Susie's mind drifted to an oft-visited subject – the possibility of a long-term future with Lee. Strikingly handsome, business savvy, and generous to a fault, he liked to surprise her with little gifts for no apparent reason. Never before had she met a man with whom she had so much in common. Susie had been waiting for a table at her favorite restaurant when Lee struck up a conversation with her. Turned out he was a fan of nouvelle cuisine, too. Sue was learning ink-and-wash landscape painting – a collection of the same artistic genre graced the walls of Lee's apartment.

"I never thought I would find someone who shared so many of my interests," she whispered to herself. "Maybe this is a sign that we are destined to be together." Before she could finish the thought, the brown and green mailbox announcing the farm's driveway came into the distant glow of the headlights.

Susie flipped on her turn signal despite the isolation, slowly negotiating the driveway.

Nestled in the foothills of the easternmost Appalachian Mountains, the farm was 40 acres of light forest and rolling meadow. The white clapboard home sported a broad, front porch, complete with a set of green metal chairs. Three huge oaks sprawled across the front yard, a few of the massive branches easy candidates for a rope swing. To the rear of the home sat a large barn, accented with a traditional metal roof and fire engine red paint. Whitewashed picket fences faded off into the dusk beyond the range of the Honda's headlights. A single florescent bulb, mounted high on a telephone pole, created a broad circle of light, shining down on the pebbly drive and parking area.

Susie parked in her usual spot and dug in her purse for the keys. She hit the button to open the trunk and retrieved the small overnight bag that held all her needs for the weekend. One of the horses whinnied from the barn, no doubt hearing the activity by the house.

For a moment, Sue was tempted to go to the barn first. It was probably Baygirl who had sounded off – the chestnut mare being her favorite. *No*, she thought, *I'll give her an apple later. Right now, I want to change out of these clothes and heat the tea water before Lee gets here.*

Susie retrieved her bag and slung it alongside her purse. As she strolled toward the back door, the slight noise of a shoe scuffing on gravel startled her. She started to turn toward the sound when the world went black.

"Lee" had actually been at the farmhouse all that day. His name wasn't Lee; he didn't work for any import business, and he wasn't from Washington. He *was* Chinese. Lee opened the back door, glad the waiting was finally over, this long mission near its end.

The two men from the van carried Susie into the kitchen via armpits and ankles, the slight girl's weight hardly perceptible to either man. They headed to the master bedroom and ungraciously flopped the young woman onto the double bed. A sheet of plastic had been spread across the otherwise bare mattress; four strands of nylon cord were used to secure her limbs to the corners.

"She will wake in approximately ten minutes," informed the passenger from the van. "Her head will clear. You should administer the first injection before she is conscious for the best effect."

The driver nodded to the bedside table where a black bag rested, its sinister contents appearing out of place in contrast to the crisp, white lace doily. "Use no more than 4mg of the serum every six hours or her heart will stop. The needles are an extra fine gauge so the puncture will be difficult to detect.

Remember to use the salve on each jab immediately afterwards. She is healthy, so evidence of the injections should resolve quickly."

Lee nodded his understanding, and without further conversation, the men left the house. Lee watched as the first man drove off in Susie's Honda. He was immediately followed by his associate, driving the van. They pulled out of the driveway without even a backward glance.

Returning to the master, Lee picked up a syringe and drew 3mg of a brownish liquid into the tube. He lifted Susie's skirt to mid-thigh and injected the entire dose into the muscle of her leg. He placed the needle back on the table and then moved a chair to the bedside, waiting on the results of his handiwork.

Swimming colors and swirling clouds crowded Susie's field of vision. Her stomach felt warm and comfortable; her limbs were numb. It was a few moments before she realized her eyes were closed, but that was okay. The scenery unfolding before her was spectacular and unlike anything she had ever seen.

Eventually, curiosity crept into her mind, and she opened her eyes to see what wonders that would bring. She found Lee sitting beside her, a look of concern on his face.

"Hi," her voice sounding whispery in her own ears, "what's going on?"

"I'm glad you're finally awake," he said in a serious tone. "I've been worried sick about you."

"Ohhhh," she cooed, "I'm just fine. As a matter of fact, I've never felt better. Not to complain, but how did I end up in here?"

"Well, I'm not really sure, but I think one of the horses must have kicked you in the head. I found you lying in the barn. I couldn't get cell service out here to call for help, so I carried you into the house to take care of you."

Susie had an overwhelming sense of well-being, coupled with a mental fog that made unscrambling Lee's story impossible. She wanted to move her arm and touch her head, but the limb wouldn't respond. It took a bit of effort, but she eventually managed to look toward her right wrist, noting it was bound. She then checked her other limbs, finding them all in a similar state. She smiled knowingly. "Why Lee, I didn't know you were so kinky."

Lee grunted, but kept his voice serious. "I had to restrain you, Susie. You were convulsing and thrashing around. I was afraid you would hurt yourself."

Again, his comment bewildered the girl. She was trying to sort it all out, but the drug flowing through her veins made concentrating impossible. She decided to close her eyes and succumb to the pretty color show again.

Throughout the night and all day Saturday, the injections continued to violate Susie's body. Her mind became foggier, as the dosage was gradually increased. Lee fed her crackers with water, the prescribed method for keeping her brain euphoric, untroubled about hunger or thirst. The restraints had become unnecessary, and blankets were issued. There were even a few comical, bumbling adventures involving the bathroom.

By late Saturday afternoon, the Chinese man believed her mental state had decayed to the point that she would believe almost anything. He sat in the bedside chair and gently rubbed his prisoner's cheek to bring her into the here and now.

"Susie," he began. "Your boss from the IRS called. He expressed concern and asked me to let you know they are all thinking about you - hoping you'll get better soon."

"That's so sweet of them," was the groggy response.

"Susie, he asked about your computer password at the office. He said he needed access to your computer while you are healing."

"My password?"

"Yes. They want to know where you keep your work and what the password is."

"Ohhhh. My password is Baygirl01," she said giggling. "Like the horse that kicked me. My work is stored in the projects directory on the 'D' drive."

"Okay Susie, I'll call back and let him know. They all send their best wishes. You can go back to sleep now."

Lee pushed back the chair and moved to the kitchen. His cell phone dialed a predetermined number, and he relayed the information provided.

The minivan followed the Honda into the Fairfax apartment complex. The Honda parked in Susie's numbered spot, as it had so many times before. The van selected an empty visitor's space close to the entrance. To the casual observer, Susie exited the sedan and approached the van. In reality, the charlatan was an inch shorter, seven years older and five pounds lighter. Without makeup, the two women didn't look anything alike. The perfect haircut, makeup, and eyebrow shaping helped create the illusion – high heels, padding and use of Susie's wardrobe rounded out the disguise.

The woman was handed Susie's purse, the contents of which were undisturbed except for the addition of a handwritten note, documenting a computer password and storage address.

Before the Susie-like female made it to the apartment door, the van was gone.

~  ~

Monday morning, Susie's Honda arrived promptly at the IRS's Fairfax data processing center. The driver exited and locked the car as normal and then proceeded to join the cue waiting to clear security. The line of federal employees looked like any other group of office workers heading in to start a new week. Carrying newspapers under their arms, sipping steaming cups of coffee, and adjusting the shoulder straps of computer bags, the government personnel slowly snaked through the screening process. The sleepy Monday morning routine looked harmless enough, but the imposter knew this wasn't the case. It was casual gatherings such as this that might prompt a co-worker to initiate a conversation. She knew there was little chance she could hold up her end of any such exchange, especially if the person knew Susie well. That would attract attention, potentially leading to discovery. To improve the odds, the pretender held a smartphone in both hands, thumbs moving rapidly as if texting and eyes holding rapt attention on the tiny screen. She prayed the effect would make her less approachable.

When it was her turn, the young Asian woman placed her purse on the x-ray machine's rolling belt and then inserted Susie's ID card into the proper slot. A few nervous seconds later, she heard a humming noise, punctuated by the metallic sound of a latch being disengaged, and the revolving turnstile was free.

Two months ago, Lee had installed a GPS tracking software on Susie's phone. The spying device had recorded Susie's movements and voice conversations. The stand-in had studied her movements, stance, and voice recordings. Her performance was worthy of an Academy Award.

After retrieving her purse, the woman avoided the elevators, choosing the less traveled staircase instead. Two flights up, she exited to the right, striding just a little too deliberately to a cubicle. When a mere ten minutes passed, she removed the 32-gigabyte thumb-drive from the workstation and switched off the computer.

The replacement Susie retrieved her purse and immediately stepped to the ladies' restroom, choosing a stall and securing the door. Taking a seat, the impersonator withdrew a small envelope of green powder from her jacket pocket. Holding the mixture of herbs and spices close to her nose, she inhaled deeply and then relaxed, waiting on the effect.

Within the hour, the snorted concoction began to do its job. The woman's throat became irritated and her vocal cords constricted. Her now raspy voice was accompanied by red, puffy, watering eyes and a sniffling nose. Gathering her wits, she proceeded to execute the most difficult part of the mission. Approaching the supervisor's office door, she casually looked inside to verify the boss was at his desk. Three raps sounded on the doorframe, causing the middle-aged man to look up from his paperwork.

"Good morning, Susan, how was your weekend?"

This was it – the hardest part. The substitute's heart raced in her chest, and she could feel her cheeks flushing, adding to the powder's effect. She dabbed at the moisture in the corner of her eyes, and her voice sounded terrible. "It was fine – thanks for asking. I think I've caught something though. I don't feel very well."

A look of concern crossed the supervisor's face. "I saw a report on the news last night, and flu season is in full swing. I think you should see a doctor – take a few days and get some rest."

The conversation was going just as they had predicted it would during her briefing. Her pulse slowed and confidence sat in. "Yes, I think that's a good idea."

The replacement then lowered her head slightly. In a low voice she continued, "Thank you for the concern."

Spinning his chair quickly to open a file drawer, the man pulled the proper form out of the cabinet. "Take as long as you need, Susan. I hope you feel better soon. I'll fill this out and take it to human resources today."

She responded with the perfect viral sequence. A sniffle and sneeze, followed by the unmistakable sound of her blowing her nose all preceded the weak, "Thank you."

"No problem, Ms. Wilkes; go on home and get well."

Ten minutes later, the White Honda pulled out of the parking lot.

Within an hour, a complete copy of the IRS's computer source code was being transmitted, routed, and re-routed over the internet. The final destination - Beijing.

Four days passed when a county sheriff's deputy pulled into the farm's driveway. The man hired to feed and care for the horses detected a horrible smell of death coming from the barn and found Susie's body. He notified the sheriff's office immediately.

Susie was discovered in the barn next to Baygirl's stall. The back of her head had been crushed by what appeared to be a kick from the nearby horse.

Section One

The Downdraft

Chapter 1

AP Press Release – Oakland, California – U.S.A. 08:00 *December* **1, 2016**
Oakland's Police Commissioner, Roger T. McLain, announced today that
the city is issuing a warning to visitors of California's eighth largest city.

Commissioner McLain explained that the police force is no longer
capable of protecting tourists and other visitors to the area. The 30-year
veteran lawman detailed the situation during a press conference held
this morning at city hall. According to McLain, the warning is
precipitated by a series of events that have unfolded over the last three
months. "A combination of budget cuts, a depressed economy, and the
resulting rise in violent crime degraded my department's ability to
respond to emergency situations. Unless absolutely necessary, we are
advising casual travelers, sightseers and vacationers to avoid Oakland
until a resolution can be found."

The Greater Oakland Chamber of Commerce protested the
announcement, calling on city hall to do its job and provide protection
to residents, businesses, and area visitors. "This announcement will only
serve to further damage economic interests in the community. The
police department has lost several lawsuits in the last few months due
to its own incompetence, and this is just a kneejerk reaction," stated
Bernard Winslow, spokesman for the organization.

Other experts agreed with Mr. Winslow's assessment. Global statistics
released by the United Nations Office on Drugs and Crime indicate that
Oakland's safety rank is comparable to some third-world nations. A rash
of robberies, homicides, and other gang-related violence has plagued
the bay area city for the last few years. State and federal courts have
awarded huge sums to the victims and families. The city reported its

insurance premiums have increased more than 300% in the last two years alone.

Oakland isn't the first metropolitan area to resort to such drastic measures. Detroit's Chief of Police issued a similar warning in 2012. In 2014, Trenton, New Jersey attempted to privatize that city's law enforcement, resulting in several months of chaos. During that period, curfew restrictions all but eliminated visitors to the east coast city.

In 2013, Chicago invoked a similar warning for the south side of the nation's third largest city. Escalating drug-related violence triggered record numbers of homicides in the Windy City that year.

The National Federation of Law Enforcement Officers places the blame squarely on staff reductions. The NFLEO issued a statement today, citing an overall reduction of 119,000 officers from 2010 levels throughout the continental United States. Ongoing budget difficulties, erosion of the tax base, inflation, and seven years of recession initiated these deep cutbacks.

Beijing, China
January 11, 2017

Wu Ling Chi leaned back in the chair, careful not to tip over the rickety contraption. Despite his meager 27 years, he was fatigued, aching, and even a little cramped here and there. He stretched his arms over his head while arching his lower back, but the discomfort stubbornly prevailed. He peered at his watch and smirked. It was no wonder he hurt; he hadn't stirred from the computer workstation for over six hours. He tried rotating his head in small circles, but that didn't offer any relief. Neither did massaging his temples. *Working this long is nothing new*, he thought. *You're turning into an old grandmother*. Always logical to a fault, his own words caused him to laugh aloud. *Are there any young grandmothers?* Pushing away from the desk, Wu stood slowly, blankly peering around the tiny, windowless office.

In the Chinese Ministry of State Security, or MOSS as it was known in Western security circles, having an office was nothing extraordinary. Having an office *with a window* was an indication of achievement. Wu hoped the results of his latest efforts would lead to such perks, perhaps more. Having a window would make the protracted days at his desk more tolerable, with the added benefit of quietly announcing to his co-workers that he was of value to the

Party. Perhaps, he would even be allocated an apartment with more square meters of space on a higher floor. The elevation meant less traffic noise from the bustling boulevards of Beijing, where every day more and more automobiles raced through the streets. Wu sneered at the thought, as his demanding work schedule meant he never spent any time in his apartment anyway. What real difference would a larger flat make?

Wu moved to the small, open area in front of the table that served as his desk. He gingerly twisted his body at the hips, hoping to eradicate the kink in his lower back. Despite his stiff frame and growling stomach, Wu was basking in a sense of self-worth. He could only hope his superiors agreed with his assessment. This closet-office was going to drive him insane if he had to work in here much longer.

There were no pictures, certificates, or other personal effects in the workspace. Such trinkets were expressly forbidden at MOSS. The bare walls were painted bureaucratic hospital green, no doubt intended to surround the occupant with a relaxing harmonic and to promote efficiency. A single guest chair and a locked metal file cabinet rounded out the contents of the space. About the only item that provided any flavor to his eye was the state-of-the-art computer equipment residing on the table. Updated just a short time ago, the hardware had been imported from one of the huge Japanese conglomerates that had no idea of its intended use and probably wouldn't have cared anyway. The thought of a greedy, capitalist computer salesman enjoying the benefits of profit made Wu shake his head. *The West was full of such short-term thinking, and it would be their downfall.* The irony of his foe providing the weapons he would use to crush them was not lost on Wu. A vision of the sloppy Yat Boon Gau (*Japanese Dog*) whoring with women while overindulging in food and wine flashed through his head. The civilized Chinese would triumph as they always have.

The sound of a turning doorknob interrupted Wu's mental victory lap.

Wu turned as the door opened vigorously, and his jang chuan (boss) appeared in the threshold. "Greetings, Team Leader Yangdong."

The older man was in his mid-thirties and carried himself with military air. His tunic was neatly pressed, plain black loafers recently shined, trouser crease razor sharp. Yangdong's shoulders were squared, and his neck appeared as though it were attached to his torso with a steel rod. There was no smile or greeting from the visitor. He took a single, measured step into the office, promptly closed the door behind himself, and then spoke. "Analyst Wu, your report, please."

Wu cleared his throat, "Comrade Yangdong, the results of our latest efforts are better than anticipated. The Americans have not yet discovered the intrusion. As of one hour ago, no countermeasures have been detected. We are ready to implement the next step."

Wu's report elicited an unusual response from his boss. Yangdong's right hand moved to his chin, stroking his clean-shaven jawbone while lost in thought. Wu had anticipated his team leader would thank him as usual, and immediately exit the office. This had been the daily routine since the inception of the project almost four years ago. Not today. His superior appeared to be surprised by the report, and was mentally exploring its implications.

After a few moments, Yangdong's eyes narrowed, focusing harshly on Wu. "You are absolutely certain of this report, Analyst Wu?"

"Yes comrade, there is no doubt."

Houston, Texas
January 12, 2017

Wyatt pulled into the driveway without even realizing he was home. He'd been so focused on the financial reports streaming on the radio; he couldn't recall navigating the last few blocks. He parked in front of a suburban residence that had been the family's home for more than 14 years. The car's engine idled while he listened to the last of the broadcast.

Even when the announcer began his rant about the Rockets' latest trade for an overpriced power forward, Wyatt didn't move. His mind was completely occupied, digesting what he had just heard. Today's grim inflation reports catapulted the stock market into a steep nosedive this morning. A lot of people had been momentarily crippled by the news. Gold was going nuts, and three major banks announced an increase in their prime interest rates. Other financial institutions were expected to follow.

Wyatt rubbed his eyes using his thumb and index finger. He turned off the car and leaned back in the seat, a deep sigh escaping. *The timing of this couldn't be worse*, he grunted.

He stepped out of the vehicle, closing the door in a single, robotic motion. A year ago, he would have slammed it shut with gusto, but not anymore. Wave after wave of bad news, bad luck, and bad decisions had taken the fight out of him - he simply didn't have the energy anymore. Besides, the old jalopy probably didn't have a lot of door slamming left in it.

He initially turned for the mailbox, but then reconsidered. The postman never delivered good news anymore, and after the report on the radio, Wyatt didn't have the heart. He knew the box would contain a dozen or so letters from bill collectors demanding their money, threatening late fees, and reminding him how badly his credit would be affected if he didn't call them soon. That final threat always provided a little comic relief. *There's nothing anyone could do to make my credit score any worse. Why do they even bother with that crap?*

Opting instead for the front door, Wyatt's path crossed the high grass and weeds in the yard. The overgrowth reminded him of the need to check on the lawnmower. It wouldn't start last Sunday, and he needed to tinker with it. *Cutting my own grass is just a sign of the times*, he told himself. A year ago, a yard crew groomed the lawn, shrubs, and edging. They weren't expensive in the grand scheme of things, but when the decision came down to paying the yard guys or buying groceries - eating won handily. On loan from a friend, the secondhand lawnmower had kept the neighborhood association and their nasty, reprimanding letters at bay. Those notices always included the mandatory threat of a fine if he didn't comply with the association's idea of a neat and tidy lawn. He hesitated at the front stoop, remembering an even better reason to mow – they were having another garage sale this Saturday.

Wyatt stuck his key in the door's lock and entered the house. Warm air hit his face, eliciting a grimace at the thought of having to reopen all of the windows. They didn't run the air conditioner any more – cool air being another victim of his financial position. At least the late winter weather in Houston was bearable today, a paltry 70 degrees outside. Wyatt didn't know what they were going to do in a few months when things became seriously hot and humid in the Bayou city. The heat in southeast Texas had been known to kill those without climate control.

Wyatt started his grand tour of the house, flipping latches and tugging at window frames. There must have been a threat of rain this morning. That's the only reason why Morgan would have closed them all before leaving for work. His wife disliked that muggy feeling more than he did. The house was stuffy, and he hoped it wouldn't take long before the hot changed places with the cool. The sun would be going down in a little bit, and it might actually get comfortable enough to doze off tonight. He made sure the master bedroom's glass was wide open.

Out of habit, he grasped the TV remote, hoping to fill in more details of the day's foreboding financial reports via cable news. He stopped just as his thumb moved to press the power button – they didn't have cable anymore. The provider had disconnected their service a little over a month ago, and he hadn't had time to hook up the rabbit ears.

All of this was so new to Wyatt and his family. Some 18 years ago, he established a small accounting and financial services firm. Its customer base increased steadily. Three years ago, the company reached its peak, providing employment for 32 workers. Growing a small business hadn't always been a bed of roses. While there had been periods when money was tight, those lean spells were normally offset by generous bonuses later. Walking the tightrope of expanding his corporate blueprint versus raising his family's standard of living constantly challenged Wyatt. It seemed like every time Morgan and he put a little money back, some company emergency required a reinvestment of their savings.

It wasn't always bad news or cash flow problems that motivated them to empty their reserves into the firm. There were times when expansion or improvements depended on cash. After remitting an ever-increasing rent for 10 years, Wyatt decided the firm's office space should be one of those improvements. An intense search resulted in acquiring a modest building in a stable section of town. The sales price was $1 million even. Morgan reluctantly agreed to allocate a chunk of their savings for the down payment. Wyatt never minded writing a check for the mortgage – it was an investment in their future. He thought of the equity in the building like a savings account.

Wyatt had always placed a high value on real estate. Reasoning that, "They aren't making any more of it," Wyatt convinced Morgan that the majority of their savings should be invested in property. He didn't believe in anything speculative or risky, just conservative, practical assets. The couple purchased the largest house they could afford in an up and coming neighborhood, thinking that it would increase in value over the years and become a wise investment. That financial plan worked well for over a decade. No one could have predicted home values would plummet in such an unprecedented manner.

The Houston Sunday paper contained a graph in the real estate section showing property appraisals in various parts of the city. Wyatt could be found with a calculator on many a Sunday afternoon, estimating the current value of his home and office investments. Until recently, the news had always been good.

Anyone who knew Wyatt and his family pictured them as a fine example of the American dream. Casual observers took note the sizeable home, nice cars, boat, wonderful vacations, and successful business. It was all real – an accomplishment by any measure.

Their financial situation began changing in 2010. Wyatt thought Hemingway described it best in one of his old novels. When asked, "How did you go bust?" the character answered, "Slowly at first, and then quickly." *I resemble that remark*, Wyatt thought. In that tragic year, clients began to pay late, claiming their business was down. Others never paid at all and closed their doors, still owing Wyatt thousands of dollars. New clients were very difficult to find, and competitors continually lowered their rates to win new business.

At the time, Wyatt believed he'd seen it all before. This wasn't the first economic downturn he had steered his little company through, and it wouldn't be the last. He had navigated these choppy waters and was familiar with them. He controlled expenses, reduced staff, and cut benefits. No matter how tightly he ran the ship, each month became more of a challenge to meet payroll and pay the bills. The business struggled to keep afloat, Wyatt and his family suffering as much as anyone on the payroll.

It was the banks and government regulation that ultimately pushed the firm over the edge. Wyatt had used credit in the past to keep his business solvent during rough times. When new banking regulations were passed, the bar was raised for creditworthiness. Wyatt's little company didn't qualify with the new restrictions.

In many respects, Wyatt felt as if the business were one of his children. Like any parent with a dying child, he pulled out all the stops. The family's life savings, college funds, IRAs – everything went back into the company, hoping to keep it buoyant until things got better. It wasn't enough. Wyatt fought like a cornered tiger, but nothing worked. Over a four-day period, he visited 16 different banks with a financing proposal and business plan in hand. He borrowed money from relatives, friends, and anyone else who he thought could help. Despite all his efforts, cash flow continued its downward spiral.

The business still had customers, but not enough of them paid on time. A true numbers man, Wyatt recognized that if only his accounts receivable were current, his business would be flourishing. The firm doubled its collection efforts, diverting resources from other departments to assist in the effort. But like a struggling momma bird flying back to the nest with a scrawny little worm, it just wasn't enough for all the hungry beaks.

The final blow came on a fateful Tuesday afternoon. He returned from lunch and noticed the few remaining employees standing outside of the company's office building. The bank had arrived with a sheriff's deputy. They had changed the locks.

His initial reaction was actually relief. It was finally over. No more stalking the postman every day to see if a client's promised payment had arrived. No more employee meetings to tell struggling co-workers that paychecks were going to be late. No more worrying whether the power failure was due to the volatile thunderstorm or the utility company fed up with not being paid on time. No more business.

Most people expected Wyatt's reaction to the repossession to be fiery, an emotional protest. Everyone waited, anticipating he would explode like a bursting balloon. When the bank's vice president explained his position, Wyatt stood motionless, paralyzed by the news. After a few moments, his shoulders slumped, and he sauntered slowly back to his car without another word. The bank's needle had little effect on the balloon that was already leaking air.

After regrouping from the shock of the foreclosure, Wyatt acted on what he considered to be the only avenue left - the last glimmer of hope. A larger firm had been considering acquiring Wyatt's business. He still had a few loyal customers and *some* revenue. What little value was left in his company wasn't big money by any measure. Still, his remaining employees would have a job, and Wyatt would receive a paycheck for at least a year during the transition.

The potential buyer was at the stage of raising financing. The partners in the firm had been waiting on an answer from their bank. Today's news regarding interest rates wasn't good. Deep down inside, Wyatt knew that radio report just changed his future.

~ ~

Minister Hong was in a foul mood. The chicken served at lunch was stringy and tasteless, and the tea was tepid at best. When the politburo appointed him as MOSS' headman two years ago, he had humbly accepted the position with only minimal expectations. One such anticipation was a properly prepared lunch. He couldn't see any justification for eating a bad meal in these prosperous times.

The minister had consumed enough substandard dishes to qualify as a food critic. He acquired his expertise early in life, born into a peasant family of rice farmers in the Jilin Province of northeast China. As a child, availability of food and variety in diet were elusive. His parents worked hard and did the best they could, but full stomachs were the exception.

By the time he was six years old, he astounded his schoolmarm by speaking fluent English, Mandarin Chinese, and French. Communist party officials whisked him from his small village to the provincial capital to quantify his gift. His math, science, and analytical skills were only slightly above normal, but his brain's capability to absorb and process the intricacies of language was off the scale.

Such a talent quickly drew the attention of the Central Communist Party. At that time, during the late 1960s, China was desperately trying to climb from behind the shadow of the Soviet Union and establish its own presence in the world. Nixon had just visited the most populated nation on the planet, and a great thawing of international acceptance was underway. China needed people who could quickly become confident in foreign dialects for trade, diplomacy and most importantly of all – espionage.

By that time, MOSS was rapidly advancing to the top tier of the recruiting hierarchy. Still underfunded, with only a regional presence, the leadership of the Red Nation was beginning to give weight to the advantages of a strong intelligence service. That realization elevated MOSS' position on the ladder of funding, influence, and ability to tap the nation's talent pool. The young man from the remote province was transferred into the best conservatories and closely monitored by the agency until his graduation. Hong's command of English, combined with an unwavering belief in the communist ideology, made him the perfect candidate to recruit.

Hong's first assignment took him to British-controlled Hong Kong. A faction within the Central Bank of China was beginning to grasp the power of currency manipulation. The government possessed few experts who understood the complexities of international finance, and the city's reputation as the "World's Fair of Food" made the assignment more palatable.

After establishing himself as a reliable agent, a string of foreign assignments soon followed. Hong served his masters in Australia, where the glass noodles had the consistency of cardboard. East Germany and the Soviet Union followed, complete with food so putrid, the thin man actually lost weight. Were it not for a six-month mission in Singapore, he would have surely died of malnutrition.

His mundane missions always involved either industrial espionage or international finance. MOSS didn't have the same modus operandi as the famous British, American, and Soviet intelligence services. There were few, if any, gunfights, kidnappings, or adrenaline pumping border crossings. In fact, risk avoidance was always a high priority. Chinese leadership was calculating and in no immediate hurry to dominate the world arena. Most senior members of the party fully comprehended the fact that economic supremacy would override military power in the long run. These men sensed the shark-like hunger of the world's more mature economies to access their country's considerable consumer base. One minister compared Western companies to a groom waiting to ravish his new bride; such was the lust to enter Chinese markets. Hong became one of the thousands who assisted the country in manipulating this blind greed to China's advantage.

His foul mood was further stimulated by the worker sitting across from him. Yangdong wasn't one of his favorite people. The team leader's desk was littered with remnants from street side food carts, and his table manners were just short of offensive. He was obviously a clod who could never appreciate the value of a good meal. Such unsophisticated, shallow thinking would surely limit his career. Still, the supervisor's performance record was adequate, and the burgeoning workload on the ministry was such that making changes at this point in time was unwise.

"You wished to see me, Team Leader Yangdong," Hong stated, more that asked.

The man seemed excited in his own way, "Yes, Minister. Operation Golden Mountain is progressing ahead of schedule. The results of stage one have been verified, and we are ready to begin the next phase. This step, of course, requires your approval."

Hong leaned back in his chair. Other than this neutral action, he showed no emotion. *The man is so good at hiding his inner thoughts*, studied Yangdong, *I envy his strength. No wonder he is the minister.*

In reality, the head of MOSS was riding a tidal wave of emotion, ranging from excitement to pure joy. Golden Mountain was one of his pet projects. He had sheltered its funding and resources like a mother bear protecting her cubs. Now, this distasteful man was telling him the plan was ready to be implemented. A celebration was in order. He would have the concierge recommend the latest in upscale Cantonese fare. This report was a long time in coming, and his mind could determine best how to proceed while enjoying a well-prepared meal.

January 13, 2017
Washington, D.C.

The Marriner S. Eccles Federal Reserve building has been a landmark in Washington, D.C. since 1937, but didn't receive its name until 1982. Forty-five years after it was finished, an act of Congress dedicated the imposing Constitution Avenue edifice to a former chairman of the Federal Reserve System, and the magnificent structure finally had a name. With an exterior of marble quarried in northeastern Georgia, the building had been designed in the mid-1930s as the primary meeting place for the 12-member board of directors. Over the years, several original nicknames described the imposing, four-story structure from "The Mount Olympus of Money," to "The Temple of Tender."

Representative Reed Wallace was touring the building with a small entourage of freshmen congressmen. Recently elected in the newly formed Texas 39th district, the Dallas-based lawyer and businessman was more attentive to this building than any of the others they had explored so far. Part of his campaign promise was to support a full audit of the Federal Reserve System, and he was looking forward to seeing the enemy camp.

The guide continued, "Today, we are in for a special treat. The main lobby was closed to daily traffic in the 1980s, but will be accessible for our group. Please follow me."

As the touring politicians ambled up the marble steps, two uniformed security guards opened the heavy bronze and glass doors. Reed had traveled to Washington many times before. He had always been impressed at how government buildings were designed to project power and security. He supposed it had been that way since Roman times. *Your government is stable, powerful, and in charge. Don't worry – and don't challenge us,* he reiterated to himself.

After finishing an uneventful walk-thru of the Eccles building, the rookie policymakers continued their whirlwind excursion through Washington, receiving a cursory introduction to the more celebrated landmarks. It was late afternoon by the time the small bus parked behind the capitol building and unloaded the smiling politicians and their families. Reed was still full of energy and eager to return to his office. He glanced at his watch and decided if he hurried, he could make it there before most of the staffers left for the day. He was anxious to get started and maintain the momentum of the election victory. Seeing none of the familiar, yellow taxis at the curb, Reed opted to walk the few blocks to his temporary offices, stretching his legs in the process. His campaign manager had secured a small space at a nearby hotel and arranged for the new representative's staff to move in. For a January day, the weather in Washington was actually quite mild, so the Texan set off, eating up the distance with long strides over the concrete sidewalks of the nation's capital.

Reed's desire to be a member of the federal government was, in truth, motivated by vendetta. His father had been a small town banker, honest and respected by the community. Reed had been practicing his jump shot when the older Wallace received a call, offering him a position at the Federal Reserve

Bank. The compensation package easily outdistanced anything the local community bank could promise; it was the proverbial offer that he just couldn't refuse.

Everything had gone well for four years, with Mr. Wallace being promoted every so often and generally enjoying his work. A pre-law student, Reed was in his junior year at The University of Texas when his father called that fateful day.

In retrospect, Reed could easily recognize there were so many things wrong with the conversation that day; he was a little ashamed it hadn't dawned on him at the time. He remembered his father's tone was troubled, the cadence of his words rushed. "Reed, I'm driving to Austin. I need to talk to someone about this. Can you skip a class and meet me?"

Reed, puzzled by the unprecedented visit, agreed. He was concerned something was wrong between his mom and dad.

His dad's journey fell short of the capital city. The next morning, the family Volvo was spotted in a truck stop parking lot, his father slumped slightly over the steering wheel. Blood trickled from his temple, and his wallet was missing.

The police wrote it off as a robbery, and eventually Reed accepted that conclusion as well. After his father was buried, the family and community mourned the loss for weeks. Reed eventually returned to school, graduating summa cum laude. Three weeks before commencement, he was recruited by a small, but growing law firm in Plano.

Over the years, the pain from his father's murder faded, but his memory of the man never did. Reed married, had children of his own, and lived the lifestyle of a successful man. There was little stress in his life until he met Mr. Agile.

It was a sizzling mid-June morning when the consultation was calendared with a prospective client. With the economic troubles hindering the nation, Reed's firm had seen a spike in business. It seemed like every contract, purchase, lease, or other corporate transaction was being scrutinized to an extreme level these days. No executive officer of any company wanted to risk a deal going south or a surprise clause adding unanticipated expense later on.

Reed strolled into the conference room that day expecting another review of a real estate lease or tax issue. Mr. Agile desired no such services from the firm.

As he walked through the streets of Washington, Reed replayed the entire meeting in his head.

Mr. Agile was a very old man, at least 80, if not 90 years of age. He wore a dated wool suit that might have seemed vintage were it not for the necktie, poorly knotted and sporting a stain beneath the Masonic Lodge pin. The older man struggled a little, finally settling in the upholstered chair. Before Reed could even begin the meeting, Mr. Agile was racked with a coughing fit, producing a faded handkerchief to cover his mouth.

"How can I help you, sir?" Reed opened.

Mr. Agile studied the lawyer for some time before speaking. "I can tell just by the resemblance, but I have to ask to be sure. Are you Laurence Wallace's son?"

Reed's first thought was Mr. Agile was an old friend of his father's. Perhaps this man had sought out Reed's firm, wanting legal help from the son of an old family acquaintance – it wouldn't be the first time.

"Yes, I am. How did you know my father?"

Mr. Agile pondered his answer for a moment and then replied in a hushed tone. "I worked with your father at the Fed. I knew him quite well. Let me get to the point, young man – my reason for being here. I have lung cancer and have been told to get my affairs in order. You, or more precisely your father, happen to be one of those affairs."

The old gentlemen started coughing again, the handkerchief receiving more work. Reed snapped the top off a bottle of water and extended it to his visitor. Eventually, the man was ready to continue. "In my condition, there's nothing they can do to me now. Ending up like your father would be a blessing in disguise. I've come here because I wanted you to know your dad wasn't a victim of any robbery – his death was premeditated."

Reed's first thought was *You are a crazy old fool*. He had, however, been raised to respect his elders and didn't vocalize the sentiment. Instead, he chose a polite inquiry. "How do you know this, sir?"

Mr. Agile smiled, expecting the question. "I'll answer that shortly, son. Unlike most people, I have a reasonably good idea when my time will be up, and I'll be standing before my Maker. I have a few things to clear from my conscious before I meet Him. The story of Laurence Wallace is one of those things."

Reed didn't react. His ability to handle surprise far exceeded his age and experience. Years of witnesses making crazy statements, surprise evidence, unanticipated moves by opposing counsel, and insane rulings by judges had all tempered his reaction to surprise. Shock was no longer in the Reed Wallace emotional repertoire.

The lawyer calmly replied, "You have my full attention, sir."

Mr. Agile smiled and nodded his head, gathering his thoughts before continuing. "Your father was on the fast track. His work was prompt and precise. Rumor was that his name was on the short list for a regional director's position."

Reed decided to play along. "Dad never talked much about his professional responsibilities. To be honest, I can't remember his ever talking about the office or his duties. I always wrote it off to a good man who left his work at the front door when he arrived home."

The older man waved off the statement, "Secrecy was expected at the Fed, young man. It wasn't an attribute – it was a requirement. The Federal Reserve Bank is the most powerful organization in the world. Many people suspect or speculate about its influence and reach, but few really know. Every nut case conspiracy junkie and rookie reporter would love to pry open the organization's inner secrets. Any Wall Street executive would sell his soul for even a crumb of insider information. Many try, but none succeed. The reason why is simple - a strictly enforced, total adherence to silence."

Reed had to admit, the old gent had drawn him in; his lawyer's thirst for intrigue was awake and hungry. "Please, sir, continue."

Mr. Agile nodded, and for a second, Reed thought he saw an expression of *Gottcha* cross the man's face. "The Fed has more security and intelligence-gathering capability than the CIA and FBI combined. Nothing happens in this world without money, and the Fed has access to every financial transaction. You can't buy a cup of coffee without the Fed knowing about it in one form or another. Even the activity at pay toilets can be monitored - if necessary. Where do you think the NSA got all of the funding and brainpower to create its supercomputer search engines? The Fed funded it and made sure the technology was shared with them after installation."

Reed's guest paused for a moment, anticipating another coughing spasm. After a few troubled breaths, he continued. "Your father specialized in an area called 'expansion reserves.' I won't bore you with details on monetary policy or the way the system works, but as the nation's gross domestic product grows, more money is needed. Money is subject to supply and demand. The more our economy expands, the greater the need to expand the amount of money in circulation to support it. If we had the same amount of currency in the system today as a hundred years ago, greenbacks would be in very short supply. Loans would be impossible. Our population has doubled in the last century. The nation produces far greater amounts of goods and services. Your dad's department managed this important aspect of the banking system – keeping up with this growth. Most folks simply refer to this as the 'money supply.'"

Reed had indeed heard the term tossed about on various news programs. The phrase was self-explanatory, or at least that's what he had always thought. "So the money supply is based on the growth of the economy. If I hear the nation's gross domestic product grew by 3%, then the Fed makes sure there is 3% more money in the system – right?"

Mr. Agile's expression changed, this time looking more like a college professor having patience with a slow student. "That's what the average citizen believes, yes. In reality, it's not that simple or straightforward. International trade, government debt, and even the time of year all have an impact on the calculation. More hard currency is needed around Christmas than any other season. It's also important to know that we are not just talking about physical money. In the US economy, physical bills and coin make up a very small percentage of the actual money supply."

Reed nodded his understanding, but didn't want or need a lesson on finance and banking today. He decided to move the conversation along. "This is all fascinating Mr. Agile, and while I appreciate you taking the time to explain it to me, I'm wondering what this has to do with your claim that my father wasn't a robbery victim."

For a moment, Reed thought he had angered the older man. Mr. Agile's eyes flashed bright for just a moment, and he withdrew his hand from the tabletop to his lap – normally a defensive posture. Whatever the man was feeling, it seemed to pass quickly, and his tone remained even.

"Most Americans don't understand the system and don't take the time to learn. If they did, I'm sure a lot of questions would be asked. Your father was learning, and he asked questions. That's why I believe he was killed. My evidence is what you legal people would call circumstantial, but I anticipate you'll find it compelling. What you choose to do with my disclosure is up to you. My only goal is to relieve myself of this burden that has been a weight on my shoulders for over 20 years. I never came forward because I was frightened. Now, the fear of carrying this to my grave outweighs that prior concern."

Finally, Reed thought, *finally, we are getting somewhere.* Mr. Agile took a drink of water and cleared his throat. He paused for only a moment and then began what Reed thought sounded like a practiced confession, repeatedly rehearsed many times through the years.

"Your father's time of death was determined to have been on March 8th, between 2 p.m. and 4 p.m. – is that correct, son?"

Reed had studied the police reports a thousand times. He knew the exact details like the lyrics to a favorite song. He nodded, "Yes, sir. That is correct."

"I was in charge of the Audit and Security Division at the Dallas office. Even in those days, the Fed had state of the art security systems."

Mr. Agile reached into his coat pocket and pulled out a folded sheet of faded, yellowish paper. He carefully smoothed the edges on the table's surface and then slid the old document to Reed. It appeared to be a computer-generated printout using a dot-matrix type of technology. It was basically a confirmation to remove one Mr. Laurence Wallace from the personnel system at the Dallas Federal Reserve regional building and lock down his office and contents. The document further stated that the whereabouts of Mr. Wallace's credentials were unknown, as he had been the victim of a violent crime.

At first, Reed didn't get it. It would make sense for his dad's access to sensitive information to be removed after his demise. Reed looked up at his guest with a questioning expression. Mr. Agile, always seemingly one step ahead, mouthed four words. "Look at the date."

Reed's vision blurred after checking at the top of the form. He rubbed his eyes and blinked several times, eventually focusing back on the print. The date on the parchment read March 7, the day before his father was killed. The time was 4:50 p.m. Reed heard ringing in his ears and felt a wave of nausea coming on. He replaced the paper on the table and peered into the blank stare of the old man across from him. "I'm sorry, Mr. Agile. Could you excuse me for one moment?"

"Of course."

Reed left the conference room with more haste than he intended. As a matter of fact, he rushed out needing different air. He hurried down the short hallway to the men's room and splashed cold water on his face. He braced himself against the granite sink with both arms locked at the elbows as if to steady his weight. Regaining his composure, he hurried to his office, fingering his keys in his front pants pocket. Once inside his personal workspace, he unlocked a seldom used, private file cabinet and retrieved a folder full of his own dusty, yellow papers.

It took him a few moments to locate the police report. He could almost recall the document and its contents by memory, but after Mr. Agile's assertion, he felt compelled to verify the dates and times once again. There it was, recorded in several places, March 8. The newspaper clippings all said the same thing – March 8.

Reed returned the folder to its correct place and locked the cabinet. He gathered his wits again and headed to the conference room. Mr. Agile and the old paper were *exactly* where Reed had left them. He took his seat, one word repeating in his head, "*Mistake.*"

"Mr. Agile, pardon my skepticism, but couldn't this paper simply be a mistake? A computer error?"

The older man displayed no overt reaction to the statement. He continued, "I considered that, but any of the Fed's coveted computers having an incorrect date would have resulted in millions of financial transactions being in error. Every check cleared through the system would have been wrong. That would have made headlines all across the world. No, young man, there was no computer glitch."

After a drink of water, he persisted, "Now I understand that until 45 minutes ago, you had no idea that I even existed, much less that I would deliver such disconcerting allegations today. No doubt I have challenged a belief you have held for many years, and I'm certain you must wonder if this information is credible." The older man paused and leaned forward toward Reed, his leathery hand resting on the lawyer's jacket sleeve just below the elbow. "There are other inconsistencies," he continued. "Do you know how much gasoline your father's car had in it when the police discovered his body?"

"No, I always assumed he had stopped at the station to fill up or use the restroom. After the car was returned to my family, my mother repaired the broken window and sold it at auction. I never wanted to see it."

Mr. Agile clasped his hands together on the conference table, apparently considering his next statement carefully. "I removed your father's security clearance on the 7th. It was the last thing I did before clocking out. Your dad was a really likeable guy, and his death – especially the circumstances surrounding it - troubled me. I was off work the following day, but received a phone call early that morning. Someone had tried to enter the building using your father's magnetic badge, and the guard caught his image on the camera. The man was confused because the intruder looked like your dad. The sentry was following procedure and had noted that I personally removed your father from the system. At the time, I still hadn't put two and two together. I told the guard Mr. Wallace was dead and to call the police. I believed it was your father's murderer trying to use his badge."

The man across from Reed leaned forward and pointed his finger at the paper. "I'm convinced your dad knew something was wrong. I think that's why he called you in Austin that morning. The car's gas tank was full, topped off at a station ten miles north of the one where he was found. I saw the credit card transaction myself. Why would your father have stopped and filled up, and then stopped again ten minutes later? I also know your father used the restroom and purchased a cup of coffee when he stopped the first time. I interviewed the clerk who remembered him a few days later. Your dad was executed, Reed, of that I'm sure. I can't tell you who or why, but this was no robbery."

Reed's head was spinning, and that was a condition he wasn't accustomed to. This seemingly harmless, old man had sent his mind into analysis paralysis, and the attorney wasn't comfortable with it. He managed to calm himself and started to push away from the table, but Mr. Agile wasn't done yet.

"Before I go, we should work on my last will and testament."

Reed absentmindedly responded, "I'm not the firm's expert on wills, Mr. Agile. I'm afraid I wouldn't do a good job for you."

The old man smiled, "It's not for me, Reed. It's for you. While I doubt anyone is paying attention to my activities anymore, there's still that chance. You may need to explain why I was here, and I don't think telling the truth would be wise."

As Reed ambled along the Washington side streets, he didn't pay much attention to his immediate surroundings. Normally, when traveling through a new place, he would be looking at nearby sidewalk cafes, secondhand shops, or perhaps even people watching. Today, he was simply celebrating his arrival here.

"Here" wasn't a location on a map. It had nothing do with the status of having been elected to a national office. By Reed's way of thinking, *here* was a place that provided the best odds of uncovering the facts surrounding his father's murder.

Reed paused, checking the street signs to verify he was turning toward the temporary offices. He waited for the walk signal to change before crossing the wide avenue, his mind drifting back to Dallas and how that one old man had changed everything.

After his visit with Mr. Agile, Reed initially ignored the man's claim. Combined, Reed's job and family required every spare minute of every waking hour. He simply couldn't justify repurposing time from the obligations of the here and now to dwell on vague allegations about past events. Deep down inside, he wondered if he were deluding himself about the reality of the allegations, or simply procrastinating from exploring them further. Some small voice kept telling him Mr. Agile's visit was a life-altering event. In so many ways, Reed didn't want his life to change. But Mr. Agile's voice kept haunting him, the man's words popping into his consciousness at the oddest times. Reed finally decided there was no choice but to spend time either debunking the old man's story or discovering what really happened.

Two years and two private detectives later, Reed was convinced Mr. Agile had told him the truth. The paid investigators brought him very little fresh information. A little excursion to Miami did bear fruit, however. The Austin police lieutenant who investigated the case was still sound of mind and subsiding on his pension in southern Florida.

When Reed phoned the retired cop, the fellow instantly remembered the case. "That whole set of circumstances was weird…just plain weird. For one thing, we never interviewed any real witnesses. No one heard or saw anything, yet the black Volvo sedan was parked no more than 50 feet from a very busy island of gas pumps – in broad daylight. The victim was found facing straight ahead. Most people would have made eye contact with an attacker in that situation. Think about it; if you were parked at a gas station, wouldn't you look up if you suddenly noticed someone beside your car? No sir, there were a million things wrong with that case, and I still find myself replaying the events, trying to make sense of it all. Come on down if you want; I can talk and fish at the same time. I'll be happy to tell you everything I can remember."

It seemed everyone was helpful with the exception of his father's employer. Several times, Reed attempted to speak with a representative at the Dallas regional headquarters who might provide even basic information. Who were his father's colleagues at the office? What was he working on? To whom did he report? All of these were legitimate questions. When he couldn't get any response the nice way, he got mean. He filed a motion in federal court for discovery. A federal judge, after consultation with the Attorney General's litigator, denied the motion. Next was the Freedom of Information Act. For months, Reed plowed through a mountain of forms and regulations, only to have his request denied in less than an hour after its submission. He had begun work on a civil lawsuit when his partners at the firm called him in.

"Reed," the senior partner announced, "you have to stop this. We just received notice from the Texas Bar Association that our firm in under investigation. My wife's brother works there. He whispered to me that someone here in our firm has angered the feds. He said he's never seen anything like it, and they want to decorate their pikes with our heads. You have to stop, man – you can't fight city hall on this."

Reed resigned from the firm that afternoon and initiated his campaign for Congress the next day.

Chapter 2
Beijing, China
January 13, 2017

Minister Hong arrived exactly three minutes before the meeting was scheduled to begin. The Zhongnanhai complex in central Beijing was synonymous with the Chinese communist government in the same way Moscow's Red Square represented authority to the Soviet people, or the White House was an icon for the president of the United States. Once a resort destination for ancient emperors, the park-like setting was hundreds of years older than any of its current occupants. Bordering on the famous Forbidden City, the walled compound was noted for its system of lakes, which had been adorned with names such as the Southern Sea or the Central Sea. In reality, the lakes had been constructed as defensive moats to protect ancient royalty, their beauty an unintended benefit.

Today's meeting wasn't on any public schedule or noted in any press release. The State Committee officially met once every six months to formally conduct the business of China. Those widely publicized events were actually carefully planned theatrics, designed to reassure the Chinese people that their leaders were working hard to move the country forward.

The day-to-day business of China was most often conducted via email and closed circuit television, as required. Only the most important issues warranted a face-to-face meeting, and even then, the entire State Committee was never invited. Ministries that wielded little power, such as environmental and natural resources and interior were often excluded.

The presentations housed in Minister Hong's briefcase documented a bold plan that could result in a change to the world's balance of power. Such an ambitious undertaking warranted the ministers' meeting in person. The State Committee had been briefed on the operation years ago. Authority had been granted to proceed with the initial phases of the operation – within certain guidelines.

Today's summit was organized to rehash the downside or unintended consequences, should the operation go awry. Hong was more annoyed than nervous. The outcome of today's conference was predetermined, Hong having already received the blessing of those who controlled his country's destiny. Still, others who might be affected needed to know what was coming and have a chance to voice their objections. In the unlikely event things did go badly, Hong might need their support.

Five of the six invitees stood behind high-backed executive chairs surrounding a wide conference table inlaid with teak and mahogany. The interwoven red and gold textile covering each chair was of the finest quality and could last for hundreds of years. Quality silk is the chosen fabric of status for the elite Chinese, who would sneer at mass-produced Western leather upholstery, believing it lacks artistic value and craftsmanship.

A respectful hush fell over the assemblage as the president entered the room and commanded his place at the head of the table. After the most powerful men in China had taken their seats, pleasantries were exchanged. They were all refined dignitaries who considered diving immediately into business boorish and rude. Ten minutes into the conference, the president nodded at Hong, signaling permission to proceed. In turn, the head of MOSS motioned to his assistant, who delivered each attendee one of the carefully prepared presentations.

Each minister studied the eight-page handout as if he had never seen the information before. In fact, a secure courier delivered the exact same documents less than 24 hours ago, to allow review prior to this forum. Information of such a sensitive nature certainly could not be distributed via email or fax.

Hong maintained a stoic demeanor while the committee completed the review of the documents. MOSS' top man was not at all surprised that the Minister of Finance took the most time to analyze the brief. The only one of the group who wasn't a hardliner, Hong trusted the politics of China's head banker the least. The room remained silent for some time, as the Red Nation's powerbrokers digested the gravity of the mission. "I apologize to my esteemed colleagues for the quality of my project update and proposal," he began, knowing full well each page represented perfection to the smallest detail. "My team is ahead of schedule, so there wasn't time to craft a presentation worthy of this council." Several heads nodded, accepting the unnecessary apology and acknowledging Minister Hong's humility. The head of MOSS continued, "My comrades, we have before us the single greatest opportunity for the Chinese people in recent history – perhaps of all time."

Hong paused to take note of the indifferent faces comprising his audience. None betrayed their thoughts, but Hong didn't expect them to. Instead, he used the short gap in his presentation to demonstrate his stoic, controlled approach to the subject.

"With Operation Golden Mountain, we can guarantee our economic growth and eventual domination of global affairs. As the only truly civilized race, we will take our rightful place at the head of the world's table. China will once again control its own destiny. As most of you know, the European Union is in shambles. The insolvent capitalist governments of Spain, Greece, and Italy have failed, and there is general anarchy in the streets. Our intelligence reports detail the ongoing battle between Muslim political groups and organized crime syndicates to establish control. Germany is withdrawing its support of the euro, causing France to be the next to fall. The British are barely holding on, a result of nine years of recession. Today the United States and India are considered global dominant forces, but both countries are weak and teetering on the edge of collapse as well."

No one spoke for almost a full minute. It was the Minister of Finance who broke the silence. "Minister Hong, first of all I wish to congratulate you on the progress of this project. I do, however, have some small reservations that I feel deserve to be aired before this wise council. As well planned and detailed as this operation is, there is substantial risk. If discovered, the United States will consider our actions as an act of war. They have numerous methods of retaliation at their disposal. If deftly handled on their part, they could unite a significant portion of the world against us."

Two others nodded their heads in agreement, but Hong seemed not to notice. His response was controlled, "You are correct as usual, Minister. There is risk, but I feel it is warranted. If our plan is discovered, it is unlikely to happen until the damage to the US is done. They will be weakened at that point and have fewer options. The People's Republic will publically deny any involvement, blaming the exaggerated claims on organized crime syndicates and drug cartels. I also believe there is a strong possibility that many nations will see a wounded beast and decide to finish the job we started. Russia, several countries in the Middle East, and most of OPEC would no doubt prefer a weakened, less intrusive United States of America."

The president began speaking without waiting for any response to Hong's statement - a clear indication of his support. "Ministers, I believe this operation is warranted for other reasons as well. Our economic growth becomes more and more difficult to sustain. Our government is less popular than ever before. Our people are being misled by the false promises of the West. Should the United States suffer the projected damage from this plan, our method of governing would be recognized as undeniably superior. The issue would be settled once and for all – what we are doing is the right choice for the Middle Kingdom."

Without further questioning, Hong's proposal was authorized. Within two hours, orders were issued to begin the attack on the United States of America.

January 14, 2017
San Jose, California

Zang examined the suit and high heels in the mirror one last time. She smoothed the nonexistent wrinkles from her skirt as she had important business today, and wanted her appearance to reflect the significance of her responsibilities. While she would never admit it, her nerves were more than a little frayed.

The 24-year-old hadn't felt such emotional turmoil since entering the United States just over two years ago. Her immersion into western society had been stressful. Extensive preparation provided by MOSS had sustained her, even as she waited in line at the immigration office. She had continued to remind herself that no law had been broken, and there was little risk of arrest – yet. Her degrees in mathematics and engineering were legitimate and could withstand any level of scrutiny. *I'm just one of the thousands of Chinese wishing to join her family in the United States*, she kept telling herself. *If I believe that, live that, and feel that, these crass, American barbarians won't suspect the truth.*

After receiving her green card, working at the Silicon Valley technology firm enabled her to establish a routine. Routines reduced stress. Her new employer performed research on advanced storage technologies for laptop computers and smart phones. Zang was stunned at the quantity and quality of scientific information that crossed her desk practically every day. It would have taken her countrymen years to develop what she saw in her email inbox and departmental updates every week. She was pleased to bundle the valuable information and send it back home where teams of engineers and students happily dissected the data.

Often, Zang wondered why she hadn't been discovered. Didn't the Americans wonder why Chinese factories were ready to produce the latest products before the specifications were publically available? Her newest project involved lab testing a micro-sized hard drive for cell phones. The electronic storage unit was no larger than a small coin and stored gigabytes of information. When her testing was completed, the US cell phone providers would seek bids to mass-produce the device. The Chinese factories would undercut even the most efficient competitors because they had been studying the plans and specifications, secretly provided by Zang, for months. The combination of industrial espionage and cheap labor was invincible.

Her covert task today wasn't criminal as far as she knew. The assignment was so unusual she exasperated her superior by her request for clarification. The raspy Mandarin voice on the other end of the phone was impatient with the junior agent's questions, and his tone relayed that clearly. After researching the mission thoroughly for the past three days, she was ready. Turning off the bathroom light, she headed to the door, scanning the flat one last time, verifying she wasn't forgetting anything.

By Chinese standards, her San Jose apartment was actually quite lavish. The one bedroom efficiency had a dishwasher, microwave, and solid surface cooktop. In her native country, only the upper echelons of society, living in the major cities, enjoyed such luxury. Zang rejected the place when she first toured the complex, because her mandate dictated that she appear to mesh with average Americans of the same socioeconomic situation. Standing out or drawing attention to oneself was strictly forbidden. It had taken her a while to realize the apartment was normal by local standards. Still, always conservative with money and image, she had opted for a third story unit, amazed that its monthly rent included a discount because most folks in this country didn't want to climb three flights of stairs. She leased modest furniture and purchased essential pots, pans, silverware, and linens at a nearby discount store. After a few months, her concerns faded with the comfort of routine.

Zang rummaged in her purse, locating her key chain. After locking the door behind her, she began her trek down the stairs to the parking lot.

Driving a car had almost been the death of her. Motor vehicles are still a rarity in China, with waiting lists of more than five years to acquire even a modest family sedan. As a college student, she rode a bike on campus. Upon graduation, Zang located a flat that was a comfortable walking distance to work. The idea of navigating through superhighways while steering around traffic snares was more than a little daunting. It wasn't like she had toured the countryside with her family, buckled in the back seat of an SUV or completed a driver's education course in secondary school. Zang had only ridden in an automobile twice in her life before arriving in the states. After acquiring legal status to work, the original plan had been for her to gain employment in the San Francisco area and use the mass transit available there. The chance job opening in San Jose had been a perfect fit for her background and qualifications, so it was decided that Zang would learn to drive.

The Chinese gent who operated the On Track Driving Academy chain-smoked cheap cigarettes with a stench that betrayed their Taiwanese origin. His late model, training sedan was fully equipped with passenger side brake pedal, extra-large beanbag ashtray and family size bottle of Tums. Normally, within four weeks, new drivers were competent enough to complete the class. Zang passed on the third time through the course. She was never sure if the instructor's nerves couldn't deal with her obvious anxiety anymore, or if she had obtained the necessary skills. Even then, she failed the official state driving test twice before being issued a State of California operator's license on the third attempt.

Purchasing her first automobile was another revolutionary experience. The glistening showrooms, fast talking salesmen, and seemingly endless options amazed Zang. She was almost at complete cognitive overload when a co-worker rescued her, explaining the process, and visiting several dealerships with her in his spare time. More than once, Zang studied the San Jose bus routes and cost associated with taking a taxi everywhere. Those options were simply impractical, so she made a cash purchase of a brand new, wonderful smelling Ford Escape. She had her first fender bender pulling into traffic from the dealership.

Zang unlocked her car and carefully maneuvered out of the apartment complex's lot. She drove only on side streets to and from her office or the occasional trip to a nearby shopping area. Today she was going somewhere new, and the concept terrified her.

Twenty minutes and numerous single-finger insults later, the harried girl parked in front of the Almaden Plaza strip mall. A bubbling, young real estate broker energetically escorted her thought the small retail space that was available for immediate occupancy. Within two hours, a new California business was born – Red and Gold Check Cashing and Postal Center would celebrate its grand opening two weeks later.

Zang rented space for three different branch locations of Red and Gold that day. She was unaware that MOSS seeded hundreds of similar enterprises throughout all 50 states, all under the operation of Chinese immigrants. The sheer number of the mail/check cashing centers would have aroused suspicion if anyone tracked such things. Most communities welcomed the fledgling establishments, replacing empty storefronts pasted with "For Lease" signs with a business and jobs.

Houston, Texas
January 30, 2017

Morgan shifted into park and reached to switch off the ignition, but then paused. Seeing the house made her contemplate staying in the air-conditioned car just a little longer. Even with the moderate temperatures this time of year, the house would be muggy and close. The occasional hot flash made it practically unbearable. Darkness came early with the winter-shortened days, and she rarely got home before the sunset. Still, the house seemed to hold the heat inside no matter how many windows Wyatt and she opened. She would never have believed a cold-water shower could feel so good.

The sauna-house didn't seem to bother Wyatt as much. She wondered if menopause was more to blame than the humidity, but shrugged off the thought – there wasn't anything she could do about either. Still deliberating about going inside, she wondered what mood Wyatt would be in. She fully understood the relationship between the current financial crisis and the bailout deal Wyatt was trying to put together. The daily newscasts had gone from bad to worse, and even her co-workers were becoming concerned. In the past, few people paid attention to events surrounding Wall Street and big banks - now, everyone did.

A year ago, she would have been anxious about her husband's health. After all, over the last few months there had been a noticeable change in him. He often seemed beyond caring or even capable of worry. Maybe he had learned not to let things get to him. At least he didn't show anxiety like he used to. Still, she wondered if the pressure wasn't building up inside like a big dome of lava under the crusty mantle of a volcano. Eventually, the volcano erupts.

The tight financial situation hadn't been a complete negative for the family. If Morgan forced herself to be optimistic, there were a few small, silver linings to be found. Wyatt often teased that his wife could find something positive in a heart attack. One reassuring point was Wyatt himself. These days, the talk around the water cooler commonly included accounts of men who lost their livelihood and took a nosedive right into the deep end. Details always involved drinking, divorce, abuse or other tales of horror. Wyatt was an exception to what had become the stereotypical bread earner who had succumbed to bad behavior after an economic demise. While he didn't smile as often or laugh as easily, he was basically the same man as before. *Quiet and surreal would be better words than moody*, she thought.

Morgan shut off the motor and walked gingerly to the front door. Her feet were killing her after the ten- hour shift. She was taking all of the extra hours she could get, but with the price of everything going crazy, many of the other nurses were working overtime, too. A few years ago, working weekend and holiday hours was easy, now there were lotteries to secure prized overtime shifts.

She found Wyatt in the kitchen, his gaze fixed on some point in space. A heaping mound of envelopes and circulars were stacked on the table in front of him. "Hey, babe," she greeted, causing him to focus and then look up.

His expression immediately put her on alert, broadcasting that something was terribly wrong. A weak "Hey," was his only reply.

"What's wrong, Wyatt?"

Wyatt's voice was low and his face grim. "It's not been a good day, hun. The phone call I've been dreading... the merger is off. Rick delivered the news as gently as possible, but it's still a no-go. He said the partners didn't want to do anything with what's going on in the markets right now."

Morgan moved to his side, "Oh baby. I'm so sorry. Why didn't you call me and let me know? I would've gotten a sub and come home right away. Are you okay?"

Wyatt looked up at her and faked a smile. He reached for the pile of mail in front of him and held up a rather thick bundle of papers. "A deputy came to the door with this a few hours ago." Morgan looked down at the top sheet, and the print was large and bold. She saw the words, "Notice of Foreclosure," across the top.

Morgan's knees suddenly felt very wobbly, and she staggered a little before sitting beside her mate. If Wyatt noticed, he didn't acknowledge anything. Morgan's eyes darted from the paper to her husband's face. His eyes were watery and red, his complexion pale. She leaned across the table and embraced him in a gentle hug. Only a few moments passed by before each was crying on the other's shoulder.

The couple realized months ago that their house was no longer affordable. Even with Morgan's extra hours and the cutbacks on household expenses, they couldn't replace Wyatt's share of the household income. The mortgage payments were the biggest single expenditure in the budget, and they knew it wouldn't be long before the bank became impatient.

Fourteen years ago, the couple purchased their home, offering a hefty down payment. Because they never missed an installment and took great pride in the upkeep of both the grounds and residence, Wyatt initially believed there was equity in the property. When the accounting firm began to flounder, Wyatt and Morgan decided they would take two courses of action. First, they would put their homestead up for sale. Even though the house encompassed a lot of memories, the kids were grown now anyway. Their son, David had enlisted in the army. Sage was in college, on a full scholarship and living off campus in her own apartment. As the only two full-time residents, Wyatt and Morgan simply didn't require 4,000 square feet of living space.

The second means of stabilizing their finances involved applying for a mortgage modification. Years ago, the government had forced the banks to offer various programs designed to help people struggling through the down economy. In the off chance that the house did not move quickly, Wyatt would maneuver through the necessary paperwork to complete this process.

Within a few days, Wyatt and Morgan stood with a young realtor after finishing a pre-listing walkthrough of their home. The house-peddler had bad news. "I'm sorry, but I don't think your home will sell for more than $200,000. It's a wonderful space, but the kitchen and master bath are outdated, and there are hundreds of competitors on the market right now."

Wyatt was shocked. "But we paid more than $400,000 for this place almost 15 years ago. I still owe $250,000 on the note. Things are that bad?"

The realtor had expected the reaction. She hated this part, no matter how many times she had to deliver bad news; she would never get accustomed to it. "Yes, things are that bad. I know you probably think I'm just trying to low ball your home to get a quick commission," she answered, anticipating their unstated objection. "But I'm not. If you have a little time this weekend, I will be happy to show you some of my listings. Once you get a feel for what the market has to offer, you will see – there are hundreds of homes larger and more modern than yours, and most are listed for significantly less than what you owe. You're not alone. I meet so many people who are in the same boat. That's why you read so much about people just walking away from their homes."

Morgan and Wyatt had taken her up on the offer and returned in a soured mood. The agent had been right, there was no way anyone would buy their property, based on what was available. Clearly, people were desperate to get out of their mortgages.

Plan-B was the mortgage modification. For two whole days, Wyatt filled out the endless forms required by the lender. The process bought them some time, but in the end, their request was rejected. Their income didn't meet the modification guidelines. The final rejection letter arrived less than a month ago.

Wyatt shook his head, thinking the bank hadn't wasted any time throwing them out.

Overcome by the finality of their loss, tears flowed freely while the two silently hugged, both of their minds racing with questions. It was Morgan who broke the embrace and reached out to hold her husband's hand. As gently as possible, she asked, "What are we going to do, Wyatt? Will they put us out in the street?"

Wyatt shook his head and pointed to a paragraph on the letter. "It says here we have 30 days. I think at that point in time, we'll have to be out."

Morgan nodded her understanding and then reached across the table, removing the paper from his grasp. She gently took his other hand in hers and squeezed. "We'll think of something, Wyatt. We always do. As long as we're together, it will be all right."

Wyatt's next statement surprised her. "Actually, I have a plan. I've been thinking about it for hours, and while it's not perfect, I don't see much of an alternative. I'm a little hesitant to tell you though. It seems like I haven't been the best planner lately."

Morgan relaxed in her chair, not sure if Wyatt had finally lost it, or if she should be pleased with his inspiration. "Okay, I'm all ears, Wyatt. I hope it doesn't involve a tent, because you know my idea of camping is sleeping in a hotel that doesn't offer room service."

Morgan's declaration set off a short session of gallows humor. Wyatt smiled and said, "No, no tent. I have a bridge all picked out. We can decorate in neo-modern cardboard, and I'll woo you with the shiniest shopping cart under the overpass."

Morgan laughed and shook her head. "Save some of that cardboard. I'll make you a sign saying, 'Will do accounting for food.'" Their snickering quickly faded, both realizing the jokes weren't all that unrealistic.

Wyatt reached for a bowl of fruit sitting in the middle of the table and pulled out an orange. He moved to the sink and dug his thumb into the skin, peeling back a long section. "Seriously Morgan, I've got an idea, but I don't want to overwhelm you so soon. If you want to wait until the shock of all this has worn off, I'll be glad to go over my grand scheme a little later."

Morgan smiled up at him, "I'll tell you what. You give me a few sections of that orange, and I'll lend you my ear. Besides, I'm not going to get any sleep tonight anyway."

Wyatt's expression betrayed the fact he was having doubts about sharing his solution. As the business was failing, Morgan noticed more and more indecision and self-doubt in his eyes. *Who could blame him*, she thought. It seemed like everything he attempted, planned, or believed in had evaporated into thin air. Any normal person would begin to lose faith in his own judgment.

Morgan rubbed her husband's shoulder in a reassuring gesture. "Wyatt, don't make me beg. I'll peel the orange if that's what it takes for you to tell me what you're thinking."

Wyatt nodded agreement with her terms and began laying out his strategy. "We've still got the boat. I say we turn all of this into a positive. Let's sell everything, walk away from the house, and go live on the water. I know it's a bit more of a drive to work for you, but we've paid for the slip a year in advance, and that fee includes all electric and water. We can sell all the furniture and the yard tools – everything except our clothes and food, and resign ourselves to a life of luxury on the sea."

Wyatt handed his wife a slice of orange and continued. "I'll find a part-time job at a gas station or maybe even get some temporary bookkeeping work. I know a big firm won't hire me because of my credit rating, but a little company needing a part-time person probably won't check. I can fish a little and maybe even pick up some cash repairing our neighbors' vessels. What do you think?"

Morgan pondered Wyatt's plan. Some time back, they had discussed retiring on the boat, but that was only daydreaming. It had never come up again because Wyatt still had faith in either the business bailout deal or the loan modification. Now, both of those options had dried up. She had to admit, compared to sleeping on the ground, the boat was the Taj Mahal. "Okay Wyatt, let's say I agree to go along with not having a yard and living in constant motion. Are we going to do that forever? Do I need to grow gills?"

Again, Wyatt smiled at his wife and teased, "Baby, I've always had a mermaid fantasy. Sing me a siren song, would ya?"

Morgan waved him off with a "Pfffff" sound and then got serious. "We won't be able to cruise or take her out. The fuel would be worse than our house payment. Let me think about it, Wyatt. Sleep might come a little easier tonight if I'm working on that question, rather than worrying about finding an unoccupied overpass."

Wyatt seemed relieved at her reaction. "You don't think I'm crazy? I know it's not a great plan, but it's all I could come up with so far."

"No, my husband, I don't think it's crazy at all. As a matter of fact, I think it's rather creative. I just need to think it through is all."

Wyatt nodded and handed her the last section of the citrus fruit. "Oh, damn. I forgot, I got so wrapped up in the bad news, I forgot about the good news. David is coming home next month. He's been granted 30 days leave."

Morgan immediately brightened at the news. Her son was coming home! She hadn't seen him in almost three months, and he was going to be here for a whole month! Wyatt pointed to the stack of mail on the table. "He sent a short letter – it's in the pile there."

Morgan shuffled through the mound of bills, collection notices, and junk until she found the handwritten note. It wasn't much, but she held it to her breast and smiled widely. "Now, I do think I'll be able to sleep."

Wyatt wasn't done yet. "I've saved the best for last. Come with me."

He led her to the bedroom door, which was closed. She gave him a puzzled look, and he motioned for her to go in. When she crossed the threshold, a blast of cold air hit her. "I decided if we're going to lose the house, we might as well go out in style, so I turned on the AC. What's the electric company going to do – repossess the cold air?"

Morgan wrapped her hands around his neck and pulled him close for a kiss. "I love you."

"I love you too, baby. Thanks for hanging in there with me. I don't know what I'd do without you."

Chapter 3

January 30, 2017
Beijing, China
MOSS Headquarters

The attack against the United States of America began with a hum, rather than a bang or boom. Spread out across China and dozens of other countries were computer servers in all sorts of configurations and clusters. Server farms, as they were called in the West, had sprung up throughout the East as well. Like the rest of the world, the populations of Asia demonstrated an unquenchable thirst for access to the internet. To feed the growing demand, thousands of gateways, hosting centers, and access points were installed throughout the region. MOSS controlled a significant number of these technology centers on the mainland. Not only did China monitor and control her people's activities on the World Wide Web, the clandestine organization fully understood the power of the internet as a weapon.

For years, the game of one-upmanship had escalated. The Chinese would hack into some sensitive network or computer system, quickly answered by a new encryption routine or firewall that eliminated the threat. The hackers would overcome the new technology and penetrate again. This cycle repeated itself on an almost daily basis. Americans read press releases and watched newscasts covering the subject, but the reports always blamed nameless, unknown attackers, and indisputable links to the Red Nation were difficult to prove.

Most Western experts believed the Chinese were engaging in what amounted to digital war games. If an actual military confrontation between China and the US were to ever occur, military strategists expected an attack aimed at disrupting the Pentagon's computers.

It was also well known that hacking was used for industrial espionage. The computers storing schematics for the latest fighter jet, or material data sheets for a new type of stealth coating were always being probed and tested. Often, ultra-valuable information was stolen and delivered to engineers and scientists working for the Red government.

In the US, exorbitant amounts of money were invested to protect both government and private computer systems. After it became public that someone had stolen this, or infiltrated that, many copycat hackers decided they too might profit from stealing other people's information. It wasn't unheard of for one US company to hack another in order to obtain a competitive advantage.

There was also a huge wave of cyber-crime associated with identity theft. Millions of Americans woke up to find themselves the victims of such activities, often having their lives ruined by criminals who were thousands of miles away. Once a person's confidential information was known, the thieves applied for loans that they never intended to repay.

Most of the money allocated to protect critical systems was focused on the industrial and military supply chains. Diplomats had been the targets of spying for years and had developed hardened, more secure systems. To the defense industry, digital skullduggery was something relatively new.

There were really two different types of hacking. The category most widespread was the theft of information. The other was destructive intrusions, often called viruses. In 2012, it became public knowledge that the United States had infected Iranian computers with a virus that slowed the Islamic nation's nuclear weapons program. There were other organized attacks that remained secret.

The beauty of MOSS' Operation Golden Mountain was that it broached new territory in the realm of using computers as offensive weapons. The software developed by the hundreds of expert programmers working for the ministry wasn't stealing or destroying anything. The target systems had been intentionally built and designed to be used exactly as MOSS intended.

The US Internal Revenue Service had caught up with the modern world some ten years before when it began allowing American taxpayers to file their tax returns digitally over the internet. Millions upon millions of people embraced the option in order to receive a timely refund. The digital returns could be processed faster and cheaper than their paper ancestors, and the system was popular both within the service as well as with the general population. The programmers at MOSS showed a high level of interest in the system's capabilities, too.

For the past few years, MOSS had been investigating and probing the IRS's systems. There were hundreds of questions that needed to be answered before any sort of operation could be mounted. Originally, the MOSS hackers started using trial and error methods. One of the most critical components to the plan involved discovering how the IRS monitored returns as they were processed, such as what metrics were reported and the reaction time after questionable data was discovered. The list of unknowns continued on and on and would have seemed daunting to most people, but not the Chinese. They had practically inexhaustible human resources available. They were patient, methodical, and tenacious.

The breakthrough came when a MOSS agent managed to infiltrate the IRS's data processing center. A complete volume of the source code was smuggled out of the facilities on a thumb drive without the IRS even knowing they had been victimized.

Once the source code was back in China, the game was over. Reverse engineering took a matter of weeks, and soon the programmers at MOSS understood every small detail of the IRS systems. Knowledge was power, and the plan had accelerated.

After a complete analysis of the IRS's software, the next step was to gather a database of information on US citizens. This part had been easy. A few strategic entities were hacked, producing volumes of files with names, addresses, social security numbers and other sensitive data needed for the operation.

Over the last year, Analyst Wu had been gradually testing the IRS. The names of actual US citizens were used to file false tax returns electronically. Most of the fraudulent returns were configured to show a refund varying from a few hundred to a few thousand dollars. Wu had been amazed when the checks were printed and mailed by the United States Treasury within a few days. They even mailed one to an address in Singapore and paid the international postage.

Wu's examination also revealed another weakness with the US system. Significant lag time existed between the death of a citizen and when the IRS's computers recognized the fact. This nuance added a layer of opportunity to Operation Golden Mountain. A method was needed to retrieve the personal information of deceased Americans.

The solution to build "the dead file," as it was named, was an easy fix. The individual states all had on-line systems used to generate the necessary death certificates and other paperwork required when one of their citizenry passed away. Even a novice hacker would find these systems frighteningly simple to penetrate.

Wu and several members of the Golden team were gathered around a workstation in the MOSS headquarters basement. After the third pass through the checklist, Wu turned to Supervisor Yangdong with a questioning look. The older man simply nodded, and Wu pressed a single button on the workstation's keyboard.

All across the globe, servers began to hum, firing their digital weapons. In the US, the IRS computers responded, but not in defense. They answered back with acknowledgements as the first few thousand bogus tax returns were filed in a matter of seconds. It was only a trickle at first. Wu had designed the software to gradually increase the volume of fake documents over time so as not to cause alarm.

The computer screen flashed the simple message of "In process," signaling that The United States of America was under attack. Wu looked to gauge his boss' reaction, and for the first time he could remember, Supervisor Yangdong was smiling.

February 1, 2017
Houston, Texas

Morgan had the day off and normally would have slept in. Her discussion with Wyatt last night, combined with the cool air in their master bedroom, allowed her to sleep soundly, but wake early. As she made her morning coffee, Wyatt joined her in the kitchen, and the couple exchanged a brief, "Good morning."

It was known, but left unsaid, how important today was going to be. If the long-married couple had been able to read each other's minds, they might have been surprised at how similar their thoughts were. Both understood that the conversation and eventual decision made that day would alter the course of their destiny. Both were deeply concerned about how that change would affect the other.

Morgan waited patiently for Wyatt to brew his morning dose of caffeine before broaching the subject. As her husband wandered around the kitchen, gathering the necessary condiments for his routine, she plopped down at the table and pondered how to kick off the tête-à-tête.

Their boat was docked at a marina on the far south side of Houston. A few years ago, a customer had gotten behind in his payments to Wyatt's company. The man had been a good friend as well as a long-term client. Since the fellow's business was failing, he approached Wyatt one day and offered the title to the vessel as compensation. "I don't want to stiff you, Wyatt. I've tried to sell the boat, but the market's been destroyed by the recession. She needs some work and tender loving care, but her hull is solid. I bought her right, and most of the parts she needs are stored nearby. I'm offering to sign her over, free and clear, if you'll accept the title as payment for what I owe you."

In those days, Wyatt's business was still trending well, and the couple had often dreamed about purchasing a boat. After a brief visit and hasty tour of the vessel, they agreed to the proposal, and the paperwork was finalized. Wyatt and David spent many weekends working on the boat. After it was habitable, Morgan and Sage accompanied the men and did their share of labor. The acquisition was one of the few hobbies the entire family could share.

After *Boxer* had been refit, the family enjoyed several voyages aboard. That first summer, they cruised from the Mexican border to the Florida panhandle. They relished the quiet weekends aboard the boat without leaving the pier, while other holidays resulted in extended cruising. When Wyatt's business turned sour, the outings to the marina declined. David's leaving for the army, combined with Sage's busy senior year in high school had all but eliminated their water getaways.

Some months ago, when things started going downhill with the business, Wyatt contacted a broker and put their yacht up for sale. The boating world had suffered worse than the housing market over the last eight years, and they hadn't received a single offer. Since the slip and insurance had been paid a year in advance, the boat sat unused and forgotten for several months.

Morgan took a sip of coffee and judged Wyatt ready to continue their discussion from last night. "What condition do you think the boat's in?"

Wyatt briefly glanced up from the toast he was buttering. "I would guess she's a little dirty, but the mechanicals should be shipshape. The last time we took her out, everything was fine."

"What would we do with all of our stuff? I mean, there's not room on board for much of anything. Would we store it?"

Wyatt thought for a moment and then replied, "I've read several articles about living aboard, and that always seems to be the hardest transition. We've surrounded ourselves with things - personal belongings and other items that just won't fit on a small boat. From what I've gathered, it takes a while to get accustomed to a streamlined existence, but most people adapt."

Morgan mulled that over for a while and then looked up smiling. "There would be a whole lot less to dust."

Wyatt continued, "It's the sentimental items that people mention missing the most. Pictures, the kid's art projects, awards and trophies...that sort of thing."

Morgan pushed back her chair from the solid oak table, suddenly flooded with the memories of scrambled egg breakfasts and Popsicle stick history projects. She rose slowly and deliberately, taking in the room and its contents as never before. She peered into the hall just off the kitchen at the ever-growing montage of school portraits, vacation snapshots, and birthday pictures she had gathered over the years. She eyed the assortment carefully, the emotion in her swelling as she remembered the whens and wheres. Wyatt joined her, draping his arm around her shoulders and pulling her close.

After gazing at the family pictorial history for a bit, the couple turned back to the kitchen when something caught Wyatt's eye. He planted his feet as he pointed out the laundry room door. Over the years, they had marked David's physical development on the frame. Varied colors of inked notches with correlating dates indicated the progress of their son's increasing height. The opposite frame documented Sage's growth. "That's the kind of thing that is priceless," he said, "That's what we'll miss the most."

Morgan waved him off, "I'm not so sure Wyatt. I pass through that doorway every day, and to be honest, I don't think I've noticed it for years. If you hadn't pointed it out, I probably wouldn't have thought about it."

Wyatt wasn't so sure. He'd watched Morgan change since the trouble began. Now, more than ever, she seemed determined to protect him from her frustrations. There had been a variety of examples to confirm his hypothesis. Her monthly appointment at the hair salon had been replaced by a bottle of hair color purchased at the drug store, and Sage was her new stylist. The first few attempts hadn't produced the desired effect, resulting in Morgan strolling out of the bathroom with slightly moist eyes and sporting a hat. Wyatt had expected a far worse reaction than what his wife presented. He often wondered if she hid the pain from him intentionally. Regular manicures and gym workouts were sacrificed as well.

Still, she had soldiered on, never complaining about the losses she was experiencing. Occasionally, Morgan would vent about the way things were impacting the children. When Sage graduated from high school, the celebration had been a much less elaborate affair than her brother's only a few years before. Sage had never complained as far as Wyatt knew, but her mother claimed to know it bothered the girl. With promises like, "We'll make it up to you one of these days, baby," the hurt had slowly healed.

Promises of better days ahead seemed to keep everyone's spirits buoyant at first. But then the days didn't really get better; in fact, they got worse. The family's positive attitude showed signs of weakening as they faced the holidays. By Thanksgiving, blessings seemed to be in short supply, and the collective outlook showed flu-like symptoms – tired and achy. By Christmas, the malaise had progressed to pneumonia, and by New Year's Eve, hopefulness was on full-blown life support. Everyone had promised each other the next year would be better and different, but the optimism seemed shallow and forced.

Wyatt cleared his head of the past and refocused on the present. Morgan had left him pensively reflecting next to the height chart, while she returned to the kitchen for a refill. When he joined her, she fairly beamed at him as she announced, "I think there's a silver lining in all this, and even if you don't agree with me, please keep it to yourself. I want to believe...no, I *have* to believe that we will be better people if this money thing forces us to shed some of our materialistic ways. Now, even if you don't think the same thing...Wyatt please, pretty please, let me believe that. It's the only way I'm going to pull through this change without being bitter."

Wyatt nodded his understanding. "I agree 100%. If we are going to do this, we have to look at it like a positive step forward. We're doing it for a simpler life...we're leading the way, not running or being chased." Wyatt swept his arm around the house, "Who needs all this stuff anyway?" He paused for a moment and used his best salesman's voice. "As far as I'm concerned, we are taking this step to purge all these petty material distractions from our relationship. We want to concentrate on our love for each other and experience more of nature and the great outdoors."

Morgan burst into hysterics. She tried to contain herself, but couldn't. Wyatt's feigned hurt look didn't help her efforts. After a few attempts, she finally managed to blurt out the words "Horse feathers," and then it was Wyatt's turn to lose it.

A good hearty laugh seemed to brighten both their moods. Morgan looked her husband in the eye and smiled. "Do you love me?"

Wyatt's look was just as genuine. "I do. With all my heart, I do."

Morgan enjoyed their connection for a moment before raising her cup in a toast. "Let's do it then." Wyatt touched his cup to hers with a loud clink, and then they kissed.

AP Press Release –New York, New York – U.S.A. 08:00 February 2, 2017

Today, Moody Investments Limited announced a downgrade on US government debt. Effective immediately, US issued treasury bonds will carry a B- rating, lowered from a previous grade B assessment. A quote from Moody's senior manager cited the continued economic stagnation and the federal government's inability to reduce the deficit as the justification for the change.

This is the third downgrade of the once bellwether bonds that has occurred in the last six years.

Analysts anticipated the move since the US debt topped $19 trillion last week, and efforts to reduce spending stalled in Congress.

Thurmond Howell, senior analyst at Bork, Sterns and Lewis, stated, "This move is going to make it even more expensive for the federal government to borrow money. The international financial markets are becoming more agitated over the staggering amount of US debt. Fiscal stimulus measures have failed, while entitlement programs have grown."

The announcement is expected to result in further downward pressure on the Dow Industrial Average, which has already lost more than 300 points in the last three trading sessions.

In related news, the US Department of Commerce reported yesterday that core inflation rose to a level of 4.4% for the fourth quarter of 2016. This news was welcomed by European stock exchanges in late trading, as analysts there feared the Federal Reserve's polices were artificially suppressing inflation.

Houston, Texas
February 2, 2017

Wyatt had been on the computer practically all day. He picked up the pad of paper resting next to the keyboard and leaned back, causing the chair to squeak. "I should've put that in the description," he thought. Yesterday, after reaching their decision to live on the boat, Morgan spent her day off inventorying household items. The couple had categorized every nightstand, blender, and knickknack to be sold, given away, or stored. They had gone to bed, emotionally and physically exhausted.

After this morning's coffee, Wyatt immediately began listing the items to be peddled on various online auction sites. Even though Saturday garage sales were a regular occurrence, he was surprised at the sheer number of items that still occupied their home. He also needed to make the rounds to the local charity drop-off, used furniture store, pawnshop, and Sage's apartment to distribute boxes of items that were unmarketable on the World Wide Web.

Wyatt glanced at his watch and whistled. For the last ten hours, he had taken pictures, typed in descriptions, and set prices. Sites like eBay, Craigslist, and other internet based secondhand portals were all familiar territory now.

On one hand, Wyatt was impressed with how much cash they could potentially raise. Going from a nicely furnished, four-bedroom home, to the bare essentials required for onboard living was a massive undertaking. The couple agreed to store some things that neither could bear to part with, such as an antique hall table that had been in Morgan's family for more than 100 years. The storage space would be paid using the proceeds from the sale of the other belongings. Hopefully there would be a significant amount of cash left over for living expenses on the water.

On the other hand, the process had been a depressing drain on them. To coldly walk through the house pointing at this, that or the other was emotional at times to say the least. Morgan, as usual, tried to keep things bright and cheery. She would point to a chair and say things like, "I never did think that went with the rest of this room, anyway."

Wyatt knew it was all a facade. While neither of them were what he would consider materialistic people, no one could casually dismiss a houseful of possessions that represented a lifetime. The children's bedrooms had been the worst of it. Wyatt felt like he was selling the foundation of his offspring's security right out from underneath them. The secure, warm place they could always return to, no matter what, was no longer going to be there.

His wife surprised him by offering up some family treasures that he believed were "off limits." At one point Morgan returned from her jewelry box with a handful of pricey-looking baubles. "These gaudy estate pieces once belonged to Aunt Barbara, and to tell the truth, I never did like her much. Can we sell them for the gold?"

Since the economy had been in the tank for years, Wyatt knew the value of secondhand items wasn't what it used to be. For a few fleeting moments, he wondered if they could raise enough money to salvage the mortgage, but quickly dismissed the notion. Their comprehensive sale was a one-time event, and in a few months, they would be exactly back where they started, only with no couch to sit on or television to watch.

Morgan's paycheck, any part-time work he could find, and the reduced cost of living should see them through. The proceeds from their going out of business sale would be the seeds of a new nest egg and emergency fund.

Wyatt was pushing away from the computer, fantasizing about a cold drink from the fridge, when his email dinged. He glanced at the screen and sighed. The small television in the spare bedroom had attracted someone's attention in Oregon, and a bid was posted. "So it begins," he said to no one. "So it begins."

Alexandria, Virginia
February 2, 2017

The computer servers located in the Internal Revenue Service's main data center didn't detect the slight increase in the number of tax returns being filed early. They processed the thousands of normal taxpayer forms with the same speed and efficiency as the bogus submissions sourced from China.

As each digital return was processed, certain tests were made for data accuracy and completeness of the file. Social security numbers were verified against that agency's primary database, and if there were no red flags, an electronic message was forwarded to the Federal Reserve to cut a check and mail it to the address indicated.

Each night, several summary reports were generated and disbursed to various managers, senior agents and others holding responsibility for the service's daily operations. None of this analysis showed anything out of the ordinary or alarming. It was very common for those owed a refund to be the first to file and receive their checks. It was those who owed the government money that waited until the last minute.

Another trend that hadn't gone unnoticed by the IRS involved the country's economy as a whole. Years ago, government analysts recognized that as the economy worsened, taxpayers wanted or needed their refunds as soon as possible. February, in a healthy economic climate, was a sluggish month. During tough times, people e-filed their returns hours after collecting their W-2s - the net effect being the service's workload increased earlier in the calendar year.

The digital gun aimed at the United States was armed with three different categories of ammunition. First, tens of thousands of returns from real, living Americans would be electronically filed. Their social security numbers were bona fide, as was their income. What was bogus was the amount of the refund claimed and the address where it was to be delivered. Wu's software was designed to file these returns first because the IRS would only accept one tax return per social security number. Millions of puzzled Americans were going to get a letter back from the IRS when they tried to submit their legitimate tax returns.

The second bullet to be fired at the US was the dead file. Millions of Americans died every year, and while most estates would eventually submit the deceased's final tax return, these filings tended to be very complex and rarely arrived at the IRS before April 15.

The final shot at the IRS computers was a series of amended returns. When MOSS received a refund for one of their bogus filings, a correction was immediately submitted. This double dipping of the fraudulent opening salvo resulted in even more US Treasury funds being mailed to addresses that were controlled by MOSS. This final wave was really not necessary, but the Chinese programmers enjoyed thinking about the bedlam they would cause in the American computer rooms.

The treasury began printing checks as requested by the IRS. There was no system in place that would recognize the high number of refunds being sent to post office boxes. Even less visible was the fact that many of the boxes were housed in businesses owned by immigrant entrepreneurs.

As the checks were delivered by the US Postal Service, the managers of the MOSS-funded enterprises, such as those opened by Zang in northern California, would gather and cash the checks. The monies were then deposited into the checking accounts managed by MOSS and almost immediately wired through a series of offshore accounts.

On the first day of the attack, a mere 10,000 returns were submitted. The average refund was $1,800, resulting in the United States Treasury being ripped off for a paltry $18 million. In reality, each false refund was actually a double whammy to the US government. An anticipated payment was converted into a liability, or money owed.

On the second day of the campaign, 90,000 false tax returns were submitted. The daily number kept growing until the tenth day, when over one million were transmitted. The relentless barrage of fraud continued to hammer the IRS's system for weeks.

February 10, 2017
Cypress Garden Apartments, Houston Texas

Sage fussed around her small apartment, somewhat anxious to see her mother and somewhat annoyed at the intrusion. The rare visit by both of her parents was welcomed in some aspects. As she glanced around the living room, she tried to envision what a few more small pieces of furniture would do for the place. Her mom tried to describe over the phone what she was bringing from the house, but Sage honestly couldn't picture some of it. *No matter*, she thought, *this place is so desolate now, anything would help.*

As she tidied up in anticipation of the parental visit, a small picture on the end table caught her attention. The picture captured an unscripted moment of family fun on the boat. She was spraying her father with a hose, and mom's timing with the digital camera had been perfect.

Setting the photograph back in its place, Sage wondered what her dad's mood would be. Constant conflict and turmoil had characterized their relationship for the last year or so. The interaction with her father was becoming more unpleasant every day, something or someone had to yield. Sage had opted for moving into her own apartment. Officially, her excuse had been a closer proximity to school; at least that was the polite justification for the change. In reality, she didn't need to be closer to the college; she wanted to put distance between a house that simmered with stress and conflict, threatening her sanity.

A wave of self-pity welled up inside of her. It just didn't seem fair that her life was so abruptly and wholly altered. The promise of an Ivy League school had been a mainstay of high school years filled more with exploring the nuances of organic chemistry than pep rallies. The household mantra had always been "If you make the grades, we'll pay for the best schools." Somewhere between receiving her acceptance letter from Wellesley and the second interview with MIT, that rug was wrenched from underneath her previously firmly planted feet. The beginning of his senior year, David had chosen a Dodge Ram dual cab truck, complete with lift kit and chilled leather seats. Sage bummed rides to campus when she could, but most often found herself sharing a bus seat with some lovelorn, coming of age junior high lad who fixated on her chest while she did her best to ignore him. The list of altered promises and disappointments stretched on and on. Memories of the ill-fitting, secondhand prom dress still caused her eyes to water.

David bailed for the army, and she couldn't blame him for that. Isolated after David's move, Sage found herself ill-equipped to manage the pressure of a crumbling family and a father who become more and more unpredictable as time passed.

She had always admired the way her dad easily managed the demands of a thriving business and bustling household. The last year before she moved out, he seemed to flounder. The strong embrace that had always grounded her in a sense of comfort and security began to weaken over time. As his hopelessness multiplied, her father withdrew and became hollow. *Didn't he realize this nasty situation affected more than just him?* She wondered. It seemed like he just gave up right when she needed him the most.

Sage wandered to her bedroom and began folding blue jeans that had been sitting in a basket for three days. She knew her mom would notice and comment. Sage thought about how close she was with her mother, thankful of the relationship. Still, mom would fuss and bluster over Sage living out of the laundry basket. *Is something wrong at school? Are you feeling okay?* Thoughts of the interrogation made her smile, but still, she didn't want to go through it today - especially not in front of her father.

As she folded a slightly worn dishcloth, Sage's mind drifted back to the time immediately prior to her move. She would never admit it, but the suggestion of her leaving home had been a cry for reassurance. Dad seemed to be focused on switching off lights to save electricity, not about her future. The final straw came the day she left a package at the discount store while she was refilling a prescription for her mom. When she had discovered the missing purchase, she had asked for the keys to return and retrieve it. Her father had become sullen and upset over the wasted gasoline. His scolding still resonated in her ears. Her protests that it had been an accident just made the situation worse.

Carrying the folded towels to the kitchen, Sage replayed that day in her mind. It wasn't his being upset over the gas that pushed her out. That episode had been just another example of his attitude. The message that day made it clear that he no longer cared about anything other than his own problems. The failure of the family business was important, and Sage understood that. Wasn't her life important too? Did everything have to be about him and the business?

Sage grimaced at the replay of the disappointment. She had to finish getting ready for her parents to stop by, and reliving all of this wasn't helping. Maybe they won't stay long. Maybe dad will be in one of his quiet moods and there wouldn't be any conformation or judgment.

Houston, Texas
February 10, 2017

The sign above the door read "Gold and Silver Buyers," and looked out of place in the otherwise empty strip mall. Wyatt noticed the sign wasn't a permanent fixture, but rather one of those banner advertisements hanging via a rope at each corner. The weeds sprouting here and there in the parking lot seemed to be competing with the random assortments of trash scattered around. A long row of dirty windows displayed montages of signage broadcasting "Space for Lease." The block walls between the storefronts held their own advertising, courtesy of some local youths and spray paint. Two years ago, Wyatt wouldn't have even considered doing business at such a place. Now, the low-rent, unoccupied strip mall was commonplace – eyesore or not.

Wyatt turned off the motor and got out. He made another quick scan of the parking lot, making sure he was alone. The wadded paper bag in his hand was full of Morgan's gold jewelry, and he couldn't help but feel like a target. There was one other car in the lot, and he was sure that belonged to the girl working in the shop. *If I were desperate*, he thought, *I would wait for some dude to come toting in his life's treasures and sell them. I would be waiting on him when he came out with the cash.*

Wyatt shook his head, embarrassed at his paranoia, and picked up the pace across the lot. Still, he watched his back. Years ago, this area was one of Morgan's favorite shopping destinations and an icon of Houston's north side. The main street was Farm to Market 1960, or FM1960. The two-initial designation a leftover from a time when this area had been farmland and the early Texans had been practical in naming their roads. Houston had experienced a boom of growth in the 1970s and '80s. The city didn't have any zoning, allowing the growth to spread outward rather than upward with skyscrapers. FM1960 became one of the main drags. For over 15 miles, scores of shopping malls, office buildings and businesses of every kind had budded and thrived. Wyatt remembered someone once saying, "If you can't buy it on FM1960, you don't need it."

All of those new businesses needed cheap labor, and apartment complexes sprouted along the corridor like wildflowers in the spring. Upscale housing, country clubs, and restaurants abounded. When the never-ending recession gripped the country in 2009, things began to change. Stores hired fewer workers, which translated into fewer apartment leases being signed. Owners of apartment buildings needed to fill their vacancies, so rents became cheap.

Inner city, low-income families suddenly realized they could afford to live in a better neighborhood and moved in.

Like so many communities in the US, urban creep began to wear down the once celebrated area. Crime slowly increased, and school rankings began to fall. Upscale shoppers moved to safer, less congested stores and shops. Businesses closed or relocated, following the consumers. Just like the apartment complexes, the commercial developers needed to lease their space, so rental rates dropped. Less desirable retailers jumped at the chance for a more prestigious address. It was a downward spiral that was almost impossible to stop.

The all but empty strip mall Wyatt was approaching was one of hundreds along the six-lane street. He remembered when traffic was an issue – but no more. He hadn't seen more than four or five cars at any one stoplight the entire trip.

The tattoo parlors, pawnshops, secondhand stores, and payday loan businesses survived, but they were like small islands in a dead sea of decay. Wyatt dismissed all of this and pushed the doorbell-like buzzer at the entrance. He'd been here a few days ago to get a quote, so he knew the process. The realization that this jewelry was the last large ticket item compelled him to be a savvy seller and solicit several bids. He'd visited four different locations, and King Midas Gold and Silver Buyers was the highest bidder.

He waited a few moments until the sound of the lock disengaging buzzed in his ears. The sparse lobby was obviously as temporary as the sign outside. A few mismatched chairs, a single end table, and crusty-looking lamp sat amid bare walls. The hastily acquired decor wasn't intended to attract repeat business. Behind a small counter sat a young woman, less than 30 years old. Her smile indicated she remembered him from a few days prior. "So, we offered the highest price for your gold?"

Wyatt nodded, "Yes, you're the winner. Is the quote still good?"

The girl scanned her computer monitor and pecked a few times on the keyboard. She paused while the machine responded and then busied herself with a calculator. Twenty seconds later, she looked up and smiled again. "You're in luck. Gold shot up again this morning, so I can actually offer you a little more than I estimated the other day."

"Well that's good news. How much more?"

The girl double-checked her calculator and the computer screen. "Almost $500 more. Gold is going nutzoid right now."

Wyatt teased, "Maybe I should wait a few more days to sell. I might get another thousand by then."

A shrug was quickly followed up with a mumble. "Up to you."

Wyatt was actually pondered doing just that, but decided against it. The precious commodity could go down as well. That was the problem with all of the turmoil churning throughout the country right now – you just never knew what was going to happen.

Wyatt shook his head and placed the heavy paper bag on the counter. "Naw, I'll go ahead and sell today. The only thing going up in price faster than precious metals is gasoline, and I'm wasting a lot of that liquid gold by driving around."

The young woman nodded and took Wyatt's bag. She began a lengthy process of pulling each piece of jewelry out and rubbing it on a black surface that looking like the ink tin of an old-fashioned rubber stamp. She then carefully squirted a drop of liquid from a small tube to check the purity.

The entire process took almost an hour, and Wyatt scrutinized her every move carefully. While his instincts told him the gal was honest, you couldn't be too cautious. When the girl had finished weighing, testing, and marking every piece, she hit the total button on her calculator with a grand gesture. Rather than announcing the total, she turned the little device around so Wyatt could see the number. *Not bad*, he thought, *not bad at all*.

He nodded his acceptance, and the attendant said, "I have to go to the safe in the back. I can't leave your gold out here while I'm gone. Do you trust me enough to let it out of your sight for a few minutes?"

Wyatt nodded again, figuring nothing in life was without risk. While the girl left to retrieve his money, he reflected on the last few days. The rise in the price of gold helped offset some of the gloom he had been feeling since Morgan and he had set off on this course. It had been so difficult selling everything. Countless trips to pawnbrokers resulted in the liquidation of blenders, leaf blowers, televisions and other man-portable items. Three different secondhand stores now displayed his family's furniture on their showroom floors. Sage welcomed the bookcase, wardrobe, 3 boxes of kitchen paraphernalia and assorted décor items into her apartment. Morgan and she had offset some of the melancholy by fussing around and arranging the hand-me-downs in the newly furnished space.

Still, it was depressing. Wyatt and Morgan had basically kept their clothing, and enough kitchenware to make coffee and eat. Last night they had slept on folding cots normally stored in a hall closet for guests visiting during times of high occupancy in their household.

Shortly, the attendant returned, counting out a significant stack of $100 bills. Wyatt, ever worried about robbery, stashed the cash in three different pockets before bidding the lady goodbye. He paused before leaving the place, checking that the parking lot was still empty.

Driving home, he reflected on how much the area had deteriorated over the last 15 years. The parallel with his life was obvious.

Until it hits you between the eyes, he thought, *you don't realize the effect of poverty.* When his credit rating began its descent, small gotchas popped out of the woodwork. The cost of his life insurance rose 20% - blamed on a bad credit rating. He tried to switch policies, but no new company would have him at any price. Again, his credit score was deemed the culprit.

Credit card companies suddenly increased their interest rates precipitously even though they were being paid every month. When Wyatt contacted the banks, they said that he was now a higher risk than before – regardless of his payment history. "I bet you guys showed up late for the battle and enjoyed bayonetting the wounded," he had angrily scolded one call center employee. It didn't help; they raised his interest rate again the following month.

Morgan tried to downgrade their satellite television to a basic cable package, but Comcable wouldn't take them as a customer without a significant deposit. The amount of the deposit was more than what they would have saved with the reduced service. It seemed to Wyatt that everyone was dog piling his family, kicking them when they were down. Job interviews for positions he could handle with one hand tied behind his back led nowhere. Finally, a headhunter returned his call and laid it out on the table – no one wants to hire an accountant with bad credit.

He had checked into bankruptcy and couldn't find a law firm that would take either his company or him personally as a client without extortionist-level retainer fees. The cost was so prohibitive; Wyatt wondered how anyone could afford to go out of business legally.

When the lease was up on his company car, he relegated to a used SUV. The "We Finance Here" car lot charged extraordinary interest rates that negated much of the savings over a new car. The repair bills for the constantly breaking vehicle resulted in it actually costing him more than a new vehicle would have.

The role of the humiliation factor couldn't be ignored. During the last few months the business had been operating, Wyatt had a lot of trouble focusing on work. It seemed like every night there was a new crisis at home, and the resolution was often demoralizing. Constant phone calls from bill collectors filled his voice mail, while endless emails offering money from loan sharks and payday loan hacks cluttered his inbox. Trying to work on a client's books during this period was next to impossible, and he often wondered if the stress didn't affect the quality of his work.

Wyatt turned into his neighborhood and noticed another house was up for sale. There were now nine homes listed on his street, four of which were in foreclosure. Thinking about a new start and leaving all this behind actually improved his mood. *We'll make things simpler*, he mused.

Three days later, Morgan and he packed the last few remaining items in the house and locked the door behind them - one last time. Each of them anticipated the need to console the other, but that concern was completely unnecessary. Both were relieved this chapter of their financial ordeal was finally over.

The couple stood in the driveway and held hands for a brief, tender moment before driving both cars to the marina. Stopping at the mailbox, Wyatt conducted a small ceremony of placing an envelope containing the keys inside. The mortgage company could wait on the US mail just like everybody else.

On the way to the dock, they stopped by Sage's apartment. For once, she was actually ready to go and hopped in her mother's car. Morgan appreciated her daughter taking a few days off so the family could be together during the transition. Since the plan was going so smoothly, she thought about taking a little of the gold money and going shopping. As the two girls followed Wyatt's SUV through Houston, their conversation centered on how to break the news that a detour to the mall was in order.

Chapter 4

February 14, 2017
Kemah Bay, Texas

That first day, they busied themselves preparing the boat. The forty-five foot trawler was really more like a floating two-bedroom, two-bath condo. Boxer had been Wyatt's pride and joy. After much debate, the family decided to name their new craft in honor of a great-uncle who once served as a naval aviator aboard the aircraft carrier USS Boxer. Wyatt had always been close to the man and thought the name matched the boxy shape of the vessel as well.

Like returning to a vacation home that hadn't been occupied in some time, all sorts of small tasks needed to be done before the couple occupied the space full time. Water tanks needed to be flushed and refilled. The septic system required similar attention. While Morgan and Sage busied themselves with dusting, wiping and washing, Wyatt performed maintenance on the numerous onboard systems.

There were three diesel motors in the engine room. Two were for propulsion, the third being a 14- kilowatt generator to power the hotel. All of them required oil and fluid checks. Boxer was also equipped with an extensive battery system. Besides the normal, deep-cycle starting batteries for the engines, she carried a bank of reserve cells connected to an inverter. If the family wanted to enjoy a quiet evening without the humming of the generator, Boxer could power all of her appliances using battery only – for a while.

Wyatt checked the filters on the air conditioning and heating system as well as Boxer's water maker. The latter device pulled seawater through a series of ceramic filters and produced fresh drinking water.

Morgan and Sage had two, full bathrooms to address. Each was fully equipped with head, shower, and vanity sink. Besides unpacking the significant amount of personal items carried from their home, the girls wanted to freshen the entire cabin, as it had not been ventilated for several weeks.

The trio worked tirelessly from dawn till dusk, as a seemingly endless amount of work was required to make Boxer feel like home. They unpacked and stowed clothes, stored pantry items, and replenished their supply of ice.

Boxer was equipped with one household-size refrigerator and a small deep freezer in the galley. A half-size refrigerator on the deck kept cool drinks handy topside.

After starting the diesels, topping off the battery fluid, and double-checking the workings of the engine room, Wyatt advanced to the bridge and repeated a similar process there.

Boxer was really a three-story boat. Seafarers boarded her transom on the middle, or deck level. Four stairs headed downward into the cabin, or hotel area, while a ladder led up to the bridge.

In the center of the bridge was the helm, the nerve center of Boxer's operation. A plush, comfortable, white, vinyl chair was bolted to the deck in front of a dash that wouldn't have looked out of place in an airplane. Rows of gauges, digital readouts, meters, and large monitors surrounded the stainless steel steering wheel.

Each of Boxer's three engines required its own set of monitoring instruments. Equipped with the equivalent of four separate electrical power systems as well, Boxer could run off shore power just like a house. She could also generate her own AC power from either the battery or generator. The fourth system was DC, powered from the large battery bank in the engine room. Each of these options demanded its own panel of gauges and meters on the helm.

Wyatt smiled as he remembered having to learn how to operate the vessel some years ago. He had studied all of Chapman's books regarding piloting and seamanship over and over again – almost memorizing the information those nautical standards contained.

In reality, Boxer was a combination house and recreational vehicle. As long as her fuel tanks held diesel and the galley were stocked, she was quite self-sufficient. She was mobile, able to handle all but the worst weather conditions without issue.

A burnt orange sunset streaked the western horizon when Wyatt finished his extensive checklists. He heard the sliding glass door leading to the salon roll open, and a moment later Sage's head appeared at the top of the ladder. "Mom says dinner's ready."

"Another five minutes and I'll be through," Wyatt responded.

A few moments later, Morgan steered her husband to the boat's bow where two plates complete with PB&J's were illuminated by a crimson, cinnamon-scented votive candle. It *was* Valentine's Day, after all.

Wyatt's cell phone buzzed at 2 a.m. He was so deep in REM sleep; he couldn't find the right buttons to answer the call. His half-functioning mind revved his adrenal glands, arriving at the conclusion that collection agencies were now dialing his cell phone in the middle of the night. He became so angry that when it rang again a few minutes later, his tone was extremely harsh. "This had better be good!"

A surprised voice on the other end responded, "Dad?"

Wyatt exhaled, his voice becoming instantly soft. "David? I'm sorry, buddy...I was asleep. Is everything okay?"

"Dad, I'm getting on a military transport in 10 minutes. I should be at Ellington Field about three hours from now. Can you pick me up?"

Wyatt's heart soared. "You bet I will, son. I'll get ready and head that way in just a bit." It was almost an hour's drive to the airfield.

"Okay, Dad. I'm sorry I woke you. You're going to have to put up with me for 30 days, ya know."

Wyatt yawned, and a sleepy smile crossed his lips. "I guess we'll figure out some way to survive. Love you, son."

"Love you too, Dad."

The line went dead, and Wyatt sat in the dark for a moment, enjoying what was a rare, good feeling. His son was coming home, and right at that moment, nothing else mattered. He felt a hand on his shoulder, signaling Morgan was awake. "Is everything okay?"

Wyatt stretched, the night's stiffness evaporating from his body. "Yes, yes it is. David's plane will land in a few hours," he stated, pushing back the covers, swinging his legs off the side of the bed, and sitting upright. "I'm going to pick him up."

Morgan grunted, "You mean *we* are going to pick him up, don't you?"

Wyatt grinned, "If you make the coffee, then you can tag along." The remark earned him a playful swat on the shoulder.

February 14, 2017
Washington, D.C.

The sounds of clicking heels and scuffing shoe leather echoed from the polished marble floor as Reed ambled toward his office. He had just been through one of the most confusing meetings of his budding political career and was trying to analyze what just happened.

The real power in the House of Representatives was measured by which sub-committees a congressman was assigned. The entire process was like a professional sports league trying to put together a multi-player deal. Draft picks, order of selection, free agents and future considerations all contributed to a system of political bartering that made Reed question the sanity of the entire process. Personal qualifications, experience, or desire had little, if anything, to do with it.

Despite this feeding frenzy for leverage and constant maneuvering for power, the freshman had managed to achieve his goal. He was now the newest member of the House Subcommittee on Domestic Monetary Policy and Technology - the sweet spot for dealing with the Federal Reserve.

Reed had sacrificed every other potential position to acquire this appointment. He had risked exposing his agenda, with one senior member of his party questioning why he was bypassing other politically powerful opportunities. Some quick thinking seemed to satisfy the curious politician, but just barely. "I believe future economic events will make this committee more influential than it is today," the junior congressman explained. The party's leadership hadn't posed any further questions.

He was running a game within a game. He had made no secret of his dislike of the Federal Reserve System during his campaign. Carefully crafting his speeches to make it a secondary issue, Reed didn't want to appear overzealous to the electorate or to elicit unwanted attention of party powerbrokers. He judiciously manufactured the image of a man compelled to reform the Fed, hoping to provide a good cover for his true intention – discovering what really happened to his father.

Reed strode through the heavy, wooden door that separated his office from the hall of the capitol building. Brenda glanced up and smiled, handing him the stack of messages from the corner of her desk. Before he could even say hello or thank her for the notes, the phone rang.

"Congressman Wallace's office," she answered professionally. "No, I'm sorry; the congressman isn't in at the moment." Reed winked at her and proceeded through the reception area toward his office, flipping through the messages as he passed. Brenda covered the phone with her hand and cleared her throat to attract his attention. When he established eye contact, she motioned with her head to one of the visitor's chairs in the corner. There, a smallish man sat with a briefcase on his lap. Wallace studied his watch and realized his appointment had arrived considerably early, but that was just fine with him. He had been looking forward to visiting with this man for a long time.

Reed nodded a silent thank you to Brenda and stepped over to address his visitor. He offered his hand, bowing slightly at the waist. "Dr. Martin?"

Peering over the rims of his coke bottle-thick glasses, the older gentleman managed more of a grimace than a smile. He nodded and weakly shook the Texan's hand. Reed made a motion with his arm, inviting the visitor to his office while saying, "Please, Doctor, won't you come right in?"

"I'm a little early," protested his guest. "The taxi driver drove much too fast despite my objections. I kept telling the maniac that I wasn't in any hurry."

"It's not a problem, sir. Can I get you anything?"

The man considered the query for a moment before shaking his head. "No, thank you; I'm fine."

Reed followed Dr. Martin in, motioning for his guest to settle in one of two burgundy leather visitors' chairs. After the doctor was seated, Reed chose the other chair, rather than sitting behind his desk. He wanted his visitor to feel comfortable and interact with him as an equal.

The congressman began, "So, Dr. Martin, how long have you been the head of George Washington University's History Department?"

"Almost twelve years now. I enjoy the research part of the position more than the teaching these days. The administrative role has never been a favorite of mine. Necessary evil, I suppose."

Reed nodded his understanding. "Do you find my request unusual, sir?"

The man reflected on his response for a little longer than Reed believed necessary. When the professor finally spoke, the pause was understandable. "No. No, not really. My department receives the occasional request from various branches of the government. I normally assign such tasks to one of our post-graduate students. Your inquiry, however, had already been made some years ago by one of your congressional predecessors. I handled his project originally, so it only made sense for me to handle this request personally."

Reed was curious. "A predecessor of mine?"

The doctor nodded, "Yes, congressman Ron Paul asked my department for a nearly identical study some years ago. I've always had a streak of libertarianism myself, and have a lot of respect for Ron. I rolled up my sleeves and dove right into the project."

Reed nodded and watched Dr. Martin unzip his briefcase, pulling out a small pad-computer. The professor continued. "Congressman, before we begin, I need to tell you something. I do this only so as not to waste valuable time. I can provide a synopsis of the information you've requested right now. I don't think it's the answer you're looking for, but it would save both of us a lot of effort."

Reed was a little surprised by the statement, but recovered quickly. "Why sure, professor. I suppose that makes sense. Please continue."

The historian nodded, "I'll get right to the point, congressman. It's no secret that you are the next in a long line of anti-Federal Reserve officials who've managed to get elected. I've reviewed your campaign speeches, scrutinized your website, and consulted with senior members of your party."

The professor paused for a moment, letting his statement sink in before continuing. "I'll be blunt, Mr. Wallace. If your intent is to replace or modify the Fed, it simply won't work. You'll be wasting your time. The Federal Reserve System is entrenched, powerful, and well-protected."

That's what I want everyone to think I'm doing, thought the congressman. *I want them all to be distracted by thinking I'm out to change the system.* The expression on Reed's face relayed a mock surprise at the academic's words. He started to protest, but the professor cut him off.

"Representative Wallace, I'm not a big fan of the Fed. I understand its imperfections more than most. The Federal Reserve should be thought of like Churchill viewed democracy, 'Democracy is the worst form of government, except for all the others that have been tried from time to time.' Well, sir, the Fed is the worst form of central banking I've ever seen, with the exception of all the other methods that have been tried throughout history."

Reed feigned cynicism, now convinced he had contacted the perfect person for his purposes. "You're going to have to expand on that, professor. I'm a little shocked by the direction this conversation is heading."

The professor smirked knowingly, believing he was one step ahead of the younger man sitting next to him. "Throughout the history of organized government, there have been two methods of monetary policy. Either the government or a powerful private entity has controlled the money. Both methods have *always* led to economic disaster. In some fashion, one can attribute the downfall of history's greatest empires to this very policy. British, Roman and Ottoman empires all failed due in some part to the management of their currency. As you know, these downfalls resulted in enormous suffering by the people of the realm. This has been the case regardless of the form of rule, be it socialism, democracy or republic. There are no historical exceptions."

Reed's gaze drifted for a moment while the professor's words rolled around in his mind. After a brief pause, he nodded for the man to continue.

"Even here in the United States, we experimented with both methods for over 150 years. The Continental Congress controlled the money supply to fund the Revolutionary War. The British overwhelmed the system with counterfeit bills. An independent central bank was then established, only to be ruined by corruption. Lincoln reversed that system, generating Greenbacks. Again, government control eventually failed. The US has bounced back and forth between the two methods since the beginning. The establishment of the Federal Reserve System in the 1920s stabilized the economy and engendered long-term growth. The Fed is a hybrid of the two methods, and it works better than anything else human society has implemented."

The Texas representative crossed his legs, leaning back in his chair. "It doesn't sound like anyone wanting to disrupt the status quo would have your support either, professor."

Dr. Martin immediately dismissed the concept. "I couldn't offer any voice about what's going on today. I don't have the unabridged facts to study and analyze." The older man's face became very serious, "Young man, it takes a while for time to erode all of the inaccuracies and propaganda put in place by powerful men. And believe you me; history is full of influential people who were experts at this sort of deception. Slowly, over many decades, the smoke and mirrors dissipated, and truth surfaced. To the historian, time is often like a knife - peeling away the deceptive skin covering the fruit of truth. That's why I'm a historian."

Reed did an admirable acting job, his expression displaying disappointment. "I'm sorry you feel that way, professor. Still, I would like to contract the study, if you please. At minimum I need the history lesson."

The professor sighed, "Who prints the money, or more accurately, who controls the money supply, is one of the most misunderstood facts about our government. Today, our government doesn't print its own money to spend – that is done by the Fed. The people who run the Fed, and thus make monetary policy, are appointed by the government. It's a shared power, with neither side having full control."

The older man gazed at his watch, standing abruptly. "My apologies, Congressman, but I've another appointment. I'll be in touch when I've finished your study."

After shaking hands and showing his guest to the door, Reed returned to his window and peered out into the gray Potomac sky. *I don't care about the Fed or the money supply or any of it. I want to find out who killed my father and why.*

February 15, 2017
Washington, D.C.

The secretary of the Department of the Treasury glared at the phone with an expression that betrayed her complete annoyance. She was only halfway through the latest status report on anti-counterfeit operations, and this call was the fourth one since she began. Reaching for the ultra-modern speakerphone, she couldn't help but notice the nine-inch high stack of additional paperwork that required her attention today. Hitting the intercom button, her voice relayed frustration. "Yes, Ginger, what is it?"

"I'm sorry to interrupt, Secretary Palmer, but there are two gentlemen here from the IRS. They maintain it's an urgent matter."

Rubbing her temples, Wanda Palmer whispered under her breath, "What now?"

Ginger evidently recognized the exasperation in the utterance, expanding, "They are *rather* insistent, ma'am."

SOT Palmer, as she was known throughout the organization, curtly responded, "Show them in please, Ginger."

A few moments later, the door to the secretary's office opened, and two men Wanda didn't recognize were shown in. Quick introductions were exchanged, but Wanda was so tired she couldn't remember their names. She almost let out an audible chortle when she recognized a resemblance between the two IRS agents facing her and the vaudeville characters, Abbot and Costello. While the two men confirmed with Ginger that they didn't need anything to drink, Secretary Palmer was trying to remember which was taller, Abbot or Costello. The taller man interrupted her memory search, speaking with urgency in his voice. "Madam Secretary, as you know, Under-Secretary Withers is on vacation at the moment. We felt this matter was important enough to bring to your attention immediately."

Something in his tone caught Wanda's ear. "Go ahead; you've got my attention."

The shorter IRS agent opened a small attaché case while his partner continued. "A few hours ago, it became evident that something was terribly wrong with the IRS's tax processing system. We believe there is a strong possibility that we are experiencing some sort of cyber-attack."

Secretary Palmer's first thought was, *"So, why are you troubling me with this?"* Rather than ask why they hadn't immediately contacted the FBI, she decided to hear them out. "Go ahead."

It was Abbot's turn to talk, "Ma'am, this report indicates that tax returns generating over 210 billion dollars' worth of refunds have been submitted electronically to our system in the last eight days. That is over 100 times the average for this time of year."

Marsha let out a very un-cabinet-level whistle. "Did you say billion – like with a 'b'?"

"Yes, ma'am, I did."

Secretary Palmer reached for the report and quickly scanned the numbers. A minute later, she glanced up and tersely inquired, "Has anyone notified the FBI?"

Abbot and Costello first looked at each other, and then Costello spoke. "No, Madam Secretary, we didn't. There is evidence that the source of the attack is offshore, and we don't have the authority to report an act of international terrorism...perhaps an act of war."

"What?"

Abbot continued, "We noticed the abnormality three days ago and sent out our own investigators at that time. It finally became clear this morning that a very disturbing trend is in play here." Abbot looked at his co-worker, who nodded that the other agent should continue.

"Ma'am, we believe the Chinese government may be the source of this attack."

SOT Palmer's spine bristled, and her gaze became piercing. "You'd better be able to back up that type of statement...and do a very fine job of it."

Secretary Palmer listened as the two men explained their logic. Agents had been sent to three different addresses that had received refund checks. All were postal service stores with hundreds of mailboxes, and all were owned by Chinese individuals or corporations. When the business owners' names were finally tracked down, the FBI's counter-intelligence desk had flagged one of the people as a potential MOSS agent.

The two IRS agents continued with the results of the investigation for a few more minutes when the secretary held up her hand and stopped them. "I assume someone has stopped payment on all of those checks?"

Abbot and Costello's reaction justified their new nicknames. The two men hesitated and stammered for a few moments before Abbot finally blurted out, "No, Madam Secretary, we haven't done that because we can't. There is no way to discern legitimate returns from bogus ones, and even if we could, the government can't stop processing on individual checks. We don't have that capability in the system. There's never been a need. We would have to stop processing on all treasury checks, including social security, unemployment and pensions. Even the military's paychecks would have to be stopped."

Secretary Palmer made her decision in less than a second. She reached for her phone and pressed a button.

"Yes, ma'am."

"Ginger, get me the chief of staff at the White House right away. Tell him it's extremely important."

The White House

The gathered staff sat in shock as Secretary Palmer and her early morning guests explained the situation to the president and his immediate staff. A hastily prepared presentation served as the primary focus of the meeting, with the attendees flipping pages as their eyes widened and narrowed during Palmer's narrative.

"Mr. President, in summary, each year the Internal Revenue Service processes approximately 153 million tax returns. Normally, about 80% of those receive refunds. The annual government collections from individual income tax are $1.8 trillion. Normally, we refund about $400 billion of that amount, resulting in a final net number of $1.4 trillion in revenue. This situation could reduce that amount by over 20%, sir."

Everyone in the room knew that China was to blame, but no one wanted to say it. The world was teetering on several different edges as it were; a war was something no one wanted to add to the mix. The president fully understood that's what this meant – an act of war. Subterfuge was often as damaging as an overt attack.

After the known facts had been disclosed, the obvious next step was to determine a course of action. This stage of the meeting was the exact opposite of the presentation, as several discussions lead to debates that escalated to arguments. As a variety of solutions rolled around the conference room, it was determined that the Federal Reserve Board must be brought into the conversation. Twenty minutes later, Chairman Gordon was on the speakerphone and being briefed. When Secretary Palmer finished her presentation, Gordon whistled loudly.

"Mr. President, I can see only two options here. Either we honor the checks that have been written or we don't. As I'm sure you've already been told, we don't have the capability to pick and choose which payments are honored versus rejected. People will take the checks to local financial institutions, and our clearinghouses will process the Treasury's account numbers, crediting the banks. It's an all or nothing proposition because Treasury doesn't differentiate the accounts for social security stipends, Medicare reimbursements, or tax refunds. It all comes out of the same bucket."

The chief executive replied, "Chairman Gordon, what will be the impact if we honor the bogus returns? And by that, I mean what will be the consequences of $180 billion withdrawn from the government's operational cash accounts?"

There was a longer than normal pause on the other end of the speaker. Finally, the nation's top banker responded. "Mr. President, that amount of money is significant in the grand scheme of our country's financial position. In reality, sir, the final impact to the nation will be about twice that. The government is going to get double-dipped because anticipated revenue will be converted to expenditure. The final number could be as large as $360 billion, sir. That is a significant sum."

The president nodded, "If in fact it is the Chinese, their absconding with only $10 will become a political hot potato." The nation's leader scanned the faces of each ally seated at the table. "We will be attacked by the other side of the aisle relentlessly. Some of the citizenry will demand retaliation, while others will lose faith in our administration." Most of the gathered staff nodded knowingly.

The chief executive downed a sip of water and continued. "Chairman Gordon, what if we don't honor the checks and other payments until all of this is resolved?"

The voice on the other end hesitated. "I'm not sure, sir. This situation is unprecedented. Historically, whenever governments have failed to meet their obligations, there have been mixed reactions. I think the outcome all depends on how it is presented to the American people. Since this would be only a temporary situation, I would hope it would be manageable."

Another 20 minutes of discussion ensued before the president issued his final statement. "I don't know about all of you, but I'm sick and tired of America playing the victim. Our friends on the Asian mainland have manipulated currency, tariffs, manufacturing agreements, international finance, and practically every other aspect of global trade, with little to any regard for anyone but themselves. They have blocked uncounted initiatives and resolutions in the United Nations, while doing business under the table with such rogue regimes as North Korea, Iran, and Venezuela."

The most powerful man in the world paused for just a few moments, carefully selecting his words. "I've had enough. I believe the American people will accept waiting a few days for their checks and deposits in order to stop this blatant attack. We've always pulled together when aggressors have sought to harm our nation. I don't see how this situation is any different. We need to stop the diversion of our funds to China. Chairman Gordon, please stop payment on all US Treasury checks immediately."

February 15, 2017
White House Press Room

The room was abuzz with hushed conversations projecting from a dozen small groups of reporters. The anticipation thickened the air, and everyone could smell the adrenaline flowing through the gathering. It had been months since an "all hands on deck" press conference had been called. These things didn't happen unless something big was in the works.

Several of the reporters noted that their sources inside the government had been very silent today – an unusual circumstance. Others speculated about the last minute changes posted to the president's calendar. The extensive line of government vehicles arriving at the White House in a steady flow served to further heighten the furor.

The press secretary marched purposefully to the podium and pushed downward on the platform with both hands while repeating, "Ladies and gentlemen…. Ladies and gentlemen, please be seated. The president will be with you in just a moment. Please take your seats."

In a few minutes, the room quieted as the owners of pad computers, multifarious hand-held recorders, and low-tech paper and pencil anticipated the coming announcement.

To everyone's surprise, an assortment of government officials strode onto the small stage. The gathered reporters faced an odd mix of familiar faces. Several members of the House Banking and Finance Committee were first, quickly followed by the secretary of treasury, the chairman of the joint chiefs and finally the secretary of homeland security.

An unspoken current ran through the rows of journalists – this was big!

When the president stepped to the lectern, everyone stood. He immediately signaled them to their seats and began speaking. "I'm going to issue a brief statement and then take a few questions. "

The tired-looking chief executive scanned the room and then glanced down at his prepared remarks. "This morning, it came to our attention that something was amiss at the Department of Treasury. Tens of thousands of suspicious tax returns have been filed using the online computer system familiar to many Americans. As of this point in time, I have ordered a full investigation by the Department of Homeland Security into the matter."

Younger members of the press corps perceived the announcement by the commander-in-chief as anticlimactic at best. Several of them wondered what the big deal was. A computer glitch? A problem with the IRS's system? Ho-hum. Those with more experience waited for the other shoe to drop. They knew that the collection of officials standing behind the president hadn't been called together over some computer error.

The president continued, "As many Americans know, the payment of social security benefits, military salaries, government pensions, and the payroll of federal employees all originate at the Department of Treasury. Temporarily…and let me stress that word 'temporarily,' the severity of this issue leads us no option but to suspend those payments."

Millions of television viewers suddenly were rapt with attention. Every person in the pressroom moved to the edge of his seat, with many barely controlling the urge to shout out questions. After a brief pause to let his words soak in, the president continued in a very controlled voice. "I want to stress to every citizen of the United States and those who do business with her, this situation has nothing to do with the solvency of our government. I want to make it perfectly clear that we expect to resolve this matter quickly and return to business as usual."

The chief executive half-turned and pointed to the secretary of homeland security. "We are taking no chances on such a serious matter. I have every branch of our government investigating not only the cause and resolution of this situation, but a method to ensure nothing like this happens again. I asked these department heads to join me today in order to assure the American people that we are taking this situation seriously, and every available resource is being used to correct this problem."

The experienced journalists in the room began immediately analyzing the collection of people standing behind the president. Every facial expression, stance and gesture was scrutinized. The diagnosis wasn't good. Even the generals from the Pentagon seemed uptight – a sure sign this was a very serious topic.

The president cleared his throat and stated, "I'll take a few questions now," pointing to a reporter from the New York Times seated in the front row.

"Sir, would you describe this as a computer glitch, some sort of fraud, or something else? Could you please expand on exactly what is happening?"

Relieved at the question, the president turned and pointed to the secretary of treasury. "I'll let Secretary Palmer answer that."

Looking absolutely shocked to be put in front of millions of viewers, Palmer took a few, small steps to the microphone. She cleared her throat and stated, "At this moment we cannot say with certainty what or who is the cause. What we know is that billions of dollars' worth of checks, wire transfers, and direct deposits have already been sent. These *will not* be honored, and all new transactions will be withheld until we are aware of all of the facts."

Palmer started back to her original position, but the Times reporter wasn't going to let it go at that. "Ma'am, are you saying if someone has received, but not cashed his social security check, it will bounce?" A low murmur hummed through the room, many surprised at the reporter's choice of the word "bounce."

Again clearing her nervous throat, Palmer replied, "Yes, that is what we are saying. We advise all citizens to hold onto any government checks in their possession. Furthermore, we advise every recipient of US federal government funds to verify that any recently deposited checks were honored. As of 10 a.m. eastern standard time this morning, the Federal Reserve is no longer honoring those checks."

While the pressroom maintained some semblance of order, Secretary Palmer's last statement had more than one unintended consequence beyond the White House walls. A large segment of the American population abandoned their televisions in order to access their online banking systems. Within eight minutes, the servers at every major US bank, as well as at hundreds of smaller financial institutions, were overwhelmed. Hundreds of thousands of people were given error messages saying "System Unavailable," which more than a few interpreted as meaning their funds were unavailable. All across America, folks were gathering their purses, slipping on their shoes, and heading to the local bank.

Secretary Palmer stepped away from the microphone, signaling with a nod to the president that she was done. Every arm shot up, and a chorus of "Mr.

President…Mr. President!" blasted the room. Calmly, he pointed at an AP reporter, which silenced everyone else.

"Mr. President, why can't the government simply stop payment on the fraudulent checks? Why stop them all?"

The chief executive smiled and nodded at the question, "That's a very good question Steve, one of the first ones I asked myself. It was explained to me that the technology used to process the millions and millions of payments issued by the federal government simply does not have that capability. Historically, any time someone has received an incorrect check or deposit, the government has simply asked for the money back. The percentages have been so small; the capability to stop one or more payments was never developed. This is one of the items we are working on, so that this situation never happens again."

"A follow-up, Mr. President! So the government is in a situation where it's 'all' or 'none,' and your administration determined the problem is big enough to opt for none?"

The president metered his answer, responding, "Yes, that is accurate. Until we gain a full understanding of the source and scope of the issue, I have been advised that this is the safest and best course for our nation."

All over the world, important phones were ringing. Bankers, investors, and government officials were being roused from slumber and having meals interrupted. The message was basically the same – the United States isn't paying its bills.

Cable news producers were dialing experts, trying to book interviews with analysts while the press conference was still in progress. The opposing political party's think tanks began creating spin, centering primarily on the integrity of the current administration's announcement – maybe they were hiding something even more dark and sinister.

~  ~

In China, several ministers watched a translated version of the press conference. While it was impolite to squeal with joy, several knowing smiles flashed.

The Minister of Finance wasn't viewing the news conference, instead enjoying the company of his #1 administrative assistant. The persistent knocking at his door resulted in an annoyed response. It was one of the Premier's messengers, delivering a simple, one sentence note:

Implement Phase II of Operation Golden Mountain.

As the paper was being sucked into his shredder, the minister was on the phone, issuing orders to the Chinese Central Bank. US Treasury notes, of which the Chinese government held a position exceeding $1.5 trillion, were immediately listed for sale on the international markets, essentially flooding the supply side and causing the price to drop dramatically. The Ministry of the Interior began placing electronic orders for oil futures, thus driving the price on the world's commodity exchanges higher.

Alternative news sources and bloggers by the thousands were spinning up conspiracy theories almost as quickly as the reporters threw questions at the president. Most of the uninformed speculation revolved around the premise of a federal government unable to pay its bills due to massive federal debt.

Communication infrastructure was stretched to the limit. American wives were hitting "1" on speed dial to make sure their husbands had heard the news. Adult children were reaching out to their retired parents to determine the status of the elders' bank accounts. Phone systems at bank branches were overwhelmed in moments, the busy signals adding to the paranoia already spreading throughout the general population. More than a handful of experienced bank managers knew what was coming and tried desperately to call for cash deliveries - their email, cell phones and landlines now useless.

Private citizens weren't the only ones in a panic. All over the nation, state controllers speculated if the suspension of federal funds applied to them. The unemployment, social services, and educational funds were all dependent on federal monies. Was Treasury stopping payment on their lifelines as well?

Every financial market in the world practically froze. Essentially, the number of shares being traded on Wall Street fell to zero while traders tried to ascertain what was really going on. Currency traders, futures markets, and commodities all followed suit, the enormous global financial engine suddenly screeching to a halt. America couldn't pay her bills. It didn't matter if by choice or not, the fact was the fact.

Neither the president, nor his staff understood the mindset of the American people. For the last 20 years, they had been subjected to an ever more powerful media whose sole purpose was to create controversy – news vultures whose sole intent was to present content according to what would generate the highest ratings against their competitors. It was no secret that good news didn't sell as well as bad. A fair fight was boring and didn't generate much advertising revenue. A clean disagreement was even lower on the entertainment scale.

This industry-of-strife had gradually extended its tentacles into practically every aspect of human life. Television, radio, newspapers, magazines, movies – even children's cartoons were inundated, tweaked and accented with polarizing conclusions that sought to minimalize the thought process of the average person. Comedy, theatre, art, and popular music stirred the pot of discontent.

It wasn't just in America or the Western nations. Arabic news outlets fueled century-old debates, fanning the flames with twisted propaganda about Israel and her allies. Few people on the planet were immune to the spreading, cancer-like business of discontent.

One of the primary side effects to this 21st century high-tech industry was jaded disbelief. Human faith in the truth, even the capability to tell the truth, had severely eroded over time. Everyone had a hidden agenda. Politicians, ministers, judges, police officers and others in authority simply couldn't be trusted. Documentaries exposed family physicians in cahoots with mega-pharmaceutical companies. Depictions of policemen being motivated by racial hatred or succumbing to the temptation of wealthy drug cartels filled the nightly news. Stories of judges poisoned by some inner binary switch, either liberal or conservative and never in-between, created a growing inability to trust leaders.

The industry-of-strife loved the television ministers who fell from grace – painting an exaggerated picture of men ultimately corrupted by money and power and no longer deserving of trust. The message to the people – you can't believe a man of God. No religion was immune. All of the Catholic Church's wonderful deeds of charity, education, and help for the downtrodden were forgotten due to the horrid acts of a few, sick men. After the exposure, the industry-of-strife congratulated itself for providing such a valuable service to the public.

Political rhetoric was intentionally elevated to the status of a gladiator match. If the candidates were boring, spin rustled feathers and polarized constituents. If that didn't work, rumor and innuendo were created, amplified, and backed with layers of connect-the-dot facts.

The unintended consequences brought about by the industry-of-strife were that no one believed the president and his statements anymore. No one trusted the government. Whatever was going on, whatever the truth, it wasn't what the man said. It was anything but what he claimed. At least that's how the vast majority of the people interpreted the situation.

February 15, 2017
Houston, Texas

Christina Perkins worked the front counter at the Trustline National Bank branch on Westheimer. It was the typical slow weekday, and her mind was occupied with the growing mountain of laundry waiting for her at home. The occasional customer drifted in now and then, requesting withdrawals and making deposits. The most exciting occurrence of the morning was a printer jam when a long-time customer requested a money order.

The first hint that something was peculiar came from a patron who returned to the bank after listening to the president's press conference on her car radio in the bank's parking lot. The middle-aged woman initially dropped in to deposit a small check, smiling and waving to the employees as she left. Five minutes later, she was back inside - to withdraw every last penny from her checking account – in cash. The branch manager, who would normally expect to be notified of such an occurrence, waved Christina off as he was clearly on an important phone call and couldn't be disturbed. Frustrated by both the manager's lack of response and the clearly anxious customer, Christina politely questioned the woman about her transaction.

"You haven't heard? The government can't pay its bills. The president is on the radio telling the country that all of the government checks are bad. I want my money, and I want it right now."

Christina dismissed the story, thinking the lady had misunderstood or someone was playing a bad practical joke. Before she could even count out the small stack of $100 bills, two more people rushed into the lobby, waiting in line and fidgeting.

Christina asked her current customer if she would like an envelope for her cash, but the woman snatched the bills and stuffed them in her purse. She pivoted quickly and rushed out the door without another word.

Before Christina finished with the next bank patron, 20 people glared at her from the line. Many of the customers clutched checkbooks, ATM cards, and other documents. To Christina, they all appeared anxious or fearful.

She turned to bid a co-worker open another teller's cage, but found the other clerk absolutely swamped with an inordinate number of cars in the drive-up lanes. Just then, the manager saw fit to exit his office, immediately hustling to the service counter. He watched as another customer withdrew his entire balance and then motioned for Christina to step around the corner with him.

"There's been an incident in Washington, Christina. I'm waiting on instructions from downtown, but I believe we can expect a run on the bank today. I want you to try and reassure people their money is safe - to not empty their accounts. I want you to be calm and act like this day is the same as any other."

Christina still didn't realize what he was saying at first. He started to expand on the situation when impatient voices began complaining. "Can we get some service here please?" The manager motioned for Christina to assist the malcontent as the line of customers grew longer by the minute, and no one looked happy.

Every single person Christina waited on demanded all - or most of their available funds. The bank's vault was on a time delay, and at this rate, the amount of hard currency in the tills wouldn't last very long. Christina glanced up to see a familiar face next in line. The older gentleman was a favorite among the customer service personnel, as he knew each of them by name. One of their biggest depositors, Max was a thrifty old gent and saved over $50,000 in his nest egg. Christina got a lump in her throat when she spotted the old-fashioned savings booklet clasped tightly in his hand. Sure enough, Max wanted his money. The manager attempted to intervene, offering a cashier's check or money order. The man would have none of it, insisting, quite loudly, that all of the banks were "going to hell in a hand basket."

By now, the line of customers was out the door and halfway down the block in front of the building. The drive-thru was completely clogged with cars, and bank patrons jammed the parking lot in the strip mall across the street. The manager decided to gamble with Max and stated, "I'm sorry, sir, but we have implemented a $500 maximum withdrawal limit per day, per customer. I'll be happy to provide the rest via certified check, but I can't give you the entire amount in cash."

Both Christina and her boss were shocked at the older man's emphatic and impassioned protest. "This is ROBBERY!" he yelled. "I've had my money in this bank for 15 years, and I want every single dime before I leave!"

When the manager started to repeat his limit, the man waved him off and turned to the people standing in line, bellowing, "They're out of money already! The news report was right! They don't have any money!"

Three things happened about then. The first incident was innocent enough. Snuggled in its mother's arms, a baby expressed discontent over the long wait, releasing an annoying screech. Secondly, a young man bypassed the queue, and howled over the crying child that the ATM machine was out of order. Another man, who couldn't understand the complaint, thought the younger man was cutting in line and began cursing the innocent ATM user.

In less than a minute, the two men were shoving. When the inevitable first punch landed, the branch manager retreated from the main lobby to notify the police. Unfortunately, all of the phone lines were lit up with customers calling into the branch. A free telephone line wouldn't have done him any good anyway - Houston's 911 systems had crashed only minutes before due to call volume. The manager grabbed his cell from his desk, but couldn't get a signal.

Glancing around the lobby, he could see the battlefield had now spread. Customers scrambled to remain out of the volatile tussle. In a panic, he pressed the alarm button mounted under his desk. Meanwhile, the fight resolved the old-fashioned way – one guy lost, and the other won. The manager reentered the lobby, announcing the police were on their way and would no doubt require statements from all witnesses. More than one customer opted to exit the building immediately. Quickly, Christina scrawled and posted a homemade sign:

Branch Closed due to computer system failure.
Please come back later or visit another location.

The sign was hastily taped to the stainless steel and glass front doors, and then they were locked. A bank employee was assigned to let the remaining customers out of the building as soon as their transactions were completed.

To the people in front of the bank's building, the sign didn't make any sense. Their angry faces were pressed against the windows, peering inside. They could see the few remaining customers already inside of the branch, receiving their money. One man posed a question to no one in particular, "If the computers really are down, how are *those* people getting money?"

Tensions escalated as more and more people surged against the bank's entrance. Max, with his $500 dollars in hand, was let of out of the branch, cursing and mumbling all the way. Weaving his way through the crowd toward his pickup truck, Max was consumed with a combination of anger, frustration, and fear. He just knew he would never see his money, and it was all he had in life. His kids were grown and lived out of state. His wife had passed away some years ago, the good Lord rest her soul. His only social life seemed to be going to the funerals of old friends. To Max, it wasn't the money itself. He couldn't have spent it even if the bank had coughed it up. No, the money was his legacy, the only tangible result of his 80 years – and now that was gone.

Max's heart began to race as he realized the futility of easily removing his Ford truck from its parking space. Wiggling the oversized vehicle back and forth, progress could be measured by the inch. A seemingly endless line of cars stretched around the block, all in line for the drive-thru windows. The blood roared in his ears, and his chest began to tighten. In the 15 minutes it took him to maneuver from the parking space, the feeling in his chest grew serious. His level of despair overrode common sense, and he ignored the sharp pains radiating from his sternum. Finally free of the parking lot entanglement, Max's foot descended hard on the accelerator, causing the back wheels of his truck to bark while leaving a short trail of rubber. The throbbing in his chest yielded to blurred vision as he began to turn the vehicle in front of the bank, the old truck going way too fast. Max's last thought was to slow down, but his foot never executed the command. His brain's dying order was to brake, but the accelerator was pressed instead, the out-of-control pickup aimed directly at the front doors of the bank.

The throng of people gathered at the main entrance scattered as Max's truck hit the curb, barely escaping harm, as the heavy vehicle slammed into the doublewide glass and steel entrance. The truck's vector wasn't perfect, and the front bumper nicked the building's structure, causing the 4,000-pound projectile to enter the bank's lobby on two wheels and bouncing. The glass, doorframes, heavy granite table, and two visitors' chairs finally brought the truck to a stop.

In the bed of the truck was a full five-gallon can of gasoline Max used to fill his lawnmower. The bouncing, rough ride had turned the container on its side, and leaking contents were now leaching through a drainage hole in the pickup's bed. In a few moments, the stream of liquid petrol found the truck's hot muffler, and a small fire whooshed into existence. Ten seconds later, the blaze was spreading, white-hot. In less than a minute, flames engulfed the truck's half-full fuel tank. In two minutes, a significant fireball of boiling red and yellow flames and superheated air engulfed most of the bank's lobby.

For the few remaining customers inside, absolute bedlam ensued. Screams and shouts filled the smoke- clogged building as the fire spread with a fury.

Christina's initial reaction to the door exploding inward and the resulting inferno was to duck behind the service counter. She crouched there, paralyzed with fear for what seemed like a long time. She felt a tug at her arm and looked up to see her manager pulling her from the floor. He barked, "Get in the vault! Get in the vault! We'll be safe there from the fire. It won't burn."

Four of the bank employees made it inside the thick steel structure. The desperate workers huddled together on the floor, surrounded by rows of safety deposit boxes and cash drawers. It is true, they were safe from the flames and smoke, but the manager hadn't realized the heat from the firestorm would radiate through the steel walls of their sanctuary. Christina noticed the soles of her shoes were beginning to smolder as the sweat poured out of her body. All of the enclosed bankers began screaming in pain, the water in every cell of their bodies so hot it was actually cooking nerve tissue. Christina fell once, but the searing heat on her skin encouraged her to stand again. At 180 degrees, her tortured brain finally seized out from the pain, and she fell to floor where she died.

~   ~

The combined number of law enforcement officers employed in the greater Houston area numbered 36,000 in the year 2017. During any one shift, the maximum number on duty was 20,000. Of these, a significant number were guarding prisoners, working court cases, or investigating crimes. In Houston alone, there were over 14,000 bank branches and other financial institutions, leaving less than one available policemen per branch. Given a run on the banks that was 100 times larger than any experienced during the Great Depression, and that simply wasn't enough manpower to keep the peace.

The first responders in Houston were actually some of the fastest in the nation, taking only two hours for the police and fire department to arrive at the Trustline branch on Westheimer.

All over the country, millions of people decided they wanted their cash, and they didn't want to wait. Gas stations were taping cardboard signs to pumps – cash only. Lines were forming within an hour of the news coming out of Washington. Nervous station managers had seen this before, having experience with hurricanes and long lines of panicked people. Calls went out for police protection, most of which went unanswered.

Online transfers and ATM withdrawals crashed computer servers all over the financial landscape, resulting in retail stores' inability to process credit cards. Surges of customers rushing to their local grocery stores were met by signs at the entrances - cash only today. Even more people flocked to the banks to secure emergency funds to tide them over this crisis. Financial institutions were overwhelmed, and they simply couldn't cope. Doors were locked, and customers were turned away. Tempers flared, fights broke out, gunshots split the air, and eventually someone threw a homemade bomb at a branch in Detroit.

Brenda stuck her head inside of the congressman's door and gently tapped on the frame. When Reed glanced up from the stack of papers in front of him, she shyly tapped her watch and said, "Sir, it's 5:30. If you don't need anything else, I'll be on my way."

Reed blinked his eyes and yawned as if to clear his mental cobwebs. He'd been intensely concentrating on a proposed bill sent him from a constituent and couldn't initially comprehend Brenda's meaning. A quick glimpse through the narrow slit in the curtains revealed the fading light of the Washington winter day, and he realized the afternoon had slipped away. "Wow, I thought it was about three, Brenda. I need to get going myself. Hang on a second, and I'll walk out with you."

After quickly shutting down his laptop while pulling on his overcoat, the two made their way toward one of the capitol building's private doors.

Brenda noticed the tickle in her throat before her nose detected the distant smell of smoke. As they continued down the hall, the two noted an unusually large number of security guards and D.C. police assembled in the passageway. One of the regular security men took notice as the two government servants approached the exit. Reed nodded at the man and was surprised at the serious expression that countered. "Representative, I would recommend one of us escort you to your vehicle, sir. There have been some reports of disturbances, and we don't want to take any chances."

"Disturbances," Reed probed. "I've not heard about any disturbances. What's going on?"

"The president made an announcement earlier today, and there have been some issues at a few local banks. We also have some reports of a large crowd gathering on the mall by the White House. If you don't mind, sir, one of us will be happy to escort you and the young lady to your cars."

Brenda was curious, "Do you know what the president talked about, officer?"

"No, ma'am, I do not."

Brenda's face flashed concern as she turned to Reed. "I'm supposed to pick up my sister from work. You know, I haven't heard from her all day. I hope she's okay; she does work at a bank."

Suspecting that local policemen generally did not chaperone federal employees to their automobiles, Reed grew concerned about Brenda's safety. His lawyer's "sixth sense" told him there was more to this story than had been relayed.

When his radio sounded, the officer moved a few steps toward the throng of gathered policemen and security personnel, listing intently. A few moments later, he turned back to Reed and Brenda, stating, "The security situation has been upgraded, Congressman. I'm afraid we'll not only have to accompany you to your car, but also provide an escort to your destination, sir."

Reed nodded his understanding, his mind churning on the information provided. He didn't have a car. He didn't really need one since he was still in temporary quarters at a nearby hotel. "Officer, I was walking home, but this young lady has quite a trip ahead of her. I'm sure I'll be fine. Can you make sure she gets home okay?"

The policeman frowned, and then added, "Well, technically I'm only authorized to provide security for members of the House and Senate."

Reed brightened, immediately thinking of a solution. "Well then, she'll just have to give me a ride home – the long way."

Brenda started to protest, but Reed's look cut her off. The policeman nodded, turned to his fellow officers, and instructed, "Luke, could you provide escort for Congressman Wallace, please?"

Luke was a rather large fellow. His closely chopped, graying hair and square shoulders would have looked more at home on a Marine Corps drill field than in the blue policeman's uniform. He managed a cursory nod and what must have been his version of a smile.

While they hurried to Brenda's car, Luke asked about their destination. Brenda mapped it out for him, and again his only response was a nod. When they arrived safely at the designated parking spot, Luke directed, "I'll be waiting for you in the cruiser at the bottom of the ramp. Please follow me and stay close. If there is any trouble, lock your doors and stay put."

The small sedan was a little tight for the tall Texan, but he managed to fold himself in while dismissing Brenda's apologies over how dirty her car was. They maneuvered down the two exit ramps and waited while the automatic arm slowly rose. Reed noticed two columns of smoke rising against the grey Washington sky. The fires looked to be less than a mile away, but it was difficult to tell in the low light.

Officer Luke was exactly where he said he would be, and waited patiently for the traffic to clear before pulling out. Reed noticed their escort's eyes monitoring Brenda's progress in his rearview mirrors. Other than the smoke, everything appeared normal until they were about eight blocks from the Capitol. Suddenly, Luke turned on the cruiser's blue flashing lights, cutting a space out of the traffic in the right-hand lane. Brenda followed, confused by the sudden change and mumbling, "This isn't the right way."

At the next intersection, they took a right, and Reed noticed a sea of blue and red flashing lights in the block behind them. Dozens of emergency vehicles cluttered the street. He turned to Brenda, "He chose a detour to avoid whatever is going on back there. I'm sure he knows what he is doing."

Brenda clutched the wheel a little tighter, as if to release some stress on the steering column. Another block later, Brenda commented, "What are all these people doing out on the street? They sure don't look happy." Reed was trying to get service on his cell phone. He wanted to see if there was any breaking news on the internet and hadn't been watching as they drove. Brenda's words snapped him back into the here and now, and the representative immediately noticed what Brenda was referring to. Clusters of five to ten people were unevenly spaced all up and down the sidewalk on both sides of the street. There didn't appear to be any good reason for it as far as he could tell. The quick images of body language he did detect caused him to agree with Brenda – these people didn't look very happy.

Three blocks later, Brenda again interrupted his futile efforts to get cell service. "What the heck is going on, Mr. Wallace?"

Reed's gaze left the tiny smartphone screen, moving to the area surrounding their ride. He almost let out a curse at what he saw. Dozens of policemen lined the sidewalk, each man wearing a helmet and carrying a glass shield. The officers held nightsticks, and the shields lowered over their faces gave off an appearance of warriors ready to enter a battle. At the head of the column was another 10 officers on horseback. "I don't know Brenda, I can't get cell service. Can we try a news station on your radio?"

"Sure," she replied, and reached for the control knobs.

Before she could power up the car's AM tuner, Reed yelled, "Watch out!" Luke's patrol car had suddenly stopped dead it the middle of the road. Brenda barely braked in time, but it didn't matter. Both of them stared in horror as a bottle of some sort arched through the air and landed on the hood of Luke's police cruiser. Another three or four rocks quickly followed. Luke's white reverse lights flashed on, a sure sign he wanted to back up. Reed didn't blame him and started yelling, "Back up...back up!"

The young girl was partially in shock from confusion, but managed to pull the shift lever into the right spot. When she checked her rearview mirror she said, "I can't back up, there are cars packed in behind us."

Reed's head pivoted around, and sure enough, the street was completely blocked by dozens of vehicles. There was no place to go. He turned to look in front of them and watched as another barrage of bottles and rocks was launched at Luke's cruiser. Reed's stomach turned to ice when the glass of the police car's windshield turned into a spider web.

Reed's head pivoted, searching for an escape, every instinct screaming that they were in danger. He noticed Luke's outline through the back glass of his cruiser. Suddenly their escort popped out with a shotgun in his hand. His appearance caused the driver in the lane beside the police car to swerve, hitting another car in the far lane. Reed saw the opening and pointed, screaming, "Go! Go! GO!"

Brenda forgot she was in reverse and punched the gas. Her car lurched backward and slammed into a BMW behind them. While Reed continued his cadence, Brenda mumbled, "Sorry," under her breath, threw the shifter into drive, and hit the gas. They barely fit through the opening. As Reed watched, Luke shouldered the shotgun as a wall of bottles, rocks and other projectiles began impacting all around him. Reed's last vision was of the officer's hard landing on the pavement, his weapon falling free of his grasp.

The side street was less traveled, allowing a reasonable speed. A few blocks closer to the bank where Brenda's sister worked, Reed began smelling smoke. Brenda signaled to turn a corner when an entire street strewn with police cars and fire trucks lay before them. Dozens of flashing lights filled the avenue, the green florescent helmets of the firefighters rushing here and there.

A building in the middle of the block showed bright yellow and red flames while it boiled coal black smoke. The car was filled with the odor of burning rubber and plastic, so thick and toxic it made Reed's eyes water. On the edge of his vision, Reed noticed something odd about the bystanders. Normally when a fire was burning so close by, the onlookers would be focused on the flames or the men fighting the blaze. The people outside of Reed's window weren't gazing at the event with curiosity or concern. They were angry and restless. The congressman watched, noting heads that rocked back and forth during speech, arms shot out pointing with strong emotion, and men who shifted their nervous weight from one foot to the other. These people were mad, and feeding off of each other's anger.

Brenda started to sniffle, managing to voice concern over her sibling. She had no choice but to remain on the side street, inching forward through the clogged intersection. They had no more made it through when Reed noticed a woman standing on the sidewalk wearing a ski cap and bright white mittens. The lady waved at their car, grabbing Brenda's attention. "There she is! That's my sister!" Brenda stopped right in the middle of the street, waving for her sibling to join them, a move that annoyed many other drivers.

With sis safely in the backseat, Brenda squealed the tires, accelerating the little car away from the troubled area. They drove into a residential area of middle-class homes where everything seemed much calmer. Brenda pulled over and stopped. Reed noticed her hands were shaking, and she was having trouble focusing. "I can't drive anymore," she stated.

The sister spoke up from the backseat, finally catching her breath. "There was a run at the bank today. I barely got out of there alive. The president announced something about government checks wouldn't be honored, and people went stark raving mad. We locked the doors, and that just made it worse. I've been standing on the corner watching the police arrest people and haul them off in vans. Someone set fire to the building a little while ago."

The two sisters looked at each other, and both mouthed the word "Mom" at the same time.

The new passenger immediately reached for her cell phone, but Reed stopped her. "Won't do any good. Cell service is out."

Reed listened as both girls expressed concern over their mother, who lived alone outside the beltway. At the same time, there was no way anyone dared head back toward Reed's hotel and the bedlam occurring in that area. The three decided on an alternative plan. They were close to Brenda's apartment, so it was agreed that Reed would wait there while the two sisters headed to their mother's house. Reed didn't like the idea of the two women travelling alone, but couldn't argue them out of it. Brenda claimed she would feel better if someone were keeping an eye on her place anyway.

Five reasonably calm blocks later, Reed hopped out of the car with a door key in his hand. The girls waved and sped off, heading west.

February 15, 2017
The White House Situation Room

The row of computer monitors along the wall displayed broadcasts of all major cable news outlets side-by-side. The pictures being displayed were disturbing to the assortment of staffers, department secretaries, and military officers seated around the room.

The president had been warned to expect limited incidents of violence. The historical evidence clearly indicated that when the American public believed their money was at risk, violence could occur. Everyone on the National Security Council had predicted the incidents would be isolated, but the news reports told a different story.

All across the nation, there was a run on the banks. Hundreds of cities and towns reported widespread disturbances. The situation was so bad even the news anchors were begging people to remain calm.

The White House phone system was overwhelmed, with several state governors unable to access the proper channels to call up the National Guard. Many executed the order on their own. Reserve peace officers often couldn't be contacted, although many knew well enough to report for duty.

Secretary Palmer finally proposed a new idea. After making eye contact with a clearly disturbed chief executive, she suggested, "Mr. President, I believe it would be wise to declare tomorrow a national bank holiday."

The statement broke the horrified daze of several staff members and one-by-one, many of them nodded in agreement. The head of homeland security muttered, "If there are any banks left to have a holiday." The remark drew a sour look from the chief executive, but he didn't say anything.

After waiting to see if anyone protested the idea, he simply nodded and commanded, "Draw up the order – I'll sign it."

It was the middle of the night in Europe, but the major cities there were preparing for a similar reaction. Singapore, Tokyo, and Sidney were already experiencing limited civil unrest, but nothing on the scale of the happenings in North America.

Within an hour, the White House press secretary was holding a brief conference, explaining the executive order. Tomorrow would be a federal bank holiday, which would provide some window of time to resolve the issue with Treasury payments.

February 15, 2017
Beijing, China - MOSS Headquarters

The translated news reports coming out of the United States indicated Golden Mountain had far, far exceeded anyone's expectations. While the original plan had been conservative, even the most optimistic analysis predicted the operation wouldn't result in any more than a significant thorn in the side of the US government. It would also serve the dual purpose of broadcasting a message that the capitalist system of free enterprise was weak, decaying, and vulnerable.

The riots, with their resulting loss of property and life, were bonuses in the eyes of senior Chinese officials. Minister Hong didn't want to lose momentum. In less than 12 hours, their efforts had left the single greatest threat to the Middle Kingdom teetering on the edge of collapse.

The global reaction to unfolding events in Washington was welcome, even if unexpected. The OPEC countries were clamoring for the US dollar to be replaced as the world's reserve currency. Not a new idea, but now the effort had the serious backing it had always needed be taken seriously.

India, Japan, Germany, and Russia released statements condemning Washington's decision to stop payment on all funds. As far as Minister Hong was concerned, those countries were getting what they deserved. *If you sleep with a dog, you wake up with fleas*, he thought.

Without firing a single weapon, his department had brought the world's greatest military power to its knees. Now it was time to finish the job. Now it was time for China to take its rightful place as the dominant force economically and militarily. Now was the time to slay the great dragon while it was wounded, gasping for breath.

There was a third, optional phase to Golden Mountain. It had not been discussed or documented to the council, but could be implemented in short order.

Minister Hong's fingers moved across the keyboard in front of him. He leaned back, waiting on the monitor to display the information requested. A map of the United States appeared with hundreds of multi-colored lines crisscrossing the country. The different hues indicated transmission capacities of the North American electrical power distribution system.

The American power grid was essentially a patchwork of loosely integrated systems. Starting in the early 1920s, the huge network of high capacity electrical lines linked power plants to individual customers. There were over 500 separate electrical companies managing the system. Almost 100 years of different technologies existed in the network.

Americans liked cheap energy, and the utilities that managed this network constantly walked a fine line between the amount of a customer's monthly charges and the cost of upgrading infrastructure. Even without outside influences, the grid often failed.

Minister Hong's engineers had studied historical data regarding these failures and the impact to American productivity and civil stability. MOSS' headman had been fascinated by the varied responses and social impact these past blackouts had produced.

One of the first modern examples was the New York City power failure in 1965. While sections of the city still maintained some electrical power, millions of citizens were left in the dark. Human error at an upstate Niagara generating plant was blamed for the failure. The economy at that time was reasonably strong, and the only civil disturbances had been the block parties and public drunkenness throughout several of the major boroughs. The US government had taken some elementary steps to avoid the occurrence of a similar event. Twelve years later, it was clear those attempts hadn't been successful.

In 1977, almost all of New York City was without electrical power for over three days. The Chinese analysts had used this outage as a centerpiece of their study, given the economic conditions in the US at that time paralleled the current environment. Unrest, violence, and arson devastated the city during that blackout. Over 4,500 people had been arrested, and 550 police officers were injured. The damage to the local economy was severe. That failure had been caused by multiple lightning strikes and human error. Again, the government reacted, applying a Band-Aid over the problem, hoping the situation wouldn't repeat.

America isn't the only country to experience widespread power failures. Supposedly, an errant lightning strike paralyzed all of southern Brazil in 1999. Almost every year there were one or more large-scale power failures throughout the world. Some caused civil unrest, while others resulted in mere inconvenience.

The analysts at MOSS believed they could predict public response, having discovered a direct correlation between the general level of morale, economic conditions, government reaction, and length of the outage. Considering the events earlier in the day, the United States was primed for a negative reaction should there be widespread electrical grid failure. Minister Hong intended to deliver such an event.

The hack was really very simple. The voltage regulation systems at key points in the distribution system had been built in China, by Chinese firms. Using what the engineers referred to as a "back door," a small bit of computer program code had been inserted years before. This normally benign code lay slumbering, waiting for the signal to awaken.

Minister Hong picked up his telephone and hit a three-digit extension. His call was answered before the first ring had exhausted itself. "Begin Phase III of Golden Mountain," he ordered flatly.

Since utility company personnel needed to control the critical switches, relays, and voltage regulators from remote operational centers, internet access was mandated. A single electronic command issued to 16 critical monitoring stations in the United States set the initiative in motion.

When the signal came from China, the Trojan software at these stations activated itself and began generating fictitious readings. Normally, North American electricity ran at 60 MHz. All across the continent, generators at coal-fired, natural gas fueled, and nuclear power plants displayed false 55 MHz readings - misinformation provided by the Chinese hardware.

Turbines at hundreds of power plants increased speed to recertify the low reading. In less than a minute, a true overvoltage surge pulsed through thousands of miles of high voltage power lines. The faster the generators spun, the lower the reading sent by the now corrupted monitoring stations.

At 70 MHz, high-tension transmission lines started sagging beyond safety limits. At 72MHz, relays at operating stations began to spark and blow. When the frequency hit 75 MHz, fires began to burn throughout the entire grid.

Generators, spinning faster than their designed safety limits, experienced fatal mechanical failures. Bearings were destroyed, overheated parts warped and melted, and hundreds of fires and explosions occurred from Maine to California.

It wasn't just the power generation capabilities that were damaged. All across the US, computers were fried, wires melted, and circuit boards became puddles of shiny green glass. One by one, the dense population centers became dark, their evening glow extinguished like candles exposed to a strong breeze.

Stoplights couldn't signal traffic, packed subway cars halted, and commuter trains blocked intersections. In New York City, elevators full of people in over 800 skyscrapers shuddered to a stop, hanging cold and dark in their shafts. The major transportation tunnels servicing Manhattan immediately closed when the critical ventilation systems went off-line.

Equipped with the latest technology, the nuclear power plants were the first to begin emergency shutdown procedures. A few minutes later, their low-tech brethren, the coal and natural gas plants, interrupted operations as well. The hydro-electrical generators were soon to follow.

Gas pumps being ravaged by lines of desperate drivers couldn't pump. Hundreds of thousands of people, already spooked by the banking events of the day were replenishing staples at local supermarkets. Bare shelves and few selections put tempers on edge, and when the lights went out, it pushed many folks to the brink of their sanity. Heated conversations led to physical confrontations, many ending in violence.

Fisticuffs, shootings, looting, robberies, and arson broke out in every major city. Not all aspects of the catastrophe were criminal or violent. Candles used to light homes and offices started fires. Fire departments struggled to respond because there wasn't any water pressure to feed their equipment. First responders all across the continent, already taxed by budget cuts, staff reductions, and low morale tried to react, but absolute traffic gridlock slowed any response.

Police departments, still reeling from the banking crisis earlier in the day, were completely unprepared for the wave of unrest that swept their cities.

Fueled by rumors, years of a downtrodden economic environment, and divisive political campaigns, the American population centers were dry piles of tender, just waiting for a spark.

The average American was already fed up and resentful. Many wanted to point a finger at someone - anyone - or everyone for a quality of life less than what he or she remembered having as a child. Closing the banks ignited the tender box; loss of electrical power fanned the flames. Many average, law-abiding citizens transformed into armed, angry, and resentful people. Rumors spread like wildfire. Ranging from foreign invasion to an EMP nuclear strike, every street corner and small town crossroad postulated a different conspiracy theory, none of the accounts forecasting a positive future. One radio station in Atlanta, running on backup generators, broadcasted that a military coup was being reported on the AP wires. Millions of commuters, stuck in traffic on greater Atlanta's streets heard the story on their car radios.

Cities like New York, Cleveland, and San Diego were recent veterans of widespread power outages. The citizens of these locales actually remained relatively calm for several hours. When reports of fried circuit boards, inoperable backup generators, and nationwide failures began airing on local radio stations, general panic set in. The common thinking of the few media that were able to broadcast proselytized the notion that the grid failed as the casualty of an EMP attack. Some churches declared that the end times were upon the sinful nation.

Section II – Bottom Lands

Chapter 5

February 15th, 2017
Kemah Bay, Texas

Wyatt stopped, fishing in his pocket for the car keys. Something odd about the sunlight prompted him to pivot and stare toward the northwest. The Houston skyline was that direction, and the amount of smoke on the horizon astonished him. The low sun provided backlighting for the ash and heat climbing in the atmosphere. A pinkish-gray cloud manifested into a dome-like shape that dominated the sky. By Wyatt's estimation, most of the city was covered by its angry haze. He shook his head, remembering that the Houston Fire Department had suffered numerous budget cuts during the last few years. "Wow! What a blaze. Those guys are probably shorthanded, struggling to extinguish whatever is burning," he speculated.

Driving to the market, Wyatt supposed a little classic rock might help dissolve his funk. He selected from the radio's preset stations, sitting back to enjoy some oldies, but goodies. The Aerosmith hit was just reaching the guitar solo when the DJ interrupted the jam with a newsflash. Wyatt became agitated, never having heard this station broadcast any sort of bulletin. As he reached to change channels, the words "hundreds dead," immobilized his finger before it could hit the button. He listened to the poorly worded, impromptu report for a few moments, eventually switching to a fulltime news source.

The words spewing from the dashboard were so shocking; he was prompted to pull to the side of the street and park. The president had conducted a press conference...government checks wouldn't be honored...riots erupted...power failed. Hundreds, perhaps thousands of people were dead.

He listened until the reporters began recycling the same information. The situation described by the media was unfathomable to Wyatt. He'd just driven through Houston a few hours ago. Everything had looked just fine. How had this happened so quickly? At that moment, two police cars with flashing lights and wailing sirens zipped past, their urgency snapping him out of the fog. Some instinct made him realize the trip to the market had just taken on a new level of urgency. *The smart thing to do is stock up with as much food as I can fit in the back*, he thought. Wyatt checked his rearview mirror and reentered traffic.

Evidently, he wasn't the only one who decided that getting a few extra supplies was a good idea. The Food World parking lot was jammed with customers, many of whom were frantically circling the already overcrowded facility, on the prowl for shoppers exiting the building. Wyatt didn't even bother looking for a close-in space. He pulled to the end of a far row, centering the SUV in the striped area that ordinarily provided drivers with adequate turning space from row to row. He locked the doors and sprinted toward the store's entrance.

The unmistakable warning of squealing tires compelled Wyatt to pivot, facing the clamor. A pickup rounded a row of parked cars, its engine accelerating while the driver focused his attention on his rearview mirror. The truck barreled straight for Wyatt, who barely managed to spring out of the way. A lone security guard chased the offending vehicle on foot, struggling to keep up. The heavyset, older man didn't have any hope of catching the speeding getaway car, but still yelled, "Stop! Come back here!" If it hadn't been for the events described on the radio and the near miss by a fast-moving bumper, Wyatt probably would have found the whole episode comical.

The truck raced to the end of the row where it swerved to avoid another car. The right front wheel struck the curb at a perfect angle, resulting in one side of the vehicle careening into the air. Wyatt watched, fascinated as the pickup tilted in slow motion, rolled several feet on two wheels, and then gradually tipped over on its side. As the truck slid to a halt in the grassy border of the parking lot, the guard stopped his pursuit directly in front of Wyatt. The man stood, gasping to catch his breath, bent at the waist with his hands on his knees.

The guard didn't look like the sort of fellow who was a regular marathon runner, and the slight raspy noise emitting from his lungs concerned Wyatt. "Hey man, you okay?"

The panting man turned his gaze to Wyatt and nodded, taking a few deep breaths in order to form words. "Yeah...I'm okay...how about you?"

Before Wyatt could respond, the massive front window of Food World exploded outwards, shards of glass raining down on the crowd trying to enter the store. As the security guard began to straighten, several teenagers jumped through the newly created opening, all carrying boxes, bags, and packages of loot. "No! Stop!" the guard shouted, and started jogging back to the building.

Wyatt observed the looters scamper off and then turned back to the pickup, now fully at rest on its side. The driver was struggling to push open the door. Wyatt scrutinized the scene as several people ignored the accident, scurrying past without even a glance. The passersby apparently were more concerned about getting inside the store before the shelves were picked clean than checking on the well-being of the motorist.

Wyatt approached the truck, shouting out to the driver, "Hey, are you hurt?"

A muffled voice came through the underside of the floorboard, "Go away! I've got a gun, so just go away!"

The aggressive response caught Wyatt by surprise. He stopped several feet away, unsure of his next steps. The driver, a young man in his early twenties, eventually pushed the door up and open. True to his word, he crawled out, brandishing a pistol, poised, primed, and ready to shoot his way out. It quickly dawned on the young fellow that no one was going to attack him, so he tucked the handgun in his belt and began examining his truck, a disgusted look on his face. When he pulled a cell phone out of his pocket, Wyatt decided the guy wasn't seriously injured and turned for the store.

Another siren came screaming down the street, drawing Wyatt's glance over his shoulder. He noticed the pistol-toting driver take off, dashing across the pavement. *Evidently, he's worried that the cops are coming to arrest him,* thought Wyatt. *That guy just abandoned his truck and left the scene of an accident. Why is everyone in a panic over a stupid press conference?*

Before he could take even one more step, a woman's scream split the air. A loud, popping racket punctuated her desperate cry. Wyatt watched in horror as the security guard stumbled backwards, hands clutched to his chest. He hadn't even collapsed on the ground before dozens of people stampeded out the doors.

Wyatt froze as he watched the throng violently overrun a young woman clutching a newborn. Employees and customers alike were streaming away from the building, many looking over their shoulders as if being chased by some horror. It finally occurred to Wyatt's overstimulated mind that the popping noises were gunshots coming from inside the building. *Enough of this; I'm out of here.*

Wyatt jogged back to his car and started to leave when movement caught his eye. He spotted a man approach the overturned pickup, glance around, and then slink away with a bag of groceries. *Now there's an idea.*

Wyatt pulled up beside the wreck and hopped out. In a few minutes, all of the remaining bags were in the SUV. A sense of guilt entered Wyatt's mind, a welling of remorse over participating in the bedlam. Climbing back behind the wheel, he sat for a few moments and pondered what he'd just done.

Why did I do that? I'm not a thief. I've never stolen anything before in my life. Is this some contagious disease? He was about to get out and return the sacks of goodies when more shots rang out from Food World. Three men, waving pistols in the air, rushed out of the building. The few people who remained in the lot scattered in all directions, their faces filled with terror. Several took cover, ducking behind nearby cars while others seemed determined to put as much distance between them and the shooters as possible. The air was filled with dissonance - grating screams, barking tires and racing engines. Wyatt, reacting with an instinct of self-preservation, shifted the SUV into drive. Leaving two trails of rubber, he made a mad dash for the exit.

Over a mile passed before Wyatt slowed the car to a reasonable speed. Just as his heart rate was returning to normal, he noticed sirens approaching from behind. His stomach knotted, absolutely sure the police were after him for being a looter. He sighed with relief as the two ambulances came into view and then zoomed past.

As Wyatt continued, he approached a bank at the corner of the intersection leading to the marina. Nearing the impressive stucco building, he could see several flashing lights in the parking lot. A large crowd, four police cars, and two ambulances surrounded the building. *What now?*

Signaling to turn, Wyatt determined that the police were in a confrontation with several members of the angry throng. From his vantage, it appeared as though the cops were trying to block people from entering the bank. Dozens of men and women were pointing fingers and shouting at the officers, who were clearly trying to protect the branch. An anxious-looking man, whom Wyatt recognized as the branch manager, fidgeted nervously behind the thin line of police.

Wyatt couldn't help himself, slowing the car to gawk – curious about what was going on. *Did someone rob the bank?* Without warning, a large man shoved one of the police officers, and the crowd surged forward. A shot rang out, and people scattered in every direction. *This looks like Food World again.* Wyatt hit the gas, speeding back to the marina.

Reaching over with his free arm, Wyatt pulled the hatch closed. The plastic handles of the cheap, throwaway bags were eating into his hand, but he ignored the discomfort. Scanning the marina's parking lot, he crossed the pavement and aimed for the ramp leading down to their pier. Boxer's slip was quite a distance, so he rested the bags on the sidewalk to readjust his load - or at least that's what he tried to tell himself. In reality, he needed to calm down. The experience at the store had shaken him badly, and he needed to regroup before Morgan and the kids saw him in such a state.

Pausing at the head of the pier, the bizarre episode kept replaying in his mind. *Why is everyone acting so irrational? Who kills for groceries?* His analyses of the events at Food World were interrupted by the distinct grinding noise of a motor starting. The sound was emanating from his pier, and he hadn't noticed anyone else around today. He picked up the bags of pilfered supplies and strode down the walkway.

As Boxer came into view, he observed David examining the shore power connection. "Everything okay?"

David spun and glanced back, immediately moving to help carry the bags. "The power keeps blinking on and off. I powered up the generator so we wouldn't drain the batteries. All of the connections are tight. I don't know what's going on."

They dropped the bags on the pier and Wyatt began checking the connection of the larger vessel to shore power. Wyatt's boat required as much electrical energy as any small house. Boxer was furnished with televisions, two refrigerators, freezer, water maker, and all sorts of other appliances that consumed electricity. While underway, a generator supplied the necessary power, but when tied up at a slip, large yellow power cables connect the boat with the land-based electrical grid.

Wyatt rechecked the large plugs that twisted into sockets mounted on the utility post. David sighed, "Dad, I already tested those. The fuses are fine, too. I think the problem is with the marina."

Wyatt patted his son on the shoulder, "I just wanted to double-check, son, you never know. Did you check the breakers in the boat?" Wyatt regretted the question even as it left his lips. Of course, he did. He's not a little boy anymore, and I've got to stop treating him like one. He's a man now and an officer in the United States Army.

David nodded, "Yes sir, they're okay, too. I even tried running the cables to another post. Hey, what's going on with all the sirens? Is it the big fire somewhere in Houston?"

Before Wyatt could respond, the cabin door slid open, his wife and daughter strolling onto the back deck. Wyatt waved to the girls before instructing David. "Let's get the groceries aboard. We all need to talk. The world is now officially insane."

After depositing the sacks in the galley, Wyatt asked everyone to have a seat. The main cabin was equipped with a table surrounded by a semi-circle of couch-like seating. After everyone had settled, Wyatt repeated what he had heard on the radio and related his first-hand experience at Food World.

David spoke first. "Should I try to get the satellite dish working? I think we need to know what's going on." Wyatt nodded in agreement. The boat was equipped with flat screens in both cabins and the salon, but the reception in the fiberglass cocoon created by the hull was terrible. The original owner had purchased a new satellite system but never installed it. Wyatt thought, "*Just another one of the endless list of things that go with owning a boat. Things you never get around to.*" As David left to gather tools, Wyatt turned to his daughter, inviting her assistance. "Sage, why don't you go to the bridge and follow the chat on the VHF radio? I'm curious if the Coast Guard is broadcasting anything."

An expression fueled by annoyance crossed the young girl's face. Sage glanced at her mother who nodded approval. The teenager sighed, "You guys just want me out of here so you can talk. Whatever."

After Sage headed for the bridge, Wyatt drew next to his wife, and they hugged. Morgan's concerned expression betrayed the fear welling inside her. "How bad do you think it is?" she queried.

Wyatt rubbed his chin and thought for a moment, "Pretty bad. As a matter of fact, I was downright frightened, Morgan. The look in people's eyes was the worst part."

Morgan digested his remark while studying his face. Finally, she offered, "What are we going to do, Wyatt? I'm wondering if we should try to make it back to Sage's apartment or something. Are we in a good place?"

Wyatt had already considered that and was quick with a reply, "I don't think we *can* make it back, even if we wanted to. The reports on the radio indicted the roads are closed. The police asked everyone to stay at home and remain calm. I think we're better off hunkering down right here. Don't we have everything we need?"

Morgan tilted her head, mentally running an inventory, "I guess so…. I mean, there's plenty of food, so I imagine we'll be okay for a while."

Wyatt racked his brain to remember anything he'd missed – any critical item they might need later. Unless they ran out of electrical power or the water maker broke, they had an endless supply of H2O. Boxer's two massive fuel tanks had been topped off with diesel. A few years ago, he'd learned the hard way to keep the reserve full. Preoccupied with the rush to return home after the weekend, he'd delayed refilling the tanks. The boat sat in the hot Texas sun for a few weeks while he was away on a business trip. Algae, feeding off of the air in the chambers, had grown and multiplied - eventually clogging the filters. It had been an expensive lesson having the tanks drained and scrubbed. *Boats are a hole in the water you throw money into*, he mused.

Boxer was also equipped with a small set of solar panels and a wind turbine. These devices were used to keep the massive bank of batteries charged while "on the hook," or at anchor. Most boaters wanted to enjoy a quiet anchorage without the constant drone of a running generator. These renewable energy sources helped extend the life of the battery bank.

He looked up at Morgan, "I think we're in good shape here. As a matter of fact, we're probably better off here than at home if the power stays out. We have electricity from several different sources, unlimited drinking water, and an ocean full of fish."

Morgan nodded her agreement, "I guess you're right. I mean I can always serve fish and chips or fish tacos or fish grilled with lemon," she giggled. "I'm going to start putting the groceries away. I hope you pilfered some good stuff. Something useful…like a five-pound tub of tartar sauce," Morgan teased.

Wyatt laughed, "Shoot. I just hope that guy lifted name brand soda. Some of those house brands are iffy at best."

Morgan laughed, extracting items from the bags. Wyatt watched her reach in a sack and remove a can. Her expression changed to "Why would anybody buy this?" Wyatt easily recognized the look; he had seen that same face on several Christmas mornings as she opened presents. He chuckled again and left to check on how the kids were doing.

After finishing the dishes, Wyatt needed some fresh air and found David reclined on deck, his feet propped on the railing, his eyes scanning the harbor. He turned and motioned with his head, "Nice night...at least it would be if it weren't for that," nodding to the north and Houston. The sun had been down for over an hour, but the sky glowed an ominous shade of red. As the crow flies, it was over 30 miles to the metropolitan cowtown, yet the distant blaze illuminated the entire marina, the faint odor of smoke drifting in now and then.

With a sweeping gesture, David motioned around the marina at the dozens of expensive homes and condos hugging the shoreline. "I think the power is out everywhere, Dad. None of these homes have a single light on. I see the flicker of candles in a couple of them, but everything else is completely dark."

Wyatt glanced around and then climbed the ladder to the bridge to get a better view. He scanned the horizon in all directions before confirming David's conclusion. "You're right, son. I don't see a light anywhere. It looks like the whole area is still without power."

David wasn't through with his observation. "Dad, since I've been out here, I've heard sirens several times. All afternoon while I was installing the dish, they were all over the place." He lowered his gaze to allow scrutinizing his feet, seemingly hesitant to broach a vital issue. Finally, making up his mind, "Dad, did you bring the guns down to the boat? I only ask because I think I heard gunshots a while ago. They sounded pretty close."

Wyatt wasn't surprised by that question, especially given what he had seen earlier in the day. "Come on, son. Let's take account of what we've got. I think it's probably as good a time as any."

David hesitated a moment, "You don't think I'm being paranoid, do you?"

"No son, after what I saw today, I think you're spot on. I stored the weapons in the cabin. Let's go dig them out."

The two men descended the steps to the salon, Wyatt opening a rarely used hatch in the floor. Morgan, busy in the galley, instantly realized what was happening. She'd never liked having the guns aboard. She put her hands on her hips, "Is everything all right? Why are you getting the guns out? Please tell me a flock of ducks just landed outside, and you're going hunting."

"Everything's fine, Mother," replied Wyatt, "We just have a few minutes and want to be sure of what's in here."

Morgan didn't buy it for one second. She gave her husband a look of "Yeah, right," and went back to arranging the refrigerator. Wyatt pulled out the two plastic cases and a large bag.

David and he carried the equipment onto the back deck, flipping on the lights so they could see. David opened the first case and removed a 12-gauge shotgun. It was a pump-action Mariner model in stainless steel.

After hearing tales of the occasional local pirate, Wyatt had brought his old skeet gun to Boxer. Even though the shotgun had a fine coat of oil, the blue finish had rusted in less than two weeks. When he took it to a gunsmith, the man had told him the salt air required either a military black or stainless finish. Anything else would rust away in a matter of days.

On his next trip to the sporting goods store, Wyatt explained his need to the man working behind the counter. Evidently, this was a common problem because the fellow reached back and pulled out a bright, shiny shotgun he called the "Mariner's model." As the two men talked, the clerk recommended Wyatt think about an AR15. "It won't rust, and that shotgun has a very limited range," the clerk advised. "If I were worried about pirates, I would get something with at least 300 yards of range."

Wyatt had seen pictures of the black rifle and knew that the military used something similar to it. He decided it wouldn't be a bad idea to have a little more firepower…just in case. The store was running a special, and the man had talked Wyatt into purchasing a case of 1,000 rounds of ammunition with his rifle. "You're gonna need to sight the weapon and practice with it to feel comfortable firing. Plus, these guns are so much fun to shoot, you'll be glad you got the ammo."

When he returned home with the guns, Morgan was upset. "Are you expecting a war? You don't even like to go skeet shooting anymore. Why did you buy that?" He hadn't been able to give her a good answer and had actually tried to return the AR15. He quickly learned guns couldn't be returned, so he packed both of them away in the boat. Neither had seen the light of day since - until now.

David whistled as his dad pulled the assault rifle out of its case. "When did you get this?"

Wyatt replied, "It was an impulse buy. I don't know…I thought it looked cool."

"I qualified with one similar not long ago. They shoot pretty well. Have you zeroed the sights yet?"

Wyatt shook his head, "Nope. It's never been out of the case. There's a bunch of ammo for it. Can you show me how it works?"

David nodded, "Yeah, it's really pretty simple. In the morning, I'll see if I can bore sight it and at least get it close. I can show you the controls in the daylight." Wyatt watched as his son expertly disassembled the rifle and examined the parts. "I'll need to clean it, too. It still has the factory grease here and there. No biggie." David examined the shotgun, a serious frown forming on his face. "Dad, I think we had better load this one tonight. I know it sounds crazy, but I'm really concerned. After what you told me today and everything I've been hearing, we should keep this one loaded."

Wyatt wasn't so sure. Everything seemed reasonably calm around the marina. They hadn't heard a siren for a while, and he didn't want Morgan and Sage getting any more upset than they already were. Wyatt decided they needed more information. Boxer was equipped with an AM/FM radio just like a car. He motioned David to follow him to the bridge, and he flipped on the receiver with the volume low. The two men sat and tried searching for both AM and FM broadcasts, but found nothing but static. Wyatt turned to David and asked, "Any chance you unhooked the antenna when you were installing the satellite dish?"

David thought about it for a second. "I suppose anything's possible. I don't think so, but maybe."

Wyatt switched off the radio, pondering his son's suggestion to load the scattergun. His thoughts collected, Wyatt was readying to voice his opinion when crackling shots sounded in the distance. David's head snapped up, and he half stood. He looked back at his father and then at the shotgun and then back at Wyatt. His father had already made his decision. "Go ahead, load the gun."

David shoved five shells into the shotgun, flipped on the safety, and tucked it under the bench seat at the back of the deck. He reassembled the AR15 and put it back in its case. He then stacked everything neatly in one corner and out of the way.

The girls decided to join them, and the family spent the rest of the night talking about anything and everything except what was going on in the world around them. Sirens whined in the distance a few times, but Wyatt was thankful there wasn't any more gunfire.

Eventually, the salt air worked its magic, and yawns quieted the conversation. Wyatt glanced at his watch, noting how the time passed so quickly. He stood, reaching skyward with both arms, stretching his back from its stationary position, and announced his intent to hit the hay. The entire family thought that was a good idea, and soon followed him inside the cabin.

Without shore power, the refrigerators and freezer concerned Wyatt. All of the devices were dual voltage, having the ability to power by AC or DC. The DC current was supplied by the boat's battery bank, but those wouldn't last long without being recharged. Before retiring, Wyatt set Boxer's controls to auto-charge. When the batteries dropped to a certain level, the diesel generator would fire up automatically and recharge them. The drone of the vibrating machine might wake the dead, but Wyatt knew that was better than having drained batteries. He flicked the switches necessary to set the controls, and then Morgan and he kissed and said their goodnights.

Wyatt never quite understood why he slept so well on the boat. The master cabin was like similarly sized boats; it sported a queen-sized bed, but offered limited headroom. When they had first acquired Boxer, Wyatt hoped that no one was claustrophobic because every square inch of wall and ceiling was carefully utilized, giving the craft a "more than snug" feel.

In addition to the tight space, every boat rocks, regardless of where it is docked or how calm the water is. Wyatt credited the soft sway of the boat, combined with the salt air and large doses of sunshine with the best rest he'd managed in years. He'd heard others comparing the experience of sleeping on a boat to that of a baby inside the womb, but never believed it. Now, he looked forward to climbing into his berth as often as possible, its magic melting away whatever the world threw at him. Morgan claimed she rested so well that she could save a fortune on makeup; after a couple of days at the marina, her skin fairly glowed.

Wyatt was deep in a REM cycle when something wakened him. Disoriented and irritated for just a moment, he recognized David's voice whisper, "Dad, you need to wake up. Dad?"

"Yeah, David…yeah, I'm awake. What's wrong?" He whispered back.

David's tone was serious. "You need to come out here."

Wyatt carefully threw off the covers and slipped on his shorts. Rubbing his eyes, he vacated the cabin as quietly as possible, sliding the door closed behind him so as not to disturb Morgan. "What's going on, son?"

David's eyes darted toward the back of the boat. "Someone is outside. I keep hearing noises. I think we'd better check it out." David was holding the shotgun.

"Aren't you a little old to be worried about the boogieman?" Wyatt teased, nodding toward the gun.

David smirked, but then a serious look crossed his face. "I hope that's all it is."

They moved closer to Boxer's stern, pausing on the deck to listen. Only the normal night sounds drifted across the water. Even the red glow over Houston didn't seem out of place anymore. The wind had shifted again, bringing with it a sharp stink of ash and burning plastic from the fires to the north. Other than drifts of the rancid odor, the marina was peaceful.

Wyatt stood, trying to decide between a flashlight and the night vision. He hadn't used the starlight device but once, a quick test long ago. He lifted a bench seat, removing a small flashlight from the compartment below.

The sound of breaking glass startled both men. David flashed a look of "I told you so," and then moved to the back of the boat. Both men stepped off Boxer and onto the wooden pier, searching for the source of the noise.

Even without the normal lighting along the pier, they could see reasonably well. The glow from the north and a nearly full moon illuminated all but the darkest shadows. They crept to the center of the walkway, a habit most boaters develop early, so as not to fall into the water. A rustling racket, followed by a thump and then whispered cursing sounded from a nearby boat.

They moved together cautiously, approaching a boat named Money Pit that was tied up a few slips down. The newer sports fisherman was owned by a retired lawyer named Bill. Wyatt couldn't remember the man's last name, which wasn't unusual among boaters. Pier mates often became good friends without knowing much at all about the normal, weekday lives of their neighbors. It was a matter of social politeness that the trials and troubles of everyday life were left behind and unmentioned while at the marina. Wyatt had one neighbor in slip #25 who stilled called him "Wright," despite four months of seeing each other almost every weekend.

David and he paused at the back of Money Pit, listening intently. They detected movement inside the boat as it shifted just slightly, small ripples of water vibrating off the hull and spreading across the otherwise glass-smooth water. Wyatt looked at David and then at the entrance to the boat, "Hello onboard Money Pit. Bill, is that you?"

No answer. Wyatt repeated his greeting, slightly louder than before. Still, there was no response.

Wyatt switched on the flashlight and directed its beam at the pier. He maneuvered carefully, stepping over the shore power cables and a BBQ grill that had been stationed on the dock. Wyatt started to step from the pier to Money Pit's transom and froze mid-stride. There were dark spots of blood presenting clearly on the glistening white swim platform. The red stains appeared wet and fresh. Wyatt glanced at David and motioned him over to examine the anomaly. With his son peering over his shoulder, Wyatt moved the beam of light up to Money Pit's fishing deck. Two more small crimson puddles shimmered in the flashlight's beam.

David was really uncomfortable. "Dad! Let's get out of here."

Wyatt motioned with his hand for David to calm down. He turned back to Bill's boat and pointed the light through the large sliding glass door that led to the salon. Again with a raised voice, "Bill, is that you? It's Wyatt. You okay, man?"

The sound of muffled movement came from inside Money Pit. Finally, a voice called back, "Wyatt, is that you? Thank God! I've been shot. Please help me."

"Go get your mother," Wyatt instructed his son. The older man stepped over to the swim platform and then onto the fishing deck. Bill appeared at the doorway, holding a towel against the side of his head. The cloth was bloody, and the man's skin an unnatural, pale gray.

Wyatt helped Bill rest in the fighting chair, gently removing the towel. A long gash asserted itself along the side of his temple, and half of Bill's sideburn was missing. Bright rose-colored trails reflected in the light, the blood running down his neck and soaking his shirt. Despite the grisly-looking injury, Wyatt knew instantly Bill wasn't in immediate danger. The bullet hadn't hit anything critical. "Bill, you're going to be okay, buddy. It just grazed you. All head wounds bleed like crazy, but you're going to be all right."

Wyatt could hear Morgan, David, and Sage rushing down the pier, the jerky motion of flashlight beams betraying their urgent pace. Words poured out of

Bill, "There was a roadblock. You know, I only live five miles from here. The police wouldn't let me pass and told me to go home. I tried to tell them…I tried to say I *was* going home. I mean, like, the boat is really my home. They wanted to see my driver's license, but I had forgotten it. Some other man was arguing with them, and then somebody started shooting. My windshield was sprinkled with tiny spots. Small little holes just appeared right in front of my face. I ducked and hit the gas. I think I hit somebody's car…maybe it was a person. I dunno. They shot me. I didn't even feel it, but then the blood started running down my…"

Morgan took Bill's hand, "Bill, it's all right now. You're okay. Shhhhhhh…just settle down, we'll help you."

David spoke up, "Dad, get pressure on that wound. He's lost a lot of blood. We need to get pressure on it ASAP, or he might go into shock."

Morgan blurted out, "David's right. Shouldn't we call an ambulance or the police or somebody?"

Sage dug the ever-present cell phone out of a pocket, checking the display. She returned her parents' gaze, shaking her head - no signal. She offered, "We could drive him to the ER, it's only a few miles away."

Bill protested, "I'm not going out on the road again. No, thank you. Not again! You guys have no idea what it's like out there."

Sage retrieved Boxer's medical kit and began digging around to locate bandages. It took a while, but eventually the makeshift paramedics stopped the bleeding and bandaged Bill's wound. They got him to swallow some pain tablets, followed by a large glass of orange juice.

While the kids kept an eye on the patient, Morgan motioned Wyatt aside. "I guess that answers any question about trying to leave. What's happening, Wyatt?"

Her husband didn't answer the question, mostly because Morgan's eyes showed she already knew the answer. Instead, he tried to reassure his wife, "We have everything we need for right now. I'm sure things will settle down. Everyone is frightened, but things have to get calmer. I don't know of anything else to do but wait it out."

Morgan nodded her agreement, "I guess I should be thankful. There are probably a lot of people in worse shape right now. At least we're comfortable."

Eventually, Bill calmed down and everyone began yawning again. After all hands were back aboard Boxer, Wyatt stared at the glow to the north and shook his head. He locked the salon door, deeply concerned over what tomorrow would bring.

February 16, 2017
Southland Marina
Kemah Bay, Texas

Wyatt woke up at six and headed to the galley, a hot cup of coffee being the first priority of the day. He filled a cup with water from the sink and shoved it in the microwave. While the water was heating, movement outside on the deck caught his eye. David was up already, apparently using the early light to clean the rifle. After his cup of instant brew was topped off with a dash of milk and sugar, Wyatt joined his son.

"Morn'n."

David looked up and smiled, "Hey, Dad, did you get any sleep?"

Wyatt winced slightly, "I'm good. Have you seen Bill yet this morning?"

His son nodded. "Yes, sir, he stuck his head out a bit ago and waved. He mumbled something about a headache, but said he was okay."

Wyatt perched on the edge of the transom, admiring the confidence with which David handled the gun. The kid seemed to know *exactly* what he was doing. After a few swipes with a rag, David snapped the weapon back together and worked the action. He then sliced open the case of ammunition with his pocketknife and began loading the two magazines that accompanied the weapon.

Wyatt cleared his throat, somehow a little uncomfortable watching his son casually prepare such a deadly device. "Hey, any chance we could get a line wet this morning? You know the flounder should be running up the lake. Remember those two big ones we caught a few years ago - down at the end of the pier?"

David smiled, "Yeah I do. Man, that one I hooked really put up a fight. Sure, Dad, let me get this rifle ready, and then let's go. Do you have any bait?"

Wyatt smiled internally, "Yup. I have a couple of pounds of frozen shrimp. It's not as good as fresh, but we might get an interested customer if we hurry."

David put the rifle away while Wyatt grabbed a couple of poles. He was excited at the prospect of fishing with his son for the first time in two years. David had been away at college and then the army. There just hadn't been time for them to enjoy what used to be one of their favorite activities together.

They ambled toward the end of the pier, and after a few minutes of tying rigs and baiting hooks, both men had lines in the water. Wyatt noted the incoming tide and realized that should help the fishing. Even though they were almost five miles inland from Galveston Bay proper, the marina still experienced an eight to ten-inch tide.

The two fishermen garnered a few strikes, David landing a rather anemic catfish. The sun rose higher in the early morning sky, and both of them knew the chances of catching a tasty, game fish declined with the light. After a little over an hour, Wyatt flashed a wry smile, "I think your mom can put away the tartar sauce today, son."

"Looks that way. We got started a little late; maybe we can give it a shot again tonight?"

Wyatt nodded, "One more cast, and then let's call it quits."

David spied some surface activity and reared back, letting fly a long cast toward the disturbance. His throw was perfect, and he let the bait settle to the bottom. After a few seconds, he began the usual motion of bouncing the rig along the harbor floor, trying to convince any fish in the area that an injured meal awaited. On his second tug, he felt resistance and jerked the pole hard to set the hook.

Wyatt grew suddenly interested. "Got something?"

David didn't answer at first. The line felt different, and he figured it was snagged. "I don't know. It doesn't feel right. I think I might be hung up on something."

David continued to work the pole and reel. He'd never felt anything quite like this before. Whatever it was, it was exceptionally heavy, yet he was able to reel in line. Over the years, his father and he hooked everything from an old Styrofoam beer cooler to waterlogged Nikes. Whatever was on his line now was moving, but heavy.

Wyatt watched, curious what was bending his son's pole almost in half. The prey didn't seem to be fighting him, yet David was struggling to bring it in. He twisted to retrieve the net when the odd tone in David's voice commanded his attention. "Dad...ummmmm...I think I've...oh my God."

Wyatt peered directly into the water before concurring with his son. "Oh, Lord."

David was slowly towing a human body to the pier. The pale, almost ghost-like skin reflected though a foot of muddy, brown water. David's line tangled in the long, black tresses of the cadaver. After a few more cranks of David's reel, they determined it was the body of a young girl, probably in her teens, but difficult to tell. The corpse was face down, her thin legs dangled a little below the surface, one of which had a crab attached. David stopped reeling. He'd had enough, his facial expression revealing his repulsion as he considered the possible fate of someone's daughter.

Wyatt caught himself before suggesting a call to the police. His next instinct embarrassed him even more – a strong impulse to turn off the water maker in the boat. Both men stood silently, gazing anywhere but at the body. Morgan's voice added to the discomfort. "You boys bringing me something good to cook tonight?"

David spun and gagged.

Wyatt turned to see his wife walking down the pier, hugging a cup of steaming coffee. Despite a rolling stomach, Wyatt managed to hold up his palm, signaling Morgan to stop right where she was. A confused expression crossed her face. "What's wrong, Wyatt?"

His voice was soft. "There's a dead person in the water, Morgan. You don't want to come over here right now."

It took the remark a second to register with Morgan. "There's a what? A dead...a body? Are you sure the person is dead?"

David spoke up. "Yeah, Mom. There's no doubt."

Morgan fought the urge to make sure. After all, she was a nurse and was quite acclimated to gory scenes. *I've seen enough unpleasant images to last a lifetime,* she thought. Her face betrayed a thousand questions that were flying through her mind, but she didn't ask any of them aloud.

David and Wyatt edged closer to Morgan, the three deliberating over what should be done about the dead girl. The final decision was to cut David's line and tie it off to the pier. That way, the body wouldn't drift around the marina or frighten any residents. It was the best solution they could construct, given the situation. When the cell signal was available again, they would call the police and report the body. Until then, Wyatt didn't even have a shovel to dig a grave.

Returning to the boat, Morgan warned Sage to stay away from the end of the pier while the two men kept busy storing the fishing gear. Everyone was quiet, a melancholy stillness having descended on them all.

It was David who broke the silence. "Dad, we need to go and find out what's going on. I ran the cables for the satellite, but I can't get it to work. Either it won't align, or no one is broadcasting. We need to know what's happening in Houston and the other cities. You know, this little marine community is pretty isolated. The worst of it is the not knowing."

Wyatt agreed.

As soon as the fishing equipment was squared away, they let Morgan know the plan. As the two men stepped on the dock, Wyatt noticed David was toting the shotgun. He thought to protest, but quickly changed his mind. *What is this world coming to when I'm relieved my son is carrying a gun?*

The first thing Wyatt noticed as they left the pier was the lack of cars. On a normal Saturday morning, the marina lot would be full with families, carrying in groceries, fishing poles, and swimwear for weekend fun. Before the depression caused the price of boat fuel to skyrocket, people had to park along the street and walk a considerable distance to get to the water. Despite the grim economic times, the marina was still an exceptionally busy place on the weekends. While most captains kept their vessels tied up to avoid the cost of fuel, the lure of the water was still strong. As Wyatt surveyed the area, he noticed three, maybe four more cars than he had seen the day before. He estimated there were about forty cars total in the lot.

He pulled the keys out of his pocket and negotiated the driver's seat, legs still hanging outside. Despite the constant dinging signal, warning him that the door was ajar, he fingered the control in an attempt to locate a radio station. David waited nearby, handling the menacing gun like it was a common hammer or saw. *He's scared, and I guess I don't blame him. It's not every day you fish a body out of the water and can't call the police for help.*

The radio identified nothing but empty airwaves on both the AM and FM bands. Wyatt scanned the range twice and then switched off the ignition and locked the door. Wyatt shared an exasperated look with David before asking, "What now?"

"I wonder if that's why I can't get the satellite dish to work. I wonder if there are any signals there to receive."

His father shrugged his shoulders. David pointed the shotgun toward the street. "Let's take a walk up the drive and see what's happening on the main road." Wyatt didn't think that would hurt anything and might provide a little better picture of what was going on. He could use a good walk anyway.

The duo progressed through the parking lot and then onto the marina's driveway, which was actually a half-mile long private street. Their path was uphill, the land on both sides open, flat and blanketed with knee-high vegetation. Originally, this area had been cleared and leveled to accommodate homes, condos or a small business plaza. The real estate investors of yesteryear held tight to their cash these days, leaving nothing but a field of weeds where the promise of commercialization had existed before. The only business ever constructed was the bank at the corner.

As father and son traveled, it dawned on Wyatt how quiet the world had become. It was almost lunchtime, and he couldn't recognize the whine of a single engine or the hum of an air conditioner. There were no airplanes in the sky and no boats on Clear Lake behind them. It was if everyone had just disappeared. In a strange way, it was a pleasant sensation. As David and he crested the rise, the land flattened out to the level, featureless terrain of the southeastern coastal prairie. The horizon was littered with the rooflines of two-story homes and utility poles. This particular area had seen a boom in construction at the turn of the millennium, giving rise to entire subdivisions practically overnight.

They were traveling in the direction of Kemah Avenue, a street that had been nothing more than a sleepy country lane less than 30 years ago. Now it was home to strip malls, large outlet stores, and numerous fast food restaurants. The ever-increasing traffic had required two different expansions of the seldom-used lane. A boom area until 2008, development ceased altogether after the depression began.

To the two men scanning Kemah Avenue, time appeared to have moved backwards 30 years. The five-lane high capacity roadway was completely void of life. David couldn't believe the difference. "Wow! This is eerie. It's like one of those old black and white 'Twilight Zone' shows – all of the people have vanished."

Even the traffic lights were dark, gently swaying in the light afternoon breeze.

The two men continued until they reached the bank where Wyatt had witnessed the shoving match earlier. A police car, lying on its side, was the only evidence of the confrontation in the otherwise empty parking lot. The patrol car had burned, giving off a rank odor of smoldering plastic and melted rubber. Both men kept their distance. Wyatt noted the bank's glass doors were shattered, the entranceway's frames bent and twisted. Neither man wanted a closer look at the car or the inside of the bank.

David moved on while Wyatt paused, pensively considering the once-vibrant business. Despite blaming bankers for the demise of his company, he didn't wish this sort of violence on anyone. David continued to the avenue's curb and scanned the street in both directions. The road was vacant for as far as he could see.

They declared any further exploration pointless. Frustrated, the duo headed back to the marina. Halfway there, an unusual sound drifted across the wide, empty field from the east. At first, both men tensed, the wind-distorted noise was like someone crying or in pain. Moving closer, they observed a small, blonde head racing around the corner of a distant privacy fence. The running child was quickly pursued by two others, one of them yelling, "Tag! You're it!"

The men watched the backyard game without comment, lost in relief and then-distant memories. Exchanging glances, it was unnecessary to speak. Both felt comfort at the previously mundane scene before them. Both realized how important it was to believe some things were normal, especially after witnessing the desolate landscape behind them.

Father and son continued their expedition in silence, soberly reflecting on the events of the day. When they were almost back to Boxer, Wyatt spoke. "I think we should reach out to our fellow boaters around the marina. They are all probably wondering about what is going on as much as we are. Maybe someone has access to news or something. Why don't you and Sage walk up and down all of the piers, letting everyone know we are calling a meeting this afternoon at six by the pool?"

David nodded, "That's a good idea. It might also help to know who is down here. Last night with Bill was scary. That whole encounter could've gone very badly."

Returning to the boat, Wyatt told Morgan of his idea. His wife agreed wholeheartedly, suggesting David leave the shotgun behind while his sister and he toured the marina. Before long, David and Sage were off, trekking from pier to pier, seeking neighbors.

Southland housed 14 individual piers, each with numerous slips. Boxer was tied up on pier two, which accommodated craft up to 48 feet. Pier one was built for larger vessels, capable of handling yachts up to 100 feet in length. The smallest vessels at the marina were about 25 feet bow to stern. There was a mixture of power and sailing vessels, subdivided into practically every class, type, and length available.

The kids returned around 4:30 and announced they identified 29 occupied boats. Everyone agreed to meet by the pool at six...everyone except Bill. He elected not to go, using bourbon as a painkiller and sleeping off the effect.

Wyatt had one last duty to perform before the meeting. Taking plastic trash bags from Boxer's stow, he asked David to accompany him back to the marina's drive. On their earlier trip, Wyatt had noticed an area filled with golf ball-sized landscaping stones. Filling two doubled-up bags with the rocks, they hefted the heavy load back to the end of the pier.

Using a tarp and two long boat poles salvaged from an unoccupied boat, the duo managed to wrap the dead girl's body in a makeshift plastic shroud. The task at hand put both men into a grim, melancholy frame of mind. The teenager was close to Sage's age, and Wyatt couldn't help but wonder about the agony her parents must be suffering – the "not knowing" where their daughter was during all this mayhem had to be the worst. David's thoughts tracked in tandem with Wyatt's, clouded with images of his sister.

At Wyatt's suggestion, David snapped two pictures of the girl's face with his cell phone. They pulled a small sample of her hair for the DNA. It was the best they could do for future identification. Bill's launch, an inflatable 14-footer with a small outboard, was used to tow the deceased out into the lake. Securing the two heavy bags of stones to the tarp, Wyatt mumbled, "Until the sea gives up her own," as the two men watched the body sink to the bottom.

~  ~

At first glance, the crowd appeared to be a normal cross-section of any social gathering. A closer inspection would reveal some minor differences. The age of the attendees was slightly older than the population at large, and the quality of clothing, watches, and jewelry indicated a little more disposable income than most people could claim these days. Owning a recreational boat during an economic depression when gas prices were over $9.50 per gallon required income. While Craigslist was littered with owners of jet-skis and sailboats desperate for cash, the monthly upkeep and other associated costs were staggering. Still, the water had an addictive lure, and there were ways to manage expenses. People didn't leave the marina nearly as often. Owning a boat and using it were now two different things. Most of the marina's residents had purchased their vessels years ago during better economic times. Some, recently joined by Wyatt and Morgan, used their floating cottages as permanent residences.

Wyatt watched his neighbors drift into the pool area, his mind reminiscing about years past when he commonly called such meetings in times of crisis. At those gatherings, his credentials had been tied to his role as the leader of a business. Now, he had no authority or responsibility to anyone other than his family. The thought helped him relax. *I'm just one of many here*, he thought. *I'm not in charge, and I don't want to be.*

Still, deep inside, there was an urge to assert control. Obscured by layers of perceived failure, the compulsion to organize, lead, and resolve wanted to speak and be heard. That voice was weak, muffled by memories of fiasco and disappointment. The impulse was easily beaten down.

It didn't take a lot of effort for Wyatt to justify his back-of-the-bus thinking. *This is different than when I ran the show. There's no money on the line, no deadline to talk about, and no deliverables to list. I don't owe these people anything. This isn't a business meeting - it's a social gathering.*

David eased close to Wyatt. "Dad, I think everyone is here. I'm the one who invited them all, should I get it started?"

Wyatt scanned the small clusters of people assembled around the pool deck. He was a little surprised at the number of folks he didn't know. He'd seen most of the faces here or there, but was a little taken aback at how few of his neighbors he'd actually held a conversation with. He nodded at David, "Sure, why not?"

David cleared his throat and spoke loudly, "Hey, everyone! Thanks for coming. I would like to suggest each boat have a representative take a turn speaking what's on their mind. We can go by pier number, largest to smallest."

Wyatt couldn't suppress a smile. David's diplomacy, the suggestion of starting with the people who owned the smaller boats first, demonstrated remarkable grace. Everyone at the marina knew the smaller your pier number, the larger your boat. His son had just sidestepped any chance those with means could attempt to flaunt their status, while at the same time making sure everyone's voice was heard. Wyatt read the body language of the group as being frightened, concerned at best. Any hint of "My boat's bigger, you should listen to me," would be rejected today.

Evidently, his son's suggestion was well received as heads nodded all around the pool. An older gentleman strolled to the center of the crowd as people began setting up lounge chairs in a broad semi-circle. After everyone was settled, a tentative voice spoke, "My name is Dale, and I'm on pier 14 aboard *Her Diamond*. I don't know about everyone else, but I can't get in touch with my family, and I'm worried sick about them." As Dale looked around, several people showed their agreement, and a few smiled. The speaker acknowledged the encouragement as a sign for him to continue. The old fellow's confidence grew as he continued. "I came down to wash the boat, and now I guess I'm stuck here. I tried to leave, but the police forced me to come back. I've got a little food aboard, but my water tank is about empty. I should have filled it up before the water stopped yesterday, but I didn't. I think fresh water might be a priority for everyone."

Wyatt hadn't thought about that. While Boxer had a water maker, smaller boats were only equipped with storage tanks. Water might be a problem for many of the residents.

Time seemed to fly as everyone took a turn speaking. Wyatt listened keenly, taking notes about everyone's issues and ideas. Always the manager, his mind was occupied by an attempt to solve the problems being voiced by his fellow boaters. Waiting for the next person to stand and speak, Wyatt suddenly realized everyone was looking at him. It was his turn.

Wyatt moved to the center of the group, introducing himself, his family, and his boat. After a short pause, he lifted the legal pad containing his scribbles and quickly examined the summary. "I've been noting everyone's concerns and needs. While there is nothing I can offer to help in regards to communicating with family or loved ones, I do have a few ideas about some of the more basic needs. None of us know how long this situation is going to last, so if I may suggest a few things, it might make these uncertain times easier for all involved."

He paused, gauging everyone's reaction. Heads were moving north and south, many of the listeners smiling. He continued, "Clearly, fresh water is a concern. As I see it, we have three sources; rainwater, the pool, and some of the larger boats here in the marina have water makers aboard. I suggest we organize some sort of water distribution until the city water is restored."

Wyatt looked up from his paper, noting the mostly positive reaction to his proposal. He smiled sheepishly and then continued. "We have a decent supply of fuel at our disposal. Most of these boats are full of either gas or diesel, and there's the marina's fuel pier to consider as well. I don't know how recently the marina's tanks were topped off, but there are probably thousands and thousands of gallons available."

He hesitated for a bit before continuing, as his next suggestion was more than a little radical. Taking a deep breath, he decided to throw it out there. "Everyone knows the marina office has a spare set of keys for all of the boats." He chuckled, "Any of us who has ever driven down here and forgotten our keys has probably utilized those spares." Several people nodded in agreement, remembering a similar experience. "While I don't count myself as a burglar, if the situation doesn't improve soon, I don't think anyone will have us arrested if we break into the office and borrow some of those keys. Most of these unoccupied vessels have food aboard, and we could even utilize the water makers on some of the bigger vessels as well."

Again, the consensus was agreement. It was suggested by one gentleman that the refrigerators and freezers on some of the locked boats may already have drained the batteries, and precious food might be going to waste even now.

The meeting carried on for another hour. It was getting dark when they finally finished, having determined that a committee would meet first thing in the morning and organize a salvage effort for the food and other critical supplies residing in the unoccupied boats. The foragers would leave notes for the owners letting them know what had happened and who to contact regarding reimbursement.

As the attendees drifted back to their respective piers, Morgan approached Wyatt and gave him a hug. "You did great, honey. I think everyone feels a little better now. I know I do."

David joined them, echoing his mother's sentiments. He'd volunteered to be a scavenger, and Sage had surprised her parents by raising her hand to join the water committee. The family sauntered back to Boxer with higher spirits and a somewhat positive sentiment about the future.

~   ~

The next day, the citizens of Southland Marina, or "Marinaville" as someone had nicknamed the community, worked together in an effort to make everyone more comfortable. Wyatt and Morgan were pleased to see their children play an active role, contributing their share of the workload.

It became painfully obvious that keeping all of the boats supplied wasn't going to be easy. The vessels without water makers were going to require the most labor. Since boats are similar to automobiles in that they require a good scrubbing now and then, buckets are a common commodity at any marina.

After a few dozen buckets had been collected, helpers organized to transport the buckets of water from one boat to another along the piers. Everyone started calling them the bucket brigade, and in the hot Texas sun, it was exhausting work.

David and another young man broke into the marina office, trying to inflict as little damage as possible. They wrote a note explaining the cause and retrieved two large sheets of plywood containing hundreds of hooks labeled with slip numbers and, of course, dangling keys.

It was Morgan who suggested the formation of the Marinaville City Water Department. A large 80-foot sailing vessel with a high capacity water maker was tied up at the base of pier one. That single boat could generate over 100 gallons of fresh water per day – enough to fill the tanks on several smaller boats. While Morgan's idea resulted in a significant shortcut for the water carriers, the bucket brigade still didn't want for physical exercise. Wyatt smiled when the jokes started circulating, most pertaining to how much money they were all going to make with the introduction of this fabulous new weight loss program.

Three of the smaller vessels didn't have generators. Their cabins were powered solely by battery banks, normally recharged via shore power. At first, this had been a serious problem. Wyatt, inspired by Morgan's water company idea, suggested one of the vessels with a generator be moved to a nearby slip, allowing the neighbor to recharge its batteries. The Marinaville Mobile Power Company was born and could currently boast a 100% customer service satisfaction record.

Another task deemed necessary was the monitoring of various radios. A team was organized to take turns, each member assigned a certain day to listen in on both the marine frequencies and normal AM and FM.

It was the second morning without electricity that Mr. Pierce came hustling down pier two, frantically waving a piece of paper. He excitedly reported that the Emergency Broadcasting Network was now working, and there was news.

Wyatt, busy cleaning a small batch of perch caught that morning, wiped his hands clean and headed for Boxer's bridge. He dialed in the AM station prescribed by Mr. Pierce and began listening.

YOUR ATTENTION, PLEASE. YOUR ATTENTION, PLEASE. THIS IS MAJOR ROBERT DANFORTH OF THE 112TH TRANSPORTATION REGIMENT, FEDERALIZED TEXAS NATIONAL GUARD. I HAVE AN **IMPORTANT** ANNOUNCEMENT. TO ALL CIVILIANS OF HOUSTON, TEXAS...THE UNITED STATES ARMY, BY ORDER OF THE PRESIDENT OF THE UNITED STATES, HAS ESTABLISHED MARTIAL LAW FOR THE CITY OF HOUSTON. IN ADDITION, ALL CITY AND STATE AGENCIES HAVE BEEN FEDERALIZED. ALL EMPLOYEES OF THE CITY OF HOUSTON OR THE STATE OF TEXAS SHOULD REPORT TO THE FEDERAL BUILDING AT 1200 SOUTH MAIN STREET AS SOON AS POSSIBLE. BRING IDENTIFICATION WITH YOU. ONLY INDIVIDUALS WITH APPROPRIATE CREDENTIALS ARE ALLOWED TO TRAVEL TO THE FEDERAL BUILDING.

ALL OTHER CIVILIANS WITHIN THE INTERSTATE 610 LOOP ARE ORDERED TO REMAIN IN THEIR HOMES UNTIL CONTACTED BY LOCAL AUTHORITIES. FOR THE SAFETY OF ALL CITIZENS, **A CURFEW** OF **1800** TO **0600** WILL BE STRICTLY ENFORCED, AND VIOLATORS WILL BE SHOT ON SIGHT.

ALL CIVILIANS RESIDING OUTSIDE OF THE 610 LOOP ARE HEREBY ORDERED TO REPORT, AS SOON AS POSSIBLE, TO CHECKPOINTS ESTABLISHED AT EVERY MAJOR INTERSECTION OF THE 610 LOOP AND INTERSTATES 45, 59, 10, 288 AND 290. ADDITIONAL CHECKPOINTS ARE BEING ESTABLISHED AT ALL MAJOR SURFACE ROADS, AS WELL.

YOU ARE REQUIRED TO BRING IDENTIFICATION AND WILL BE ASSIGNED TEMPORARY HOUSING AND DUTIES. THE UNITED STATES ARMY WILL PROVIDE BASIC SHELTER, SECURITY, FOOD, WATER, AND MEDICAL CARE.

FAMILY UNITS MAY BE TEMPORARILY SEPARATED IN ORDER TO PROVIDE SHELTER.

NO WEAPONS OF ANY KIND ARE PERMITTED INSIDE OF THE 610 LOOP.

PERSONAL PROPERTY IS SUBJECT TO CONFISCATION.

ABLE-BODIED ADULTS, BETWEEN THE AGES OF 16 AND 65, WILL BE EXPECTED TO PERFORM ASSIGNED TASKS AND LABOR.

THESE ORDERS ARE ISSUED BY GENERAL T. WILSON ADAMS, MAJOR GENERAL, UNITED STATES ARMY.

END OF MESSAGE.

THIS MESSAGE WILL REPEAT IN 30 MINUTES.

The message repeated all day, and Mr. Pierce traveled from boat to boat, ensuring everyone heard it. By late in the afternoon, an impromptu town hall meeting was taking place behind Boxer with practically the entire population of Marinaville present.

Wyatt was shocked at the variety of reactions. More than a few of the boaters were ready to pack up and do as the army ordered. Others seemed determined to use any excuse as justification for why they shouldn't follow the instructions. "We don't live in Houston, and the message was specifically directed to the 'citizens of Houston,'" they argued. The debate raged for over an hour.

An older gentleman remarked that the whole thing sounded like being told to report to a labor camp. He compared it to WWII and the orders given to the citizens of Japanese descent living in the US. Others backed his observation, passionately making the point that they would prefer to stay at the marina and be free.

There was also a heated plea for the Marinaville residents to stay together. After all, they were all well fed, comfortable and isolated from the mayhem. The order for martial law had been instituted to bring order and provide food and shelter for the citizens of Houston. Why should such a well-functioning community be divided?

Back and forth the conversation flowed. Point and counterpoint were debated, sometimes leaving angry faces and seldom resulting in any consensus.

Wyatt wanted to stay put. He didn't know the specific reasons why the president had made this decision, nor did he believe the army could control a city the size of Houston. Finally, it was David who seemed to resolve the conflict. He innocently asked, "Why don't the people who want to follow the instructions head to Houston, and the people who want to stay can remain here?"

No one could debate that logic - it was free choice. The congregation settled on mulling it over, most pledging to announce a decision in the morning. Wyatt was relieved at having avoided being drawn into the dialogue.

The next morning, two of the families occupying smaller boats apologized to everyone, packed up, and left. The others all decided to stay, at least for the time being. Wyatt could understand why those folks who were leaving had made their decision. A smaller boat was fine for a weekend or even a short trip. Living on one fulltime had to be cramped and stressful, especially when combined with the unknown of the conditions surrounding your primary residence and worldly possessions.

Everyone turned out to wish those heading to Houston well. Hugs and promises of "See you soon," abounded. "We'll be sharing margaritas at our reunion pool party within a month," one captain predicted. Wyatt and David flashed each other a knowing look - both having doubts of a return to normalcy so soon.

After the farewell, Marinaville settled back into routine. The daily tasks of keeping everyone supplied with enough water, fuel for generators, and food kept all of the residents busy. There really wasn't the time to second-guess any decisions.

A few days later, Wyatt rose early and was making his coffee as usual. Morgan joined him, discussing the day's upcoming events, and whispering a few comments about how the children were accepting of their new lifestyle. Morgan casually meandered to the salon's door and glanced out. She quickly turned to Wyatt and excitedly reported, "It's snowing!"

Wyatt, puzzled, joined her and was astonished by the scene. Greyish white flakes of what appeared to be snow were falling all around the marina. He ventured outside and caught a speck in his hand, but it wasn't cold, nor did it melt. It was ash. He looked north to the fires raging in Houston and then at a flag on a nearby sailboat. The wind had shifted, and they were receiving an ash storm that would have made any volcano proud.

Southland Marina, Texas
February 18, 2017

Sage sat on the bridge, slouched in the captain's chair with her legs resting on the dash. The VHF radio was switched on, but she wasn't paying attention to it. Instead, music from her cell phone pulsed through earphones, her duty of monitoring the marine radio ignored. With her hearing blocked, Sage didn't detect her father's climbing to the bridge until it was too late.

Wyatt shook his head, sitting across from his daughter with a stern look on his face. Sage noticed the look of disapproval, questioning his expression until she realized she was shirking her responsibilities. Jerking out the earphones, she flashed an embarrassed look of apology and then turned up the volume knob on the big radio.

"Sage," he began in a gentle voice, "I know this is all kind of tedious for you, but I need you to take it seriously. I'm not sure what's going on in the world right now."

His daughter shrugged her shoulders and focused her gaze on her toes. "Daddy, I'm sorry. I'll pay attention. I just got bored listening to the static. No one is saying anything, and I just downloaded this new song the other day…." She was interrupted by a voice on the radio.

"Houston Yachting Club…Houston Yachting Club…this is the Serendipity. Houston Yachting Club this is Serendipity. Over."

A static-filled minute passed without any response. The captain of Serendipity repeated his hail. More seconds ticked by, and again there was no answer. Sage and Wyatt glanced at each other, both wondering why. The Houston Yachting Club was one of the high-end marinas on Galveston Bay. The expensive, private organization was known to have a waiting list for new members and an excellent reputation for service. Before either could speak, the radio sounded again, "Any vessel, any vessel, this is the sailing vessel Serendipity requesting a radio check. Over."

Wyatt realized the captain of Serendipity knew what he was doing. While he wasn't familiar with the boat or its master, the request for a radio check was logical. *If you don't receive the expected response in a given amount of time, make sure your equipment is working.* Wyatt waited a few moments for someone else to respond. No one answered the call. He motioned for Sage to hand him the microphone. "Serendipity, Serendipity, this is the motor vessel Boxer, docked at Southland Marina – we read you loud and clear. Your radio is operating fine, Captain. Over."

There was a buzz and then a click. "Captain, could you please go to 62? Over."

Wyatt frowned at the request. The initial hail had been on channel 16, the official frequency for contacting other vessels and listening for coast guard alerts. For that reason, boats equipped with a marine radio are required to monitor 16. The rules basically read that you hailed another vessel on 16 and then switched channels if you wanted to converse further. Wyatt didn't know anything about the sailing vessel Serendipity, as there were thousands of boats in the area. It was unusual for a stranger to want to talk unless there was a problem. Wyatt keyed the microphone, "Serendipity, this is Boxer. Going to channel 62, Captain. Over."

Wyatt nodded at Sage who started spinning the large dial. He watched as the big green numerals increased, finally displaying "62." He spoke again, "Serendipity, this is Boxer, now on 62. What can I do for you, Captain? Over."

Most recreational boaters tried to play by the rules when broadcasting on an official channel. It was a matter of professionalism, a courtesy to others, and the fact that every other boat in the area was listening in.

When two vessels were communicating on a side channel, the conversation typically became more casual. The same voice came across the airwaves, "Boxer, sorry to bother you. We're coming up the ship channel and can't raise Houston Yachting Club. Their radio might be down, and I was wondering if you could try a landline for us. We can't seem to get a cell phone signal. We struck a submerged object a few hours ago and are taking on water. Our bow thruster is out, and the rudder is fouled. I'm going to need help getting this big girl in. If things get much worse, I'll have to call 'Mayday.' Over."

Wyatt looked at Sage, pointing at her phone. She checked the display for signal and verified what they both already knew. She eyed her father, shaking her head - no cell service. Wyatt transmitted, "Serendipity, we don't have cell service either and are not equipped with a landline onboard. Captain, how long have you been out?"

A few moments passed, followed by a concerned voice. "Boxer, we've been offshore for over 20 days on a return run from South America. Why do you ask? Over."

Wyatt shook his head. *This guy has no clue what has happened. He's coming in blind.* He pressed the talk button, choosing his words carefully. "Captain, I would drop anchor if I were you. The world has changed significantly since you put to sea. Martial law was declared a short time ago, and our pier has been without power since the 15th." Wyatt didn't end his transmission there. "Captain, I know you don't know me but...drop the hook, sir...catch up on the news...brace yourself."

Wyatt could imagine the look on the sailor's face. How would he react to a strange, metallic voice sounding over the airwaves, claiming apocalyptic events and offering bizarre advice? The man was almost home with a crippled boat. He was probably looking forward to walking on dry land after such a long voyage. He's almost there, almost home - and then this weird radio message comes out of nowhere telling him to drop anchor before he finishes the voyage.

It was over two minutes before the radio sounded again, "Boxer, can you repeat that? Did you say martial law? What in the world is going on?" Wyatt snorted at the lack of "over" ending the transmission. Clearly, the distant captain was a little shaken up - who wouldn't be?

"You heard me clearly, Captain. I've heard news reports of a government failure...riots...out of control fires... causalities – social collapse. The same news channel reported the president was declaring martial law. Let me warn you, sir, the world isn't the same as when you left. Over."

The distant voice's tone changed - softer than before. "Captain, I've got serious problems here. We have five crew and twelve passengers aboard. The bilge pumps are barely keeping up with the water we're taking on. I've got to get these people off this boat."

Wyatt considered the situation for a bit. "Captain, can you make it to Southland Marina? We have enough people here to help tie her off."

The response was almost immediate. "Negative, Boxer. We draw nine feet. Clear Lake isn't deep enough."

Wyatt's next idea made Sage's head snap up, a concerned expression on her face. "Captain, I can come out and tie up alongside. We're big enough to ferry that many people to shore."

"Boxer, thank you for that. It helps to know someone is out there. I'm going to anchor for the time being and see if we can affect repairs. Right now, I can't justify declaring an emergency, but it's real close to that."

"Captain, that's your call. I wouldn't know what to do with your passengers after I had them. They might be better off right where they are. I'll check in with you later. For now, we'll stay on 16. If you need us, hail."

"Roger that, Boxer. Again, thank you for the offer. Serendipity to 16 – out."

Wyatt keyed his microphone, "This is Boxer – out to 16."

Sage was staring at him. Wyatt realized his face must be very troubled, but it was too late to hide it from his daughter. She reached over and stroked his hand. "You're really worried aren't you, Dad?"

"Yes, baby, I am. These are troubling times. For the first time in my life, I have almost no idea what's going to happen – how things are going to work out. I guess we'll just have to keep the faith that we'll be okay as long as we stick together. After talking to that captain, I think we should be thankful we're doing as well as we are. How would you like to be out on that boat right now?"

When Sage didn't answer, Wyatt reached across and squeezed her hand. He flashed the most genuine smile he could muster, and she returned the gesture.

Neither of them seemed to be genuinely comforted.

Sage needed a restroom break, and Wyatt agreed to cover her watch. Alone on the bridge, Wyatt stared blankly at the radio, fighting an impulse to pick up the microphone and hail the captain of Serendipity. There was an unavoidable parallel between the sailor's predicament and Wyatt's life. He couldn't ignore the comparison any more than he could disregard the empathy that dominated his thoughts.

Serendipity's voyage was a microcosm of Wyatt's existence, the role of the yacht's master no different than the responsibility of running a company, or being the head of a family. Wyatt's soul was troubled by the reflection of a lonely, isolated man, now denied the security of home through no fault of his own. Wyatt wanted to tell the man he understood the pain and loneliness.

Despite the absence of detail, Wyatt had little trouble relating Serendipity's journey to the path his family and he had recently traveled. The captain of a vessel held responsibility for passenger and crew, the same relationship between manager and employee. Piloting a vessel through troubled waters wasn't much different than steering a company through troubled times. Entering an exotic port of call could be compared to penetrating a new market. The analogies could go on and on.

Returning home from a long journey was a unique experience, especially for a seaman. Even a large boat like Serendipity would've required exhaustive efforts and a high level of skill to accomplish such a voyage. That last leg to homeport was always a complex paradox of emotions, even during normal times. In sports, it was referred to as "closing out the victory." The barons of finance referenced "signed, sealed, and delivered."

Wyatt had been there, both on a boat and behind a desk. He'd felt the sense of relief when finally getting close to the end, of knowing your boat and crew would sleep safe and secure that night. The sensation wasn't so different from knowing that a business tactic was paying off – that the workers would have a paycheck...job security.

Most captains wouldn't admit it, but shedding responsibility for the lives of everyone aboard was a welcome void. Hardships, such as pulling an overnight watch or fretting over every odd little noise made by the vessel, wouldn't be missed. Weather would cease to be the most important information of the day; no longer would the supply of water, fuel and food be the primary concern. No more adrenaline- pumping battles with storm-driven waves or early morning incidents with misbehaving navigation equipment. Wyatt remembered the warm glow of accomplishment, that sense of victory over the sea when the ship was finally tied off at her final harbor. It was an identical experience to a successful sales campaign or landing a new, profitable customer.

In Wyatt's mind, there was little difference between Columbus setting sail for the new world and Steve Jobs creating Apple in his garage. Both were risk-taking explorers who could be ruined by uncontrollable circumstance. Wyatt grunted at the thought. Mr. Jobs didn't have to worry about a storm crashing his fledgling prototype against the rocks - he wasn't going to perish due to the wind and sea.

It then occurred to Wyatt that perhaps the captain going down with his ship was the lucky one. Was that end better than losing it all...than having nothing left? Death before dishonor?

There was also a negative aspect to coming home. The letdown of knowing the adventure was almost over, that life would soon return to a mundane, shore side routine. Any chance to explore or experience something unique while at sea would soon be absent. No more steering the boat into a strange harbor, anxious to explore a new locale. The opportunity to sample different foods, make new friends and see exotic sights soon to be over. A smirk crossed Wyatt's face when he realized it didn't matter how you arrived at the end point – it sucked. A successful business generated money, respect, and gratification, but that's not what Wyatt would miss the most. He would never again experience the thrill of quest – the challenge of the game. His last business voyage had ended the day the bank closed his doors.

Just like Wyatt, Serendipity's homeport no longer existed, her final destination dissipated. Someone had taken it away. The captain's well-planned, properly executed voyage was all for naught. Wyatt imagined the crushing weight of despair the sailboat's master must be facing. He was familiar with the experience. It wasn't just empathy for what the man on the other end of the radio was feeling at that moment, there were future tortures to look forward to. Wyatt knew that joining the Fraternal Order of Failure led to being a card carrying member of Club Inactive. Eventually, you ended up with a Fellowship at the Society of It's-all-behind-me-now.

Sage's head appearing at the top of the ladder snapped Wyatt out of it. She tilted her head slightly and asked, "Daddy, are you all right?"

Wyatt's face flushed for a moment, concerned that his internal pity party could somehow be perceived by his youngest child. "I'm fine, Sage. Did everything come out okay?"

His daughter swatted his arm, trying not to laugh at the crude humor.

Wyatt left the bridge, convinced that occupying himself with double-checking the satellite installation would distract him from such melancholy thinking. The dish was already mounted; his son was following the cable-run down the mast.

Boxer was considered a motor-sailor and was equipped with a single mast. In reality, she was a powerboat. Somewhere, in one of the numerous storage compartments was an emergency sail. Wyatt had no idea how to rig or use the large sheet of canvas. He seriously doubted it would work very well.

David and he adjusted and readjusted the cables until almost dusk, quitting when Morgan opened the salon doors and announced supper was ready. She didn't have to tell them twice.

Chapter 6

Charlie Beckenworth was feeling like Charlie "Becken-worthless." Being unemployed for over a year had initiated a downward spiral in his life – a seemingly unending series of blows to his esteem. The crushing waves of bad breaks eventually wore him down to the point where he began to simply not care about much of anything. The fact that his wife had become the primary breadwinner for their family had been the final straw.

When he'd first been informed his employer was downsizing, he hadn't been overly concerned. His wife had a good job as a software analyst, and he had never had any problem finding work as an electrician. After two months of countless online applications, resume mailings, and untold hours searching through web-based employment databases, he realized the first pangs of panic.

Charlie's wife, Rose, had been supportive, and the couple initially worked together, trying to make the best of what both of them thought would be a temporary situation. The couple agreed that Charlie would stay at home with the kids in order to avoid the cost of daycare.

Raising children wasn't Charlie's forte. While he loved his kids as much as any father, the day-to-day activities associated with being a stay at home dad didn't agree with him. That's when the drinking began. It had only been a beer or two at first. A cold one now and then to take the edge off of the relentless boredom and ceaseless chores. Doing laundry, preparing meals, and taxiing the kids was not how Charlie had seen his life playing out.

His buddies didn't help much. At first, they said all the right words and at least pretended to support him. As time wore on, the positive reinforcements became cruel jokes, with Charlie taking the ribbing badly. Over time, he was invited to fewer and fewer get-togethers, and his friends drifted further and further away.

Rose began accepting extra hours for a bigger paycheck. This eventuality led to even more responsibility for Charlie, and the occasional brewski became a six-pack by early afternoon. There had been a major disturbance in the Beckenworth household when Rose returned home one evening to discover the children crying in a bathtub, the bathwater icy, and the kids shivering with purple lips. Charlie was lying in his favorite lounge chair, passed out drunk.

Rose wanted to believe things would get better, and Chuck would snap out of it. She gently suggested her husband seek counseling or find a group of stay at home dads. Her loving efforts were angrily rejected, and Charlie continued to slide down the slope of despair.

The civil unrest, power outage, and subsequent martial law really had little effect on the Beckenworth homestead – at first. Charlie stashed several cases of beer in the garage, and a small gasoline generator had been purchased for hurricane season. The kids were a little fussy at first, but Rose and he would simply shoo them outside to their swing set - a quiet home restoring order to the universe.

The morning of the sixth day, Rose announced they were out of cereal for the kids.

On the seventh day, the last can of soup was prepared for lunch.

By the ninth day, Charlie realized he was down to his last beer. By the ninth day, Rose metered out a single can of corn accompanied by the last sleeve of saltine crackers.

On the afternoon of the tenth day, the kids were whining about the hunger pangs. Rose did her best to distract them, rummaging around in her stash and producing a new coloring book. The present had distracted the two from their empty stomachs, but only for a few hours.

Charlie knocked on the door of every house on their street. Most of the neighbors didn't answer. Those that had opened their front doors were apologetic, but didn't have anything to share. One older gentleman went so far as to remind Charlie he should have allocated more money for meat and potatoes and less on beer. A shoving match had ensued, the final result being Charlie returning home with empty hands, a mouthful of curses, and a bruised ego. To make matters worse, he was beginning to get the shakes from the sudden lack of alcohol in his system.

The kids were inside with Rose, so he waited outside to be alone while he licked his mental wounds. He craved different air, thinking the change would enable him to conjure up some method of feeding the family. After a pilgrimage around the cul-de-sac, he found himself inside the garage. His unstable hands were failing in their attempt to repair his fishing pole. Frustrated and out of patience, he was just about to splinter the misbehaving pole when the unmistakable aroma from an outdoor grill drifted by.

The fishing pole was pardoned.

February 26, 2017
Southland Marina
Kemah Bay, Texas

The citizens of Marinaville weren't suffering from the blackout nearly as severely as most. There were minor inconveniences, such as the constant droning of generators and the ever-present task of refilling fuel tanks. Compared to the rest of America, those ten days without electricity resulted in a mere fraction of the hardships endured by the vast majority of citizens.

The pier-people understood their good fortune, at least to some degree. A celebration was in order, a pseudo-Thanksgiving of sorts. Word passed up and down the docks that all were invited to a citywide cookout to be conducted by the pool. A pot luck extravaganza, the main course comprised of several pounds of frozen steak discovered a few days earlier in the freezer of a large sports fisherman located on pier one.

Everyone was feeling upbeat about the way the community had banded together. In a way, the marina was like a small island ecosystem. Everyone pitched in, no one was left out, and a few people even commented that life there was actually better than before the collapse. There was a positive sense of belonging to something important and working together to solve problems.

Part of the optimism was based on a swell of confidence that life would soon return to normal. This faith was due to an increasing number of indications that some sort of recovery was in process. Occasionally, people reported hearing car motors in the distance. One of the captains residing on the far side of the marina watched a group of strangers skirt around the edge of the water. He believed they ventured from one of the neighboring subdivisions. Over the last few days, there had been a few sirens, but only a single gunshot from a far distance. The fires still lit the night skies toward Houston, but the reddish glow and associated pillar of smoke seemed to be getting smaller. As reports of these encounters passed from one boater to the next, the typical reaction was a knowing smile – a sign of confidence that mankind would soon recover.

Charcoal was a common commodity on the piers. Practically every boater loved to fire up the grill and smoke up a mess of ribs...or steak...or whatever culinary indulgence satisfied the weekend mood. High praise, ultimate glory, whispered reputation, and hushed respect were won and lost via the pier-side smoker.

The problem wasn't rolling two portable grills up to the pool, nor was it difficult to start a proper fire. This issue was completing the day-to-day jobs required for life in Marinaville. The announcement of a cookout was to blame for more unfinished tasks than any other single event since the collapse. Instead of completing daily chores, everyone was busy mixing special sauces, baking family favorites, and polishing prized grilling tongs. Top-secret spicy concoctions were assembled behind closed doors while shadowy figures stalked between boats, creating clandestine marinades on the hush-hush.

As the citizens of Marinaville drifted poolside, David and Wyatt were standing ready, a wager already in place regarding which of the two men could devour the most food.

~ ~

Charlie stuck his head inside the house and told Rose he'd be back soon. Still stinging from the fight with the neighbor, he unlocked the car and retrieved a revolver from the console. It took him a little while to determine the source of the wonderful smell, now wafting over the area stronger than ever. After a quick stroll around the block, his nose triangulated the source as the marina bordering the neighborhood. "Why hadn't I thought of that before," he said to himself. "Those boats would be full of food and fuel. I'll just take whatever we need and replace it later."

Strolling through the empty lots to the marina, he spotted a trail of grey smoke slowly rising from the pool area. Charlie had only been to the marina a couple of times, but knew the layout well enough. He decided to head directly for the pool and ask nicely if those fortunate enough to have all that food would share with his hungry kids. He tucked the pistol in the back of his belt, reminding himself to be polite.

~ ~

David noticed the stranger first. He gently nudged Wyatt and pointed with his eyes toward the man approaching their get-together. After relinquishing grill duty to another boater, David and his father slowly made their way through the crowd to intercept the newcomer.

David took the initiative, and with a firm, but polite voice said, "Good afternoon, how can we help you?"

Charlie didn't hesitate. The smell of cooking steaks was drawing him in, thoughts of how proud Rose would be giving him courage. Bringing home a load of food would make him the breadwinner again, the hero, the man of the house. When he saw one of the men standing poolside raise a can of beer, he actually began salivating.

Charlie refocused on the guy who greeted him. "Afternoon, neighbor. I live over there and smelled your fire. I have two kids and a wife at home, and we've not eaten in a while. I was wondering if you could share a little of that wonderful-smelling food."

Wyatt and David looked at each other as some of the other boaters began wandering over to hear what was going on. Before either could reply, Hank Weathers spoke from the crowd, "We've not got a lot of extra ourselves, friend. Can't your neighbors help out?"

Charlie was a little taken aback by the response. "Well, ummm, pretty much everyone is in the same spot we are. If they don't lift the martial law soon, there are going to be a lot of very hungry people."

Hank didn't even hesitate, "Sorry friend, we are all tapped out, just like you. The only reason we are eating so high on the hog tonight is because all this food was about to spoil."

Charlie thought about that for a minute and then scanned the marina. He scratched his head and replied with a sharp tone, "Why are you lying to me? I can hear all of those generators running. Every single one of these boats probably has food onboard. You mean to tell me you won't share just a little?"

Charlie's response clearly offended Hank. Taking a step forward and pointing a finger at Charlie, his response sounded menacing. "Look buddy, everyone has their own problems. You come walking over here on private property, uninvited, and then accuse me of being a liar. I think you should head on home before there's trouble."

Charlie shifted his gaze from face to face in the crowd. Some people were nodding their heads in approval, while others showed puzzlement at Hank's aggressive stance. Charlie started to turn away when he remembered the pistol in his belt. Hunger, fear of losing another confrontation, and the cooler full of beer pushed Charlie's buttons. The thought of going home empty-handed and Rose's disapproving face gave Charlie the courage to spin back around, pulling the gun. His shaking hand aimed the weapon directly at Hank's face. Charlie growled, "You're a liar, and I'm not going home empty- handed. Now give me some of that food, and no one will get hurt."

Wyatt spoke up, "Now hold on, friend. No sense in all that. Just put the gun down, and we will get you what you want." He turned toward the stunned assembly, exaggerating the nodding of his head, "Won't we, everyone? We can all pitch in and give this man a little food for his family, can't we?"

A murmur spread around, everyone supporting Wyatt's move. One of the women took it a step further, picking up an empty cardboard box and filling it with various dishes from the table. Someone else wrapped two of the steaks in tin foil. After the box was full, David took it, slowly approaching the gunman with the offering extended. "Here ya go. Now please put the gun away, and leave us alone."

Charlie's eyes darted around the crowd. He started to take the box from David and then remembered. "How about you throw in a few cans of that beer, sonny? A man can get thirsty."

David grunted, but did as requested. He returned the box to Charlie, who hefted it in one arm while still keeping the pistol pointed with the other. He backed up a few steps and then turned and hurried away.

~  ~

After being robbed at gunpoint, the response from the marina crowd ranged from outrage to relief. Everyone seemed to start talking at once as soon as they realized no one was going to be shot. Hank was furious, going on and on about how someone should have rushed the bandit. Other men, including Wyatt, weren't so sure. Hank's voice carried a warning tone, "Mark my words everyone, he'll be back and probably with several of his friends. Our little secret is out. Every Tom, Dick, and Harry who is hungry or craving a beer will be sticking a gun in our faces from now on."

One of the other men disagreed, "Oh come on now Hank, the man had kids at home and was desperate. It's the proper thing to share. We've plenty of food, and the government will get its act together soon. I don't want to go to bed tonight worrying about hungry kids when we have so much."

The debate raged back and forth for several minutes when Morgan decided to assert herself, "Oh now come on, folks! We're not going to let one little ole holdup ruin a good Texas barbeque, are we? Let's remember why we're here and eat up. Come on now, everyone get a plate. Y'all can argue better on a full stomach anyway."

Eventually the crowd settled down and began to plop spoons of potato salad and coleslaw onto paper plates. The mood was different, but the gathering carried on. Small groups of people mingled here and there, and conversations carried on in low, hushed tones.

David sat in a lounge chair next to his father. Slowly chewing a piece of steak, his voice was serious. "Dad, you know Hank is right. This is trouble. If anyone sees that guy walking back with that package of goodies, they're going to demand to know where he got it. If any of his neighbors come to his house begging for food, he'll tell them where to go. The marina just became the grocery store for that entire neighborhood. They could pick us clean in a matter of days."

Wyatt nodded and took a sip of iced tea. He gestured around the perimeter of the marina with his hand. "David, there are probably 2,000 homes bordering this place. If the government doesn't fix this soon, we are going to have more of a problem than anyone here can imagine."

A foreboding mood dominated the rest of Wyatt's afternoon. Several times, he started to express his inner concerns to David or Morgan, but he always stopped. *I'll let them relax and enjoy the day*, he thought. In Wyatt's mind, the robbery had been more than a temporary interruption of a cookout. He believed the act was a true indicator of a troublesome future.

Absentmindedly, Wyatt used his fork to toy with the few green beans remaining on his plate. He glanced around the pool, mentally taking stock of the group. Almost all of them were desperate to see law and order reestablished. He had watched, studying their faces when the grind of a motor was detected or tale of a stranger was passed around. He'd noted that more than anything else, these folks paid attention to stories and rumors about the old world coming back. It cheered them up – gave them hope.

They're frightened, he deduced. They're practically scared stiff and only going through the motions to survive. They're hanging their hat on recovery, trying to hang on until rescue. How long can they survive without liberation? How long before they simply give up?

Wyatt lifted his cup of iced tea, smiling at the lady who offered a refill.

The world's not coming back anytime soon, decided Wyatt. Those little signs are false, creating a veneer that's hiding the rot underneath. The gunman today scratched the surface, exposing everyone to a little bit of the truth. I sure hope all these nice people can handle it when reality hits them between the eyes.

Charlie's family dug into the steak dinners. Rose instantly suspected the meal had been stolen, but didn't ask any questions. Already-cooked steak, uncovered dishes of green beans and corn, combined with the pistol sticking out of her husband's belt made it clear the banquet was of dubious origin. She was so tired, so worried about the kids, she didn't even care.

She settled on rationing the groceries, placing limited portions on everyone's plate. Charlie took a break from the beer he was enjoying, grunting disapproval when Rose sat his share on the table. He threw a questioning look at his wife, "What's up with this? Wasn't there enough in that box for everyone?"

Rose responded with a short tone. "We've got to make this last a few days, Charlie."

He waved off her concern. "There's plenty where that came from, Rose. I figured out all those boats over at the marina are full of food. There's got to be barrels of gas for the generator, too. I only brought back what I could carry this first trip."

Rose's hands went to her hips, her voice dripping with sarcasm, "Charlie, I'm *sure* you found this meat already cooked. Or did you decide to grill it on the way back? You took this food from someone. Don't lie to me."

Charlie shrugged his shoulders, "I got lucky and ran into a picnic. They were happy to share since they had so much."

Rose shrugged dejectedly and shot him a look of "whatever," moving to break up an argument between the kids. She was so hungry she really didn't care where he had gotten the food, promising to take it up with him later. Charlie ate his share and finished off another can of brew. His mind was smug with relief as he gazed toward the marina, plans for the next visit forming in his head.

After one and all had eaten their fill, the ladies divided the leftovers while the men gathered at one end of the pool. Hank had settled down and was trying to sound reasonable, "I want to start off by apologizing. I should not have accosted that guy, no matter what I felt at the time. Someone could've gotten hurt, and that's the last thing I want." Looking around the group, he was relieved to see his apology was generally accepted.

Wyatt, in a way, was relieved the episode had turned out as it had. Hank had always been a little bit of a hothead. Wyatt believed fast tempers could be extremely dangerous, now more than ever. Calling 911 wasn't an option, and justice wasn't real anymore - for good guys or bad. *Maybe this will cool his jets a little*, he thought.

Wyatt wasn't sure why, but several of the men looked at him as if he were the leader of the group. The gathering became quiet, the men mulling around and glancing his way as if they were waiting on Wyatt to start the meeting.

Reluctantly, Wyatt said, "I think we need to keep an eye out for a few days. I don't know what else to do. Everyone is pretty busy keeping up with battery charging, fuel transfer, and searching the boats. If we organize some sort of neighborhood watch, it's going to draw down on our manpower."

Several of the men voiced their agreement. A few, however, did not. One of them was David, and he spoke up, "I'm willing to pull extra hours to keep an eye on things. I think it's obvious we're going to have visitors, and I, for one, believe we should be ready to deal with them."

Another man stepped forward. "What are we going to do? Shoot people? I think there is a higher moral question here – does everything in the marina really belong to us? Is it really ours to defend? What if the looters are women or children? Do we hold a trial? I have a lot of issues with all of this."

Wyatt was quick to respond, "I agree. I've already run through all of this in my head, and it's a difficult situation at best. Are we really going to be in an 'every man for himself' environment? I can't answer that right now, and I don't think anyone else can either."

David chimed in, "Let me ask everyone this – if we were all at home right now, wouldn't we want our neighbors at the marina to protect our property for us? If any of the absent boaters arrived here tomorrow, we can look them in the eye and say, 'We only took what we needed.' If we let random looters start raiding the marina, they may damage the boats and could take a lot more than food."

David's comment caused everyone to pause. No one had really looked at things from that perspective as the focus had been on surviving day to day. Almost a minute went by before David continued. "If I may, how about we at least agree to meet in the morning, take an inventory of what weapons we have and begin to work on some sort of plan in case more strangers start showing up and causing trouble?"

Procrastinating seemed to agree with everyone as most of the men wanted time to think, perhaps talk it over with their spouses and families. Hank suggested meeting at the head of pier two at 8 a.m., and all agreed. The summit broke up, and everyone meandered back to their boats, carting the leftovers and dirty dishes.

~ ~

As Wyatt's family made the way back to Boxer, father and son dawdled, staying back a piece from the girls. David sensed his father's discomfort, but misread the reason. "Dad, I'm sorry, but I had to speak up for what I felt was important back there."

Wyatt stopped walking, uncertain where his son was going. It took a moment for David's concern to sink in. Wyatt had to smile, "Son, I raised you to have respect for other people, but also to voice your own opinion. You didn't show any disrespect to me at all. I'm proud of the way you handle yourself. The army's done well with you."

David stared down at his feet. "I just…I don't know. It seems funny to disagree with you."

Wyatt reached up and took him by the shoulder. "David, what you did back there was leadership. You're a man now, and again, I'm proud of you. Don't worry about it. We've got so much on our plate right now. Always do what you feel is right. You can't let the fear of being wrong now and then cause you to freeze up."

Father and son embraced, and then picked up the pace to catch up with the girls. It dawned on Wyatt that he was being hypercritical of himself. Here he'd just given David a big, long speech that he hadn't been able to live up to.

Wyatt reflected back on his actions when the business was failing. Deep down inside, he couldn't identify any one decision or action that had instigated the decline. There wasn't any single event where he made a bad call. Yet, it had all come crashing down around him. There had to be a reason, some catalyst or trait that prompted it all to happen.

Just because I can't make a good decision, doesn't mean David can't, thought Wyatt. *This wouldn't be the first time a father had told his son to be better than he is.*

After everything had been stowed away on Boxer, Morgan came out to the deck and sat next to Wyatt. She made small talk for a few minutes and then asked, "Everything okay with you and David?"

Wyatt's head snapped up and he looked at his wife, amazed at the woman's perception. Did she really have eyes in the back of her head? "He's just trying to get comfortable in this new pair of shoes he's wearing. The shoes are called 'manhood,' and they can be a tight fit now and then."

Morgan smiled at her husband's use of an analogy. It was one of her favorite things about him. She patted her Wyatt on the knee, "Do you male types ever get comfortable in them? It seems like a constant struggle, even for those of you who have been wearing them for years."

Wyatt smiled and glanced skyward, "No, they never seem to fit right. Sometimes tight, and sometimes loose. He's a good kid, Morgan – you did one heck of a job with him."

"*We* did a good job with him, my husband. We both deserve credit. I see so much of his father in him. The older he gets, the more he reminds me of the young man I fell in love with so many years ago."

Wyatt put his arm around his wife and drew her close. He couldn't help himself and smirked, "Which young man was that?"

Morgan playfully slapped at him and kissed his cheek. "You know very well who I was talking about."

Wyatt kissed her forehead and smiled. She let him settle for a moment and then said, "It was Jimmy Thompson...you remember him, the captain of the football team." They both started laughing so hard, Sage stuck her head out of the cabin door to ask if everything was okay. She realized her parents were doing that crazy lovebird thing again, and that made her smile. She made a waving gesture as if to say, "Never mind," and ducked out of sight.

~  ~

The task of getting the kids to bed was much easier since their tummies were full. Charlie and Rose had tucked blankets, said prayers, told stories, and answered questions for a few minutes before wishing sweet dreams and blowing out candles. One bed had required a detailed checking for monsters suspected to be lurking underneath. None were discovered.

Charlie made his way to the back stoop, seemingly mesmerized by the dark skyline. His thoughts turned to the harder questions about life, wondering if the world would ever return to the way it had been. The screech of the screen door opening prompted him to turn, even though he knew it was Rose. She sat beside him without comment, pretending to be interested in the stars. She had to admit, without all of the city lights, their twinkle was much more intense.

She sighed, "Charlie, we need to talk about that food you brought home."

Her husband looked at the grass that hadn't been mowed in almost two weeks. He wanted to change the subject, but decided the effort was useless. "I told you the truth. I smelled someone cooking on a grill. The smell was coming from the marina. I went over and asked if they would give me some food. It took a little convincing, but they filled the box, and I brought it back."

Her tone was sharper than she intended, "It's the *little convincing* part I'm worried about."

Charlie exhaled deeply and proceeded to tell his wife the entire story. The only part he left out was asking for the beer. Rose listened quietly. After he had finished, her voice became softer. "Thank you for telling me the truth. I understand why you did what you did. I have a question for you though. Something I want another truthful answer to. What would happen to me and the kids if one of those men had shot you dead?"

He started to respond, but she cut him off, "Just think about that for a while, Charlie. You don't need to answer me right now." She stood, reaching for the door, but paused. She bent over and kissed him on the head, "I love you, and the kids love you, too. You're a good man who's been through some tough times lately. We're all better off together. Just keep that in mind, Charlie. I'd rather be hungry and together than fat and alone."

~  ~

Rod was sitting on the front porch in a lawn chair, his position partially concealed by a pillar and a tall bush. His sister's house was way too muggy to stay indoors, so he spent as much time as possible out here where the air wasn't so close. He preferred the front porch so he could keep a watchful eye on the street and the neighbors.

He'd been locked up for twenty days awaiting an arraignment for armed robbery and assault with intent. He owed some serious people a significant sum of money, and they had grown weary of waiting to be paid. The interest was mounting, and the collection efforts grew more intense every day. Rod had progressed from worried to downright panicky, eventually ending up at desperate. After a rather heated confrontation, where Rod's head had been smashed into a brick wall, the message was clear. Come up with some cash, or the misery would escalate.

His normal source of income, stealing bags and unsupervised purses from the 5th Street Beach, didn't pay all that well. Jacking the occasional car stereo was risky, barely providing cigarette money. Still, every now and then, he got lucky, or so he had thought.

Rod was making his way back to his room after a fruitless evening searching for inebriated tourists to pickpocket. He hadn't had any luck finding a victim who was beyond noticing the removal of a wallet. The lack of success was frustrating, but not all that rare. It had always been spotty work, but a guy had to do whatever he could to get by.

He stumbled upon the Porsche convertible, sitting in a remote overflow parking area. The top was down, making the expensive sports car an irresistible draw. As he approached from the shadows, he noticed an empty bottle of rum perched on the hood. Casually strolling alongside the sleek machine, he glanced inside and almost freaked.

Slumped over the center console was a tiny blond-headed woman, apparently sleeping off an eventful Saturday night. Rod scanned the vicinity, nervously checking for potential witnesses. There wasn't another soul in sight, which was to be expected, given the early hour and isolated location. In the seat beside the woman was an expensive-looking handbag. Rod moved to the passenger side, reaching in to snatch the potential bonanza.

That's when he made a big mistake. While bending over to grasp the purse, his eye caught the glimmer of an even bigger prize. The streetlight above illuminated the diamonds surrounding the gold-tone face of a Rolex wristwatch. Like a packrat drawn to a shiny object, Rod's attention fixated on the twinkling jewels, his hand immediately releasing the purse strap and grasping the expensive timepiece.

Normally, Rod would have absconded with both items, but the woman moaned and shifted positions. Seeing no sense in pressing his luck, Rod trotted off into the darkness, thrilled with the rewards of a hard day's toil.

Rod's excitement over his haul kept him from sleeping. Waiting for the pawnshops to open on Monday morning was out of the question. By lunchtime

Sunday, he'd found Mohawk Billy's caddy parked outside of Lefty's Pool Hall. Rod didn't frequent Lefty's often. The clientele typically consisted of violent, more sophisticated criminals - men who didn't like to associate with petty, beach bum riffraff.

Still, Rod knew Billy would extend credit as long as sufficient collateral was offered. After what amounted to a 20-minute session of sweaty palms, veiled threats, and one-sided negotiations, Rod paraded out of the pool hall with five crisp Franklins. He also carried a commitment to repay eight of the $100 bills by midnight the next day.

That Sunday afternoon was one of Rod's most glorious days. Ten dime bags, a new tattoo, and one rusty .38 special revolver later, he found himself broke, but happy.

The next day, Rod managed to roll out of bed and stumble to the closest pawnbroker before they closed. He thought his heart would fail when the bearded man behind the counter shoved the watch back and said, "It ain't worth nothing. It's a fake."

A hastily obtained second opinion didn't change the appraisal.

Two days later, a couple of big dudes claiming to be Billy's cousins found Rod. Despite assurances of making good on the loan, the large gentlemen didn't accept his sincerity. Rod would carry the scars from that beating for the rest of his life, which wasn't a long-term prospect at that moment.

The Stop N' Fill on the corner had been busy all day. Rod followed the manager out of the store after the night supervisor clocked in. He knew the guy would take the day's proceeds to the night deposit box at Second National Bank. He would have gotten away with the heist were it not for the Galveston County Sheriff's patrol car cruising the area. A man sprinting away from a bank attracts attention. Things really get interesting when the runner is carrying a gun and a bank deposit bag. The police tend to notice such things.

Still, the goonies couldn't collect the debt while he was in the slammer.

When the power failed, the guards kept the prisoners in the courtyard of the Galveston county jail for the remainder of the afternoon. After the third day without electricity, the deputies started calling in sick. On the fifth day, only one guard showed up.

The inmates hadn't been fed or allowed any time in the yard, which led to a rapidly deteriorating situation. That lone officer must have feared a full-blown riot, or perhaps he was a softhearted individual. Right before abandoning the jailhouse, he hit the battery-powered emergency switch that unlocked the cell doors.

It took the prisoners about two minutes to break through the outer metal doors of the jail. When the final barrier to freedom fell, all 119 inmates strolled back into society. Rod was one of them, and after milling around the island for a while, he began the 20-mile trek to his sister's house. He avoided the highways and busy thoroughfares, expecting the police to be searching for the escapees. He arrived early the next morning at his sis' place, only to discover she was on vacation. That was just fine with Rod. Sis had disowned him months before, a domestic dispute initiated after his third arrest for drug possession. Her being out of town would save him the trouble of begging to stay for a few nights until he could come up with another plan.

Rod was enthralled with his sister's neighborhood. An entrepreneur of sorts, he was quick to recognize opportunity, and this subdivision was a target-rich environment. He was in awe as he crept around, peeping in people's windows. All of these well-to-do jerks had big screen TVs and tools in the garage. He could make quite a haul out of here. Then it dawned on him that there wasn't anywhere to sell the goods. He didn't have a car, and even he was smart enough not to try and pawn something so close to where it had been stolen. No, he needed to think through a plan.

In the meantime, his sister had plenty of food and a nicely stocked liquor shelf. The bathroom cabinet contained a ready supply of prescription painkillers as well. He didn't see any cops patrolling the local streets, so he would just stay put until another prospect presented itself.

When Rod spied Charlie carrying a cardboard box with a pistol sticking out of the back of his pants, his interest was naturally sparked. He didn't know Charlie, per se, only having observed the guy canvassing the neighborhood door-to-door a few days ago. Rod had naturally assumed Charlie was casing the street - seeing who was home and who wasn't.

At first, Rod's criminal mind was frustrated, the thought of having competition for the neighborhood's plunder being unacceptable. He'd considered trying to scare the man off, but his nemeses carried a pistol, and Rod didn't. His sister hated guns and wouldn't allow one in the house. He'd double-checked anyway. After thinking about it for a little bit, he decided a partnership might in order. He was hanging out on the front porch watching for either the cops or Charlie, hoping the latter would show first.

~ ~

Charlie replayed Rose's little lecture, writing it off as too much drama and emotion, not enough common sense. He finished the fourth and last beer, but wasn't overly concerned. Knowing there was plenty more just a few hundred yards away put him at ease. *Hell*, he thought, *all of those guys with boats were lushes anyway. I'll bet there are all kinds of goodies over there.*

The alcohol running through his system was affecting his judgment. His bravery and sensation of invincibility was elevated while his fear of Rose's wrath was minimized. He would show Rose it wasn't any big deal. He'd bring back a big load of food...and drink.

Charlie's garage was hot and sticky, so he raised the overhead door to catch the sea breeze. He was a little concerned the noise might wake Rose, but she had crashed over an hour ago and was probably deep in dreamland after consuming a big meal. Using a flashlight, Charlie quietly dug out an old camping backpack and located his crowbar. At the last minute, a hammer and pistol were added to the arsenal - just in case.

The hour was late, and he figured all of the boaters would be asleep. He would just sneak over, pry open a few boats and fill the pack with food. *I wonder where boaters keep their booze*, he mused.

Rod saw Charlie's garage door open, and figured the guy was up to something. The sweeping beam of a flashlight soon confirmed his suspicions. Rod had conducted surveillance on Charlie's place for hours and was about to call off his stakeout. When he noticed Charlie hoisting a bulky bag down the street, he moved to the stoop for a better vantage. Charlie was right in front of Rod's hiding spot when the unseen man cleared his throat.

Charlie jumped at the racket and fumbled for his flashlight. Before he could even get it out of his back pocket, a voice called out from the nearby porch. "Hey man, you going hunting for some treats?"

Charlie's anxious tone proved him to be a novice and clearly unpracticed liar. "Who is that? Do I know you? I'm just going for a walk to get some fresh air."

The shadow said, "No problem, man. I'm not a cop. I know you're heading back over to that boat place. I thought you might want some help."

The man's approach confused Charlie's already buzzing head. The voice seemed nice enough and having someone along would probably help. Two guys would be safer than one. One guy could keep a lookout while the other searched a boat. He decided to test the stranger, "I'm only going to get the kids some food. What are you looking for?"

Rod stepped down from the porch, edging closer to Charlie, "I'm just bored. I don't need food right now, but I might soon. Really man, I'm just looking for something exciting to do. No TV sucks, dude."

Charlie could relate to that. He'd been bored out of his skull since losing his job and becoming Mr. Mom. This guy didn't seem so bad, and after all, he was a neighbor. Why not? Charlie decided he would clarify with the newcomer who was leading the expedition. "Sure, you can tag along, but let me warn you – this is my little treasure trove, and what I say goes. Okay?"

Rod smiled in the dark, "Sure, man – whatever you say."

The two men headed toward the marina in almost complete darkness. The moon was a small, yellow sliver, and a haze dampened the field of stars. They could barely make out the masts of the sailboats in the distance. Reaching the edge of the parking lot, they both squatted down and listened. The only noise coming from the piers was the constant "...Ting, ting, ting..." of rigging ropes, lightly thumping against the masts in the breeze. They couldn't hear any voices or music or see a single light.

Charlie looked at Rod triumphantly, "I *figured* everyone would be asleep by now. Let's move over to the far side - the bigger boats are over there."

"Sure nuff, man."

The two men worked their way slowly across the lot, moving between parked cars and trash bins until they were at the head of pier three. Charlie motioned, holding his hands far apart as if to say, "These are some big boats." Rod nodded, sneaking down the ramp onto the pier, Charlie right behind him.

Hank Weathers had just switched off his reading light a few minutes before. He was lying on the master berth, visualizing the meeting scheduled for the following morning. He didn't feel any strong regrets about the encounter with the stranger today. *These are good people*, he thought, *but they have no idea how bad things can get.* He wanted to get his point across in the morning. It was important that the people in the marina organize to protect themselves. They had been lucky so far, but it wouldn't last.

Hank had served in Bosnia as part of the United Nations force manned partially by US troops. He had seen firsthand the results of desperation and brutality. For the most part, the people of Bosnia weren't hungry. They were motivated by prejudice and religious hatred. To Hank's way of thinking, it really didn't matter what motivated extreme behavior.

In Eastern Europe, the people had been whipped into a frenzy by a perceived threat to their way of life. That conflict didn't involve desperate hunger. The people there felt threatened by someone who believed just a little differently than the mainstream philosophy. Yet, the temporary madness here mimicked the Bosnian furor. Here, now, starvation would be the catalyst.

Hank shuddered at the memory of the mass graves and the thousands of orphans he had seen in Europe. He had spent six months in that living hell, every day thinking he had seen the worst mankind had to offer. The worst was often outdone days later by an even greater discovery of barbarian acts or atrocious behavior.

Why did his neighbors think everyone was going to light a bonfire and sit around holding hands while they sang "Kumbaya"? He needed to make them understand that when things got really bad, a door opened inside of man. Opening that door liberated a beast – a demon of dark behavior that would release ultimate violence on its own kind.

Hank had witnessed this monster. He'd seen it firsthand, in person – up close and personal. He had to figure out how to convince his neighbors of its existence before it was too late. *How do you make them understand that the boogieman truly exists?* he wondered.

Rod approached the second craft on the pier. He shot Charlie an inquiring expression of "Why not start here?" and stepped aboard. He hopped over the transom gate and tried the large, sliding glass door leading to the salon. It was locked. Charlie set his backpack on the deck, digging around until he pulled out the crowbar. He handed Rod the long, steel tool, expecting his partner to pry open the door. Rod glared at the implement, hefted it in his hand, and swung it hard at the glass.

Hank heard an unusual "thump," or at least he thought he did. He was in that in-between state, partially asleep, but still vaguely aware. He thought for a moment that perhaps he'd been dreaming. Despite the mental fog, his senses focused quickly, inventorying the assorted noises from the marina. More from his military training than consciousness, his hand reached into the bedside drawer, feeling for the 9mm Glock stored there.

Rod's first strike only created a spider web in the thick glass. So stunned by Rod's overt, imprudent act, Charlie couldn't will himself to speak. Before he could stop the idiot, Rod swung the crowbar a second time. The impact shattered the glass inward, the crashing shards creating more of a racket than the first blow. Charlie finally found words, spitting them at Rod in an angry whisper. "What are you doing? Are you trying to announce to everyone in the marina that we're here?"

Rod shrugged his shoulders and handed Charlie the pry bar. His whispered sneer seemed ironic to Charlie, "There can't be that many people here. And what are they going to do anyway? Call the cops?"

Hank was wide awake now, alert, and sure of trouble after the second strike echoed across the marina. The sound of shattering glass was clear, the volume disqualifying the possibility of a dropped bottle or other such clumsy act. He rolled off the berth, fumbling for his shorts. He racked the slide on the pistol and chambered a round.

Hank's racing heart caused his fingers to tingle as the cocktail of blood and adrenaline surged through his veins. He slipped on his deck shoes and moved to the door with purpose, all the while his senses were probing the night – intently seeking input about what was going on.

Charlie realized he was holding the crowbar with a dumbfounded look on his face. The beam of Rod's flashlight moving around inside the cabin caught his eye, bringing him back to this grim reality. He fought the urge to turn and run. There was no way the people on the boats didn't hear that noise. He looked around anxiously, half expecting to see lights switching on inside of all the surrounding windows and to hear the voices of angry men. When there was only darkness and the murmur of leaves displaced by a light breeze, he calmed down for a moment. He was moving to the entrance of the salon, curious as to what his crazy partner was doing inside, when Hank's menacing tone made him jump. "Freeze! Don't move, or I *will* shoot you."

Charlie instinctively raised his hands, desperately seeking to convey a message of "Please, don't shoot," to the voice behind him. He fought the urge to turn around and face the threat. The overwhelming fear iced the very marrow in his spine.

The voice sounded again, "Put the pry bar down...very slowly." Charlie couldn't help himself. As he bent to place the tool on the deck, he pivoted his feet and stood facing Hank. In the dark, neither man had any clue they had met just a few hours before at the picnic. Hank's blood rush began to ease. He had his man, but wasn't sure what to do with him. Charlie simply stood in front of the salon door with his hands in the air, unsure of where this was going.

Charlie sensed movement behind him. Seconds later, Rod reached up and pulled the .38 caliber revolver from Charlie's belt. In one motion, Rod aimed the pistol around Charlie's body and began pulling the trigger as fast as his finger could respond to his brain's command.

Several things all seemed to happen at once. Hank was completely shocked by the gunshots, as the man he was watching had his arms up in the air. It never occurred to him that there was more than one intruder on the boat. His mind froze for just a moment as his eyes adjusted to the bright, muzzle flashes exploding not 15 feet away.

After a few hundredths of a second, he managed to send the command to his finger to pull the trigger. The Glock pistol in Hank's grip held 17 rounds of 9mm ammunition, but not for long. Hank's brain was sending repeated impulses: PULL THAT TRIGGER and KEEP PULLING.

Rod's neurons were imitating Hank's. Rod didn't intend to use Charlie's body as a shield. As he attempted to move from behind and get a clear shot at Hank, his feet got tangled up, and he began a downward descent. He reached out and grabbed for something to balance himself, pulling Charlie down with him.

Hank saw both men collapse on the deck and was unsure if he had shot them both or if they were diving for cover. He took two quick steps forward and started firing into the transom. Both Rod and Charlie were struck multiple times. Even if they hadn't been entangled, there was no avenue of escape. Hank fired 17 shots into the two men, but only five found human flesh. Five was enough, and when the empty pistol finally locked open at battery, both burglars were already dead.

Hank watched the two men lying on the deck for over a minute, waiting for any sign of movement. He felt very weak and realized he hadn't taken a breath for a long time. He opened his mouth to inhale and a sudden, sharp pain racked his chest. His legs became weak, and he desperately needed to sit down.

The deck and surrounding boats began swimming around wildly, swirling in his vision as he tried to sit. Something warm against his skin compelled him to touch his sternum. When he pulled his hand away, it was covered with a warm, wet liquid. *What is this?*

Hank tried to hold his blood-drenched hand up closer to his face, curious about what was causing the sensation. His last sight was the wooden planks of the pier rushing toward his face, and then total blackness.

David sprang out of bed first, followed quickly by Wyatt, still rubbing the sleep from his eyes. "Were those gunshots?" both men asked at the same time. David grabbed the AR15 and inserted a magazine, then handed his father the shotgun.

Morgan and Sage were up by then, the entire family curious what was going on. David held his finger up to his lips and made a "Shhhhhhhh" sound. Sage instinctively switched on one of the overhead lights, and David snapped at her, "No light!" His sister quickly shut it off.

While motioning his family to stay back, David peeked out between the curtains. The darkness prohibited him from seeing much of anything, but one thing was obvious – there wasn't anyone close to Boxer, and the back deck was clear.

Using hand signs, David motioned to his family that he was going to the back deck. He made it clear he didn't want company. Wyatt was upset, but couldn't stop his son in time. As Wyatt watched his oldest child reach for the door, a terrible angst flashed though his mind. "David has his whole life ahead of him. Mine is almost over. I should go first."

Wyatt lurched, grabbing his son by the shoulder and stopping him. David was stunned by the act, throwing his father a questioning look. Wyatt pointed at his chest and made it clear, "Me, first."

As Wyatt ventured out onto Boxer's back deck, he felt silly scanning around with the shotgun pointing wherever he looked. His feelings of inadequacy were highlighted by the realization he hadn't chambered a round. Wyatt grunted at his mistake. In its current state, it wouldn't have mattered if a herd of stampeding zombies was boarding the boat - he couldn't have fired the weapon. He was relieved at hearing the deck creak, a signal that David was right behind him. After checking all around Boxer and discovering no threat, Wyatt whispered back to Morgan that it was clear.

There wasn't any way to tell where the gunshots had come from. For a few minutes, Wyatt and David began to question whether they had actually heard anything at all. David mounted Boxer's bridge to scour the marina. He reported seeing lights coming on in several boats. Evidently, others had heard the same sounds. It wasn't long before flashlight beams were sweeping all around the slips.

Rose awoke with a start, automatically reaching for the other side of the bed. The sheets were cool and empty, no Charlie. She stretched and rubbed her eyes, calmly believing him to be asleep on the couch. She had to use the ladies' room anyway, deciding she would weather his ire at being rousted and coax him back to bed. It was the lesser of two evils, as he would complain all day tomorrow about his sore back if she allowed him to spend the night on the sofa.

After relieving herself, she padded into the living room to find an empty couch. Still not overly concerned, she began to search the house for her husband. The kids were fine, sleeping deeply in the odd positions that little ones always seem to work themselves into. She picked up a stuffed bear from the floor, tucking it back under the small arm that would be seeking it later.

A chill that originated on top of her head traveled down her back, resolving in her toes. Rose had discovered the open garage door. *That* was very unusual and she wondered where Charlie would have gone. Her mind, still fighting to clear the cobwebs, took a few moments to recall the stolen food and the pistol. *No, Charlie*, she thought, *I hope you didn't decide to do it again.*

~  ~

The rest of the night, most of the boaters were denied sleep. The residents of Marinaville checked their respective piers and didn't identify anything unusual or threatening. It was the following morning before someone noticed Hank's body, lying in a pool of dark red. Moments after the first grim discovery, the two dead prowlers were discovered.

Everyone seemed to need to congregate at the scene of the crime. Despite the men warning several of the women not to look, they all did, and many turned away in pale shock. There was a natural desire to try and figure out what had happened, but no one was a homicide detective. Amateur sleuths abounded, spouting suggestions born of wisdom garnered from reruns of NCIS and Monk.

It was impossible for anyone to know for sure exactly what happened. Clearly, the two dead strangers were breaking into a boat. The pry bar, broken glass, and physical position of the bodies made that clear. But how had Hank managed to get shot? Who had surprised whom?

After all the rampant speculation engendered by the throng of would-be crime scene investigators, the crowd slowly started breaking up and going about the daily routine. It was David who recognized one of the dead thieves from the pool party. He reached underneath the body and removed a wallet and located a Lone Star state driver's license, complete with name and address.

There was another discussion about what to do with the bodies. The GPS in Wyatt's car verified that one of the strangers lived close by. It was decided that several of the men would wrap the two burglars in an old sail and return them to the address. They would bury Hank at sea, the same way as the dead girl. As they were gathering bags of landscaping stones, Wyatt couldn't help but look around and say, "I sure hope we don't run out of rocks before this is all over."

Rose was up early, busy getting the kids ready for the day. She jumped slightly at the knock, these days they rarely had visitors anymore. Instinctively, she sensed something was wrong and was somewhat relieved when she peered through the peephole and didn't see a policeman. She had been expecting either her husband or a deputy there to inform her of Charlie's arrest.

The clean-cut young man she could see through the warped view of the peephole was a stranger. Her brief hesitation was chased by thoughts of her missing husband, so she answered the door.

David had been chosen to knock because he was the youngest and probably the least threatening of the pallbearers. When Rose opened the door, he cleared his throat. "Ma'am, does a Charlie Beckenworth reside here?"

Rose paused, wondering how to respond to the question. As her eyes darted right and left, David understood her reluctance to respond. "Ma'am, there's been an acci...ummmm...there's a problem."

It clicked with Rose immediately. David's tone of voice and body language said everything. Rose's gaze became intense, her head shaking as she uttered a chest deep "Nooooooo."

Pushing past David and tearing into the front yard, she didn't seem to notice any of the men standing there. The distraught woman saw the two wrapped bodies lying in the grass and rushed to kneel beside the closest one.

Wyatt edged next to Rose, not sure if he should let her unwrap the sail or stop her. In the end, it didn't matter. Rose took only a moment to pull apart enough of the fabric to see it was her husband inside. She looked skyward and screamed, "Charlie! Oh my God, Charlie! No, no, no!" Rose started to fall over, and Wyatt caught her. She was wailing and trying to breathe at the same time. The situation was made worse when the kids, looking for their mother, streamed out the front door, immediately confronted with the ashen face of their father wrapped in the pale, white sailcloth.

The sight of four unfamiliar men carrying what was obviously two dead bodies through the middle of the subdivision drew the attention of several neighbors. Mrs. Beckenworth's cries, now almost constant, attracted even more residents. David looked up to see a growing assembly at the edge of the front yard with even more folks drifting down the street, naturally curious about the peculiar affair.

David tried to get his father's attention, but Wyatt was busy supporting the distraught widow so that she would not crumble to the ground. David was struck by how unhealthy and unkempt everyone from the neighborhood looked. The crowd was marked by sunken faces framed with oily, stringy hair. David noticed the smell of body odor wafting from the people closest to him. *They don't have water*, he thought.

Two of the local women threw David a sour look as they passed by, intent on helping Rose inside. Another lady moved to distract the children.

One man stepped forward from the crowd and said, "My name's Roger Wilson. I'm an attorney. What happened?"

Wyatt, distracted by the suffering woman, didn't even look up before speaking. "These two tried to break into a boat at the marina last night. Hank must have heard them and went to investigate. We found all three men dead this morning." Wyatt paused and pointed at Charlie's body. "We had a run in with this gentleman yesterday. He showed up at the marina, demanding food and pulled a pistol on us. We gave him some food, but it must have not been enough. The other guy, I've never seen before. We buried our dead neighbor this morning."

A murmur rumbled through the crowd as two of the men bent down and unwrapped Rod's body. Several people exchanged glances and then shook their heads indicating they didn't recognize the man either.

Mr. Wilson digested Wyatt's story and then spoke in a harsh, pointed voice. "So Charlie was trying to break into a boat and get food? And you guys shot him for trying to feed his family? Was it the owner of the boat that shot these men?"

Wyatt didn't like the man's tone, but responded anyway. "No, it was a neighbor who discovered them. He's dead, too. We really don't know what happened. The boat they were trying to break into was unoccupied."

Several of the men eyed each other, hushed comments floating through the crowd. David reached out to take his father's arm, sensing the disapproval that was building around them. Before he could convey his concern to Wyatt, the lawyer spoke again. "So you shot two men who were trying to scavenge food for their families? I mean, you said the boat was empty."

Unhappy expressions and outright disdain surged through the surrounding throng of neighbors. A few comments of "That ain't right," and "They didn't deserve to die for that," circulated among the bystanders. The mood turned even uglier when Rose's renewed crying sounded from inside the house.

Another man stepped forward and poked Wyatt in the chest with his index finger. "So you just shoot anyone who wanders into the marina? Who appointed you the sheriff?" Several voices expressed agreement with the agitated fellow.

Wyatt understood what was happening and tried to defend himself. "Look pal, none of us shot anybody. We found this entire mess this morning and only want to return the bodies, so back off."

Two younger men pushed their way to the front of the crowd. One of them inquired, "So there's food over there on those boats? Is that what they were after? How much food is over there?"

David had seen enough. He stepped forward and whispered to his father, "We are out of here – right now." Wyatt agreed and motioned for the other marina residents to follow.

They started moving away when someone yelled out, "He never answered the question! I want to know how much food they have over there. There must be a lot if they are shooting people to protect it."

The four men from the marina walked quickly down the street, leaving the crowd behind them. As soon as they were clear, one of the boaters spoke up. "You know we probably just delivered a death sentence to that woman and those kids. Yesterday at the pool, that guy said he was after food for his young ones. It took some guts to come back and try for more – he must have been really desperate. How is his wife going to feed those children now?"

David gave the man a questioning look, "What are we supposed to do? I mean, from my perspective we tried to help that guy out yesterday and look what happened – Hank is dead. We can't feed everyone."

The man started to counter David when Wyatt changed the subject. "We have a whole bunch of people who now realize we have food, and they don't. I think we have a bigger problem than the widow and her children."

After Wyatt's assessment, everyone became sullen at the thought. No one said a word until they were back on the marina's grounds. The four men milled around in a group, unsure of what to do next.

David spoke up. "I think we better get everyone assembled and discuss defending ourselves. Those folks over there will sit and stew over all this for a while. I don't think it will be long before a mob ventures this way. Even if only one or two muster up enough guts to sneak in, if they return home with food, all of the others will know. That entire neighborhood will descend on us like locusts and pick the marina clean."

The men all agreed to a meeting. The powwow would be held at the head of pier four as soon as possible. As they were breaking up to spread the word of the gathering, thunder sounded in the distance.

Wyatt turned toward the western sky, the dark, rolling clouds of a front tumbling toward the marina. *That rain will be a good thing*, he thought.

A few hours later, after huddling under an overhang by the pool bar to keep dry in the storm, the men of Southland Marina broke off their discussion, having agreed on a plan. The primary issue now facing the group involved workload. While everyone agreed that a sentry was necessary, it was also obvious that the community was barely maintaining a status quo completing the daily activities required for living. Diverting two or three workers to guard the marina would overtax the effort.

The solution was to arm a single sentry throughout the night. A shift schedule was established so that the men of the marina would all lose sleep evenly. If the sentry spotted any trouble, he would activate an air horn, and the cavalry would come running. Just like Paul Revere, the sentry would give warning that Redcoat-looters were approaching.

There was a logistical problem with the plan. The marina's piers were constructed in an "L" shape. At the moment, there weren't any vessels in the right place to observe the entire harbor. The strategists decided to tow a larger, unattended sailboat to an empty slip on pier nine. The 20-foot high crow's nest would provide a great vantage point for the sentry.

The other significant outcome of the meeting was an inventory of weapons. It came as no surprise to David that Boxer was far and above the best-armed vessel in the marina. One of the boaters on pier ten was an avid hunter. Luck would have it that two of his long-range deer rifles were nestled in the trunk of his car. While there were only 20 rounds of ammunition for the sporting guns, they were quality weapons with significant stopping power and excellent range.

Other than his father's two long guns and the two deer rifles, there was an assortment of pistols, very little ammunition, and not a lot of combat or military experience among the group.

Wyatt and Morgan sat on Boxer's bridge, enjoying an inspiring Texas sunset. They couldn't be sure if the brilliant red and orange hues were due to the last remnants of the fire in Houston or were the result of the front that had passed through that afternoon. One way or the other, they were determined to relax and enjoy the peace and quiet. Wyatt sensed trouble was on the way, and after hearing of the day's adventures over dinner, Morgan had to agree.

"Morgan, I don't believe we're going to be able to stay here long. I think there's going to be a host of issues we haven't even considered. What's even worse, I don't think we can go home."

Morgan looked down at her feet and sighed. She looked at her husband, a hint of fear shining in her eyes. "I know...I've been thinking about it since that man came to the pool with a gun. If the government doesn't get control soon, things are going to get really insane. Where would we go?"

Wyatt stretched out his legs and leaned back. "The only thing I can come up with is to put out to sea. Not deep water mind you, just Galveston Bay. We know some pretty remote little coves where we could hide out for a while."

Morgan wasn't sure. "I don't know about that. Wouldn't we be sort of marooned? How would we know when to come back?"

Wyatt chuckled, more to relieve stress than from actual humor. "Before all of this happened, we would've looked forward to gunkholing for a long weekend. We would've been excited about the prospect of peace and quiet. Now, I'm kind of with you. If we leave, can we ever come back? What happens if the boat breaks – I can't just radio for help anymore."

There I go again, he thought. *I'm unable to make a decision – unable to lead.*

The couple sat in silence as the last sliver of sun vanished. There was a light breeze blowing from the south, and the evening seemed perfect. As the warm glow of dusk settled into night, they held hands and thought about the future - many of the considerations only tolerable because they had each other.

Chapter 7

March 1, 2017
Kemah Bay, Texas

While Morgan and Wyatt shared the sunset, another meeting was taking place in Rose's side yard. After the boaters had dropped the two bodies at her house, the throng of neighbors mulled about for almost an hour.

If anyone had stepped back and evaluated the events of that afternoon, what transpired would have seemed out of place and surreal. Normally, when a resident suffered the loss of a family member, covered dishes of food, delivered by a parade of neighbors, would have been commonplace. Offers of help and condolences would have accompanied the visitors.

Rose received only two offers of assistance. The first was to bury her husband. The other gesture of kindness was from a widow who lived down the street and offered to take care of the children – if Rose had something for them to eat.

The debate over the disposition of the bodies had raged in the front yard for some time. All the while, tempers rose and fell as people got worked up and then blew off steam with harsh words and empty threats. As with any group of desperate people, an enemy was soon identified. An enemy was required because they needed someone to blame. The inhabitants of the marina became the focus of their shared frustration and anger.

It was finally determined to bury both bodies in Rose's yard, on the windowless side of her house. No one had any idea who Rod was or where he had come from. A few men, unsure of how else to help, had retrieved shovels and spades and began digging. The first gravesite had been in the backyard, close to the children's swing set. A fast-thinking woman informed the burial detail they were idiots for digging the graves where the kids would see them while playing. The fact that Rose would be reminded of her sudden lack of a husband every time she looked outside was harshly communicated as well.

The men apologized and moved to the side yard and began digging all over again. When the final spade full of dirt was tapped down, the small group of dirty, sweaty men rested, leaning on shovel handles and wiping their brows.

An older man, absentmindedly picking at a newly formed blister on his hand, commented. "You all know this probably isn't the last time we are going to do this."

"You're probably right," commented another, "but the next time it will be from hunger or sickness. At least the bodies will be lighter." The man's attempt at gallows humor was met by a few chuckles and opened the door to the subject that concerned them all.

He continued, "There is food down at that marina. I never thought old Charlie here was all that bright, but he figured it out. Those guys looked well fed and clean to me. I don't know about y'all, but by my way of thinking, that food down there belongs to us as much as anybody."

After the subject had been broached, the small group of gravediggers debated the situation while the sun set behind them. Everyone in the neighborhood was already out of food or running low. Fresh water was a problem, and only one man had any faith that order would be restored soon. His voice of reservation was quickly overridden by those who wanted to raid the marina and scavenge food.

The man with the blisters spoke again. "I don't think those boat people are going to let us just waltz in there and take what we want. They have a good thing going, and they know it. If we are going to do this, we had better be prepared to fight."

"I don't think they'll do squat as long as we leave their boats alone. If I were them, why would I give a rat's backside about an empty boat that belongs to someone else?"

The older gent responded, "Those empty boats are their grocery stores. At least that's how I would look at it if I were them. They are just as scared and worried as we are. Just like us, they have no idea when the stores will open again. No, boys, I have to believe they will try and stop us. We had better be willing to put up a fight if we are going to do this. I, for one, am hungry, and my wife is already having coughing fits every morning. I'm thinking it's every man for himself."

And so it was decided the group would pass the word to meet at the edge of the community in an hour. The more men they could recruit for the raiding party, the better. The concept of strength in numbers wasn't lost on anyone, and neither was the suggestion that they bring whatever guns were available.

~  ~

The men of the marina had planned to move the tall sailboat first thing in the morning. The vessel was equipped with a reasonably comfortable crow's nest, the height providing an excellent observation post for the night watch. Moving the tall vessel proved to be difficult, as the boat wouldn't start. Towing a large, powerless sailboat in the confined spaces of the piers would take some additional planning.

Everyone was nervous, speculating what the people from the neighboring community might do. The fact that one of their own had been killed the night before wasn't lost on any of the boaters. Since there wasn't a watchtower as of yet, several volunteers offered to patrol Southland throughout the night.

David and Wyatt decided to split their turn at the watch. That way, there would be a male aboard Boxer at all times. Wyatt was still keyed up, like everyone else, and decided to take the first watch along with Mike from pier five.

Mike was a middle-aged, middle sized, middle management, oil company employee. Since his divorce two years ago, he had lived on his modest cruiser and made the daily commute to Houston. He met Wyatt in the parking lot, carrying an old .32 caliber pistol his brother had given him. He had never fired the weapon and had only five shells. Those rounds had been in the magazine for years. He wasn't even sure the gun worked.

Mike and Wyatt were both alert and nervous as they guarded the marina. Wyatt felt silly at first, questioning the need of carrying the shotgun. Now that he was out patrolling the dark marina, he had to admit it felt comforting to have the weapon. The two sentinels slowly moved around the sidewalks and public areas, whispering now and then, but mostly listening to the sounds of the night.

The men gathering for the raiding party were all a little unsettled. Most of them had expected 15 or 20 men to join the dangerous excursion, but only 11 had arrived so far. After deciding to wait another five minutes before heading to the marina, several jokes and negative comments filled the air, most centered on how so-and-so's wife wouldn't let him out of the house for the party or the general lack of guts being demonstrated by those who didn't show.

While the men milled around, one fellow produced a flask and several shared a nip of the cheap whiskey. More humor followed when one gentleman commented the liquor helped take the edge off of the chill in the night air. Everyone was sweating, and while the sun had gone down, all present had to agree, it was still quite warm outside.

One man finally raised his shotgun to his shoulder and announced, "I've waited long enough. Screw the others, it's now or never." As he stomped off toward the marina, the rest of the men all looked at each other for agreement, shrugged their shoulders, and followed.

As the group trekked toward the marina, one man switched on a flashlight. This drew a harsh reaction from some of the others, "What are you trying to do? Warn all the boaters we're coming?"

Wyatt caught a glimpse of a short-lived beam of light. He nudged Mike, who had been scouring the marina's landscape in the other direction. "I think we have company on the way. I just saw a flashlight turn on over there."

Mike scanned where Wyatt indicated, but couldn't see anything. He whispered, "What do you think we should do?"

Wyatt kept his gaze in the general direction where he'd seen the light. He motioned Mike to follow, and they scurried behind a parked car. The moon was providing just enough illumination to outline the gang of looters as they rounded the corner of the marina's property. Wyatt's heart was racing in his chest, and he could hear a ringing in his ears. The back of his knees felt wet, and he noticed his hands were shaking. *Just go away*, he thought, *just go away, and leave us alone.*

There was little doubt in Wyatt's mind who the men were or what they were after. As the group approached, he heard a rustling of cloth and looked down to see Mike had drawn his pistol. Wyatt shook his head "No," but didn't think Mike noticed the signal. He was busy peeking over the trunk of their cover, inspecting the advancing raiders.

Wyatt waited until the group progressed to within 150 feet of their position and stood up. As he rose up from behind the car, he chambered a round in the shotgun. The noise was unmistakable - the last sound anyone sneaking onto a property with ill intent wants to hear. Everyone froze.

Wyatt flinched when his own voice projected at a much higher pitch than normal. "Good evening. Could I be of assistance to you gentlemen?"

A nervous voice answered, "We are...uh...we're on our way to get some food. Do you have a problem with that?"

Wyatt found his resolve, responding in a calmer tone. "Well, friend, that depends on where you plan on finding this food. If you're just passing through, I have no problem at all. If you're planning to shop on any of these boats, then we have an issue."

Wyatt's remark caused the men he was facing to begin whispering among themselves. Clearly, they hadn't anticipated meeting any resistance, or if they had mapped out a course of action, it wasn't something they seemed eager to implement. The longer their discussion went on, the more confident Wyatt felt.

Mike was standing right behind him, and that bothered Wyatt more at the moment than the approaching group of looters. Wyatt knew that their standing adjacent to each other was a poor tactical position, opening them up to more danger. He motioned for Mike to move away just a little, to put some space between them. His co-sentry did move, but not nearly far enough to be fully effective. Wyatt let it go, the man seemingly uncomfortable putting too much distance between them.

After what seemed like a full minute of conversation, another voice rang out from the crowd. "You don't own all these boats, buddy. We have just as much right to anything on them as you do. We won't bother any that have people onboard."

"How's that going to work? Wyatt asked. "Ding, dong. Avon calling? You don't have any way of knowing which boats are empty. People aren't going to answer their door when they look out and see a bunch of armed strangers standing around."

"We'll figure it out," was the terse response.

Wyatt had anticipated the tactic. "Now let me ask you something, partner. Let's say a big group of men strolled over to your neighborhood and started breaking in unoccupied homes. Wouldn't you and your friends have a problem with that?"

Again there was much whispering and discussion, but of a shorter duration than before. The same voice answered back, more pointed this time. "There's a difference between a man's home and a boat. Unless someone lives on his boat, it's a toy…not a residence. Like I said, we'll leave any occupied boat alone."

Wyatt decided to bluff his way through. "We don't look at it that way. These boats are owned by our friends and neighbors. We all look out for each other because any one of these owners might show up tomorrow. Didn't you see the fires burning in Houston? These boats may be the only shelter some of our friends have left."

That rebuttal caused even more hushed conversation. While the shadows of the night limited the view, Wyatt thought for sure one or two of the group walked away. *Good*, he thought, *divide and conquer*.

While the invaders were discussing his logic among themselves, Wyatt turned to Mike and whispered, "If they start to move forward, fire the first shot into the air. That will bring help and serve to warn them. If your pistol doesn't go off, I'll do it." Mike nodded nervously and moved a little closer to Wyatt, only to be shooed away…again.

The same voice rang out once more. "I don't think you're willing to kill another man over the slim chance someone *might* show up and *might* need their boat."

Wyatt thought the fellow had a good point there. He was trying to think up some macho, bravado-laced answer when the looter's voice continued, "Besides, if you don't let us gather up some food, you'll be killing people anyway. We've all got family that is hungry and starting to get sick. Little kids and old people, too. Someone's going to die. Do you want all that blood on your hands?"

Mike grunted, "Bull hockey."

The interloper's words got to Wyatt. He fully understood what the guy was saying, and his mind started drifting off, wondering how he suddenly was in this position. No one had elected him mayor of Marinaville. He didn't want the job. His momentary introspection was interrupted by the urgency in Mike's voice. "Something's happening. Somebody's moving over there."

Wyatt's head snapped up, and he could see Mike was correct. It looked like three or four of the looters were splitting off. *They're trying to get around us*, he thought. *What's the term? They're trying to flank us.* Wyatt turned to Mike and said, "Fire a shot in the air. This is getting out of hand, and we need help."

Even in the darkness, Wyatt could see the pitiful look on Mike's face. There was a hesitation for a moment. Wyatt thought the man wasn't going to do it, but then he pointed the small pistol in the air and pulled the trigger. Click.

Mike looked helplessly at the gun and then muttered, "Oh, crap." He racked the slide, sending a round into the chamber and tried again. Boom!

The discharge echoed across the water surrounding the marina and caused both men to jump. Not only were their ears ringing, but the flash from the small handgun's muzzle left white streaks in their vision. *Crap*, thought Wyatt, *now I am deaf and blind.*

Nothing happened for what seemed like several seconds. Wyatt was peeking over the hood of the car, trying to get his vision back so he could check on the gang of looters. Mike was shaking his head, trying to get the ringing out of his ears.

Evidently, one of the trespassers didn't understand it was a warning shot and fired back. Wyatt saw the cloud of white light silhouette the shooter and immediately heard the bullet impact the sheet metal he was hiding behind. Everything became a blur after that.

Wyatt popped over the hood of the car, firing and pumping the shotgun.

Wham!...shszit...Wham!...shszit...Wham! Mike was absolutely frozen by the escalation, having trouble commanding his limbs to move. Finally, the message got through. Without looking over the trunk, he extended his arm and blindly fired two shots in the general direction of the threat.

The muzzle flash from the shotgun had really screwed up Wyatt's night vision. The effect of the blood racing through his veins was negligible, given the bells that were ringing in his ears. He kept rising and ducking behind his cover, head pivoting left and right, stretching to see anything in the darkness. He kept expecting a surge of dozens of furious looters, charging at any moment.

Wyatt sensed, more than heard, movement over his shoulder. His first reaction was to spin the scattergun around, sure one of the attackers had gotten behind him. "Coming in! Coming in!" David's voice yelling registered in his mind before his muzzle was pointed at his son.

David sprinted, bent at the waist, the assault rifle cradled in his arms. Using the side of the car to break his forward momentum, he took a few deep breaths and then scrutinized the patch of land past the hood of the car. Once, twice, three times he raised his head, each time exposing himself a little longer, scanning back and forth.

"What are you shooting at?" the United States Army officer asked of his father.

~  ~

Morgan and Sage were scrambling around Boxer's cabin, preparing medical supplies. They pulled out the large shipboard medical kit from its storage area. Morgan had always insisted on having a first class inventory onboard. She was verifying the contents while Sage searched for the spare pillowcases to use as bandages. Both women were reacting to the shots, both now doubly concerned after David had charged off the boat to help his father.

Fear filled Sage's voice, "Do you think they're okay, mom? What are we going to do if they're hurt?"

Morgan rubbed her daughter's head and reassured, "I'm sure they'll be fine, sweetie. Nothing we can do about it right now except get ready - just in case. Besides, this is good practice. Your brother's an army officer; he'll take good care of your father."

Sage calmed down a little, but then her eyes got big again. She blurted, "What if those men come on the boat with guns? What are we going to do?"

The mother inside of Morgan wanted to console her frightened child, but the nurse took over. "Sage, stop that. Calm yourself, and help me find the tape. If someone is wounded, we are going to need bandages and lots of tape. Look in that drawer over there." As soon as her daughter turned her back, Morgan went to the galley silverware drawer and pulled out the biggest knife she could find. She held it for a moment and then strategically placed it on the counter – just in case.

~ ~

Every light on every occupied boat in the marina was on. David could hear snips of conversation as anxious, frightened neighbors asked what was going on. With the background lighting now illuminating the marina, David made out three more men reluctantly moving to reinforce Marinaville's guard. He finally got their attention, waving them to a nearby pickup truck, so everyone wouldn't be bunched up in the same place.

The next ten minutes were tense, but after a few scrambles toward the looter's last known location, it became clear that all of the invaders had retreated. A flashlight beam located a spent cartridge, evidence of the shot fired at Wyatt.

Mike was shaking so badly he couldn't light his own cigarette, and Wyatt wasn't much better. Both men shuffled around, initially burning off the adrenaline rush. Before long, they had to keep moving in order to cope with the crash. Incomplete, rushed sentences poured out of their mouths while nervous feet paced pointlessly from one spot to another.

David organized the relief watchmen and then convinced his father to return to Boxer. On the way, they attempted to put everyone as ease. Responding to anxious questions, the answers all started sounding the same. "We're all okay," or "Everyone is safe, get some sleep," and a lot of "No one was hurt," was spread around Marinaville. Despite their reassurances, Wyatt didn't think anyone would get much rest that night.

David called out when his father and he reached the stern of Boxer. "Mom, we're coming aboard...everything's fine." Morgan exhaled with relief, Sage immediately moving to open the sliding glass door. Wyatt was pale, immediately taking a seat while giving Morgan a look of "You wouldn't believe what I just went through."

"Do you want a cup of coffee, Wyatt?" she asked.

Wyatt nodded his head, but then confessed, "What I *want* is a stiff belt of bourbon, but coffee will do. Thanks."

Sage longed for details, but her brother waved her off, mouthing, "Later." The warm light of the cabin, combined with the company of his family, finally helped Wyatt relax a bit.

By the time Morgan positioned the steaming cup of instant java in front of him, Wyatt's hands had almost stopped trembling. He managed to take a sip without spilling any of the hot liquid – a major accomplishment. All of a sudden, he felt the need to talk and started recounting the night's events. He couldn't stop himself; the story just began pouring out of him.

When he finished, Morgan's reaction surprised him. "Those poor people," she said, "Can you imagine how desperate they must be to have tried that?"

Sage jumped right in, vocalizing what Wyatt and David were thinking. "*Those poor people?* Mom, what are you saying? Dad and David almost got killed, and you're worried about '*those poor people*'?"

Morgan shook her head, indicating everyone misunderstood. "They're people just like us, Sage. If we weren't so lucky, if we didn't have this boat, your brother and father might have been on the other side. Being desperate doesn't make them evil. Your father did the right thing. I'm just upset it came to that."

Everyone was silent for a moment, digesting Morgan's words. David was the first to speak, "You're right mom, being desperate doesn't make people evil, but it does make them dangerous."

Wyatt eyed his son. "Yes, and I've got a feeling it's going to get a whole lot more dangerous around here from now on."

Morgan started to add something else, but Wyatt caught her eye. She followed his gaze to the kitchen, where the large blade was sitting out on the counter. Quietly, almost under his breath, he reiterated, "Desperation does funny things to people – doesn't it?"

The morning after the shootout, an impromptu gathering began forming in the parking lot, most of the boaters exhausted from a lack of sleep. Clearly not an organized event, the attendees consisted of the same core of Marinaville's citizens, but this time small clusters of roving socialites joined in. Most of the residents showed up with the limited firearms available to them, many glancing at the rooflines of the neighboring subdivision as if massed hordes of barbarians were preparing to invade.

Boxer's occupants were some of the last to join the "festivities," and when Wyatt mounted the ramp leading to the parking lot, a hush fell over the crowd. Conscious of the abrupt silence, Wyatt glanced around and inquired, "What? Did I say something wrong?"

The joke was flat, but managed to break the ice somewhat. One of Morgan's friends, a kind soul named Marion, owned the vessel *Tilley's Girl* with her husband Jim. Showing her typical grace, the woman approached, first touching Morgan's shoulder while addressing Wyatt. "Are you guys doing okay?"

"We're fine, thank you for asking." Wyatt replied.

Everyone continued to stare, as if waiting for guidance. Marion continued, "Wyatt, what are we going to do? Jim and I couldn't get back to sleep last night...I don't think anyone did. What are we going to do, Wyatt?"

The first thought that went through Wyatt's mind was "*Who elected me boss?*" These people didn't realize his previous leadership had cost a lot of people their jobs. He threw a helpless expression at Morgan who reassured him with a smile. David seemed to sense his father's hesitation, moving closer to his father's side.

"I don't know what going to happen folks." Wyatt said at a slightly raised volume. "I'm as surprised as anyone how quickly this has gotten out of hand."

Everyone began talking at once, many of the responses aimed at Wyatt. He let it go for almost two minutes, politely nodding here and there; responding only when someone's tone of voice made it clear the speaker wanted his attention. It was all too much for his sleep-deprived brain, causing him to become frustrated. He held up his hands and shouted, "Please...please...one at a time...please!"

An uncomfortable hush fell over the group. Wyatt waited a moment and said, "Why don't we go in order of pier number, and everyone can speak their piece?"

There then ensued some confusion over where to start. Boxer was on pier two, so it was decided to start there. *Great*, thought Wyatt, *just great*.

"My instinct is to run away." Wyatt's blunt opening raising more than one eyebrow. "I'm not sure how to do that, but honestly that's what I'm feeling this morning. We are maintaining a reasonable existence here, but it won't last. Eventually, our food and fuel is going to run out, and we will end up like those people over there." Wyatt's arm swept in a semi-circle, indicating the neighborhoods surrounding three sides of the marina.

He continued, "I don't see any way we can defend ourselves. There just aren't enough of us to maintain a vigilant watch and keep up with the work required around here. Those men last night were chased off with a few shots. The next time it will take more than that. The next time, they might decide to shoot first. It's only logical to assume that as time goes on, they and others like them, will become more desperate...more willing to take risks...more aggressive."

Wyatt surveyed the faces in the crowd, realizing they were hanging on his every word. Most of the expressions conveyed agreement with Wyatt's position, one man even flashing a thumbs-up sign of endorsement. Despite the strong opening, Wyatt was out of gas. Uncertain of what to say next, he decided to go with his gut. *Now comes the bad part*, he thought.

"I don't have the answer. I wish I did, but right now, I'm just as concerned as all of you. Last night, all I wanted to do was fire up Boxer's engines, untie the ropes, and head out of here. The problem with that course of action is we don't have anywhere to go. Every marina around here is going to have the same problem – maybe worse. We can't all just untie and go float around Galveston Bay for the rest of our lives." He hesitated, the brain fog now consuming him. "That's about all I've got to say."

Several conversations broke out at once. Wyatt listened to the hum of the crowd, noticing the little excerpts that made it through here and there, things like "He's right," and "What are we going to do?"

Slowly the gathering quieted down, and folks began taking turns holding the floor. Many passed without speaking, indicating their feelings had already been voiced. Most wanted it known that they were willing to do whatever was needed. Practically everyone wanted to stay together as a group.

When the last person finished speaking, Wyatt sought the closure they all so desperately needed. "Does anyone have anything else to add?" He was surprised when David took a step forward.

"I'm not a boat owner here, and I know most of you still think of me as a kid. I've studied at the army's war college, and I have one thing I want to add – something I think all of us need to consider. My father is absolutely correct – we *cannot* defend this marina. There isn't enough manpower or firepower to do so. Whatever all of you decide, you need to keep that *fact* in mind. There's absolutely no way we can hold this ground."

The reaction to David's statement ranged from agreement to fear. Wyatt had mixed feelings himself, proud that his son had stepped forward to contribute, and yet unhappy with the timing of his delivery. Wyatt again raised his arm, asking for the floor.

"Folks, none of us have had much shut-eye. I suggest we reconvene this meeting later this evening, one hour before sunset. I suggest everyone try and get some rest and think about how we can fix this problem. All ideas will be considered, and everyone will get to speak."

The group had been milling around, discussing options for over an hour. The initial excitement was now wearing off, everyone becoming weary of the topic. All quickly agreed with Wyatt's recommendation and then began to disperse.

As Wyatt's family headed back to Boxer, it was Sage who sparked an idea. "What we need is our own deserted island." Her statement caused Wyatt to stop mid-stride and stare at her for a moment. "That's not a bad idea, Sage. Not bad at all."

Washington, D.C.
March 1, 2017

Reed peered out the window again, unsure of what else to do. Parting the drawn blinds ever so slightly, he scrutinized what could only be described as the surreal remains of chaos. The scene outside the window could've been Beirut in 1983 or London during the blitz. The once-pristine Georgetown avenue was littered with the debris of conflict, the scraps of war. The Texas congressman sighed, unable to reconcile the waste, and disappointed that nothing had changed.

Everything was still there, exactly the same as the last time he had checked. There sat the burned out postal truck, the police car with the broken windows, and the piles of shattered glass from the corner dry cleaners. Nothing had changed. The bullet holes in the police car looked as though they had rusted a little more, but perhaps that was a trick of light. The carcass of the policeman's German shepherd looked a little more deflated. Just the sight of the dead animal made his nose crinkle with imagined stench.

The thought of odor prompted him to smell his own armpits, and the results weren't daisy fresh. If it rained one more time, he might have enough water for a sponge bath. Reed sighed at the thought. That would probably be the biggest decision of his day – bathe…or save the water to drink.

At least the burning and looting had stopped. Several times during those first few nights, he'd seriously questioned the chances of his survival. Hiding in the apartment, he'd observed mobs of angry people parading up and down the street. Some carried homemade torches, others toted armloads of bricks and stones – all of them boiling mad, a lust for violence in their eyes. The rioters set about destroying anything they couldn't eat. Before the power failed, the D.C. police had made a valiant attempt to maintain order, but they were vastly outnumbered.

The first night, scattered news reports flashed video, featuring lines of officers with riot shields and helmets. Initially, Reed believed the trouble to be just another series of protests that had somehow gotten out of hand. The first hint that something more serious was underway came when the scope of the unrest was reported. Reed had watched with despair as one station used a city map plastered with red lightning bolts, each small icon indicating a problem area. It wasn't long before the map was completely covered.

Washington's local news stations began airing footage of tear gas canisters arching into the throngs of citizens. Before long, those attempts to disperse the crowds were answered with waves of rocks, bottles, and eventually gunfire. Once the bullets started flying, any hope of containment was lost. The nation's capital became a full-fledged battlefield.

Glued to Brenda's television, Reed's initial perspective of the entire affair was limited. Watching the clash unfold on the small screen was more akin to attending a Hollywood disaster movie than a real life catastrophe. It just didn't seem real. The local stations dispatched reporters all over the city, zipping around in logoed vans mounted with satellite dishes. The footage flooded in, crews rushing from one hot spot to another while transmitting their signals back to the parent station.

Initially, there seemed to be a competition for who could report the most atrocious story – or uncover the most horrific images designed to shock the viewers at home and increase ratings. As Reed viewed the broadcasts, he realized the media was feeding the frenzy – throwing fuel on the fire. At first, Reed screamed back at the yellow journalists, demanding the editors and producers realize they were making things worse. After a while, he sat back quiet and helpless, observing the entire city spiral into the deep abyss of anarchy.

In previous political disturbances, the press had been a neutral bystander. During the civil rights protests, Vietnam War demonstrations, and harsh labor disputes, reporters operated with impunity. In those days, people, no matter how motivated, angry or partisan, respected the press.

This time, it was different. Government, police, press, and even private citizens were caught flatfooted by how quickly things escalated - the population rapidly moving from rage to desperation, the final destination being a place where there was a complete disregard for rule of law.

Like a dome of magma exerting pressure on a mountaintop, the frustration, anger, and general discontent had been building for years; an eruption was inevitable. It wasn't the lack of electricity or the government's announcement that initiated the final release. Those events were merely the catalysts, only serving to unleash an already existing, pent up flood of rage.

The outburst wasn't isolated to any one segment of the population or specific silo of society. Affluence didn't make any difference; age wasn't a factor, and race played no role. It didn't matter if the discord was due to a threatened foreclosure, the price of milk, a scheduled IRS audit, or frustration with government regulations. The root cause might have been the recent loss of employment, a deep-seeded fear of global warming, or the ban on assault weapons. Government infringement was as much a contributor as government inaction. Those who believed in the redistribution for equality were just as motivated as those who despised redistribution of wealth. Progressive left and conservative right both joined the rampage, equally contributing to a caldera of violence.

The reporters were unprepared for both the intensity and longevity of the collective fury. As society fell off the cliff, many of them lost their lives in the ensuing turmoil. In the hours leading up to the final power outage, fewer and fewer live reports were transmitted. One of the last involved a female reporter broadcasting live in front of the Channel 31 news van. Four men casually approached, nonchalantly watching as one guy opened the van's door while another pulled a pistol and fired inside. In the ensuing chaos, the cameraman was knocked down, but his camera kept filming. The last sideways images were of the attractive newswoman being dragged off, desperately kicking and pleading for her life. The picture went dark shortly afterwards, her screams echoing through the television's speaker.

Reed rubbed his temples, trying to ease the memories of those first few nights. Stumbling back to the kitchenette, he reached for the pantry door, subconsciously rummaging for something to eat. He stopped himself, realizing it was just as barren as the last time he'd checked. He had consumed the last packet of instant oatmeal - two days ago? Or was it three? His stomach chimed in with a vote for three days without food. *I wonder if having a conversation with your stomach is a sign of starvation*, he thought.

Representative Wallace began questioning the election and his motivation of revenge. Was his current predicament some sort of karma? A punishment from God?

The members of his household should be safe back in Dallas, or at least that's what he hoped. Thinking of his family, Reed's throat began to tighten, and his eyes became moist. The constant conjecture about the safety of his loved ones was torture. His last cell phone call had been to his wife and children. They were heading to her parents' home in rural Texas. What he wouldn't give right now to be there with them, or at least know they were secure.

An unusual noise outside prevented a deeper dive into the pool of despair. It was a grinding sound that he hadn't heard in days – a car engine. Reed sprinted to the window and peeked around the blinds. Yes, there was an SUV and a car outside. He rushed to the other side of the window for a different vantage, still too frightened to peel back the vertical slats. There was a military Humvee as well. Four soldiers with black rifles piled out of the Humvee, quickly followed by some serious-looking gentlemen exiting the cars. The civilians were all very clean cut, with short hair and pressed shirts. As one man moved to shut his door, Reed noticed he was wearing a handgun under his coat. One of the men was holding a piece of paper in his hand, looking at the street addresses and then referring back to the paper. Reed almost jumped for joy when the fellow pointed at his building. The soldiers immediately double-timed in the direction indicated, and in a few minutes, a knock sounded at the door.

The congressman ventured to the threshold and answered, "Who is it?"

"We are looking for Congressman Reed Wallace. This is Lieutenant Thornton, Virginia National Guard."

Reed opened the door, smiling at the soldiers. "You've found him, Lieutenant, and none too soon, I might add." Ten minutes later, Reed was being hustled to Fort Meade, the capital policemen not seeming to notice his slight body odor.

The United States House of Representatives was going to convene and conduct official business of state. The new capital of the United States of America was temporarily going to be the Maryland army base, a facility named after the Union general who defeated Robert E. Lee at Gettysburg – George Gordon Meade.

Reed wondered what his colleagues from south of the Mason-Dixon line would think of that.

Southland Marina
Kemah Bay, Texas

Morgan knew Wyatt hadn't slept well. She didn't need her intuition or the intimate knowledge that comes with over 20 years of marriage to reach such a conclusion. The fact that he had either thrashed about wildly or remained perfectly still throughout the night was proof enough.

She didn't bother asking him about it. The last few years of struggle had worn out what little complainer existed inside of the man. She decided the best cure was to spoil her husband just a wee bit, so she went about making a cup of coffee and his favorite breakfast sandwich. She did manage to slide in a few comments about the importance of a good night's sleep while she flipped the fried eggs.

While Morgan was busy fussing over his lack of rest, Wyatt climbed to the bridge and retrieved a set of Texas coastal charts. After thanking his beloved, he got comfortable and began pouring over the waterway maps while consuming the excellent meal.

He startled Morgan when he suddenly jammed his finger onto the map and declared, "That's it! That's it, right there!"

Morgan peeked at the chart over his shoulder, slowly pronouncing the words, "Matagorda Island."

The rest of the afternoon was spent scouring guidebooks that covered the Texas coast and finding out if any of the neighboring boaters had recently visited the island. Wyatt had formed the foundation of a plan when he realized it was almost time for the meeting. He really didn't want to attend, thinking it more important that he continue and finish his work.

By the time the assembly was convening, Wyatt had done as much research as possible. Two other boaters had visited the isle, and confirmed the information in the guidebooks. The original agenda of the gathering had been for everyone to take turns presenting solutions or strategies. Excited by Wyatt's idea, one of the captains immediately superseded the proceedings.

"Wyatt has a plan, and I think it's a good one. I suggest we hear him out first and then go around and see what everyone thinks."

The reaction from the gathered boaters left a surprised Wyatt with no alternative.

A wave of doubt swept Wyatt's mind. He hadn't expected to be leading the ordeal. He was just trying to do his part, secretly hoping someone else had a better plan. Being in the spotlight suddenly became uncomfortable. *Didn't these people know his ideas didn't typically work out?*

Wyatt pushed down his welling insecurity, taking a moment to organize his thoughts. "Let me start off by repeating what I said this morning - I don't think we can stay here. I would like to...I really want to, but I think David's right. So if we can't stay, where would we go?" Wyatt scanned the assemblage, verifying he had everyone's attention.

"I've thought about Galveston, floating around the bay, heading out to the gulf – I've thought about a lot of different destinations. All of them have deal-breaking issues. The city of Galveston is probably just as bad off as our neighbors – maybe worse. Floating around the bay isn't going to work. The first storm that came along would scatter us all around, and we will need land-based resources at some point in time."

One of the men at the back of the crowd interrupted Wyatt by yelling out, "Wyatt, did you buy a Caribbean Island and not tell anybody?" Everyone laughed, and Wyatt felt a sense of relief. *At least they're not taking me too seriously*, he thought.

Waiting until things settled down, Wyatt's response surprised many of the listeners. "Well, not exactly, but I do know where there's something almost as good."

Now he had their attention. "You've all heard of Matagorda Bay, and the town of Matagorda, but has anyone other than John or Ross been to Matagorda Island?"

Several people started commenting all at once. Wyatt heard people say things like, "I've cruised by there on the way to Corpus," and "We used to fish around there when I was a kid." One man stated his father had been stationed at the old airfield after WWII.

Wyatt held up his hands, again requesting quiet. "The island is a little over 38 miles long and for the most part over a mile wide. There are no permanent residents other than a few million birds and some deer. The only way to get out there is via boat. There aren't any roads. There is a small marina with a few docks and bulkheads called 'Army Hole.'"

Wyatt gauged the group, observing several heads nodding in agreement. Others were hanging on his next words. "I think we can form up a flotilla and head down there. We can fish and hunt on the island and even plant some crops if it looks like society isn't going to recover quickly."

More people were grasping the concept, but the vast majority remained silent, trying to absorb the idea and anticipate the ramifications of the plan. Wyatt expected some people to immediately declare him a lunatic and lobby against the idea, but no one did. There were, however, some questions.

"Wyatt, what if those park rangers don't want us occupying their territory?" someone asked.

Before Wyatt could answer, another woman asked, "What if some other group has beaten us to it? What if we go all that way, and the place is already full of unwelcoming people?"

Wyatt held up his hands, "I know it's not a perfect plan, folks. There are a lot of things that could go wrong. But when I compare this strategy to the certain danger of staying here, I think it's the better option. We've got some people here who are really experienced seamen. We have all kinds of vessels at our disposal, including jet-skis, motorized launches, and dinghies. The small harbor at the park's marina is sheltered. We've got Matagorda Bay for fishing. I think it's at least worth thinking through."

Morgan had brought the charts showing the island and surrounding waters. As Wyatt spoke, the oversized maps circulated through the crowd. One of the boaters noted, "I see inland lakes depicted here on the island. Does anyone know if those are freshwater?"

As the meeting progressed, more and more of the crowd engaged with the idea. Questions and concerns were raised by several people. As the sun began to set, Wyatt was pleased that so far no one had raised any issue that was insurmountable. As the light dimmed, everyone's attention reverted to protecting the marina and appointed the security patrol for the night.

The gathering dispersed, with the determination that everyone was going to consider the plan and talk it over. Several people approached Wyatt, shaking his hand and patting him on the back. Morgan noted that he was becoming the de facto leader of the group, and that concerned her. Once, he had been the sort of man who would accept that role and take it seriously. She had hoped their new, simplified lifestyle would reduce his stress and allow some time to heal after all they had been through, but that was clearly not going to be the case.

As Morgan meandered back to Boxer, the thought occurred to her that in reality, she couldn't think of anyone else she would prefer to be leading the group. Perhaps this new responsibility would be a better therapy than idleness and relaxation. Maybe some of his old self-confidence and swagger would return.

~  ~

The poolside at Southland Marina was converted from a place of recreation and tanning to command central of a sizeable naval campaign. Over a dozen boaters arrived with charts, guidebooks, portable GPS units, and pads of paper.

While the route was important, it was the formation of the boats that received the most attention. Since the flotilla would include vessels of different sizes, speeds and rough water capabilities, the planning wasn't simple.

The first task was to determine the emergency mooring points. Even in the year 2017, pleasure boats weren't all that reliable. Propellers hit obstacles or ran aground in uncharted shallows. Engines overheated or failed. Fuel lines became clogged. There wasn't any capability to call a wrecker or a towboat, if equipment failed. Deep water anchoring was beyond the capability of the average recreational boat as well. A common requirement for "setting the hook," was ten times the amount of anchor rope as the depth of the water. The fleet would be voyaging through areas where the depth was 50 feet or more, and no one carried 500 feet of line. This meant that a damaged boat would need a safe, protected shallow-water mooring, and a harbor with those specs must be reasonably close by. Areas that met these requirements were identified and noted on the charts.

The next order of business was security. The fleet would be traversing through several different areas where the shoreline was close. All of the captains attending the meeting shared a common concern over being big floating targets in these narrow passages. People might just be desperate and crazy enough to shoot at them. Pirates and waterborne assaults were another potential threat. No one believed Marinaville had the only functioning boats in the region. It was well publicized that there were over 25,000 pleasure craft in the Houston and Galveston area alone. Were there people out there using boats for dubious purposes?

It was finally determined that the flotilla would use tactics similar to the configuration of a military fleet. The nimble, faster craft would form an outer ring and scout ahead. The medium-sized vessels would be a second ring of defense, with the larger, slower boats in the middle. Their fleet would travel south using the same formation as a US Navy Carrier Battle Group, steaming with its aircraft carrier in the middle and several rings of defense around it. This formation would work well except for just a few areas on the route. There were two narrow passages that would require everyone to motor through in single file.

The final stage of the meeting was devoted to determining which boats would be used on the trip. While each man knew his own vessel better than any other, some of the boats didn't make any sense to take along. This was the most emotional part of the planning, as no captain wanted to leave his vessel behind, surely to be looted by the surrounding neighborhoods. On the other hand, a boat without a working generator was a liability. Water making capacity, food storage capability, and fuel consumption were all valid selection criteria.

Some boaters fought an internal struggle fostered by ethics and morals. None of the captains wanted to take someone else's boat. It just didn't seem right, regardless of the circumstances. The inventory of suitable vessels was finally agreed upon. Charts were noted and diagrams of the fleet's formation were drawn.

It was getting dark, and everyone was exhausted. The final decision of the day was to call it quits until the morning when Marinaville's citizenry would reconvene, and a vote would be taken at first light. If the plan were approved, the rest of the morning would be devoted to reviewing the details so that every single person on the trip would be fluent with the plan. A target departure date was set for three days out at sunrise.

Chapter 8

March 4th, 2017

The eastern horizon was just beginning to glow with a new sun when the first boat fired up its engine, disturbing the pre-dawn calm with the rumbling of its powerful motor. While the vessels of Marinaville had promoted an almost constant humming of generators, these trifling, sound-shielded motors were nothing compared to the roar of twin 600 horsepower diesels reverberating across the landscape. That first yacht was soon joined by dozens of internal combustion engines as their chorus shattered the calm.

All over the marina, radar antenna began to spin, radios hissed to life, and GPS plotters booted. Crews scrambled, performing last-minute system checks, preparing for the long voyage ahead. They would travel half the distance to Army Hole today, spend the night at anchor, and hopefully arrive tomorrow around noon. That was the plan anyway.

Wyatt hesitated on Boxer's bridge, observing as Sage started untying the inch-thick lines that secured the heavy vessel to the wooden finger piers. The radio crackled to life on the preselected channel as the captains began to report in. Every boat was assigned a number - Boxer was number 11. As each vessel pulled out from its respective pier, the captain would announce the boat number and the single word status, "Departing."

The fleet's waverunners were first. Two of these fast, maneuverable craft would act as the scouts and escorts for the main body of vessels. Each carried two men onboard, the driver and a passenger armed with a rifle and a handheld radio. The waters along the central Texas coast were still chilly this time of year, so all of the riders donned neoprene diving suits, adorned with life vests in case the worst occurred. Initially, Wyatt had disagreed with arming the escorts. The miniature hulls were unstable, and it seemed ridiculous to think anyone could aim a rifle while bobbing around on the water. He had eventually been won over by the logic that "looking ready for trouble" might avoid an actual confrontation. Someone quoted the famous old Roman idiom, "If you want peace – prepare for war."

After the waverunners reported the channel to the lake was clear, the next set of boats began their parade down the passageway. These were the smaller cabin cruisers and sport boats. Ranging between 30 and 36 feet in length, each was a small floating apartment, capable of accommodating up to four people in reasonable comfort.

The third set of vessels to depart was the sailboats. This group had caused the most controversy during the planning for several reasons. The charts indicated the waters around Army Hole were shallow, and sailboats typically drew the most water because of a deep keel under the boat. They also were the best equipped for self-sufficient living. The average sailing vessel had more food storage, water making and renewable power generation onboard than the equivalent size motorboat. Many people bought sailboats with visions of extended trips to distant islands where land-based replenishment wasn't an option. Their equipment might prove invaluable.

Fortunately, Marinaville was home to a few large catamarans, which afforded a reasonable compromise. Well-equipped for independent voyaging without drawing as much water, the three, immense, multi-hulled "cats" motored out of Southland next.

The final group to unite and leave its mooring was the larger motorboats. Boxer fell into this category of 45 to 60-foot diesel powered cruisers. While large and comfortable, these vessels sucked fuel at alarming rates while underway. *Yachts are like automobiles and pizza*, Wyatt thought. *Everything's a compromise.*

At Wyatt's signal, Sage loosened the last mooring line and hopped aboard Boxer. Morgan climbed the ladder to sit on the bridge with her husband while Wyatt's deft touch on the throttles spun the heavy craft out of its slip and into the fairway.

The tension in the air was thick as the captains checked in on the radio, but there was also a sense of freedom and adventure in everyone's voices. Morgan loved cruising in the boat. It was a completely different feeling than driving or flying in an aircraft.

The sun cleared the horizon as the last of Marinaville's vessels cleared the harbor, an unusual, eerily quiet settling over the remaining, unoccupied boats.

The route to Army Hole began with a three-mile jaunt down an inland waterway known as Clearlake. Wyatt had once been told by an old sailor that Clearlake was neither clear, nor a lake. The shallow, brackish body of water was directly connected to Galveston Bay and could boast one of the largest concentrations of pleasure craft in the world. On any normal weekend day, hundreds of vessels in all shapes and sizes plied the lake, most on their way to or from the bay.

This morning, the waterway was empty with the exception of the 27 boats departing Southland Marina. As Wyatt increased Boxer's engine speed to keep his place in line, he couldn't help but notice pillars of smoke rising from several different locations close to the lake. While the dome of smoke over Houston to the north was no longer visible, the sight of the smaller fires reminded everyone that this wasn't a vacation cruise. The single file of boats formed a straight line almost a mile long. As Boxer made it to the middle of the lake, the waverunners leading the column were entering Clearlake Channel, a narrow, twisting path leading to the wide-open spaces of the bay.

The channel resembled a medium-size river lined with homes, businesses, and even a theme park. A little less than a mile long, the waterway was home to the most densely populated portion of the lake. David was riding shotgun on the lead waverunner, and Wyatt jumped a little when his static-laden voice crackled over the radio. "We see people along the edge of the channel. Can't see what they're up to just yet, but there are small fires burning along the northern bank."

Less than a minute went by before David reported again, "I think there are lots of people camping along the channel. I see tents, a couple of RVs and even two guys fishing. No problem so far."

~  ~

Todd was designated as the driver of David's patrol craft, the thirteen-year-old controlling the small jet-powered boat as if he had been born on the thing. David had seen the teenager around the pier now and then, but didn't really know him all that well. The kid's father swore Todd was an ace with the craft, adding the family would be much wealthier if it weren't for Todd eating up gasoline, running around the lake every weekend.

When they first detected people along the bank of the channel, David nudged Todd to move on ahead of the fleet. The slight, two-man craft had quickly accelerated away from the first boat in line, blasting past the shoreline at almost 50 miles per hour. When they had approached within 100 yards of the first group of people, Todd slowed to a stop, floating in the gentle current of the channel.

An audience began to gather onshore, gawking at the approaching line of boats coming down the lake. To David's eye, many of them acted like they never seen a boat before. The few children in the group were pointing; most of the adults stood and blankly stared. In reality, the channel hadn't seen much action of late.

David surveyed the campsite, noticing an odd collection of items. Several 50-gallon drums served as fire pits, while other spots of smoldering ashes dotted the ground all around the area. Much of the ridge was bare earth, the once thick carpet of green grass worn away. The men were unshaven, and all the spectators appeared tired and unkempt. As the outgoing tide slowly pulled them closer, David counted more than 20 people congregating on the water's edge, all of them now staring at Todd and him.

They looked more like refugees of some third world nation than citizens of the USA. Dark eyes, sunken cheeks, and lazy gaits painted a picture of little nourishment, minimal esteem, and less hope. Their camp enhanced the image – cardboard lean-tos braced with scrap lumber were mixed with two old campers and three faded tents. Tools, fishing poles and other items were scattered throughout the area.

One of the children waved, and both of the guys on the jet boat returned the gesture. None of the adults made any motion, friend or foe. A few moments later, they had drifted within shouting distance of the shore. One of the men yelled out. "Hey, do you guys have any antibiotics? We've got some pretty sick people here and zero medical supplies."

David, remembering the incident by the pool, decided to play it out. He yelled back, "I don't know. Let me check," and then raised his small portable radio to his ear. "These people along the shore want to know if we have any antibiotics or medical supplies. They have sick among them."

No one answered the radio call, and David hadn't really expected a response. After a reasonable pause, he lifted the device to his ear and pretended to be listening to an answer. Looking back to the shore, he carefully chose his answer. "No one in our group has anything. As a matter of fact, I was going to ask you folks the same thing. We're low on just about everything."

One of the other men laughed and then replied, "We've got plenty of fish, but that's about it."

The first boat in line had caught up by now, quietly gliding past on the smooth water. The people onshore could now clearly count the number of vessels on the move. David had to admit, it was probably a weird sight. Even during normal times, this many boats out so early would've been a little unusual.

About half the fleet had passed when David detected movement a little further down the channel. A man, obviously not part of the group he had been addressing, appeared on shore. The fellow began shouting something to one of the passing boats, his body language displaying agitation. David pointed out the new arrival, and Todd throttled up the jet-ski, accelerating the water bike in the stranger's direction.

David couldn't make out what the gentleman was saying, but the look in his eye was clear. The guy was wearing shorts and a dirty white shirt, torn and sporadically stained with sweat, blood, and clay. His crazed expression and body motions defied explanation. It was almost as if the guy was trapped on an anthill, jerking his arms one minute, performing a bad dance step the next.

Without warning, the man screamed, "Take me with you! God have mercy – take me!" The stranger then dove into the frigid water, swimming directly at the nearest boat.

"Block him," shouted David, and Todd steered to do just that. All of the boats from Marinaville were propeller driven, many of them spinning blades large enough to suck a swimmer underneath the passing vessel. The propulsion units would then become meat cleavers.

David's waverunner intercepted the swimmer about 20 feet from shore, acting like a football player blocking for a halfback. The demented fellow splashed around for a bit, and David realized he was becoming fatigued. Having nothing else handy to give the struggling man, David stuck out his foot for the guy to grab and hold.

Initially, the desperate swimmer gripped David's ankle and held on for a few moments, gasping for air. He then proceeded to climb up David's leg, looking more crazed than ever. Not only did David have to adjust his balance to remain seated, the guy's weight started to tip the waverunner over. Again, having no other option, David shoved the barrel of the AR15 in the guy's face – right on the bridge of his nose. "That's enough!"

Something about the sharp pain of the barrel's flash suppressor made it through to the swimmer's brain, and he curtailed his ascent, panting for breath and just hanging on. "Take us in close to shore," David told Todd.

Slowly the water bike moved closer to the embankment. When the trio reached shallow water, David pressed down hard on the weapon until the fellow let loose. "Now go," he instructed.

As the jet boat idled off, David glanced over his shoulder and watched as the man just stood there in waist-high water, seemingly content with watching the rest of the fleet pass by. With David's urging, Todd increased their speed in order to move to the front of the formation again. They were almost back on point when the radio crackled. "Someone had better get up here, this looks like trouble."

David nudged the driver and instructed, "Go...hurry to the front."

As they rounded a sharp bend in the channel, the issue became clear. The narrow passageway was blocked by a rather large sports fisherman that seemed to be abandoned. The 60-foot-plus vessel must have come untied and drifted to its resting place, bow wedged into the bank and blocking the deepest part of the channel. There was no way to pass around the boat.

David keyed the microphone, "Everyone hold in place. The channel is blocked."

Boats don't have brakes or a parking gear. While there wasn't any wind yet, the channel always had a current, one direction or the other, depending on the tide. It was very difficult for a floating vessel to maintain a fixed position with even slow moving water pushing on her hull. For the smaller boats, this wasn't much of a problem as they could circle in the narrow channel. For Boxer and the larger boats, it was a very tight squeeze, requiring no small level of skill. Adding to the general apprehension of potential collisions, the captains all sensed that the longer the fleet was in this tight passage, the higher the risk of shore-born problems.

The other waverunner motored to David's boat and a quick discussion ensued. The scouting party determined that David would board the boat while one of the mid-sized cabin cruisers came forward to tow the relic. Dock lines would be used to pull the big hulk out of the channel.

David climbed aboard the ghost ship and right away noticed a horrible odor. Before he could even register what the offending aroma was, he saw a gash in the transom's fiberglass that looked like a bullet had impacted at a low angle, carving a groove in the white material. That image immediately connected with the odor in his brain. Within seconds, he discovered the bodies and turned away from the gruesome sight. A man and a woman both lay dead on the bridge, their decomposing corpses resting in a large pool of dried blood. Scavengers, most likely airborne vultures, had visited the deceased. He noticed two more bullet holes as he hurried back to the swim platform and gagging into the channel.

The driver of the other waverunner saw what was happening and motored up. "You okay, man?"

Despite his churning stomach, David signaled he was fine. "Can you bring me some water when you get a sec?"

Todd rummaged for a second, "Here, take mine. You look like you need it about now," and tossed the clear plastic bottle over.

In a few minutes, one of the small cruisers maneuvered close enough to throw across two lines. David used a hitch knot to quickly secure the ropes to the bigger boat, and then motioned for Todd in to pick him up.

The little cruiser revved its engines and began pulling on the ghost ship. There was a moment of suspense when it looked like the bigger vessel was going to stay aground, but after a few moments the ghost ship budged. As soon as the passage was clear, David again boarded the offending sport boat and untied the towlines, hastily flinging them back in a high arch. He wasted no time getting off her, and into some fresher air.

News of the bodies traveled up and down the line on the radio. As the flotilla passed the big sports fisherman, several of the captains veered slightly off course. Much like gawking rubberneckers driving past a wreck on the interstate, they couldn't tear their gaze from the carnage. Wyatt, following Morgan's lead, tried to find a "silver lining," in the incident - his hope being that everyone in the group would take the situation a little more seriously after the incident.

The next obstacle was the highway bridge. Giant concrete pillars were set into the channel to support the huge structure looming over the waterway. The navigable space between the supports was the narrowest part of the entire journey. It was the only place where the boats would get close enough to shore that someone could jump from land onto one of the vessels as it passed. David and the other scouts were relieved to see the entire area was void of spectators. Two large grey gulls were the only inhabitants at the moment, and they didn't seem to pose much of a threat to anything other than the finger mullet schooling next to the supports.

After clearing the bridge came Shrimper's Row. Large steel-hulled commercial shrimping vessels lined the north side of the channel, moored to the wooden bulkheads lining the bank. A small seafood processing plant resided immediately behind the big ships, ready to accept the delicious bay crustaceans immediately after the shrimpers docked nearby.

David knew most of these commercial fishermen were Vietnamese. His father and he passed by these boats hundreds of times over the years. Most of the families actually lived on their boats. It was a common sight to see small children playing aboard while mom and dad hosed off equipment or scrubbed decks. During the holidays, many of the boats would decorate with traditional Buddhist lanterns and other décor. At night, it was commonplace to see young mothers on deck, reading stories to their children or fishing with regular rods and reels into the nearby channel. Once, David had observed a school bus unload several small Asian children next to the shrimpers. He watched as the tallest of them peeked into a mailbox along the nearest street.

Even at dawn, the shrimping boats buzzed with activity. The first sign of life was the movement of a fishing pole, swinging in a wide arch as its line was cast out into the channel. *That's to be expected, given the tide*, thought David. The next thing that caught his eye was a man, standing beside the fisherman, carrying a double barrel shotgun.

David pointed out the sentry to Todd. "Stay right here. We don't want to look like a threat."

The first boat of the Marinaville fleet was still a little behind them. David wanted to make it clear to the man with the shotgun that Todd and he were only there for escort duty, not to harass or threaten the fishermen in any way. "Wait until boat one catches up a bit, and then stay directly between him and the guy with the shotgun. No fast movements, but be ready to hit the throttle if I yell out."

The shrimper's guard could now see at least the first few boats in line behind David, and the approaching armada caused quite the stir aboard several of the commercial boats. Evidently some warning was given, because suddenly there were people scrambling all over the big steel-hulled boats.

Within a few seconds, David counted at least seven people aiming guns at them.

"Okay," David whispered to his driver, "go up there real slow. I'm going to see if I can communicate our peaceful intent."

"You better," came the nervous response.

David took the AR15 and swiveled the weapon around to his back. He held up both hands in a "Don't shoot" position as they approached the closest boat. "Good morning," he called out.

He could hear voices coming from the shrimp boats, and while he couldn't understand the language, he was reasonably sure the greeting had caused some disagreement. A few moments later, a young teenager appeared next to the man with the scattergun. "What do you want," he called out in perfect English.

"We are only passing through to the bay. There are over 20 boats behind us, and we are just escorting them."

David could hear muted discussions going back and forth on the closest vessel. His answer came back, "If you don't bother us, we won't shoot at you."

David smiled and yelled back, "Fair enough." He also noticed none of the guards on the shrimpers relaxed. *Trust, but verify*, he thought.

Beyond the shrimpers, the last significant landmark before the bay was the Boardwalk. A popular attraction for tourists and locals alike, the Boardwalk consisted of a long row of seaside restaurants, shops, and a small amusement park.

The Boardwalk brought back childhood memories for David. As the flotilla motored past, it seemed so odd for it to be abandoned. When the waverunner got closer, he could clearly see the shops and restaurants were more than closed – they had been ransacked. Shards of broken window glass piled in mounds on the wooden walkways, and chairs were scattered haphazardly, most resting on their sides, very few of them upright like he remembered. He noticed two doors that had been splintered, and all of the buildings appeared to have been gutted by vandals.

David had to look away, the reckless destruction of the Boardwalk making his already distressed stomach flutter. Instead, he focused his gaze out to the open bay just beyond the plundered shoreline. The sun was still low on the horizon, its yellowish orb reflecting off of the glass-smooth water. One of the primary reasons for leaving so early was to cross as much water as possible before the winds whipped up the bay. While very shallow across most of its 23-mile width, Galveston Bay could develop a nasty 2-3-foot chop. Such waves were no threat to the boats of Marinaville, but they could make the ride feel like a car going over a washboard road.

The green and blue water was interrupted here and there by manmade objects. A straight line of channel markers marched off into the distance, many slightly misshapen by the gulls that constantly rested on their tops. To the south were a handful of platforms and wellheads. Mostly rusty relicts or capped gas wells, the structures provided good fishing spots and were favored by numerous species of birds.

Todd gave their ride some throttle, and the small craft accelerated out of the channel and into the bay. David relaxed somewhat, the wide-open spaces seemingly fresher – the air easier to breathe. Normally, he would love riding on such smooth water, but there was no time today for fun. He thought about the last time he was out on open water this early - a fishing trip with his father and a high school buddy before leaving for the army. They hadn't had much luck that day, but it didn't matter. He loved the ocean and salt air.

As the jet boat skimmed across the surface, David made himself sit back and enjoy the experience. There was something unique about a boat, any boat, gliding across smooth water. It's such a different sensation from riding in an automobile or airplane. It was almost as if the cushion of water deadened the sense of motion. *My eyes see I'm moving quickly, but my body can't feel it*, he thought. *I bet this is what the weightlessness of space feels like.*

A quick glance showed the line of boats exiting the channel one by one. Radio chatter settled down. The next 20-mile leg of the trip involved traveling south toward Galveston Island and should be stress-free, a welcome change from the first part of the journey. David scanned the water around them and then shifted his weight to stick his leg into the chilly bay. He had always wondered if the water would clear up without the huge tankers and freighters traveling up and down the Houston Ship Channel. Those enormous vessels, combined with thousands of pleasure boats, had to stir up tons of silt. As he sank his foot into the water, he was curious if the two weeks without traffic would make much difference, but it didn't. He could only see the outline of his foot down a few feet under the surface. The wind probably stirred up more bottom mud than propellers and hulls. Galveston Bay had probably been a cloudy body of water going back thousands of years.

Exhaling and righting himself back on the seat, David felt a slight twinge of guilt. Even though he was technically still on leave, he wondered if there wasn't something more he should be doing for his country via the army. He hadn't received his assignment before graduating from Officers' Candidate School. Technically, he didn't have a unit to report to right now. He had been told that his orders would be both mailed and emailed to him, but neither form of communication now existed. The collapse had caught him in limbo, and he had zero idea what to do about it. Right now, his family needed him more than anything. As soon as communications were restored, he would call in and find out where he was supposed to report, and how he was to get there. *Where's a good carrier pigeon when you need one*, he mused.

March 4, 2017
Fort Meade, Maryland

The auditorium at Fort Meade was designated as the temporary capitol building, and now housed both the House of Representatives and the Senate. Rather than the normal pomp and circumstance of graduation ceremonies, the large hall was now filled with elected officials engaged in wild speculation and grandiose scheming to insure the country's future. Folding chairs, small tables, and a mismatched assortment of furniture occupied most of the open floor, hurriedly assembled tools required for the legislative branch to function. The exposed steel beam structure of the roof and bare concrete floor were a far cry from Washington's Capitol building, but no one complained. While the military base wasn't adorned with world-class art, beautiful chandeliers, or marble floors, the bare bones facility did keep the cold, Maryland winds at bay, and there was enough space to conduct the business of state.

Shortly after arriving, Reed was assigned quarters in what must have been facilities normally allocated to military officers on temporary duty assignments. The living space was essentially on par with a three-star budget hotel, comprised of a double bed, closet-like bathroom, and two guest chairs. Plain, zero-frills furniture adorned the room, accented by mass-produced, soulless prints hanging from the walls. A mattress, just shy of marble slab on the hardness scale, rounded out the accommodations.

After his experience in Brenda's apartment, the congressman from Texas felt like he had just checked in at the Four Seasons. From Reed's perspective, the list of amenities offered by his new abode was practically endless. There was running water, both hot and cold, tiny bottles of shampoo, miniature bars of soap, and a plastic wrapped toothbrush. The first shower was a marathon event, the first shave just shy of euphoria. *It's all a matter of perspective*, he speculated.

An aide soon delivered a parcel of clean clothes so distressed, they could have been leftovers from a recent garage sale or rejects from the latest charity drive. In Reed's mind, the experience of donning the clean underwear, unsoiled pants, and odor-free shirt was akin to preparing for a Broadway opening in a stylish tuxedo.

It wasn't just his ordeal of isolation in Brenda's flat that shaped his newfound appreciation. On the drive from Washington, the surreal images outside the plain government sedan reminded him of news footage of a war-ravaged section of Syria or Libya, not the capital of the most powerful nation on earth.

Fires still raged unchecked, some consuming entire blocks. Freeways were jam-packed with abandoned vehicles for as far as the eye could see. Overturned cars littered the surface streets, often competing with smoldering ash heaps of bonfire-roadblocks ignited during the riots. When his escorts pulled away from Brenda's apartment, one of the men had turned and offered Reed a handkerchief. "Here, you'll need this in a bit." Puzzled, Reed thought perhaps they would be passing through areas of intense smoke, but that wasn't the reason. It was the dead, twisted, decomposing corpses. After the first few miles, Reed became acclimated to the view, and he stopped counting the fallen bodies of his countrymen. But it wasn't only people – the cadavers of horses, dogs, and cats were scattered among the ruins.

Many of Washington's broad avenues were impassable, blocked by relic traffic or the rubble of collapsed buildings. Here and there, military vehicles and soldiers patrolled the streets. The driver commented, "It took the National Guard almost three days to muster and enter the city. It took another two days to establish order, but only in certain areas. We held the Capitol building and White House, but a lot of government facilities weren't so lucky. Much of this town is still 'no man's land.'"

After what seemed like hours, they successfully maneuvered to the Maryland countryside. The earth sported a "just rained" clean smell, and Reed felt an even stronger urge to bathe. The foul, oily smoke from the city clung to his skin and clothing like a coating of grease. He recognized he hadn't smelled daisy-fresh in the first place, but the drive through Hades-on-the-Potomac had saturated his soul.

Feeling physically refreshed, Reed's mental outlook was bolstered as he absorbed the frenzied level of activity around the base. If it weren't for a desperate longing to speak with his family, the congressman's attitude would have appeared optimistic. Having no communication with his wife and children was practically unbearable. He was sure they were in a much better place than the average citizen was, but he didn't *know* that for a fact. He craved some sort of confirmation. *It's impossible right now, so get busy and do your job*, he thought. *Roll up your sleeves and occupy your time. You won't fix a thing by worrying about them.*

Reed's mood was elevated further as he began to acclimate to the current of energy that flowed through the gathered politicians. The country was in trouble, and these people had been elected to serve her. He forced himself to put aside his personal apprehensions, and began looking for his party's leadership to report in.

Representative Wallace finally found a cluster of familiar faces and strode over to join the group. Hands pumped with a little more vigor than in the past. Standard political banter was replaced with seemingly heartfelt comments like, "Really glad you made it," and "Good to see you're alive." Reed was a freshman and relatively unknown, so he remained on the fringe and just observed. The majority of the conversation concerned other parts of the country and what little news had filtered back to D.C. The legislators from rural areas believed things had remained stable in their districts, while those from districts that included larger cities were hearing bad news.

As best as anyone could tell, the chaos in Washington was the norm, not the exception. The congressman from Chicago had received a report that the second great fire to ravage the Windy City was blazing out of control; the burning skyline was apparently visible clear across Lake Michigan. Others had similar status reports from back home.

A loud, pounding noise sounded from the minute stage at the front of the room, commanding the attention of all present. "Please come to order and take your seats. Please come to order, ladies and gentlemen," the vice president instructed, pounding his gavel.

Reed found his assigned folding chair and sat wondering how all of this would play out. The House Majority Leader joined the V.P. behind the podium and tested the microphone. The room quickly became quiet.

"Elected representatives of the United States of America, I hereby call this session to order. As you all know, our country has experienced a catastrophic chain of events, and I'm sure every single one of you has a million questions. As many of you already know, the president has declared martial law throughout the country. Federalized forces are making every attempt to reestablish order throughout the land. The president has tasked the legislative branch with recovery and recuperation. When I spoke to the commander-in-chief this morning, he asked that we have a plan, ready to implement, the moment order is restored. He assured me that the executive control and the declared state of emergency would be lifted as soon as possible. So, our first order of business today will entail a situational update and briefing from several different speakers. First up will be, Director Morton of the Department of Homeland Security."

Reed was relieved. He had worried that his peers would opt for the usual political theater and positioning, and he just wasn't in the mood for a bunch of long-winded speeches. Evidently, everyone else felt the same way as he did — time to get down to business and be Americans first, politicians second.

Galveston Bay, Texas

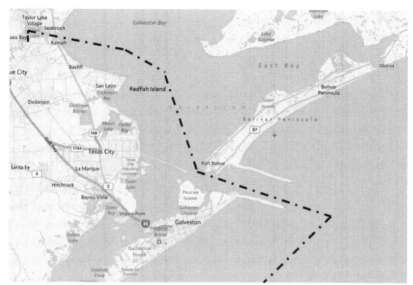

The last boat cleared the mouth of the channel, heading southeast toward Galveston Island. David was readying to move closer to the line of boats when something in the northern sky caught his eye. A dark line of clouds was just visible over the horizon, and his heart sank at the sight - a northerner was moving in.

This time of year along the gulf coast, the weather patterns were mostly mundane. About the only serious disturbances were the massive cold fronts rolling down from the arctic north. These powerful storms were strong enough to push the warm, humid air of the gulf out of the way. While frosts and snow were rare along the coast, these massive fronts were known to generate violent thunderstorms, high winds, and very cold temperatures. *What a time to lose the Weather Channel*, he thought.

Clouds normally trekked from the southwest to the northeast. Only a northerner came from the northwest, and that's where this line of clouds was coming from. David keyed the microphone on his handheld radio and called out for Boxer. When his father answered, he asserted, "Dad, look over your left shoulder at the clouds."

Everyone could hear the broadcast, and several of the boats were close enough that David could see heads pivoting to look. In a few moments, Wyatt answered for everyone. "We need to find a port – right now." It wasn't good news.

Wyatt turned and looked at Morgan who was already pulling out charts. While he had a very accurate picture on Boxer's large screen GPS, the scale wasn't large enough to pick out details, like finding a place to ride out the storm. But even without a map, Wyatt knew the bay quite well, and there were

167

only a few options. The sailboats in the fleet simply were not fast enough to outrun the front. Maxing out at about six knots, or seven miles per hour, they would be caught out in open water when the weather turned bad. Riding out the storm on open water was taking a big risk.

The danger wasn't sinking or capsizing, even the smallest of the fleet's craft could handle all but the worst weather. The risk was collision, equipment malfunction, grounding, and exposure by the crew. Boxer could handle anything short of a hurricane and survive relatively unharmed. Wyatt had piloted the boat through extremely bad weather and didn't want a repeat event. He had once likened the experience to driving a convertible car through a tornado with the top down and no windshield wipers. The driving sheets of rain had reduced visibility to the point where he couldn't see the front of the boat. The waves had slammed her so violently, Morgan had become ill. Later, she claimed to know firsthand what a pair of sneakers felt like in the dryer. The crews of the smaller boats would take an ever worse beating.

As Wyatt mentally pictured this end of the bay, there were only a few options that would provide shelter from a north wind. Of those, only one was isolated from sizeable human populations, and after what they had witnessed in the channel, avoiding other people seemed like a good idea.

"How about Redfish Island? We can anchor and then raft up on the southeast side and ride it out," Wyatt suggested, all the while scanning Morgan's expression for evidence of her true reaction.

Morgan took her finger and measured on the chart. At their current speed and distance, they just might make it. Without a weather report, there was no way to tell how fast the front was coming on, but the boiling clouds behind them appeared to be catching up. "I can't see or think of anything closer unless we turn around and go back to the channel," she said.

Wyatt reached for the radio and asked if anyone had a problem heading for Redfish. After a few moments with no response, he continued, "Let's make for the southeast side of the island."

Morgan waited to see if anyone responded on the VHF, and after a period of silence, her voice was calm, but serious. "We are just over eight nautical miles away. At our current speed, it will be 70 minutes before we get there. I suggest the faster boats move ahead because it will take a bit to secure the anchors. By the time everyone else catches up, we can be ready for them."

"That's a good idea. It's hard enough to set the hook without worrying about running into another boat. If we have everyone drifting around all over the place, there's a good chance for a collision." Wyatt glanced over his shoulder again, watching the churning, black clouds that were chasing the fleet. He picked up the microphone and announced, "We all can't arrive and anchor at the same time – there's not enough space, and we'll be crashing into each other. Every boat should make its best speed. If possible, the smaller vessels should raft up to the larger ones."

A few of the captains came back with comments such as, "Good idea," and "Good luck."

Wyatt pushed Boxer's throttles forward, and the big diesel engines increased their thunder. The heavy fiberglass hull rose slightly when she began to plane across the top of the water. As they passed the slower vessels, many of the captains signaled their support. Nobody wanted to be in open water during a northerner.

As Boxer and five other large powerboats surged past the fleet, their wakes created a bouncy ride for the vessels they passed. There wasn't time to follow the rules and slow down, but no one seemed to care. The wakes produced by the passing craft were nothing compared to what the bay would kick up with a stiff northern wind.

After fifteen minutes, the outline of Redfish began showing on Boxer's radar. At twenty minutes, he could see the northernmost tip of the island.

Redfish had been a natural oyster reef for thousands of years. An extension of Eagle Point, the small island housed trees and even a few buildings many years ago. Really more of a peninsula than an actual island, it was said that a person could walk across from the mainland at low tide.

Many people thought the island had a primitive feel to it. Some described it as being similar to wandering around ancient ruins of long-lost civilizations. Part of this was no doubt attributed to its being an isolated place where people once tread, an experience similar to visiting a ghost town. All kinds of seaborne debris was known to wash up on the unhabituated speck's shores - containers from the passing vessels, bottom refuge washed up by storms, and of course, everyday items blown from the decks of passing pleasure craft.

The Houston Ship Channel was less than a mile to the east. As this major shipping artery saw more and more tonnage, Redfish began to erode and shrink. The huge ocean-going tankers, freighters, and tugs plying the waters of the bay generated bow wakes that could exceed 10 feet in height. Dozens of these commercial vessels journeyed up and down the ship channel every day, and the small island couldn't handle the change from the normally tranquil waters of the bay. Throw in the occasional hurricane, and the small patch of dry land didn't stand a chance. By the 1970s, there were no longer any trees. By the 1980s, the island was nothing more than a crescent moon-shaped spot, less than an acre in size. By the 1990s, the island was below the surface except at the very lowest tide.

Wyatt felt the wind shift out of the north just as Boxer turned out of the ship channel toward Redfish. In a matter of moments, the air temperature dropped several degrees, and Morgan scrambled down the ladder to fetch jackets. The dark line of ominous clouds was now almost directly overhead and moving quickly. On the horizon, flashes of lightning illuminated the sky.

Pointing Boxer the right direction was tricky through this section of the bay. Numerous shallows, oyster beds, and mud reefs dotted the area, many of them randomly shifting position over time. Boxer drew almost five feet of water, and the charts carried warnings of one to three foot depths at mean tide. Hitting a razor-sharp oyster bed, even at slow speed, could peel away the hull of the big boat. More likely, the outcome would be a broken propeller or two. If Boxer lost a wheel, she could continue with a single shaft. If she lost two, they would have to abandon her and all she carried.

Wyatt's eyes constantly moved from the depth gauge to the chart plotter to the water ahead. The numerical depth readings were accurate, but under the hull of the boat. It was like trying to drive a car through a hole in the floorboard – by the time you ran over something it was too late.

Still, he could identify and anticipate trends, and right now the line indicating the bottom of the bay was going the wrong way. He watched as the numbers read 8…8…7…7…6, and reached up, pulling the engines into neutral. If he hit bottom, it might save the propellers if they weren't spinning. As Boxer coasted, the numbers began to increase, finally reaching nine feet of water again. He threw the engines into gear and turned toward the leeward side of Redfish's protected anchorage. This area had been dredged and was a known depth of 10 feet.

After navigating the shallows, Wyatt had a moment to study the island. When a Corps of Engineers project to widen the Houston Ship Channel had been announced, several groups banded together, asking the government to use the dredged materials to rebuild the now all-but-submerged landmark. Several preservation groups, as well as the recreational boating community, thought it was worth the endless petitions and emails to their congressmen. Finally, after an exhaustive effort, the proper authorities agreed, and Redfish was slowly rebuilt. Ever since, the small strip of dry land had served as a bird sanctuary, natural tidal break, and great weekend gunk-hole for the pleasure boaters.

The engineers dumped thousands of tons of soil onto the old island, topping it off with loads of basketball-sized rocks. While not exactly a sandy oasis for swimming and walking, the authorities had ensured all of that soil didn't wash back into the nearby ship channel. Almost three acres of manmade land reappeared in the bay. Barely fifty feet wide and stretching almost two football fields in length, the island made an excellent breakwater. A small cove was protected from the large wakes rolling in from the ship channel and was enjoyed by dozens of craft every weekend. Right now, Wyatt wanted protection from the wind-driven waves that would soon start howling in from the north.

Typically, a layer of soft mud covered the bottom of the bay. Anchoring in such material was difficult at best, and often next to impossible. One of the reasons why Redfish was such a popular destination was that the bottom contained a bit more clay than was normal in the area. The sticky, thicker material increased the chances of setting the hook securely.

Wyatt nudged Boxer's bow toward the center of the island and watched until the depth began to decrease. He flicked the safety cover off of the anchor chain's release while Morgan made her way forward to release the manual safety on the heavy links. More than one vessel had been sunk by an accidental release of the anchor while underway, thus the redundant safeties.

Boxer's engines were again shifted into neutral, and in a few moments, the wind started pushing her back from the island and over deeper water. When the depth returned to 10 feet, Wyatt signaled Morgan, and she released the safety and stepped back. Wyatt flipped the switch, and the anchor fell free of the pulpit, splashing into the dark water below. The first 20 feet of anchor rod was chain, and that fed out quickly, rattling noisily over the pulley. After the chain, a heavy rope started playing out as Boxer continued to drift backward.

Proper anchoring normally involved some ratio of depth to the length of the line. In calm waters, a ratio of five or six to one was acceptable. In rough seas, over seven to one could be required to hold a vessel in place. Boxer was in ten feet of water, so over 70 feet of anchor scope needed to unwind to provide a secure hold.

The rope had markers every ten feet. Morgan watched and counted, holding up fingers so Wyatt would know how much line had played out. At 90 feet, Wyatt flipped the switch on the dash, and the pulley seized the line. Now began a waiting game to see if the hook had caught and buried itself in the mud. It took a few more moments for the line to pull tight, halting Boxer's backward drift. Wyatt set the waypoint on the GPS and then pushed the throttles into reverse, giving the engines just a touch of power while watching the readouts on the screen beside him. She held! There was no movement at all except the expected side-to-side drift on the line. They had a good anchorage. Wyatt picked up the radio and let the other captains know.

The follow-on boats behind Boxer had to be aware of how far she was swinging to and fro on her line before they could repeat the same process. Any boat at anchor can swing several degrees port to starboard, and collisions were always a concern when anchoring in tight proximity.

The last of the five larger motorboats managed to set anchor as the rest of the fleet began arriving. The first boats in line had just motored into safe positions when the squall line slammed into the group. Wind gusts topping 50 mph whipped across the water, quickly followed by stinging sheets of ice-cold rain. Wyatt was on the Boxer's bridge wearing a raincoat, but it didn't do much good. The storm blasted a nearly horizontal torrent at the boaters, each individual drop feeling like a needle pricking flesh. The gale whipped the wave tops into an airborne mixture of sandblasting froth and biting salt spray.

Flying water found every nook and cranny in Wyatt's rain gear, immediately soaking his freezing cold body from head to toe. Visibility dropped to nearly zero, and it was difficult to stand without support. The bay waters instantly turned black, swelling into confused whitecaps that tested every captain's skill.

The blow was howling so loudly it became impossible to hear the radio, and bedlam set in. Out of the blinding rain, Wyatt made out the running lights of a small cruiser headed directly at Boxer. A ringing alarm began sounding from the dash as the radar's collision avoidance system engaged. Wyatt double-checked that his anchor light was on and functioning and then grabbed a large flashlight from under the captain's chair. He shined the light at the approaching boat, attempting to use the beam to warn it off.

At the last minute, the captain of the charging boat recognized Boxer and swerved off, avoiding a collision by mere feet. Wyatt got a glimpse of the man as he went by, observing as he tried to steer the small boat in the screaming wall of wind and rain. Wyatt tried to yell for the man to tie off on Boxer, but his shouts were like trying to hear a mouse squeak at a rock concert. The clearly shaken and partially blinded helmsman of the offending cruiser went past at an angle pointed directly at Boxer's anchor line. "Noooooo!"

Wyatt would never understand how, but the intruding vessel missed his anchor rope. The captain realized at the last moment where he was and swerved sharply to avoid tangling the line in his propellers. That catastrophe avoided, Wyatt then watched in horror as a crewmember attempted to climb forward onto the deck. *This guy is going to try and anchor his boat right there*, Wyatt thought. *He's going to sink both of us.*

Even with the protection of Redfish Island, the sea had built to a three-foot slop. Morgan managed the climb onto the bridge, observing the offending boat while shielding her face from the blistering rain. She bellowed out something, but Wyatt couldn't hear. He stepped closer, and she tried again. "No life jacket!" Wyatt followed her pointing finger to the crewman bobbing violently up and down at the front of the nearby vessel. Sure enough, whoever was out on that precarious perch didn't appear to have on a flotation device. He instinctively knew this wasn't going to end well.

The crewman pulled the safety on the cruiser's anchor, and Wyatt could make out the silver-colored hook dropping into the sea. The line started playing out rapidly as the wind caught the boat and shoved it backwards. The crewman started to move back toward the cabin and slipped, banging hard into the safety railing surrounding the deck. The captain left the wheel to help, and the small cruiser started to spin around in the wind.

It only took a few seconds for the pilotless boat to spin 180 degrees, centering the propellers directly over the boat's own anchor line, wrapping the thick cord tightly round the shafts. Before the captain could even turn back toward the helm, the torque on the shaft pulled it clean away from the transmission, ripping a two-foot gash in the bottom of the hull. The sound of splitting fiberglass sounded like a bomb exploding and was audible even over the storm. The other engine immediately stalled.

Now the small boat was without power and taking on water, flooding the engine compartment. There hadn't been enough anchor line out for the hook to catch on the bottom. Wyatt watched as the crippled, out-of-control vessel started to pass Boxer. He literally slid down the ladder into the cockpit, almost falling overboard himself. He grabbed a curled dock line and heaved one end to the other boat, screaming at the top of his lungs for the man to "Tie this off!"

By some miracle, the rope landed along the transom of the wayward boat, and the captain managed to see it. Wyatt immediately began wrapping the sizable line around his aft cleat as the looped coil unraveled.

Wyatt had just moved his hands out of the way when the rope snapped taunt. The fiberglass surrounding Boxer's cleat moaned and popped, but the line held the small cruiser, the tension pulling it so that Boxer's superstructure blocked some of the driving wind. Wyatt threw a second line to the captain. Once it was secured, Wyatt relaxed and tried to catch his breath. After a few deep inhalations, he yelled over, "How much water is she taking on?"

The other captain immediately began moving cockpit carpeting out of the way, and Wyatt watched as he lifted the engine hatch. After a few moments, he returned to the transom and yelled back, "She's taking a lot of water! The bilge pumps can't keep up. I can't get at the breach to stuff it with anything. She's going down."

Wyatt could see the bilge pump working, its efforts discharging a solid stream of water overboard. He could also tell the boat was becoming heavy in the back. It wouldn't be long before the water rose over the batteries and cut off the power to the bilge pump. Then she would sink quickly.

He held up one finger to the other man and lifted a seat cushion to access a storage area. Another blast of wind caused him to momentarily lose his balance, almost falling to the deck. It took a bit of digging, but he finally located a small bag containing an emergency pump. Boxer's previous owner had known his boats, or better yet, his emergencies. The kit contained a long battery cord and a hose of similar length. He held up the bag, motioning for the other boater to catch.

One for the money – two for the show – three underhand practices, and away she goes. The three pounds of pump, cord and hose flew, caught by the deft hands of the crippled boat's master. He looked inside, and quickly motioned a thumbs-up sign to Wyatt.

It took the man a few minutes to unwind the hose and plug in the emergency pump. Through the sheets of driving rain, Wyatt could see the engine hatches opened again, and then the exit-hose was propped over the edge of the vessel. He exhaled as a second stream of water joined the already hardworking built-in pump.

Wyatt waited a bit, and then yelled back at the man to start his undamaged engine in neutral, so as to keep the batteries fully charged. The fellow nodded and did just that, the reassuring hum of the motor barely audible over the howling wind.

After a few minutes, the captain checked the water level in the engine compartment again. He smiled at Wyatt and then shouted across, "The water has stopped rising. I think we are holding our own as long as the pumps hold out."

Morgan brought up a steaming cup of coffee from the galley, and it was a lifesaver. The two stood with their backs to Boxer's superstructure, a reasonable attempt at blocking the stinging rain. The hot liquid tasted great, the warmth spreading though Wyatt's freezing-wet torso.

The rain began to let up after an hour; the wind quickly followed suit. While the air temp had fallen into the 50s, the calmer breeze didn't chill the bones quite as badly. Visibility improved, and Wyatt started counting boats while keeping an eye on the crippled vessel behind him. He relaxed somewhat after verifying all were present and accounted for.

The sky remained gray and overcast, low clouds threatening to dump another deluge on the flotilla at any moment. Wyatt heard a new engine noise and looked up to see Todd and David coming over on a jet-ski, the small craft having weathered the storm tied to a nearby trawler. David was soaking wet as well, but forgot all about his discomfort after Wyatt explained what was going on with the crippled vessel behind them. "I'm going to have Todd take me over and see if I can help out," he said.

A few moments later, David was climbing aboard the damaged boat, the owner and he peeking down into the engine compartment while Todd circled nearby on the waverunner. Wyatt couldn't hear any of the conversation, but within minutes, he could see the captain rummaging around in the cockpit while David shooed Todd further away from the boat.

Before Wyatt or Morgan could voice their protest, David dove into the water and disappeared under the surface.

~  ~

The jolt of the cold water searing through his body surprised David, despite mentally preparing for the shock. The wetsuit he was wearing was designed to provide some insulation, but it sure didn't feel like it was working. He didn't have a mask, gloves or fins, but that shouldn't hamper things since he did plan on going to a great depth.

His first task was to locate the gash in the bottom of the hull. Judging by the force of the torrent of water insistently pushing its way topside, David figured this shouldn't be too difficult. He mentally inventoried the list of potential risks involved with the exploratory mission. First and foremost was avoiding the anchor line. Getting tangled up might trap him below the surface where he'd suffocate before being able to free himself. That potential death-trap was closely followed by the sharp edges of the functioning propeller. Lastly, he wanted to circumvent any damaged gear that might still be hanging beneath the vessel.

The process was agonizingly slow, having to feel his way with numb fingertips, along the curved hull of the boat. There was zero visibility in the chocolate-colored water. He hands rubbed along the smooth shell until he identified the opening. There was some good news – the damaged shaft was clear of the hull.

David kicked hard to swim out from under the boat and surfaced slowly so as not to strike his head on anything above. It was so easy to lose one's sense of direction while submerged in the black water. He popped up a few feet behind the swim platform and treaded water while taking a few deep breaths.

"Give me that sheet of plastic, and I'll stuff it in the hole. We can repair it from the inside as soon as the pumps remove the standing water."

The owner of the stricken vessel handed David a folded sheet of blue plastic tarp and then stared at the murky surface, as the young man took one last breath and disappeared under the water again.

Once more, David fingered the hull until he felt the rip. He unfolded the stuffing material and began tucking it into the breach as tightly as possible. He sealed as much of the gap as he could in a single breath and quickly resurfaced, lungs aching for air.

Allowing a few seconds for his body to readjust, David addressed the captain of the incapacitated vessel, "Okay, now give me the knife. I'm going to try and clear the line around the good shaft."

The older man paused, reflecting briefly on one of the most treacherous hazards of his own youth – having believed himself invincible, coupled with a complete lack of respect for the inherent limitations of the human body. In his experience, such a condition had often precipitated poor decisions. He shook his head at the brave man before him. "David, I'm not so sure about that. That's dangerous, son. If you get tangled up in the line, we might not be able to get you out before you drown. Are you sure?"

Something about the confident manner in which he spoke the words, "I got this," convinced even the jaded captain. A few additional lungs full of oxygen, and David was again surrounded by a black, silent world underneath the boat. He realized that additional precautions were required on this trip, as the sharp blades of the propellers could slice off a finger or sever a tendon. Despite his carefulness, David's knuckle found the prop first, the gash almost causing him to cry out in pain. He paused to recover his bearings for a moment, thinking about how screaming out while under water wasn't a bright idea.

Gently, he probed with his open hand until he knew the general locale of the razor-like edges. Finding the rope twisted around the propeller's shaft was easy. He fluttered his arms around until he found a loose end and began unwinding the cord. Before he could make much progress, it was again time for air.

On the fourth trip under the boat, he finally worked his way to the end of the line. He dropped the worthless rope to the bottom and felt all around the propeller's gear and rudder to make sure it was clear, resurfacing for the last time.

As David was pulled aboard the crippled cruiser, he informed the captain of what he'd discovered. One propeller and shaft was completely gone, probably lying on the bottom somewhere nearby. The other prop seemed undamaged. David was sure he'd removed all of the fouling line.

The captain and his crew were thrilled, not being able to thank David enough. His boat could still function on one propeller for the remainder of the trip after the leak was sealed.

~  ~

Wyatt and Morgan had forgotten all about being cold. Watching their son make what seemed like an endless number of dives under the crippled vessel was nerve-racking to say the least. When Sage appeared next to them in her swimming suit, her father unleashed his most demanding tone, "And just what do you think you're doing, young lady?"

"If he gets stuck under there, I'm going in after him."

Morgan started to protest, but Sage cut her off. "You can't stop me, Mom. I'm not going to just stand here and let my brother drown. Five summers pulling overconfident swimmers from the lake makes me the most qualified for the job."

When David finally scrambled onto the swim platform and signaled he was finished, everyone relaxed.

Wyatt looked at his wife and fairly beamed, "He's got a pair; I'll give him that. No way would I dive under a boat in this water. He must have gotten that recklessness from your side of the family."

Morgan playfully swatted her husband, "I'm not sure whether to say he's as brave as his father, or as hardheaded. Either way, you're not going to blame it on my DNA."

They both laughed, a release of stress that had built while watching their son risk his life. Before long, Todd brought David back across on the water bike. After climbing safely aboard Boxer, David thanked Todd and protectively observed as the teen spun the machine around and headed off to tie up on his parents' boat. Morgan was waiting with a towel.

David exhaled. "What a day. I was worried this was going to be a boring leave. Can you believe I was upset because I couldn't find a book to read while I was here? The army's easy compared to what you guys go through."

Wyatt patted his son on the back. David answered the gesture with a smile, and then added, "I need a hot shower and something to eat. I think I'll sleep pretty well tonight."

Sage perked up, wanting to contribute. "David, I'll take your watch tonight."

"Thanks, sis," and then noticing her marine attire, "So what's up with the suit? You looking for a fella out here?"

Sage flushed, "I was going to go in and get you - if you didn't come up."

David spread his arms and hugged his sister. It always gave Morgan and Wyatt a unique, warm feeling inside to see their children demonstrate love for each other. Wyatt often wondered if it wasn't some sort of parental relief - knowing that the kids could rely on each other after Morgan and he were gone.

Morgan made for the galley, trying to think of an evening meal that would go well with rattled nerves and queasy stomachs. Wyatt wandered to the bridge, wanting to check in with a few of the captains before sunset. The storm had caused a delay and now they were behind schedule. Wyatt sighed, thinking the schedule wasn't a big deal. *So far everyone is safe, and given the condition of the world right now, I think we're doing pretty well.*

~  ~

Buck cleared his throat and launched a mouthful of phlegm at the bay. His face was furled in a grimace as he turned away from the shoreline and hiked back to the campsite. The old, Ford pickup sat hunched down on her worn out suspension from the weight of the camper-shell. He strode to a cut-rate, green and white striped folding lawn chair and rested without concern for the frayed nylon strands hanging beneath.

He glanced at the small fire, making a mental note to have Robbie gather some more wood, even though it would be wet after the rain. He was thankful they had snatched a few logs and flung them in the truck before the storm hit. With the dry wood, they could still cook the trout and make the last of the coffee.

The windstorm had scattered his few earthly contents around the thicket, but it hadn't taken long to gather everything back up. His cousin and he only had one spare outfit each, and those had been hanging on a line after being washed in the bay. There had been time to put them away, but Buck thought a fresh water rinse would soften up the saltwater stiff shirt and pants. At least they didn't stink...as much.

The rain had really been a blessing. They had been evaporating salt water to drink, but the process was slow. When the storm appeared on the horizon, Robbie and he had scrambled to set out every makeshift cistern they could find to gather rainwater. The squall scattered most of the small bowls and containers, but a tarp strung between two trees withstood the gale, catching a respectable amount of potable water.

Buck sighed, scanning the landscape. *Now where did that simpleton run off to,* he thought. "Robbie?"

"Coming," sounded the voice from behind the truck.

Buck's cousin trudged around the back of the camper, annoyed at the interruption. Buck ignored the attitude and began needling the boy. "I'm sick of this whole thing, cuz. We've been stranded here almost two weeks, and I'm just tired of it. The fishing's lousy, and you snore like a lumberjack. We need to do something different."

Robbie protested, "I snore? Why you piece of crap...you're the one that scares off all the game around here."

Buck waved him off. "The snoring don't mean nothing, cuz. We're out of gas, out of food, and almost out of water. We need a change of scenery."

Robbie contemplated Buck's statement for a moment before asking, "Whatcha got in mind?"

Buck stood and hitched up his pants. He expelled another round of mucus, and then motioned to his cousin. "Follow me."

The two men returned to Buck's vantage point beside the bay. Buck pointed at the armada of boats now anchored less than a mile away.

Robbie's reaction was a long whistle, followed quickly by "When did they get there?"

"They must have made for Redfish to ride out the storm. They weren't there this morning. Must be close to 30 of 'em, and I bet they're all full of gas and food."

Robbie was never the brains of the outfit. "Now cuz, why would them folks give us a ride anywhere? They don't know us from Moses."

Buck's shoulders slumped a bit; his gaze turned to his feet, and he was shaking his head side to side in exasperation. His voice became low and serious. "I wasn't thinking about asking for a ride. I was thinking about taking one of them boats for ourselves."

Robbie's head snapped up, his eyes wide open. He started to speak, but Buck held up his hand and said, "Now, hear me out."

Robbie tilted his head to the side, skepticism written all over his face.

"Lookie, cuz, the world ain't coming back. At least not for one hell of a long time it ain't. I've been out of work for months, and since the layoff, all you could find was a job running the cash register and cleaning the restrooms at the gas station. That barely keeps you in chaw. If I hadn't poached that doe a few weeks back, we'd be going hungry. Am I right?"

Robbie's expression mellowed a little, but it was clear he wasn't sold on anything just yet. After a short pause, he finally nodded, giving his cousin the signal to continue.

"I broke the law then, Robbie. Wasn't nothing serious like, but I was still illegal and all. Sometimes a man has ta do what a man has ta do. Besides, I don't think there *is* any law anymore. I don't think there *is* any government. I think it's every man for his-own-self."

"Now what makes you think that? You don't know nothing more than I do for sure."

"Oh, is that so? Well let me ask you when was the last time you saw an airplane in the sky? When was the last time one of them big freighters went up or down the channel? Son, when was the last time you heard an engine running?"

Robbie rubbed his beard and thought for a bit. He surprised his cousin with a question. "Why don't we just see if they'll trade for something? Why go and stir things up?"

Buck shook his head, downplaying his cousin's idea. "And what, pray tell, do we have to trade? Some deer jerky? The lawn chairs? What do you propose we offer up?"

Robbie looked around the campsite like he was honestly trying to think of something. The effort was futile, but he didn't want to give it up. "I don't know – maybe they would want something other than fish. Maybe all's they've had for days is seafood. Maybe some deer jerky would be worth something to 'em."

Buck laughed at the man's weak effort. "Sure...sure Robbie. We'll row our little boat all the way out there and offer them up some squirrel hocks and dandelion greens in exchange for gasoline and beer. Works for me...."

Robbie pointed his finger at Buck, "Now don't go get'n all mean and such, Buck. I'm just trying to do my part and help think this thing through. There's more than one way to skin a cat, ya know."

Buck held up his hands and nodded silently, letting his cousin know he didn't mean it. "I'm sorry cuz; I'm just worried is all. I am worried we are going to be skinning that cat for food pretty soon. The fishing sucks, and we ain't seen nothing with fur on it for days."

Robbie couldn't disagree with that train of thought. His stomach had rumbled more the last two weeks than anytime he could ever remember. Besides, he was down to his last can of Skoal, and that wasn't good. "I'm listening, cousin. You go ahead and tell me what you've got in mind."

Buck thought for a moment and then laid out his plan. "I say we row the boat out there after dark. I worked part-time down at the boatyard a few summers ago. Them big boats all have generators, so we'll be able to see their lights after dark. We'll take the rifles and climb aboard real quiet like. Whoever is on the boat, we'll put them in the row boat and then take off with our new prize."

Robbie mulled the plan over and then asked, "And where might we take our prize to?"

Buck smiled, already having thought of that. "We'll drive it over to Mud Creek. There's an old discarded boat ramp I know of over there. It's only about a mile from here. We can tie up the boat, hike back here and get the truck. We'll move our camp over there and use up whatever is aboard the boat. Why, if more people keep going up and down the bay, we might become pretty good pirates." Buck elbowed the simpleton in the ribs, all the while humming, "Yo, ho, ho and a bottle of rum."

Robbie snorted at Buck's lack of musical ability, but had to admit the plan sounded well thought out. He tried to imagine actually going through with it. "So what happens if we row out there, and they put up a fight? What if they start shooting?"

"Then we shoot back - plain and simple. We gotta have guts to do this, cuz. This ain't no high school prank. If we're going to the party, we gotta be ready to dance."

~  ~

Reed's fork toyed with the green beans, pushing them around subconsciously while deep in thought. The food at Fort Meade wasn't bad. Any of the government workers who mumbled a complaint were quickly reminded that over 300 million other people would probably give anything for the canned veggies and frozen chicken being served. The remark typically turned elite-sounding complaints into short tinges of guilt. In reality, Reed was surprised at the non-partisan manner in which all of his colleagues were acting.

A slight shadow interrupted the overhead fluorescent lights, causing Reed to glance up from his plate. It was Senator Conley carrying a tray of food. "Mind if I join you, young man?"

"Why no, Senator, please do."

The elder statesman from Ohio sat his meal on the table across from Reed and managed the bench seat without complaint. Carefully draping the paper napkin on his lap, the senator scrutinized the contents of his plate for a moment before speaking. "It just dawned on me why this reminds me of army food. That's because it is army food. You can tell what day it is by what they put on your plate, and most days you're glad to get it."

Reed chuckled politely at the comment. He consumed a fork full of beans and studied the older man. The honorable gentleman from Columbus, Ohio had been a common figure in American politics for over 30 years. His face was well known, having been beamed into American living rooms on a regular basis during his five terms of office.

As a freshman congressman, Reed had experienced little exposure to the real power players in the nation's capital. Now, one of them was sitting across from him, eating frozen chicken and drinking milk from a carton like a schoolboy.

"Have you had any contact with your family, son?"

"Yes, sir, I've had a single phone call over a military channel and two written letters exchanged. They are doing as well as can be expected."

The senator nodded and continued to eat. Reed thought the man must have skipped a few meals because he was digging in with considerable gusto. Conley sensed he was being watched. "You'll have to excuse my lack of dinner conversation today. I've been in committee meetings all day and didn't get lunch. We are supposed to reconvene in ten minutes, and I don't want to disrupt the proceedings with my stomach rumbling."

Reed smiled at the remark. "No worries, Senator. I wouldn't want to be accused of denying a ranking democrat his substance."

Conley's smile was genuine. "I wouldn't have been caught dead having lunch with a junior Republican representative a few weeks ago. It wouldn't have helped your career either. People would have wondered why you were fraternizing with the enemy. Now neither I, nor anyone else here cares."

Congressman Wallace had to agree with the senator's assessment. He was actually proud of how everyone here had been working so hard to solve problems in an attempt to get the country moving again. Gone were any disputes between right and left. Egos and platforms had truly been set aside because the country was in trouble – real trouble.

The senator swallowed a sip of milk and said, "Didn't your father work at the Federal Reserve Board, Mr. Wallace?"

"Yes, Senator, that's correct."

"If memory serves, he died in a robbery some years ago."

Reed hesitated, a flood of different answers filling his mind. Despite knowing better, he couldn't suppress his response. "Officially, yes, it was a robbery. Personally, I've always had serious doubts about the incident."

The response seemed to trouble the senator from Ohio. A fleeting glimpse of annoyance crossed the man's face. The emotion passed so fast that Reed couldn't be sure he was reading it right.

"I'm sorry to hear that, Mr. Wallace. It must be a difficult thing to live with…the not being sure, I mean."

Senator Conley continued with his meal, Reed believing the topic was exhausted. He was wrong.

"My brother-in-law worked for the Fed in those days, Congressman. I'm curious, what do you believe happened to your father?"

The question sent Reed's sixth sense to high alert, the senator's approach and conversation now entering the realm of suspicious. Pretending to having trouble swallowing, the Texan bought some time to compose his answer.

"There were a number of inconsistencies with the final police report, Senator. In addition, new information about the case has recently come to light. Why do you ask?"

Conley was a master politician and had no trouble waving off Reed's inquiry. "No reason, Congressman. I was just trying to make conversation. I'm sorry if I broached a sensitive subject."

"No problem, sir. It's not a sensitive topic at all. I just thought it unusual lunch conversation."

The two men continued with their meal in silence. Conley signaled he was done by wiping his face with the napkin, wadding the paper into a proper ball, and depositing it on his tray. As he stirred to stand, he said, "Nice meeting you, Mr. Wallace. I promise to keep my dialog a little lighter next time. Good day, sir."

Reed smiled as the man rose. "Good day, Senator."

Conley picked up his tray and turned to walk away. To Reed's astonishment, the man paused and then spun back. "If I may, Mr. Wallace…a little advice from and old-democrat-dog to a young-republican-pup. Don't allow your official actions to be driven by any personal agenda. It will taint your term and poison your service to our great nation. I'm telling you this because I hear you're a bright young man who truly cares about his country. I'd give anyone the exact same advice."

Without waiting on any response, the senator left, greeting someone at each table on his way out.

Reed immediately replayed and analyzed the entire conversation. The discussion could have been what it appeared on the surface – a casual discussion between two elected officials. On the other hand, Conley might have been issuing a friendly warning. Was he trying to say, "We know what you're up to, don't even think of trying anything?"

God, you're paranoid, he thought.

The whole exchange put Reed into a funk. As if he didn't have enough to worry about, now the senator's words added another layer to his fog. He'd been struggling to keep his chin up and remain functional as it were. He'd even considered visiting the base chaplain and having a conversation about depression.

Just as he was beginning to feel like things might improve, the man from Ohio had thrown a proverbial wrench into his gears. Reed was just realizing his melancholy state wasn't entirely attributable to missing his family. His internal strife was based on the struggle to set aside what had been his primary motivation during the last few years of his life – the mission to find out what had really happened to his father. Now, the collapse of society demanded he put those private concerns behind him and work for the good of the people. He was struggling to accept that change.

The Texan supposed he wasn't the only one battling an internal struggle. The national crisis impacted everyone a little differently. Some of those he worked with had lost family members in the riots, while others had loved ones who were missing, the military unable to account for their whereabouts or status. Many people knew for certain that their homes had been destroyed. It seemed like everybody had a different worry, loss or concern.

Reed chewed another bite of chicken, realizing the man that had shared a table with him was causing a flood of guilt to wash over him. *He's right of course. I should be that focused*, he thought. *I shouldn't be worried about anything other than putting the country back together again.*

Everyone at the makeshift capital realized the citizens were hurting. The elected leadership of the country was doing everything in its power to repair, resolve and organize. *All the folks here are pulling together to utilize their strengths to contribute except me*, thought Reed. *I need to get onboard and push down this selfish desire for revenge,* he resolved.

~ ~

Sage yawned and pulled the blanket tighter over her shoulders. The northern gusts carried an arctic bite into the normally humid region of Texas. Her iPod was plugged into the cigarette lighter on the bridge, but she had turned off the device, feeling like her ears were becoming fatigued. The only audible melody playing now was the orchestra of groaning anchor lines and the random splashing of a fish striking the surface of the bay. Most of the boats were running generators, but the dull, constant drone of the machines faded into a constant background hum – a kind of white noise – so relaxing it was coaxing her eyelids to close.

Before he had gone to bed, her dad had told her to wake him up if she got too sleepy. "Pulling anchor watch is about as boring as it gets. If you get tired, don't hesitate to wake me up. I'd prefer to lose sleep versus lose the boat," he advised.

Being the youngest, she had always felt like she didn't contribute as much as everyone else. It seemed like she was always too slow or too weak to help out in any meaningful way. David was always so big and strong and fast. She loved her brother, but for years had secretly wished he would mess up at least once. Living in the shadow of perfection wasn't easy. Tonight, she would pull her weight and do it flawlessly – no matter how mind numbing it was.

Besides, Sage was troubled about her dad. His life had been hell the last year. And every time she saw him, she seemed to notice another visible sign of accelerated aging – greying at the temples, a few more wrinkles here and there, an apathetic gait. For a while, when the business was failing, her heart jumped into her throat when mom called unexpectedly. Sage was sure Wyatt was going to have a heart attack or worse yet, take his own life. Tonight, she could let him rest.

Time to do the checklist, she thought.

She glanced at the radar screen mounted on the dash. The glowing display was the size of a small television. Unlike its stereotypical depiction in old war movies, there wasn't a sweeping arm circling from a central point or nested rings indicating distance from the epicenter. Sage saw a picture that looked similar to a paper chart, where the white background coincided with the water, and land was colored grass-green. She could zoom the picture in and out, her father explaining that a five-mile range was optimum.

The radar served as an electronic watchman as well. The device contained a function called a collision avoidance alarm that sounded an alert if another vessel were on a course to collide with Boxer. Sage knew the alarm was set, but her father had warned her it wasn't flawless. "It will only start beeping if its computer brain is certain. It helps, but you can't trust it."

The boats around Boxer showed as blue dots on the radar. At the five-mile range, the Marinaville fleet appeared as a blob around the middle of the map.

Sage's real job was to make sure an anchor didn't pull loose during the night. That anchor could be Boxer's or any of the other boat's. One vessel could drift into another if it lost its grip on the bottom. Floating onto an oyster reef or one of the well platforms that dotted the bay were other possible hazards.

The lower right-hand corner of the radar screen had two big numbers – Boxer's longitude and latitude. Those values were Sage's charge; slight fluctuations could mean the anchor was dragging. The numbers hadn't changed.

More for entertainment than duty, her dad had left the night vision on the bridge. "If you get really bored, look at the stars through the night vision," he had advised. "They didn't name it a starlight scope for nothing." Tonight, however, the clouds weren't going to allow any stargazing. Sage had toyed with the scope a little, sweeping her gaze over the bay, picking out the other boats and some seabirds standing on Redfish.

She had also spied on her fellow watchmen. Three of the bigger boats had someone keeping an eye on the anchors. The larger vessels had been chosen for the task due to their having more folks aboard who were better able to share the duty, plus their hulls rose higher off the water, allowing for a better vantage.

Sage was pretty sure one of the other lookouts was napping. Until about an hour ago, the man had lit his pipe every 30 minutes like clockwork. She hadn't seen the flash of his lighter for over an hour now. She couldn't see the other sentry on watch from Boxer's bridge. At one point in time, she had been tempted to call out on the radio just to have someone to share her solitude, but had decided against it. The noise might wake up her father or brother and that would taint her contribution.

While Sage was inspecting the huddled boats, she didn't notice a new blue dot appear on the radar screen. This dot wasn't close to the fleet, but hugging the shoreline a mile away. Boxer's radar detected the new presence for a moment, and then it was gone. A few minutes later, it found it again, but then it disappeared. *No matter*, decided the radar logic circuits, *the new contact wasn't headed directly in, nor was it going fast enough to worry about.*

~  ~

Buck was beginning to think his idea wasn't so hot, but his ego wasn't about to allow any public admission of flawed planning. Robbie and he had pushed their little 16-foot aluminum skiff into the bay an hour ago. The flat-bottomed Johnboat wasn't designed for the oceangoing experience, but rather for calmer lakes and rivers where waves and currents weren't such a factor. Their boat didn't like even the light chop on the bay and made them pay for the trip with a rough, jolting ride.

To make matters worse, the small outboard motor had been left ashore. The last of the gas had been used a few days ago trying to get to more productive fishing grounds. Tonight, it was human oar power propelling them across the water, and that was a poor substitute.

Buck sat in the front of the rowboat all smug and satisfied because he had outmaneuvered his cousin with regards to who was going to man the oars. Robbie had fallen for the same old trick of "You go first, and I'll take over in a bit." There was no way the two men could switch positions without tipping over the small boat. Buck looked forward to the time when Robbie finally realized he had been had. Hopefully, they wouldn't be rowing back.

As they tentatively navigated from the shoreline, Buck realized it was going to take longer to reach the anchored boats than he had thought. The wind kept blowing them off course, and Robbie wasn't exactly an Olympic class sculler.

Buck grunted and half-turned to Robbie, "Those dumbasses, they all have on their anchor lights like is required by the law. Haven't they noticed there ain't no other boats around? What are they worried about – the coast guard?"

Robbie peered around his passenger, nodding at the white twinkling lights in front of them. "They look like Christmas lights, cuz…. I sure do hope they know it's better to give than receive."

After what seemed like half the night, the interlopers were finally close enough to make out individual boats. Buck signaled that Robbie should take a break, and then leaned back and whispered, "We need to pick one out - one of the big ones on this side."

"I don't care which one you pick, cuz. Just make sure it's one that's close, cause my arms are about to fall off."

Buck nodded and swiveled on the bench to gain a better perspective of the fleet. He wanted to choose the largest possible boat because it would have the most supplies onboard, and probably the biggest fuel tanks. He wished there was a way to tell which ones were diesel and which were powered by gasoline, but that was just a chance he would have to take.

Finally, he spotted one on their side of the formation. He pointed it out to Robbie and whispered, "Let's get this over with, cuz."

Robbie began rowing a little faster than before, adrenaline kicking in over the anticipated heist. Buck reached for his shotgun.

~  ~

Movement caught Sage's eye as the small craft steered from behind the big catamaran anchored a few boats over. Her first thought was the small launch was from one of the other members of the fleet, but the rowboat was too big for any of them to carry as a dinghy. She picked up the night vision, studying the two men as their paddling brought them closer to Boxer. She could make out enough detail to realize they were strangers. *What the heck were they doing out in the middle of the bay at 3 in the morning?*

Her next line of reasoning concluded they were fishermen. She had watched her dad and brother leave at all kinds of crazy hours in order to catch fish. These two were just a couple of fishermen from the shore who were out for a day's catch. Satisfied she had figured it out, she leaned back in the captain's chair as the men rowed closer and closer to the anchored flotilla. When the guy in front reached around and pulled up a big gun, Sage doubted her original hypothesis. When the small boat clearly made a turn for Boxer, she became frightened.

Sage's mind raced with all kinds of options. They were tired and just wanted to tie off on Boxer, perhaps needing to rest for a bit. They were having an emergency...maybe their boat was leaking or something. Maybe they were from one of the other boats, and she just didn't recognize them. While she tried to justify whom and what they were, the small rowboat made directly for Boxer's stern.

By the time she snapped out of it, the approaching vessel was too close for her to slide down the ladder and reach the cabin. She was hiding behind the captain's chair, peering over the top, sure the two men had not seen her yet. She thought about yelling out and stomping on the floor to wake everyone up, but the man in the front of the boat was now pointing the shotgun toward Boxer, and she froze, certain the guy was going to shoot her.

Panic tore through Sage's chest when the boat stopped right behind Boxer's swim platform, one of the men grabbing onto the deck to stabilize their tiny craft. The man in front looped a line around one of Boxer's cleats, while the other set down his oar and picked up his own huge gun. Sage ducked even lower behind the chair and for some reason began rummaging around for something to throw at the men...maybe she could scare them off.

She opened a small storage hatch beside the helm and found one of Boxer's emergency kits. Inside the clear plastic box was something that caught her eye – a flare gun. Her dad had taught her how to use the bright orange pistol a long time ago. It was fairly simple, and she quickly pulled off the safety pin and rose up to get a clear view of the strangers below.

The first guy was now standing on Boxer's transom, steadying the small boat so his partner could get out. Sage pointed the armed flare pistol at the two men and screamed, "Get off our boat!"

The sound of the screeching voice made Buck jump, and he lost his grip on the rowboat at just the wrong time. Robbie, wobbly and rocking, tried to shift his weight to get balance, but was instead thrown overboard into the chilly waters. Buck watched his cousin fall, but was more concerned about whoever was yelling from aboard his prize. He turned, raising the shotgun.

Sage pulled the trigger. The hammer fell on the 12-gauge emergency flare, striking the primer and igniting the propellant. The red-burning magnesium rocket was designed to shoot several hundred feet into the air as an emergency signal. It left the short barrel and flew directly at Buck, striking him square in the chest.

Buck was stunned by the impact, which reminded him of being hit by a well-thrown baseball. He dropped his shotgun, watching in horror as it bounced off the deck and rattled into the water. The loss of the weapon enraged him beyond control. The bright flare ricocheted off his body and slammed into Boxer's deck, where it was pinned into a corner, fizzling and pulsating blinding light.

Sage immediately sprang for the ladder, desperately wanting off of the bridge and into the cabin. She slid down the steps and reached for the cabin door when a strong grip seized her from behind, tossing her to the deck like a rag doll.

Sage gazed into the meanest pair of eyes she had ever seen. The crimson glow from the burning flare caused the filthy, unshaven man hovering over her to look like a demon, staring down at her with the intent to consume her very soul. He raised his arm, and her heart stopped. He was grasping a long knife, its shiny steel blade reflecting like fire in the throbbing radiance from the flare. Every fiber of Sage's being focused on that dagger. As if watching a movie in slow motion, she detected the man's arm muscles tighten, and then the blade curved downward. Sage closed her eyes, waiting on the inevitable agony she knew was going to rack her body in less than a heartbeat.

The pain never arrived. Sage peeked up and noticed the knife almost exactly where it had been, but there was something new. Another hand was part of the image, firmly clutching the wrist of the dagger- bearing demon. She detected a shifting shadow behind her attacker and then watched puzzled as his eyes changed from an expression of pure hatred to one of surprise - and then pain.

David clasped the man's knife arm with both hands, squeezing with all his might on the wrist. He sidestepped and planted a vicious kick to the attacker's weight-bearing knee. The resulting sound was a grotesque chorus of breaking bone, popping ligaments and an animal-like howl escaping from the victim's throat. David's furry was unbridled, the desire to stop the man about to slaughter his sister becoming a bloodlust roaring through his veins. The tension in the arm holding the blade dissipated, allowing David to let go with one hand. Pulling the freed hand back, David's fist shot out with all of his rage, striking the attacker in the Adam's apple and throat. Again and again and again, David threw his considerable strength into the blows – rapid firing as fast as his arm could reset and strike.

Buck's last effort was more instinct than conscious thought. His brain commanded his body to twist away from the source of the searing pain that was abusing millions of nerve endings. The movement was more convulsive than controlled, yet still so violent it pulled the two men off balance. Both combatants became entangled with Sage's legs, the girl desperately trying to kick her away from the knife. David sensed he was falling and commanded his hand to keep its grip on the arm holding the blade. *Nothing else can hurt me*, he told himself as he plummeted toward the deck; *hold onto that knife no matter what.*

The two combatants landed with a thud on the fiberglass floor of the boat. David was on top, trying to regain his leverage and position for the next attack. He felt the man underneath him spasm once, twice, and then go limp. It took a second, but he quickly deduced what had happened. Just in case the man was faking, he cautiously shifted his weight and rose. There was the hilt of the knife, the blade completely buried in the man's sternum.

David couldn't take his eyes off of the weapon. He didn't notice Wyatt rushing out of the cabin, shotgun in hand, rushing to kick the flare overboard.

David never heard Morgan yell for his sister, nor did he see the two girls embrace in a desperate hug.

Wyatt stood above his son and the dead man, not sure what to do. "David...It's okay now, David.... come on, son.... It's okay."

In a trance, David regained his feet, his gaze never leaving the body lying on the deck. Wyatt wrapped his arm around his son, pulling him close. Wyatt noticed Morgan's flashlight beam focusing on the knife. "Morgan!" He whispered with emphasis. When his wife looked up, he shook his head as a signal to shine the light elsewhere.

Morgan realized what her husband meant, and with a flush in her cheeks hastily turned off the torch. This seemed to snap Sage from her silence. "Where's the other one?"

Wyatt's head snapped up at the question. "What other one? What do you mean?"

"There were two of them in the boat...I know there were. Where's the other man?"

Wyatt let loose of David and immediately headed to the back of the boat with the shotgun. Wyatt could not see anything but a small johnboat. He turned and grabbed Morgan's flashlight, using it to probe all around, but couldn't see anyone.

Sage's memory kicked in, replaying the horrible sequence of events. "I shot one of them with the flare gun. I think the flare hit the guy. There was a splash...a big one. I think the other man might have fallen out of the little boat."

"David, did you see another man?"

There was no answer. Instead, David moved to the side of the boat and began to vomit over the side. Morgan moved to comfort her son. "Sage, please go get a glass of water."

Wyatt climbed the bridge and retrieved the night vision. He scanned all around Boxer, again discovering nothing. He flipped a series of switches on the helm, and Boxer's deck was immediately flooded by several bright lights. Wyatt picked up the radio. "All boats, all boats...this is Boxer...we had some guys attempt to board us with guns. I believe one of the men fell overboard. We don't know if they were alone. There could be more pirates in the area."

Wyatt knew most of the boaters were asleep, but wanted to let the other lookouts know what was going on. Seven boats over, one of the lookouts must have come to the same conclusion. "Boxer, Boxer...I'm going to fire a warning shot to wake everyone up," crackled the radio. Shortly after the message, a loud boom echoed across the bay.

The gun blast did the trick. Throughout the fleet, lights illuminated the water, and the radio transmissions clogged the air.

~ ~

188

By dawn, all of the boaters had checked in – all were just fine except for a lack of sleep. A frantic search swept the area around Redfish, spotlights and flashlight beams probing the night. Robbie's body was never found.

Two different men approached Boxer in another dingy. They helped Wyatt lift the dead man into his rowboat and secured his body to the hull with rope. The shotgun found in the johnboat was added to the fleet's arsenal.

Wyatt pulled the drain plug in the bottom of the boarder's craft and gave it a good shove. It would take a bit, but the small vessel would eventually sink after filling with water.

Everyone stood and watched the floating tomb drift away into the rising sun as the current carried it toward the Gulf of Mexico.

Chapter 9

Washington, D.C.
March 5, 2017

The thin, typeset report landed on the otherwise clear desk with significant force. The president of the United States used his fingertips to rub small circles around his eyes. The exhausted man sighed and then focused on the four men standing in front of the oval office's historic desk.

"Gentlemen, I'm sure you all know what this report means."

The four subordinates muttered a collective chorus of "Yes, sir."

It was the chairman of the joint chiefs, the second highest-ranking military officer in the country, who spoke first. "Mr. President, that report leaves no doubt that the Chinese government has attacked our nation without provocation. It is an overt act of war, even though no shots were fired."

The president's chief of staff quickly chimed in, "I agree, Mr. President. The Red Chinese did so without regard for human life. We cannot let this act of aggression go unanswered."

The commander-in-chief stood and moved from behind the desk. He stopped, looking out the window lost in thought. After a few moments, he half turned his head. "I'm ready to hear recommendations, gentlemen. I'm sure all of you have strong feelings about how we should respond."

The Secretary of State wasted no time. "Mr. President, I strongly urge we carefully meter any response. It's my belief that we should make the facts known to the United Nations and our allies. I recommend we use all avenues of diplomacy and our nation's economic power to retaliate."

The admiral snorted at the suggestion, and wasn't embarrassed about it. "Our economic power? The United Nations? No offense, Mr. Secretary, but we don't have any economic power right now. The United Nations doesn't even have electricity as of this moment. What are they supposed to do? Throw our candles at the Chinese?"

The president interceded before the Sec-of-State could respond. "Admiral, I appreciate your position. What would *you* recommend?"

The question wasn't unanticipated. "Sir, normally, I would offer up a menu of military-based options. Unfortunately, I cannot do so at this time. Our cities are in turmoil, our supply chain is non-existent, and our forces are mobilizing to support our own territory and local law enforcement. Starting a shooting war right now isn't wise."

The president grimaced and shook his head in disbelief. "Are you saying that we are helpless, Admiral? Are you saying that the greatest military force on the planet has been beaten?"

The chairman didn't back down. "No, sir, I intended no such representation. Our territory is not at risk from invasion or military attack. Our national sovereignty isn't threatened at this time. What I *am* saying, Mr. President, is that our prolonged offensive capabilities are severely hampered until such time as we can restart America's manufacturing, distribution and logistics infrastructure. Without resupply, sir, we can't sustain any significant offensive operations."

It was the chief of staff's turn to address the military man. "Admiral, what do you anticipate the next move by our Asian friends will be?"

The admiral's initial answer to the question was a grunt. "If I were the Chinese, I wouldn't do anything. I would sit back and pour as much salt in our wound as possible. I would do so with financial moves and currency manipulation. They get stronger while at the same time making us weaker. In a way, sir, I envy their position right now."

The president turned back to the window again, clearly deep in thought. "Admiral, can we at least rattle our saber? Can we at least make them think we are going to hit them?"

Before the chairman could answer, the sec-of-state interrupted. "Sir, if I may. The British are barely hanging on. The same can be said of Japan and much of South America. Our allies in the Middle East will undoubtedly beg for a calm, measured response. The financial markets worldwide are in complete disarray. I advise caution in our reaction, sir. I believe it wise to consider the global ramifications of our next move."

The admiral's input surprised everyone. "He's right, you know. Mr. President, you can order six carrier battle groups to stream toward the South China Sea right now. We can start rotating long-range bomber flights on penetration vectors. The Chinese will see them - no doubt. We can move dozens of fighter aircraft to Japan and Guam. But I ask you to consider how the rest of the world will react."

Staring at nothing specific, the chief of staff added, "What will the American people think? How will *they* react?"

Frustration showed on the president's face. "We have to do something. We cannot let such an attack on our country go unanswered, gentlemen. My tendency is to have faith in the American people, not to underestimate them. Always before, when our country has been threatened, the people have pulled together. Right now, given what is happening all around the nation, I believe we need a catalyst to accomplish just that. I'm convinced that once the people know the facts, that a foreign power caused their suffering, it will act as a uniting force...a reason to rally around the flag."

The Pentagon's top man wasn't convinced. "Mr. President, I agree with the premise, but recommend caution with the timing. Let's get the country functioning again. Let our forces establish order and then basic services. The American people's support will be so much stronger if they are fed and have electricity. I can provide many more options if we know we can refuel our planes and feed our troops."

The secretary of homeland security nodded in agreement. "Mr. President, it's been just three weeks since the upheaval began. I'm already receiving reports of starvation along the eastern seaboard. Less than 10% of the country has electrical power. The transportation system is completely shut down. Hospitals are out of generator fuel and medications. Fires are burning out of control in eleven major metropolitan areas that we know of. Fewer and fewer first responders are reporting for duty. National Guard units are reporting higher and higher levels of non-reporting personnel..."

The president cut the man off. "Okay, okay...I get the picture, Mr. Secretary. I understand." The chief executive walked around to the front of his desk and calmly leaned on the corner. He studied each man squarely, his voice steady, "Gentlemen, we cannot let the Chinese, or the rest of the world for that matter, believe for one moment we are going to let this assault go unanswered. Each of you makes a valid point, but the final responsibility resides with me. While I don't like it, I'm willing to compromise. Admiral, surely we can at least begin to position assets where they will cause the Chinese to sweat a little?"

Thinking for a moment before responding, the senior military official said, "Yes, Mr. President, we can take some preliminary steps and begin to move forces to the region. I can move an armored brigade to South Korea, and we can reroute a few carrier groups to the Pacific."

The commander-in-chief smiled with pleasure. "Draw up the orders, Admiral; I'll sign them. I also want it understood that the vast majority of our military forces are to be used domestically. Let's see if we can manage to send a message to the Chinese and get back on our feet at the same time. We'll have our retribution after we make sure our people are secure."

~ ~

The city of Galveston, Texas possessed a long and colorful history – much of it involving corruption, skullduggery, and the darker attributes of mankind. As the Marinaville armada approached the Bolivar Roads, Wyatt got his first glimpse of the island city's skyline. The Moody Plaza high-rise tower was normally the first structure viewable on the horizon, but this afternoon it was columns of smoke and ash rising heavenward that landmarked the town. Clearly the citizens of Galveston had suffered yet another in a long string of hardships.

Houston was nothing more than a B-player in Texas during the early 19th century - Galveston being where the action was. Once a booming coastal port, the businessmen and longshoremen who ran the city had become greedy and corrupt. The situation had gotten so out of hand, a far less desirable and clearly inaccessible docking facility gained favor with many of the Lone Star state's reputable businessmen. Fifty miles inland and to the north, Houston's port facility should have never existed, but graft drove visitors away from the Galveston Island's natural deep-water harbor.

Over the years, Houston grew and prospered while Galveston struggled - the hurricane of 1900 all but eliminating any hope of reestablishing the town's prominence. Still distinguished as the greatest natural disaster in the history of the United States, an estimated 7,000 people perished in the storm.

During the prohibition years, prostitution, gambling, and speakeasies were openly known to exist in Galveston. The citizens of the island supported the illicit activities which translated into the burg becoming a very popular tourist destination. Wyatt grunted thinking about those wild times on the island, it must of have been the Las Vegas of its day. *What should anyone expect*, he thought, *the place was founded by a pirate*.

The fleet had no intention of steering anywhere near the island today. During normal times, boaters from Clearlake commonly motored the 28 miles south, in search of a location to dock and enjoy some of the finer seafood restaurants along the east end. No such dining excursions were in order today. After the pirate attack early this morning, avoiding people was a high priority on everyone's list.

As the group of boats plied south through the bay, they passed the site of another historic disaster, this one manmade. To the southwest, Wyatt could discern cranes looming over the port of Texas City. In 1947, while the small town was enjoying the post-war economic boom, an explosion there killed over 500 people and injured thousands more. A German freighter loaded with fertilizer exploded with such force its anchor was recovered several miles away. The event caused two nearby ships, both full of the same ammonia nitrate, to catch fire and then detonate. This second set of atmospheric eruptions completely wiped out the first responders heading in to fight the flames. The people of Galveston, 14 miles away, were knocked to their knees by the blast wave.

That catastrophic event and the subsequent recovery resulted in the small community referring to itself as "the town that refused to die." Wyatt hoped the same resolve that had sustained the citizens of yesterday worked as well for the current populace.

The flotilla was approaching the Bolivar Roads, one of the busiest intersections of commercial marine traffic in the world. At this spot, the Houston Ship Channel, the Intracoastal Waterway, and the Texas City Channel all met in what amounted to a Times Square-like interchange of water-borne tonnage. Normally, Wyatt and the rest of the skippers in the fleet would be on high alert in this area, but not today. Probably more than anything he had witnessed so far, the lack of super-tankers, football-field-sized container vessels, and oceangoing tugs made it clear how bad the situation was. The radar showed the roads were completely void of any traffic.

To anything other than a large commercial vessel heading southwest out of Houston, there was what amounted to a fork in the road ahead. Galveston Bay essentially ended leaving two choices – west along the Intracoastal Waterway or east to the open waters of the Gulf of Mexico.

The Intracoastal, or "The Ditch" as it is commonly called, is a manmade channel of water that winds its way from Brownsville, Texas all the way along the United States coastline, eventually reaching New Jersey. In the early 1900s, construction began on the system that eventually resulted in a maritime superhighway. A system of dredged channels connected the country's natural bays, lakes, and rivers, providing one of the longest protected passageways in the world. The system was designed so commercial traffic could avoid the dangers of open ocean transport. It was possible to float from the Mexican border all the way to upper eastern seaboard without navigating into the open, often dangerous waters of the Atlantic Ocean or Gulf of Mexico.

Normally, the fleet of smaller boats from Marinaville would have chosen The Ditch for its protection. It had been decided that avoiding the Intracoastal was the lesser of two evils, and the group would head offshore and into the Gulf for this leg of the journey. Wyatt recalled the intense discussion over this choice. Going offshore was a risk. The rambunctious waves of the gulf could make the transit rocky for hefty vessels, let alone the least seaworthy of their group.

On the other hand, several sections of the Intracoastal were lined with housing developments and communities along the banks. The boats would be easy prey for anyone wanting to cause a problem from shore. The Brazos River locks posed an insurmountable challenge and so determined the course of the flotilla. Without electrical power, the mechanism wouldn't be operational, and there was no way of knowing if the locks would be open or closed.

One of the primary concerns with going offshore was the sailboats. These vessels weren't built for speed. Their hull design was such that they could maneuver and maintain course at a slower pace. Powerboats posed an entirely different, but equally threatening challenge. Most of these smaller vessels were much, much faster, but couldn't steer nearly as well at low speeds. Even in moderately rough water, these smaller boats needed to maintain twice the speed as their wind-powered cousins to keep their bows pointed in the right direction and ride the waves properly. Keeping everyone together might be a serious problem.

After the fleet crossed the Bolivar Roads, they began the turn southeast, heading for the gulf. As Boxer rounded the bend, Wyatt was stunned at the scene that appeared off the bow. Boxer's path was blocked by dozens and dozens of anchored ships. For as far as his eyes could see, a congestion of freighters, tankers, and cargo vessels crowded the Galveston entry channel, the line of ships stretching far out into the gulf.

The radio instantly came to life with an indecipherable gargle of hails.

Wyatt glared at the radio with a confused expression, not recognizing any of the voices. It took a few minutes, but finally the broadcast traffic settled down, and one voice came through. "Pleasure boats in Galveston Channel, this is the Estes Marie. I repeat, pleasure boats exiting Galveston Channel, this is the Estes Marie. We are anchored off of your starboard bow and are in desperate need of assistance. We have a medical emergency. We are out of food and cannot raise anyone on land. Please respond – over."

No sooner than that message had made it through, the frequencies were again flooded with garbled traffic from several of the ships. Wyatt could isolate a few calls for assistance, another request of ferry service to the shore, and one offer to barter. All of the radio operators scrambled for airtime - talking over each other - and it was nearly impossible to untangle the mass of chatter.

Movement caught Wyatt's eye as a slender and sleek speedboat suddenly roared out of Galveston, its course on an intercept for the Marinaville boats. Wyatt hit the intercom button next to the radio and commanded, "Morgan, I need David up here right away."

A few moments later, David's head appeared at the top of the ladder. "What's up, Dad?" His question was quickly punctuated by a distinct wolf whistle. "Wow...look at all those ships," he remarked, admiringly, as he took in the surroundings.

Wyatt nodded toward the approaching speedboat, now close enough to determine four men toting rifles, riding in the craft.

"Oh, crap," was David's response, and he disappeared to fetch his own firearm. Wyatt slowed Boxer, hoping some of the other friendly boats would catch up. They would need reinforcements if there were going to be trouble.

The speedboat came alongside Boxer, staying out about 100 feet. One of the men held up a handmade sign that read, "RADIO – 4."

Wyatt acknowledged the sign, flashing a curt nod toward the bobbing craft, and switched to channel four on the VHF. A gravelly voice spoke through the speaker. "Stay away from our ships, buddy...unless you want trouble."

Without thinking, Wyatt keyed the mic and responded, "Your ships? I'm not sure what you mean."

"These ships out here belong to us. We're handling all of the business with them. We ain't going to have anyone nosing in on our territory."

Wyatt shook his head, still not quite comprehending what the guy meant. Two of the fleet's boats were catching up now, each one brandishing a shooter. *This is turning into some sort of waterborne showdown at the O.K. corral.*

After a moment, Wyatt responded. "We are just passing through, friend. We don't want any trouble," and then cursed himself for the B-grade Western movie response.

The answer seemed to cause a debate on the speedboat. Wyatt could see from the body language that there was disagreement among the crew. David's voice sounded from the deck below. "Dad, I see two more boats full of armed men heading toward us. I think these guys have called for reinforcements."

A few moments later, "Dad, we need to either get out of here, or let me sink these guys. We are going to be way outnumbered in less than a minute."

Wyatt weighed the options while scrutinizing the four men. Their gestures were very animated, waving arms and pointing fingers. Wyatt didn't believe they had spotted David just yet. The other robber-boats were coming closer; he had to do something.

Picking up the radio mic, he switched to the fleet's channel and announced, "Everyone go around Boxer and hurry...full speed...we'll hold these guys off."

Wyatt looked down into the cockpit. "David, go tell your mom and sister to lay flat on the floor." He watched as his son's eyes flashed large with realization. David nodded, immediately turning to the cabin door and delivering the message.

The Marinaville boats started passing by Boxer, going to full throttle as soon as they were clear. Wyatt turned the radio back to channel four and announced into the microphone, "Hey, you guys still on this channel?"

The response came quickly, "Yeah. What do you want?"

"What I want is for you to back off and send those other boats away. We only want to pass through. I'm getting tired of watching you guys argue."

"We're trying to decide if we want your boats, too. I wouldn't be getting up in anybody's face if I were you, bud."

Wyatt held the radio down to his side and exhaled. *I don't want this*, he thought. *I wish there was another way.*

Taking a deep breath, Wyatt's voice was so calm; he didn't recognize it as his own. "David, shoot out their engines."

David fired the first shot a few seconds later. It was the signal Wyatt was waiting for. He pushed the throttles forward for full power while turning the steering wheel at the same time. David's first round took the crew of the small boat by surprise. Before they could recover, Boxer was barreling down directly at them, gaining speed. Round after round flew at the small boat. Small geysers of water erupted into the air around the hull of the pirate's vessel, soon followed by sparks flaring from the hood of its outboard motor. David was adjusting his aim, his bullets now hitting the mark.

Boxer covered the distance in a few moments, her massive bow bearing down at almost 12 knots. Men started jumping overboard, motivated by Boxer's clear intent to ram their tiny craft. At the last second, Wyatt swung the wheel hard, barely missing a collision. That first boat wasn't his main concern. He was more concerned over the two new vessels and holding them off until the rest of the fleet could get by.

David shifted his fire toward the next enemy craft, small splashes of water rising in front of the rapidly approaching threat. Wyatt saw small flashes of light blinking on the oncoming craft and instinctively ducked low behind the dash – they were shooting at Boxer. The cracking-thump of a round impacting a few feet from Wyatt confirmed the nightmare. The bullet punched a small hole in the fiberglass bulkhead of the bridge, missing critical helm components by mere inches.

Boxer was rolling at full speed now, her 45,000 pounds plowing through the sea and leaving a huge V-shaped trough of water in her wake.

As best as Wyatt could, he tried to ram the first boat, but it was far too nimble and easily veered away. What it couldn't escape was Boxer's stern wake, a six-foot high wall of fast-moving water. The driver hit it at a bad angle, causing the attacking vessel to ramp high into the air. Wyatt watched as the airborne boat rose over the crest of Boxer's stern-wave, gradually turning on its side. The boat-turned-aircraft slammed down into the water, the jarring impact throwing all aboard into disarray. The landing was so violent, the driver instinctively slowed his boat down, providing the window David needed.

The twin outboards began receiving lead as David's barking rifle poured round after round into the motors. The outboard closest to Boxer caught fire, initiating even more scrambling by the already confused crew. Men were climbing all over each other in an effort to escape David's withering hail of bullets and find the vessel's fire extinguisher.

The skipper of the third boat saw what was happening to his predecessors and decided to turn around, engines wailing as it sped off, back toward Galveston.

Wyatt swung Boxer around in a wide arch and slowed the big yacht down. He yelled for David to check on the girls while he remained on vigil, watching as the Marinaville boats scuttled past. It would be a few minutes before the last of the armada was safely headed out to the gulf.

Father and son gazed from the bridge as the men from the burning attack boat began swimming, kicking hard for the nearby rock jetties. Finally, David broke the silence. "Dad, I gotta hand it to you - *that* took a rather large pair of nads."

Wyatt held up a trembling hand for his son to see. "Right now, I don't feel so brave. I have no idea why I just did that. Seemed like the right thing to do – I guess."

Morgan and Sage appeared from below, shaken, but okay. The crew of Boxer had just finished exchanging a round of hugs when the last of the fleet streamed past.

~  ~

Boxer hung back from the long line of Marinaville boats heading out into the gulf. Progress was slow in order to avoid the obstacle course of anchored ships occupying the narrow passage. The route was bordered on both sides by the Galveston Jetties. The 800-foot wide space between the protective walls of concrete and rock was congested not only with ships, but also their long anchor scope of chain and steel cable.

The jetties stretched for over 35,000 feet into the open waters of the gulf. Boxer was just closing the gap when the first of the fleet's vessels reached the end of the breakwaters and entered the open, unprotected waters beyond. The captain of the lead cruiser didn't report good news. "We have 5 to 6- foot seas out here. They're rolling in pretty strong. I'm not so sure this is a good idea."

The captain of the second boat in line quickly chimed in. "Ouch! This is going to be one very rough ride. Is there any alternative?"

Wyatt's family, gathered on the bridge heard him grumble. "We can't seem to catch a break. What are we going to do now? Those guys from Galveston are going to come back with a bunch of buddies if we anchor. Unless we go back up the bay, I don't see any way to wait for calmer seas. We only have enough fuel to do that once or twice. Talk about a rock and a hard place."

Six-foot waves weren't normally associated with shipwrecks, and all of the vessels in the armada were designed to handle them under normal operating conditions. There was an old saying among boaters – the boat will handle more than you will. Six-footers would pound the smaller boats to death. At good speed, this trip required almost four hours of offshore travel. The high seas would lengthen that time considerably. In addition to the crews having their dental fillings jarred loose, there were other ramifications to a rough water passage.

In rough seas, things broke more often. Wiring bounced loose, hoses popped off, and machinery gave out. There wasn't a single skipper in the fleet that wanted to spend an hour in six-foot rollers. In addition, all of the boats were loaded with hundreds of pounds of extra supplies. Having a twenty-pound box of canned food acting like a pinball inside of the cabin was a recipe for someone or something being damaged.

The lead boats were circling at the end of the jetties, waiting on the rest of the line. Several of the captains were discussing the situation as Boxer approached. Their conversation was interrupted by a new voice crackling over the radio. "Pleasure boats at the mouth of the Galveston jetties, this is the Diego Maru; my ship can offer shelter on our leeward side. We would also like to discuss a trade."

Wyatt's eyebrows lifted, and he drew David in close. "Now there's an idea. One of the massive tankers could protect us from the waves until things calmed down. I wonder what they want to trade."

David shrugged his shoulders. "Ask 'em."

Wyatt picked up the radio mic. "Diego Maru, this is Boxer. Go on, Captain, what do you have in mind?"

"Boxer, we are a Suez-Max class tanker of 290 meters in length. We are anchored two miles off the jetties. I'm watching your group right now. I can offer a place to tie up, my hull providing shelter. I also have diesel fuel aplenty, and would consider bartering."

David whistled, "Wow, 290 meters is a lot of ship. That's bigger than all of Redfish."

Wyatt radioed the other boats, "Captains, what do we have to lose? Anybody have a problem with nestling up to big brother until things settle down?"

No one voiced any objection. Twenty minutes later, the fleet approached the giant ship - and a giant she was. Just over three football fields in length and standing almost 10 stories high, the Diego Maru was a floating mountain of a vessel. Even the short, two-mile ride out to the tanker had banged and thumped all of the smaller boats. As soon as the vessels starting pulling alongside the tanker, the water's surface became almost flat.

Boxer approached what appeared to be a solid, endless wall of steel. The black hull of Diego Maru seemed to rise straight out of the water and disappear into the sky. Wyatt felt odd being so close to something so massive. Normally, when these huge carriers were underway, pleasure boats avoided them like a mouse avoids a stampeding elephant. New boaters are warned over and over again that the huge ships can't stop or turn. If your little fiberglass hull gets in the way, it will be crushed by the bow and whittled to toothpick-sized bits by the truck-sized propellers. It's a visualized lesson that doesn't often have to be repeated.

From somewhere above, giant dock lines were lowered. These ropes were as thick as Wyatt's leg, but provided a secure point for all of the pleasure boats to tie on. A quick exchange of radio messages resulted in the captain of the supertanker agreeing to visit Boxer. Wyatt radioed for one of the jet-skis to pick up the hitchhiking shipmaster. Before long, a single man lowered himself via the steel ladder bolted to the side of the large vessel's hull. After a descent of several minutes, the man managed to climb aboard the Jet-Ski, and before long a passenger was aboard Boxer.

The captain of the Diego Maru was much younger than Wyatt had imagined. In his late 30s, Captain Roland Ripple was dressed in deck shoes, khaki pants, and a bright yellow polo shirt. He sported a trim, short beard and wore a baseball hat with the logo and name of his ship underneath the embroidered title of "CAPTAIN." Wyatt liked the man immediately.

As Captain Ripple was introduced to Wyatt's family, he bowed slightly at the waist and shook everyone's hand in turn. When he finally reached Wyatt, the man addressed Boxer's master as "Captain," a sign of respect.

Morgan fussed over their guest, offering something to drink and eat. A glass of water was accepted and everyone sat down to talk.

"Do you have any news of what is happening? We came through the Panama Canal 21 days ago. Since arriving here, I can't raise the harbormaster or my owners on the phone. The shortwave is dead. Other than the rest of these ships here, we don't have any source of information - no satellite television or phone."

Wyatt relayed what he knew, which wasn't much. When he described the conditions onshore, Captain Ripple's eyes conveyed a solemn, almost sad understanding. "I'd pretty much assumed there was some sort of collapse or attack."

Morgan asked, "What about your crew? Is everyone all right?"

Captain Ripple nodded, adding, "We're lucky. We have a top quality sick bay and well-trained medics onboard. Most of these other vessels here are short-range haulers with limited resources. We are fully equipped and stocked for weeks. It won't last forever, but right now I've only cut back on rations for a few items."

Sage was calculating the number of heads peering over the tanker's rail above Boxer. "How many crewmen does it take to run a big ship like this?"

"We have a total crew of 28. My seamen and officers hail from 11 different countries. I'm sure several of them are observing us right now."

Morgan cleared her throat and asked, "Are we the first people from shore you've seen?"

The captain shook his head, "No. About ten days ago, a small boat approached and hailed us, indicating they wanted to trade. They tried to rob us, but my men kept them away by blasting them with our fire hoses."

Wyatt grimaced, "I think we met your friends a little while ago. They weren't very welcoming."

Captain Ripple nodded. "I was listening to the play-by-play on the radio. You did a lot of people a favor. Those guys were pure thugs, career criminals. They've been extorting most of the vessels anchored here for several days now."

David glanced at Wyatt, smiled and shook his head, still not believing his father had pulled that off. "So captain, you mentioned something about a trade. What is it that you need?"

The tanker's skipper reached in his pocket and removed a piece of paper, passing it to Wyatt. "Anything on the list would be appreciated. We have diesel fuel, some medical supplies, and a small machine shop onboard. I'm willing to make a fair trade. I'm taking the position that we are going to be here for a while. Many of the other ships have reached the same conclusion."

Wyatt examined the list while his family peeked over his shoulder. He grunted at the first item, fishing poles. Most of the list made immediate sense, but a couple of the items defied explanation.

"Captain, what do you mean by 'ferry service'?"

"We have plenty of diesel fuel, but only a few weeks of food." The man pointed at a nearby cargo ship, "That bulk carrier over there is full of rice and other foodstuffs. Their captain wants to trade because he's short on diesel fuel for his generators. The problem is, neither of us have a launch that can ferry cargo back and forth."

David looked skyward at the deck of Diego Maru, shielding his eyes from the sun. "What about your lifeboats? Can't you use them?"

Ripple grimaced, "Our lifeboats are flotation units only. They don't have any propulsion. We're working on that right now, but even if we do rig something up, it will probably only get us to shore. Some of the other vessels you see anchored here have already been abandoned. They had the old-fashioned boats with oars or motors, and many of them headed to shore days ago. I'm not sure how they fared."

Morgan wanted clarification. "So you need a boat to haul supplies back and forth between these big ships?"

"Yes, ma'am, that would be a big help. Some of these vessels have cargo aboard that will keep the crews on other ships alive."

Wyatt surveyed the towering behemoth beside them. "How would we load and unload the cargo, Captain? I can't see carrying a lot of weight up and down that 10-story ladder."

Again, Ripple had thought that through. "We have a small davit on deck. We use it to lift supplies aboard. We can raise or lower up to 2,000 pounds."

The conversation continued back and forth for over an hour. Several times, Wyatt and Captain Ripple moved to the bridge, talking to nearby ships over the radio. By mid-afternoon, an itinerary was organized.

Wyatt looked up at David, "This is going to be a complex. It makes going to the mall with your mother and sister look simple." The remark drew a punch on the shoulder from Morgan, who playfully snatched the list from Wyatt's hand and examined it critically. She shared the plan with Sage, who smirked at her dad. "Piece of cake compared to our normal Saturday shopping sprees."

Wyatt filled the airwaves with a flurry of conversation between Boxer and the other boats in the Marinaville fleet. After he explained what had been planned, the other captains agreed, and everyone received their assignments. At first light, four of the small pleasure boats would become bulk goods haulers and shuttle supplies between their ocean-going neighbors.

The jet-ski taxi returned, and Captain Ripple shook hands with Boxer's master. "Wyatt, you can count on our help should you good people ever need it. I think we're going to be here for a while."

The ocean conditions were better the following morning, but the wind was blowing onshore, and everyone knew the seas would continue to grow as the day progressed. Wyatt was glad they didn't have to attempt the next leg of the journey south just yet.

Four of the Marinaville boats were tasked to become merchant ships of a sort, while the rest remained tied to Diego Maru. One by one, the captains of the small vessels untied and moved off to load their assigned cargo. Boxer's job was to haul three 50-gallon drums of diesel fuel to a nearby cargo ship in exchange for several dozen bags of rice.

Back and forth the nimble boats traveled, redistributing bartered goods ranging from a few small cans of yeast to several pounds of flour. The captains of the commercial vessels had evidently been communicating with each other for days; everyone knew exactly what they needed for their crew to survive.

As the day wore on, Morgan sought to coordinate a similar list of items that were in short supply with the fleet. By late afternoon, the final load was being lifted from Boxer's deck – winched skyward to the deck of an Argentinian bulk carrier.

David and Sage were covered in sweat, having lifted, shoved, tied, and guided several loads onto and off of Boxer's small deck. "Who needs a gym membership with a job like this?" Sage had commented.

The fleet of little boats benefited as well. Before leaving the marina, every scavenged fishing pole, reel and tackle box had been bartered. For the sailors stuck on the commercial ships, fishing over the side would be an important food supply, so the tackle was in high demand.

Another valuable commodity was firearms. International law prohibited the big ships from carrying any weapons. The recent encounters with the pirates made everyone in the Marinaville fleet wish they were better armed. Not a single one of the pleasure boaters wanted to give up any of their limited supply, so only the salvaged pirate shotgun and a few odds and ends were offered up for trade. At one point, a crewman on a natural gas tanker had offered five gold Rolex watches as payment for Wyatt's shotgun. "You can't eat or shoot a wristwatch – sorry, no deal," was his response.

The only real problem with the massive exchange occurred at dusk. Wyatt was topping off Boxer's fuel tanks using a hand pump attached to a 50-gallon drum, when a radio squawk requested that he visit one of his neighboring pleasure boats. After finishing with the fuel transfer, Wyatt rode the waverunner to the nearby cruiser and was welcomed aboard.

Kenny and Clare McClure were long-time boaters in their mid-60s. Wyatt could tell something was wrong immediately by the expressions on their faces.

Kenny shook Wyatt's hand, and then Clare kissed the visitor's cheek. The older man began, "Wyatt, I'll get right to the point. We've been offered a cabin aboard one of these freighters. The captain proposed room and board in exchange for our ferrying cargo back and forth until things return to normal. Clare and I are going to accept their proposition."

Wyatt was initially angry. Recruiting new crew was never part of *any* bargain with the ships. *Still*, he thought, *it wasn't excluded either*. He attempted to keep his expression neutral. "Kenny, Clare, I'm not sure what to say."

Clare spoke up. "Wyatt, we appreciate all you and the others have done, but we're not cut out for this. We almost wrecked your boat back at Redfish because we don't have the skills necessary for this kind of adventure. And while we aren't leaking anymore, we're down to one engine. The thought of living on this small little boat for a long time just doesn't sit well with us. Our boat isn't set up for the long-term like a lot of the others. I think we'll be more comfortable on board that bigger ship."

Wyatt's momentary flash of irritation subsided. *Imagine attempting this expedition 15-20 years from now when you're their age.* He nodded, thinking it all made sense. Kenny wasn't done yet. "We're not the only ones. Bill and his Anita have made the same decision."

Again, Wyatt couldn't blame them. He didn't like the thought of the fleet breaking up or losing a single able-bodied hand, but it wasn't going to be an easy lifestyle at Army Hole.

"I think I speak for everyone on this – I wish you all the absolute best of luck. If it's not the right decision, you can always rejoin us later at the island."

Clare stepped forward and gave Wyatt a final embrace, her eyes searching for evidence of Wyatt's understanding of their decision, if not his endorsement. "We wanted to let you know first, Wyatt. You've gotten us through so much and we...well, we wanted you to know before we let everyone else know."

Kenny pumped Wyatt's hand one last time. As Wyatt hailed the water taxi, Kenny got on the radio and made his announcement to the fleet. It was a poignant moment for all – Marinaville was losing four of her esteemed citizens.

Gulf of Mexico
March 7, 2017

The following morning was calm and crisp. The sun was rising in the east, when Marinaville's fleet began firing engines up and down the lines from Diego Maru. Wyatt looked up to see several men peering over the tanker's rail. As Boxer and the other vessels edged away, the men above waved farewell.

Boxer turned south, loaded to the hilt with diesel fuel and about 300 pounds of supplies strapped to her decks. Most of the craft in the flotilla carried similar loads of additional supplies, but the extra items didn't seem to make up for the loss of two of their own. Boxer was laden with four huge bags of rice and three brand new 12-volt batteries. Wyatt steered the bow into the slight two-foot rollers coming across the gulf. If the fleet could make good progress before the sun heated the air, the morning's journey would be much smoother.

It was 88 miles down the Texas coast before the fleet would head into Matagorda Bay. The inlet was a maintained channel used by commercial traffic, and Wyatt wasn't concerned about that portion of the excursion. Once inside the bay, however, the fleet would have to trek through several narrow passages, and the possibility of outside contact was high. The potential danger in that leg of the trip was not something that could be calculated from maps and guidebooks; it was a complete unknown. What the voyagers would find after landing at Army Hole was a nagging concern as well.

Wyatt glanced down at the radar display and navigation systems. They were making just over seven knots, or almost eight miles per hour. They should arrive an hour or so before dusk.

Sage and David were sitting on the bow. Since they had begun boating, the front of the boat had been the kids' favorite position. There was less engine noise up there and always a fresh breeze. On calm days, the ride was very smooth. So much so that Sage liked to call it "her magic carpet ride."

Morgan was just ascending the ladder to the bridge with a fresh cup of coffee when Sage squealed in delight, pointing toward the water. There, riding in Boxer's bow wake were four bottlenose dolphins, frolicking in the waves. The graceful, grey mammals were a common site in the gulf, but still generated a warm reaction from all aboard. They would swoop up and break the surface and then slide smoothly back below. Wyatt didn't know, but he guessed the water being displaced by Boxer's passing provided the intelligent animals some sort of challenge or game.

Wyatt sipped his coffee and looked to starboard where he could see the coastline in the distance. The fleet was about four miles offshore, and he wondered if they were visible to the naked eye from land. The water was less than 30 feet deep out here, crystal clear and a royal color of blue.

To port lay open waters, the horizon broken here and there by the giant offshore drilling platforms and wells. Wyatt couldn't help but wonder if the men manning those floating rigs had been rescued or relieved. Shaking his head to clear the bad thoughts, he focused his attention back on the navigation system.

The fleet's route was taking it past one more potential danger point – the City of Freeport, Texas. While Freeport wasn't a big town, it was located right on the coast and had a significant level of marine activity. Wyatt made a mental note to watch the radar with more diligence as they approached that area.

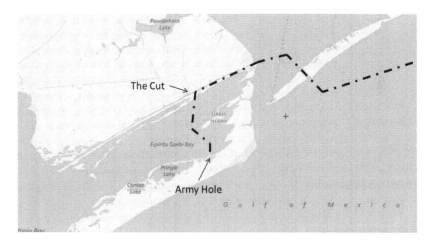

Chapter 10

Matagorda Island, Texas
March 8, 2017

"Dad, I've got good news and bad news," David's voice sounded over the radio.

Wyatt had been waiting on the call since the jet-skis had sped ahead of the fleet, their goal to scout Army Hole. The fleet was almost there.

"What's up, son?"

"First the good news – there's nobody here, and it doesn't look like anyone has been around in a long time."

The information improved Wyatt's mood immediately. His biggest fear was they would travel all this way and find out someone else had the same idea.

"The bad news is the approach to Army Hole is very shallow. I'm not sure everyone can get in."

Wyatt sighed. He knew that for years a passenger ferry ran from the mainland to the island and that would've kept the approach from silting in. No one in Marinaville knew for sure when the park department discontinued the ferry, but it had been some years ago. Without any activity, it was only natural the bottom would shoal.

"How shallow?"

"Dad, I can't tell for sure. I can see the bottom here and there. I'm coming back for a boat pole to measure the depth. I suggest all the boats slow down until we make sure we can get in."

"Okay David, see you in a bit."

Morgan stood up. "I'll get the pole ready for him."

Wyatt added, "Grab one of the good flashlights too, please. It'll be dark soon, and he may need it."

Morgan nodded and made for the ladder.

Wyatt stared over his shoulder at the long line of boats behind him. They only had about 90 minutes of daylight left, and that bothered him. Docking all of these boats in an unknown, tight area would be difficult enough in broad daylight – doing so at night would be asking for trouble.

Before leaving Southland, everyone had gathered all of the cruising guides, charts, and tour books available. These sources provided little information. Army Hole wasn't very popular. Isolated and lacking amenities such as water and electricity resulted in few visitors and no publicity. Still, they had been able to estimate the size of the docking area from the various descriptions and nautical charts. No one liked depending on such limited data, but it was a chance they had to take. They all hoped everyone would fit.

Wyatt could see David's waverunner scooting across the water, heading in at almost 50 mph. The craft slowed, pulling up to Boxer's swim platform where Morgan handed David the boat pole and flashlight.

As the jet boat blasted off, Wyatt had to laugh at his son. David held the long, aluminum pole like a lance, pretending to be riding his trusty steed in a jousting match. *At least he's not lost his sense of humor in all this*, he thought.

The fleet continued to creep its way into the Matagorda Ship Channel, barely making enough speed to maintain their course. The short waterway provided an entrance from the Gulf of Mexico into Matagorda Bay, a body of water over twice the size of their home waters, Galveston Bay.

Before long, the radio crackled again with David's voice. "Dad, this is going to be tricky. At the entrance to the approach, the bottom has shoaled to about three feet. It's very soft silt, so we might be able to plow through. We've found a channel of sorts that runs four to five feet the rest of the way in. It zigzags a little, but we can guide everyone in."

Wyatt took a moment to digest the report. Three feet was shallow – very shallow. Boxer required at least four, and some of the other boats in the fleet needed five. This was going to be a knuckle biter. Wyatt responded on the radio, "Okay David, I'll use Boxer to bust through the entrance. Say a prayer there aren't any big rocks in that silt."

As the fleet entered Matagorda Bay, the Intracoastal branched off to their left. Wyatt pointed Boxer toward the ditch, suddenly feeling a little claustrophobic with the closeness of the shoreline. The entrance to Army Hole was only a few hundred yards south of where The Ditch met the bay. Up ahead, David and the other jet boat idled, waiting on the fleet.

Two large poles were set about 20 feet apart to mark the entrance. A thin strip of land separated the Intercoastal Waterway from the shallow inlet of the state park where Army Hole was located. The entrance was a small cut, probably dredged years ago. The area David had found shoaled was like a speed bump for boats leaving The Ditch and heading into the park's waters.

Wyatt was worried about two different problems. The first was tearing off or bending one of Boxer's big propellers. Those wheels hung the lowest below the waterline. There were no propeller shops anymore and no boatyards to haul a damaged vessel to dry dock for repairs.

The second potential issue would be running Boxer aground and not being able to back her off. The entrance was barely wide enough for Boxer to fit. If she were stuck on the bottom, others boats wouldn't be able to pass. Towing her off in the confined waters of the Intracoastal would be extremely difficult.

David glided next to Boxer and yelled up at his father, "I've poked around as much as I can. I think it's all soft silt as far down and the pole will go. Good luck!"

After the nimble jet boat was clear, Wyatt spun Boxer around with her bow pointed at the entrance. He pushed the throttles forward, and the big boat started its charge at the cut. There was only enough room for her to reach five knots before the entrance, but that still seemed awful fast to everyone on board.

Right before impacting the bottom, Wyatt threw the throttles into neutral, taking all of the power away from the props. "Brace for impact!"

When Boxer hit the bottom, it was like hitting the brake of an automobile in an emergency - everyone pushed forward by the sudden loss of momentum. The sound coming from the bottom of the boat was like sandpaper rubbing wood. Right before she came to a complete halt, Wyatt slammed the transmissions into reverse and applied throttle. Boxer's twin diesel power plants roared with power and the hull vibrated from the torque. For a moment they didn't move, held fast in the mud. The expression on Wyatt's face said it all – if they were stuck it was big trouble. A few anxious moments passed before Boxer's big propellers bit into the water, causing her to sluggishly begin backing off the bottom.

As Wyatt backed the vessel to its original starting point, a cloud of stress fell over the bridge. Wyatt searched Morgan's expression for some level of confidence in his waterlogged strategy. "You know, if we can't get to the island we're screwed. The gas boats won't have enough fuel to get back- even if we decided to return. There's no place around here we can go. I hope I haven't led us all to a dead end."

Morgan reached over and touched Wyatt's arm. "You'll get us in there. I know you will. Don't give up."

Wyatt stopped Boxer and stared at the cut in front of him. He shook his head. "I should've kept my mouth shut, Morgan. Who was I to suggest any sort of plan? Everything I touch seems to turn into a big disaster."

"Wyatt, you've got to keep trying. We've made it too far to stop now."

Wyatt's expression changed from helplessness to determination. "You're right as usual, Morgan."

He looked over at a very concerned wife and daughter. "What do we have to lose now? Here we go again - hang on," and pushed the throttles forward.

Boxer thundered at the cut again. This time the impact wasn't nearly as noticeable, and without slowing much at all, they busted through. A cheer rose up from the bridge; the radio came alive with renewed hope and excitement. They were in!

Wyatt glanced over his shoulder at the muddy water boiling behind Boxer. He had never imagined using his boat like a snowplow, but it had worked. Even the vessels behind him that required more water should be able to make it now.

One of the waverunners led Boxer through the estuary to Army Hole. The shallow inlet bordering the park was less than a quarter of a mile wide, with a few small fingers of land between the cut and the dock.

The sun was just touching the western horizon when Morgan and Sage tied the last line on the port side. There wasn't enough room for each vessel to have its own mooring, but that had been expected. Fenders were draped over the starboard side of Boxer's hull to provide cushion for the next boat in line.

One by one, the fleet arrived in predetermined order. The next boat pulled in beside Boxer, and with Wyatt's help, was pulled tight against the fenders. All in all, there was enough dock space for six of the larger boats to tie up against the concrete bulkhead lining Army Hole. The rest of the vessels secured themselves to one another, a formation called "rafting."

The light had faded to late dusk when Wyatt finally had the chance to step off of Boxer and onto dry land for the first time in two days. Morgan and Sage wasted no time in joining him. He smiled at them, "Being a land lover isn't so bad, I think."

As the three explored around the edge of the port, all of the boaters appeared to be in good spirits. Excited voices resounded from many of the travelers, "We made it!" and "What a trip!"

Many of the captains made a point to hop off their boats and pump Wyatt's hand. Morgan received her share of hugs, and when David joined the small gathering onshore, he received a fair dose of thanks and congratulations.

Wyatt let the good feelings flow unabated. His sixth sense told him the others needed to let their hair down after the harrowing trip from Southland. Deep down inside, he was still worried. There was so much to do, so many things that could still go wrong.

As he quietly watched the celebrations, Wyatt couldn't help but run through a mental checklist of potential glitches. Having enough food was always going to be a struggle. Medical care was another concern, as one strong bout of flu could devastate the entire community. Division of labor was a long-term problem that might become a serious matter. Would the younger members of the workforce resent doing the majority of the daily jobs that were required for their survival? Would they begrudge the older folks who couldn't perform as much physical toil?

Morgan noticed the serious look on her husband's face and pulled him aside. "You okay, hun?"

"Yeah...I'm fine. We've got a lot of challenges ahead of us, Morgan. This isn't going to be easy. You and I moved to the boat with the promise of making our lives simpler. I think that promise has been broken."

Pulling Wyatt's hand into hers, Morgan searched his eyes. "Wyatt, if I didn't know better, I'd say you're acting like a leader. In a way, it's good to see you thinking about the next hurdle...the next problem. It makes me feel better knowing someone is looking that direction."

Morgan stood on her tiptoes and kissed his cheek. "For now, let it go. We've done very well so far, my husband. We'll make it through somehow – we always do. As far as your promise, don't worry about it. 'Robinson Crusoe' was one of my favorite books. Now I get to live it for real."

Wyatt chuckled and looked around for a few seconds. "I hope we don't have any cannibals on this island."

Morgan's expression flashed serious, but only for a moment. "Let's hope it doesn't come to that."

Matagorda Island, Texas
March 9, 2017

The first day at Matagorda Island dawned clear and bright. Despite the exhausting journey and late arrival at Army Hole, most of the boaters were up early to view their new surroundings for the first time in broad daylight.

Gradually, sleepy heads and stretching bodies appeared up and down the rows of boats, many throwing weak greetings or groggy gestures at their neighbors. The smell of coffee drifted around the docks, most of the vessels still having a small stock of the precious bean.

The sun barely up, an informal crowd began gathering on the seawall. An hour later, the entire community was mulling around.

The formal meeting began when one of the land lovers raised his voice and asked what the new place was going to be called. Everyone knew the issue was frivolous, but most of the folks thought it was a good way to start off. Several suggestions were bandied about, with Morgan coming up with the winner. It was decided by unanimous vote that their little colony would be named Crusoe.

Exploring the island was a top priority for several reasons. There was the practical, long-term survival need to inventory what was available, as well as the plain-old curiosity about a new neighborhood and surroundings. There was also a strong desire to stretch one's legs after being on a small boat for a few days.

One of the primary questions on everyone's mind was, "Are we the only people occupying the place?" The chances were low that someone else inhabited the atoll, but after the past few weeks, almost nothing would've surprised the boaters.

Teams were formed, each armed with a radio and a weapon. The team leaders huddled around a map of the island, while sections of the landmass were assigned to each small group.

Initially, David and Sage were on the same team, but Morgan pulled Wyatt aside and quietly asked for a change. "I don't want them both doing something dangerous together. I've been thinking about this ever since David dove under that boat, and Sage stood ready to jump in and rescue him. I couldn't handle something happening to both of them."

Wyatt thought Morgan was being a little too paranoid, but wasn't going quibble about it. He decided to keep Sage with him. Sage flashed annoyance when told of the change, her expression making it clear that she wasn't happy about working with her father. Off into the unknown the two-man teams went, scattering their separate ways to explore their new domain.

Wyatt and Sage hiked together, their objective being the ranger station in the middle of the island. The maps indicated a miniature, house-like structure, as well as a few outbuildings apparently constructed by the Parks & Wildlife Department many years ago. The primitive complex was at the end of a lane leading from Army Hole, a little less than a mile away.

"Dad, you and I need to talk. I'm 18 now, and you need to stop treating me like a little kid," began Sage.

Wyatt kept his expression neutral, already mentally plotting the course of this conversation. "Baby, I'm your father, and I'll always have a protective instinct when it comes to both David *and* you. But you're reading this one wrong. I put you on my team because I enjoy spending time with you – not to keep an eye on a little kid."

"I don't buy that excuse, Dad. Really, why did you switch teams? It sure looked like you wanted to keep me under your wing."

Wyatt smiled, knowing Sage wasn't going to like the answer. "It wasn't my idea to separate David and you. Your mother wanted her two children divided in case this venture turns out to be dangerous, Sage. That's why I made the change."

The response wasn't what his daughter anticipated. She stopped in her tracks, her hands firmly planted on her hips, jutting out a defiant chin. "I'll have a talk with mom about this when we get back, but you're not off the hook yet," she snarled. "Every time I'm around you, I feel like you're smothering me. It's like you think I'm still 12 or something. The way I see it, our lives are going to suck bad enough as it is. If you keep treating me like a little girl, it'll be worse."

Wyatt felt a mixture of feelings welling up inside. The first was anger at her attitude, the words coming into his throat to verbally smack her down. He choked back the urge, excusing the uppity speech to having the world collapse around her. He was sure Sage was as frightened as everyone else. His next inclination was to hug her, but he skipped that impulse as well. Her body language spoke clearly – she *wanted* a confrontation. Wyatt was no newcomer to the parenting game and would not be drawn in to a fight. "Sage, I'm not perfect – far from it," his voice calm and reassuring. "You've always been in such a hurry to grow up. Sometimes that makes my chest stick out with pride, other times it scares me to death. It seems like the last few years we're on a different wavelength or something. When I pull, you need a push. When I push, you're craving a tug. If we're going to fix this, then you have to acknowledge one simple thing – it's not all about you."

Sage's cheeks got hot, and her throat tightened. She wanted to lambast her father for those words, beat him over the head with them. "Self-centered? Is that what you're saying – I'm selfish?"

When her father didn't take the bait, she decided to use his words against him. "I thought you wanted me to be independent...to take care of myself. You've always said you can't trust anyone but yourself, haven't you? You're being hypocritical. I'm doing what you wanted, and now it makes you mad."

Wyatt again fought the compulsion of an angry retort. His voice sounded far calmer than his emotions. "It's not binary, Sage. It's not on or off. It's a give and take that comes with maturity...plain and simple growing up. You'll eventually find the balance, and it's my job to help you get there."

The girl rolled her eyes at the word maturity. She hated the word. She was also a little taken aback that her father would not be baited by her emotional tirade and had answered her with calm and logic instead. He hadn't bothered with that tactic for a long time, and she needed to think about this new change of events. Sage spread her arms in frustration, "This conversation is going nowhere. I'm not going to stand out here in the hot sun and argue the same old crap over and over again." After the pronouncement, she marched off toward the ranger's station, not even looking back to see if her father were coming along.

Wyatt was following, a smug, little smile on his lips. *Spunky little thing. She'll digest all that, and I need to give her some space while she does. She'll roll it over a thousand times in that super-smart brain of hers. I can't wait to see what pops out,* he thought.

The duo continued without speaking for the next 15 minutes. Their path wound its way through open areas of sea oats and occasional strands of small ferns. Sage observed the roofline of a building before Wyatt, and pointed it out. "Finally," was Wyatt's only remark.

The ranger station was really a small ranch-style home. The structure wouldn't have been out of place in most suburban neighborhoods. It was also clearly abandoned. Clumps of waist high weeds and grass dotted the foundation, creating an appearance of neglect. The few landscaping bushes were overgrown and showed uneven growth. A pea gravel path that served as a walkway was littered with fallen twigs and small branches from the large pecan tree that had somehow survived years of storms to remain standing in the yard.

The front door and two front-facing windows were boarded over with plywood. After Sage had taken it all in, she abandoned the silent treatment and sassily observed, "For sale, two bedroom fixer-upper. Available for immediate occupancy."

Wyatt laughed at the clever remark. "Let's see what's around back. I think there's a shed around here somewhere."

Sage pointed to the far side of the home. "I'll go around that way. Meet ya in back."

Wyatt hesitated, "Sage? I'm not so sure we should separate..."

His daughter's stern look stopped him. "Dad! I am not going to trip over a root. I don't think the ticks are out yet. And I promise to keep an eye out for zombies! Cross my heart," her words trailed off as she mockingly crossed her chest.

Wyatt shook his head, "Okay baby, I'll see ya around back."

The two split up with the father managing to look over his shoulder to check on the daughter once. Sage rounded the corner of the station, her attention divided between curiosity over the interior of the home and looking for any recent sign of people being in the area. She saw the outline of what looked like a small shack or barn a short distance away. Deciding to begin her investigation there, she began picking her way through the brush.

Keeping an eye on the building, Sage reached to push aside a limb when a noise she had never heard before arrested her very soul. She instinctively knew what it was, but her brain was so terrified she couldn't force her eyes to look. A constant, vibrating sound like a baby's rattle was coming from the grass at her feet. It was close, and it was louder than she had ever imagined.

Slowly, ever so slowly, she moved her eyes downward toward the source of the warning. The rattlesnake was so well camouflaged she almost didn't see it. Only a step away, the animal was coiled in a tight circle with only its head and tail sticking into the air. It was the head that drew her attention. Broad and flat with unblinking eyes, it appeared to be both evil and massive at the same time. While the multi-hued scales blended almost perfectly with the arid background, the eyes did not. Vertical black slits surrounded by reptilian-gold irises tried to hypnotize the frightened girl. The spell was broken only by the revulsive, flickering tongue. Sage wanted to recoil…to turn and flee, but her legs wouldn't move. She thought to call out for her father, but her voice wouldn't work. It was a standoff, and neither side wanted to make the first move.

Most humans eventually adjust to fear, and Sage's mind managed to clear the fog. In a few seconds, the orders being screamed by her brain finally translated into commands to her body. Her leg jerked - the initial movement of an effort to pivot and run.

The snake didn't want to eat Sage. The animal only wanted to protect itself. The blurred image of her leg moving combined with the fear it sensed on its tongue unleashed the strike.

The reptile's six-foot long muscle structure began to uncoil with tremendous speed and force.

Sage and the snake were both stunned when the sound of Wyatt's pistol split the air. The round struck the striking reptile three inches behind the head, practically severing the body into pieces. Momentum carried the wide mouth and angled fangs forward, but the interrupted strike fell just short of Sage's calf. The girl had almost completed her turn, but the shock of pistol noise combined with the image of the flying reptile caused her to stumble.

Without warning, Sage suddenly felt weightless, and then she was flying. The ground rushed upwards, a jolting impact, and then the scraping sensation of the sandy soil on her skin. Sage rose up on one elbow, surprised to find she was several feet from where she had been standing. She looked behind her just in time to see her father steady the pistol, sending three more bullets at the vicious monster.

Wyatt stirred the reptile's remains with his shoe, verifying the snake was dead, and then turned to his daughter.

Sage's gaze bounded back and forth between her father and the beast that had almost consumed her. Her emotions spun out of control, jockeying from fear to anger and settling somewhere close to confusion.

Wyatt hurried to his daughter's side, bending slightly and offering his hand. "You okay, Sage?"

Sage didn't answer at first, concentrating on trying to replay the scene in her mind. "Where did you come from...how did you...you threw me down...is it dead?"

Wyatt waved his extended hand, an offer to help her up. After Sage was standing, she began dusting herself off while glancing at the dead snake as if to verify it was truly no longer a threat.

"Where did you come from, Dad?"

"When you didn't meet me behind the ranger station, I scanned the backyard and noticed you heading this way. I decided to follow. When you froze mid-step, your body language said it all. It kind of reminded me of a cat surprised by a big dog - arched back and everything. I knew something was wrong. I actually thought it might be an alligator."

Sage gazed at her father with a pained look on her face. "You didn't want to separate. You tried to tell me. If that thing had bitten me...I might have...I might be..."

Wyatt took his daughter in his arms and held her tightly. He could feel her shudder and then begin to weep. The two of them held each other for a long time. Wyatt could feel Sage's hot tears soaking through his shirt. *Let it all go baby, just let it go*, he thought.

~  ~

Wyatt was still hugging Sage when he remembered the radio on his belt. Patting her on the shoulder, he ended the embrace and reached for the handheld VHF. He figured some of the other boaters had heard the gunshots and might be concerned. He was adjusting the volume when David came crashing through the bushes at a full run. The expression on his face showed anxiety, his body motion indicating he was expecting to fight.

"Dad! Dad! Are you okay?"

Wyatt held up his hands to slow down the charging bull. "It's okay David...everything's cool. It was a snake, and I got it before it ate your sister."

David was somewhat relieved, but immediately inspected Sage for evidence of injury. "You're bleeding?"

Sage examined the scrape on her leg and responded with a faked hurt tone, "Yeah, dad threw me down. The brute."

David thought about her remark for a moment, figuring it out quickly. Winking at his father while putting his arm around his sister, David displayed sarcastic pity. "Poor sis, it's hard to tell what's more dangerous around here – dad with a pistol or the rattlesnakes."

Before Wyatt could respond, Morgan's voice sounded over the radio. "This is Morgan – someone better tell me who is shooting and why…and they better do it quick."

Wyatt keyed his radio and said, "Morgan, this is Wyatt. Everything's okay, Mother. Sage wanted to bring home a pet snake, and I wouldn't let her. Everyone's fine."

"A pet snake?"

"We'll explain later. We're on our way in."

~ ~

Morgan, along with several other boaters, waited anxiously for the wayward explorers. Wyatt noticed his wife's stance - crisscrossed arms, steel-rod-straight posture, and an expression that said, "What have you done to my child?" When Sage and David strolled into the clearing, the protective lioness was relieved to see her cubs, a whisper of a smile touching her lips.

After tending and fussing over Sage's scrapes and cuts, Morgan went looking for Wyatt.

"So, I heard Sage's side of the story, now I want to hear yours. Did you really let her go walking through a snake-invested forest alone?"

Wyatt was a little taken aback by his wife's aggression. "Ummm…well…I completely missed the "Posted: Snake-Infested Forest Ahead" warning signs. I didn't realize there were any snakes."

Morgan's finger became a pointing device. "Oh, that's right. You only were worried about alligators."

Wyatt shook his head, "Morgan, up until that point, I hadn't seen anything more dangerous on this island than a sand flea. Still, I asked her to stay with me, but she's got this independence thing going on and would have none of it."

"Why did you take a gun along if this is such a tranquil place?"

"Ummm…I don't know. I guess I felt it was better safe than sorry."

Morgan stepped in a little closer to him, almost in his face. "It would be greatly appreciated if you took that same attitude with your children."

She started to turn away, but Wyatt stopped her. "Now just a minute, Morgan. That's not fair…not fair at all. What am I supposed to do? She wants to be little Miss Independent and hates me if I treat her like a child. When I let her have her way, then you're mad at me. I can't win."

Morgan spun back to face Wyatt, her tone on edge. "Since when does fair have anything to do with it, Wyatt? Where is it written that parenting involves winning?"

Wyatt could feel a domestic disturbance coming on. Arguments were rare with Morgan, but did occur. Such disagreements always involved the children, it seemed. He stood for a moment, trying to gather his thoughts and calm emotions. Morgan seemed to sense his feelings, and her voice and expression suddenly changed. She looked down at her feet, shaking her head slowly.

"I'm sorry, Wyatt. I shouldn't be so upset. It's seems like I've been losing everything lately. It's more than just our home and all our stuff. My world has suddenly disappeared. The kids are one of my few anchors with reality. They're my tether to our past, and my link to the future."

Wyatt's blood pressure went down several notches, and he felt the muscles in his back relax. He nodded his understanding while saying, "I understand, Morgan...believe me, I understand."

Morgan stepped forward and wrapped her arms around her husband. "You'll forgive me if I'm a little overprotective?"

Wyatt returned the embrace. "I think we're all going to find ourselves forgiving others a lot more often."

~ ~

After the excitement of the snake attack subsided, the exploration of the island was begun anew. The teams regrouped and marched toward their designated sections, everyone paying a lot more attention to the ground. David and Todd were assigned to scout the beach.

The island was a long, thin piece of land. A sandy path led from Army Hole directly to the gulf, a walk of slightly more than a mile. The duo's mood was solemn after the incident with David's sister, Todd wisely remaining unobtrusive, allowing time for the adrenaline rush to subside.

They had walked several hundred yards when the path intersected a very unusual sight. Stretching as far as the eye could see to their right was a long, broad slab of concrete. Looking like a superhighway extending through the middle of a deserted island, the visual effect was so stunning the two explorers couldn't help but stop and stare.

"Wow, that's awesome!" exclaimed Todd. "I didn't think it would look like that."

"I know. That's huge," answered David.

The pair was gawking at one of the runways constructed for the Army Air Corps during World War II. Matagorda Island had been converted into a training station and used as a practice area for bombing runs. David knew from the charts and guidebooks that in fact, part of the island further south was severely cratered from the blasts.

While weeds sprouted through the seams and cracks, the expanse was still impressive. Built to handle the huge B-29 Superfortress aircraft, the wide lanes of concrete were 8,000 feet long. David commented, "It's kind of spooky in a way...almost haunted. There was so much activity here at one time – now there's nothing."

After a few minutes of fascination, the two continued down the path toward the ocean. Whiffs of salt air manifested themselves as the two negotiated waist high sand dunes crowned with sea oats and cord weed. Before long, they could hear the surf tumbling onto the beach, and then they were there.

Matagorda State Park was described in the tour guides as having one of the last untouched beaches along the Gulf coast. Given the remote location of the isle, humans rarely visited the park. The first thing both of the guys noticed was the seaborne litter dotting the yellow-white sand.

Unlike the pristine shorelines often visited on vacations, Matagorda's sand was cluttered with debris. Some of the refuse was natural, some manmade. Driftwood, vegetation, seashells, and dead jellyfish littered the sand. Even though they might be hundreds, if not thousands of miles away, people had left their mark here as well. Plastic bottles, fishing line, garbage and other discarded remnants of civilization could be spotted along the coast.

The pair automatically headed for the water, crossing a flat beach area that was over 100 yards wide. Todd was the first to pull off his shoes and wade in knee deep. He didn't stay long, "Oh! Wow! That's cold."

David laughed, "It won't be for long. Another month or two, and it will be like bath water."

They decided to hike south for a while, mainly to see if anything significant had washed ashore. David kept an eye out for footprints while they were walking.

They soon noticed another difference with this place. Larger, more colorful varieties of seashells were lying around. Unlike public beaches, there weren't any people combing the sand for souvenirs or retirees with metal detectors seeking treasure. David also noted the amount of driftwood and scrap lumber scattered about. The potential fuel source might be important.

After following the water's edge for 20 minutes, the duo decided to cut inland and return with their report. Before long, they were crossing the runway again, and this time they could see the outlines of hangars to the south. Another team was supposed to be scouting this area, but the guys decided to go explore just a little more before heading back.

As they approached what was once the main operations area of the old airfield, the amount of land covered in concrete grew exponentially. Taxiways, ramps, and parking areas constructed to handle dozens of large aircraft spread far and wide across the island. It was an eerie, almost apocalyptic landscape with the skeletons of old hangars bordering the paved surfaces. The hefty buildings had mostly collapsed from lack of upkeep and the occasional hurricane that swept the area. Rusted steel beams rose skyward, some several stories tall. Large sections of roof had collapsed or been blown away. Rotted shreds of wood and sheared strands of red rebar poked out of random piles of rubble, mimicking the shape of sea grass strands poking out of small sand dunes. The whole place reminded them of a Hollywood movie set – one constructed for a film about the end of the world.

It dawned on David why the airfield felt so eerie; it was the disconnect between the scene that lay before them and the hush that surrounded it. Other than a mild breeze lightly stirring the dunes and the drifting sounds of passing seabirds, this place was absolutely silent. He tried to think of somewhere else that had mammoth structures of iron and concrete but were without sound. He couldn't come up with anything. *That's what it is*, he thought. *My brain is used to engines, horns, people and machines whenever I'm next to manmade structures this large. There isn't any of that, and it's messing with my head.*

Todd's voice was low, respecting the ghosts. "This looks like those pictures of German cities after the bombers hit them."

David nodded, his tone trying to sound mature and calm to the younger man. "Yeah, but this is just nature reclaiming what is really hers. This is just neglect and lack of maintenance. I'm actually surprised there's this much left after all these years."

After walking through a few of the more complete structures and finding nothing of interest, they decided to head back to the boats. David turned, glancing back at the site one last time. He hoped the cities back in the real world didn't look this bad.

Something woke Wyatt, and he was confused for a moment about what or who had been so rude as to interrupt his dream. He lifted his head off of the pillow and stared into the darkness that filled the inside of Boxer's main salon. Evidently, David heard it as well because the door to the rear cabin slid open, and his son strolled out into the night air, carrying the rifle.

"David," he whispered. "Any idea what that was?"

The cabin's nightlights illuminated his son enough to see him shrug his shoulders while mouthing the words, "No idea." David motioned that he was going up to the deck and check things out. Wyatt swung his legs over the edge of the berth and slipped on his shorts. The shotgun in his hands comforted him as he followed his son up the steps.

As soon as David opened the sliding glass door, both men could hear voices. The first one they made out was female. "I'm telling you it was a bear! There were two of them on the boat. Not big bears, but still, they scared the crap out of me."

A man's voice responded, "There aren't any bears on this island, honey. Are you sure?"

David looked at Wyatt and mouthed the question, "Bears?"

Before Wyatt could answer, the woman's voice shouted, "Look! Look! Over on that boat! There they are!"

The blast of a weapon sounded next, instantly followed by the report of a second shot.

David moved quickly, heading toward the ruckus. Since the boats were all rafted together, passing from one vessel to another required caution. Wyatt was trying to follow, but couldn't keep up. A third shot ripped through the air just as David made it to the cruiser where all the fuss had started. Wyatt was taking his time to avoid falling overboard into the cold water.

Throughout Crusoe, lights were coming on, quickly followed by people sticking their heads out and asking what was going on. Wyatt, trying to reach the vessel under siege from the local wildlife, was stunned when David shouldered his rifle and fired a shot. *This must be serious*, he thought.

He heard David say, "I think I got that one." The woman screeched again, "There's another one over there." David shouldered his rifle and let loose another blast.

Wyatt was still two boats away, carefully hopping from swim platform to transom, desperately trying to avoid a midnight swim. Up ahead, he could see his son standing beside a man and woman, all three of them desperately peering into the night like an invading army was attacking their boat.

"What are we shooting," Wyatt asked when he finally climbed aboard.

The woman answered, a little annoyed, "Bears. What else would we be shooting at?" She immediately turned back toward the dock, her head pivoting as it searched for the massive mammals.

Wyatt didn't buy it. "David, what's going on?"

Without taking his eyes from the shore, David responded, "I dunno, Dad. I'm not sure they were bears, but they were pretty big and very fast. I think I hit one of them."

"How big?"

"Bigger than the average dog, I'd say. Dark brown fur – very fast and the one stood on its hind legs. I bet it was over three feet tall."

By now, several people were awake and gathering on nearby boats. Most of the men had guns, and everyone wanted to know what all the fuss was about. Again, the woman who had first spotted the creatures turned, an in an annoyed voice instructed the crowd, "Shush now – we're killing bears over here."

Wyatt rolled his eyes, tired of the whole thing. "David, come on with me. Show me where you think you hit one of them. I'll grab a flashlight."

Before the two men could climb off of the cruiser, the sleepy captain of a neighboring vessel yelled out, "Who shot my boat? Somebody shot my boat!" Wyatt almost laughed - the image of the boater standing in his underwear and pointing at a hole in his fiberglass just seemed so out of place.

Wyatt put his hand on David's shoulder, "This is getting out of hand. Did you shoot his boat?"

David immediately shook his head, vigorously denying the charge. "No, sir. But I know who did."

Someone, Wyatt couldn't tell who, responded. "I shot at your boat. You had a bear on your swim platform. Did you want me to let you get eaten by the bear?"

Before Wyatt could comment, the woman screamed again, hopping up and down and pointing toward the shore. "There's another one." Her husband fired again.

Two flashlights zeroed in on the spot and Wyatt couldn't believe his eyes. In the beam's weak glare, he watched the backside of a large, furry butt waddling away at a rapid lope. "What the dickens," Wyatt said to no one in particular. It actually looked like a small bear from the rear.

Wyatt mumbled again, "This is turning into a circus."

Flashlights were now probing the shore in search of attacking wildlife. The whole dock looked like a WWII city using spotlights to search the sky for enemy bombers. Wyatt raised his voice over the dim of the crowd, "Hey! Everybody stop shooting! Right now – no more shooting. David and I are going to go over and check it out. We are NOT bears."

Some wisecracker at the back of the crowd did his best Yogi Bear imitation, "Ummm...Mister Ranger, sir, I was just looking for a pic-ah-nic basket." The remark eased the tension somewhat. Someone else added, "Hey, Boo Boo - let's go check out those boats."

As the two men scrambled toward shore, Morgan met her husband with a concerned look. "We've not had great luck with the local wildlife lately. Are you sure you want to chance being eaten by a bear?"

Wyatt rolled his eyes and passed by Morgan without further comment. David and he climbed onto the concrete wall of the dock, now tentatively walking to the location where David thought he had scored a hit.

There were knee high weeds and underbrush in the area, and it took them a while to find the body. Sure enough, David had plugged the offending animal. David rolled the beast over, and Wyatt found himself looking at the biggest raccoon he'd ever seen.

On a scale of raccoons, this guy had been a monster. Wyatt estimated it would stand almost four feet tall on its back legs. The creature must have weighed over 35 pounds. David nudged the body with his rifle barrel, attempting to verify it was truly dead.

"That's not a possum, son – that's a raccoon."

David looked up and played along with his father's sarcasm. "Really? I'm so glad you're along, Mister Ranger, sir."

Before they could return and report there weren't any bears, shouts of alarm rose yet again from the boats, excited voices and flashlight beams seemingly everywhere.

Wyatt and David rushed back to the dock to find two more of the animals silhouetted by the lights. They were huge! David raised his rifle and Wyatt stopped him. "What are you doing?"

"Dad, those things will eat us out of house and home. They will chew dock lines, electrical wire and eat every bit of food we have. They're like 30 pound ultra-smart rats."

Wyatt didn't like shooting things that weren't shooting at him. While he thought David was exaggerating just a little, his point was valid. Still, shooting a wild animal in these circumstances?

Before Wyatt could respond, the animals ran back into the underbrush and out of sight.

Great, just great, Wyatt thought. *That's all we need. We've got the world falling apart all around us, and now we are besieged by racc-zillas coming out of the woods. What's next?*

New York City, New York
March 10, 2017

The sun breaking around the curtains woke Helen. She managed a glance at her watch – 6:47 a.m. Pushing back the multiple layers of blankets, she gasped as the cold air overpowered the snug, warm cocoon of her bed. The frost around the window confirmed what she already knew – it was going to be another cold one today. Glancing down at West 36th street, she could see people were already up and milling around. *Ya gotta love the city that never sleeps*, she thought. Twenty stories below and three blocks down, she could see the line was already forming at the FEMA distribution center. Hopefully, the trucks would be on time today and not cause a long wait - again.

Helen dressed quickly. She mused at how simple life had become since everything fell apart. She didn't have to worry about her outfit being too heavy or too light. Her "fashion statement" varied little day to day. These days, she donned multiple layers of clothing even if she didn't need to venture outside. Thinking about the cold gave her a moment of panic as she realized the buckets might be frozen again. Rushing to the bathroom, she was relieved to find only a thin layer of ice on top. She used the facilities, not bothering to pour any water into the back of the toilet – it was an unnecessary waste, unless she had to flush solids.

Using the handle of her toothbrush, she poked a hole in the ice and stirred the frosty water around. She had run out of toothpaste days ago and now brushed with only water. She seemed to feel better after performing even basic hygiene.

Glancing in the mirror, she felt a pang of guilt. She had used extra water yesterday to wash her hair. The combination of her scalp itching and one of her bouts of depression made the splurge mandatory. She just couldn't help it. She would hide it though. She would tuck her still shiny tresses under a hoodie. These days, simple things like that made you stand out. Clean hair or clean clothes could cause someone to question where the water, detergent, or shampoo came from. Things could really become edgy if people thought you might have more. The situation could become dangerous if they decided they wanted to take it from you.

Helen made her way to the kitchenette and nearly tripped over the bag of garbage that had gathered. She had meant to take it down with her yesterday, but had been behind schedule and procrastinated performing the chore. The garbage heaps smelled so rancid she loathed even passing close to them. One lady in the food line a few days before had shown Helen where a rat had supposedly bitten her on the ankle. The woman had warned about getting too close to the huge piles of rubbish gathering in the empty lot down the street.

On the counter were the remains of last night's meal. Helen sighed as she realized there wouldn't be any breakfast this morning. She had left the unfinished portion of the military MRE (Meal Ready to Eat) uncovered. The roaches would have no doubt visited the food, and there had been warnings about the insects spreading disease posted all over the city. Without the constant cycle of spraying, the roaches were taking over Manhattan.

Glancing again at her watch, she knew it was time to get going. Dropping off the trash would take 20 minutes, and that would still put her way deep in the line to get food. Rushing to the bathroom, she consolidated her water into a single container. With her empty buckets in one hand and the bag of trash in the other, she left her apartment and began the considerable hike down the 20 flights of stairs.

The stairwell was especially busy this morning. The footfalls of several tenants echoed in the cathedral- like openness, most of them probably heading off to receive their handouts of food and water.

As she reached the 14th floor, Helen had to sidestep quickly as another tenant's trash bag had torn, spilling the contents down several steps. She couldn't help but wonder if rats would climb 14 stories to eat. She supposed they would. After all, she did.

When she reached the first floor, she pushed open the emergency handle and entered the building's modest lobby. Passing the row of mailboxes made her nostalgic for the normal life of just a few months ago. It had been so long since there was any postal delivery; she wasn't sure where she had put the mailbox key.

Helen paused at the doublewide glass door that signaled the entrance to the building. It was always wise to scrutinize who was loitering on the street these days. The buckets in her hand were valuable, and there had been rumors of people being killed for less.

She exhaled when she noticed the National Guardsmen were on the next corner this morning. They looked like science fiction robots with their uniforms, helmets, and black guns. Seeing their breath streaming away from their faces enhanced the creepy effect. If they kept to their normal routine, they would be posted there all day, and that meant there wouldn't be any trouble. *Perhaps things are looking up*, she thought.

Rushing out into brisk winter air, Helen hurried toward the trash heap. She passed by a young soldier keeping vigil at the corner, and he smiled at her. *I bet he's lonely*, she thought. Without thinking, she paused at the curb and glanced at the crossing signal. She had to grin at the habit – there hadn't been any signals for a long time, let alone any traffic to dodge.

When she reached the other side, a different guardsman whistled at her. *I bet he's **really** lonely*, she mused. Paying no attention to the flirt, she hurried down the street to dispose of her garbage. She made it to within two blocks when a wall of stench assaulted her nose. It was too far to hold her breath the entire way, but she tried. The odor was so overpowering, she knew it would hang on her clothing for hours. *I wonder if that solider would whistle at me if he could smell this*, she thought.

The vacant lot was almost completely full of trash bags of all colors. Weeks of rotting garbage festered in the open air. Small rivers of goo ran from the dump and into the gutter, slowly making its way toward the nearest sewer drain. Helen gagged once, but managed to toss her bag onto the ever-growing pile.

A woman leaning from a nearby open window was watching Helen. After the bag settled on the pile, the lady yelled out, "Thanks for that. I hope the new dump is next to your apartment."

Ignoring the taunt, Helen retreated toward the elementary school where the FEMA trucks would deliver some sort of rations. She hoped today would be cheese and bread. After that, it was just a few blocks to where the water trucks would fill her buckets.

The line at the elementary school was longer than she expected. Hundreds of people formed a single file that snaked for almost six blocks. At every intersection, a soldier oversaw the crowd. At every other corner, a military vehicle was parked. Helen was glad they were there. When the FEMA trucks arrived with their first delivery, there had been a lot of trouble. Some people didn't want to wait in line, while others thought they should be given extra food. A single punch lead to out and out rioting in the street. Helen had witnessed one man pull a gun and start shooting. The military guys would keep the peace.

Helen scurried to the back of the line and took her place. The trucks weren't there yet, so it would be a while before the line started moving. Ten minutes after arriving, she glanced behind her to see the line had now grown, extending another full block in length. *If those trucks don't show up soon*, she thought, *there's going to be trouble. I can just feel it.*

It was smart for a single girl not to make eye contact. It had always been that way in New York, but especially now. Helen couldn't remember the last time she had seen a policeman. Gunshots were an almost nightly occurrence. As she waited for the line to start moving, she could hear the conversation of several men behind her.

"I had to hike all the way over from 52nd this morning. I waited in line all morning, and the trucks didn't show up yesterday at all. It looks like all the people from that area had the same idea, and the line here rivals a Coney Island roller coaster. I'm going to be here all day," said one.

Another man asked, "How did everyone react when they figured out there wasn't going to be any delivery?"

"Oh, there was plenty of foul language and upset people. The army guys put it down pretty quick. Ya know, I'm surprised they still maintain control. There ain't that many of 'em. I heard they ain't even issued bullets."

A third voice chimed in, "I've heard that, too – but who wants to find out for sure?"

Helen relaxed a bit when the assembly behind her broke into laughter. Such talk made her nervous, but she had to admit wondering about the same thing. She was still living with her mom when Hurricane Sandy had hit five years ago. They had an aunt that lived up in New Rochelle, so Helen's mom had decided it was a good time to visit her sister before the storm arrived. Still, they had been without power for a few days and had watched, horrified, as the people on Statin Island and Queens suffered for weeks. There had been violence and looting then, but that was just a small part of the city. Now, even with things much worse, she never saw more than nine or ten of the soldiers at the same time. If things continued to degrade, that didn't seem like enough to maintain order.

The rumble of an approaching engine drifted down the street drawing her attention to the front of the line. *Great*, she thought, *the trucks are finally here*.

Standing on her toes, she craned her neck to see if the line had started moving. A few moments later, she recognized the now familiar echo of a bullhorn, and a muffled male voice sounded up ahead. A minute later, a military vehicle came rolling down the street, a male voice broadcasting, "Please disburse – there will not be any FEMA deliveries to this location today. Please disburse. Deliveries should resume tomorrow."

The line of stunned and disappointed people didn't react at first. Helen saw some people simply hang their heads in despair while others stared, mesmerized in disbelief at the truck bearing the bad news. Helen felt a twinge of hunger in her stomach at the news. This wasn't the first time the trucks hadn't shown up, but now she didn't have any reserve food. She decided to take her buckets and head for the watering trucks – there was nothing else to do.

As she began to move away from the line, the background din of voices began to increase in volume. Grumblings and curses floated through the air; she could feel the stress level starting to rise. Helen quickened her pace, searching for an escape, not able to cross off of this street for another block. Up ahead she noticed several people gathered around the Humvee at the corner. She had to pass by that intersection on the way to fill her buckets.

The crowd gathered around the soldiers numbered about 50 people. Most of them were either asking questions or venting their frustrations at the stone-faced troopers standing beside their ride. As Helen scurried closer, she noticed a few of the more animated individuals pointing fingers at the troops. A couple of steps later, she quickened her pace, recognizing an angry fist as it waved in the air. Dozens of frustrated, hungry people were joining the throng. One of the older soldiers hopped up on the bumper of the truck. He spoke into a radio, scanned the mob and spoke again. Helen jumped when he pointed his rifle into the air and fired a shot.

The discharge echoed off the buildings on both sides of the street. Some passersby ducked, others began running. Most of the crowd near the military guys hurried away, scurrying half-bent at the waist and holding their ears. But not everyone ran.

She was sure that the incident had the opposite effect than the soldier intended. Rather than disperse the crowd, it attracted attention, and Helen was shocked to see lots of men and women change direction and step toward the guardsmen.

The crowd reformed so quickly Helen couldn't see a way to get past without pushing her way into the dense and angry group. She decided to go around the opposite corner and watch for an opening, partially protected in a nook older architecture frequently affords.

The soldier who had fired his gun roared into the radio again while peering over the top of the growing throng. People were yelling insults, shouting questions, and screaming curses at the guardsmen. Helen noticed the stoic faces normally displayed by the soldiers had been replaced with expressions of fear and concern. She didn't blame them.

More and more people entered the area, most attracted by the spectacle of something different. Movement from up the street caught Helen's eye, and she noticed another army truck rolling to join the first. The driver started honking his horn to warn the people overflowing into the middle of the pavement.

A woman clutching a baby in one hand while guiding a toddler in the other was trying to circumvent the mob. Helen didn't see exactly what happened, but suddenly the newly arriving truck's tires screeched and smoked as the driver slammed on the brakes. Helen glanced over just in time to see the small child and the woman flying through the air, landing on members of the crowd, and knocking a few people to the ground.

Almost complete silence followed the event. For what seemed like a long time it was very quiet, everyone too shocked to make noise. The calm didn't last.

All at once, a chorus of angry voices split the air. Two guardsmen from the new truck sprang out of the back, attempting to push their way toward the injured woman and children. Several men blocked their way, shaking fists and screaming insults. Helen watched as an older man grabbed one of the soldiers by the shoulder – an effort to spin him around and get his attention. The uniformed man slammed his rifle butt into the fellow's stomach, sending him reeling to the pavement. After that, insanity ruled and mayhem ensued.

Out of nowhere, bottles, bricks, rocks and even a street sign flew through the air, impacting all around the soldiers. Ducking behind their trucks, the guardsmen seemed stunned and unsure of what would happen next. The barrage of projectiles kept increasing as more and more people joined the fray.

There was no way Helen could make out the object, one small projectile in a blizzard of flying debris. Nor could anyone know who threw it with hundreds of arms launching spit at the soldiers. A bright flash and then a whooshing sound, quickly followed by yellow and red flames sprouted around one of the army trucks. Someone had thrown a bottle of gasoline. Before anyone could react to the blaze, shots began tearing through the air. Helen instinctively ducked low, the supersonic ripping noise of bullets flying over her head. She saw bodies fall in the street as hundreds of people began screaming, fleeing in every direction.

Not everyone ran, however. Helen couldn't believe it when several men carrying baseball bats, shovels, and rakes charged the army trucks from a different direction. Again, a volley of bullets tore into the attackers, but they didn't stop. From all four directions, the frenzied crowd descended on the soldiers, and within seconds, it was over. Angry men were standing above the dead guardsmen, some of them kicking the bodies and shouting profanity. Others were rummaging around inside of the trucks. Helen saw several men running away with the black rifles, evidently scavenged after being dropped by the dying peacekeepers.

As she watched the throng pillage the army trucks, the ground under Helen's feet began to feel odd, almost like it was trembling. A distant buzzing turned into a full-fledged vibration, and Helen actually thought for a moment that New York was having an earthquake. The shaking pavement was soon joined by a whining drone that Helen had never noticed before. She chanced a peek around the corner and realized a huge tank was rumbling at high speed straight at her. Its gun was pointed into the center of the crowd. As she watched, mortified, small white twinkling lights shone from the front of the tank. The blacktop and concrete around the mob erupted. Spouts of debris jumped off of the street like small geysers of black water as a wall of lead bullets slammed into the main body of rioters. Blaring shouts of tortured panic filled the air, the confused mob scattering in every direction except toward the death spewing from the front of the steel monster. In a few seconds it was done; the survivors scattered, scurrying away.

Helen couldn't tear her eyes from the street scene before her. There were twisted, mangled bodies everywhere. Dark, crimson pools steamed into the cold air, the crackling fire engulfing the military transport. A few people were only wounded, their cries of pain and anguish filling the air.

The tank rumbled to a stop right in the center of the intersection, an electric hum sounding as its massive gun surveyed left and right. Two truckloads of men closely followed its arrival. The new soldiers leapt from the back, spreading out in an arch, their weapons at their shoulders, ready to fight. Other troops rushed to the wounded, carrying green bags stenciled with red crosses.

Helen's mind begged her to get out of there. She was scared the soldiers would think she was involved in the riot. She pulled herself from the pavement, willing her legs to work, and began to move away when a voice yelled, "Halt!"

Helen froze mid-step. The back of her knees felt like ice, she was so frightened. A soldier approached her from behind, scrutinizing the empty buckets still clutched in her hand. She managed to meet his gaze, discovering it was the same guy who had smiled at her this morning on the way to the trash heap.

"I know you," he said. "What are you doing here?"

"I...I...I was in l-l-li li line for food," she stuttered.

"Did you see what happened here?"

"Ye...yes."

"My lieutenant's going to want to talk with you. It's okay – you're safe now. No one's going to hurt you."

On wobbly legs, Helen stepped where he pointed, using the barrel of his gun. She marched around the corner, and they headed toward the closest truck. She tried desperately not to notice the bodies and gore that filled the street, choosing instead to focus on the activity of the living in front of her.

A slightly older soldier was obviously in charge, issuing commands in a staccato voice and constantly pivoting his head to observe the area. As Helen and her escort approached, his expression changed to annoyed curiosity. The man beside her saluted and informed, "Sir, I found this woman crouching around the corner, she claims to have witnessed the entire event."

The officer's eyes softened as he took Helen in. The moment faded quickly, but she would have sworn there was something more to his gaze than would be expected.

"Ma'am, I will need to take a statement from you. Are you injured in any way?"

Helen blushed at the concern for her well-being. It seemed like it had been a long time since anyone had asked, let alone cared. "I'm fine, thank you."

He nodded and smiled. "My name is Lieutenant O'Connor. Patrick O'Connor. My first priority is to secure this area. I'm afraid I have to ask you to remain here for a little while until I can take your statement."

Helen didn't want to be there. After witnessing the terrifying, horrific massacre of so many people, her first instinct was to go home and cry into her pillow. She started to refuse the officer's request, but something stopped her. Why didn't she turn and run? It was all so confusing, her mind flashing images of the people falling dead in the street. Trying to make an excuse to leave, Helen looked at her watch, the concern showing on her face. "I need to get back. I live on the 20th floor, and I have to use the elevator to carry water up to my apartment. The electricity will be turned on soon, and I don't want to miss it."

Lieutenant O'Connor understood the young woman's reluctance, reading her excuse for exactly what it was. "Ma'am, trust me on this...you'll feel better if you give a statement. Talking about what you experienced will help. Later, you'll be glad you did. I can tell already this incident should not have happened. This was badly managed and wrong. Your words might ensure something like this never occurs again."

Helen didn't know how to respond. O'Connor was so confident, so reassuring – just listening to him was calming. More and more soldiers were arriving on the scene, many of them gathering around, waiting on the lieutenant to give them directions. He looked at Helen and said, "I'll see to it you are escorted home safely, so don't worry about that. And, I'm sure we can help with your water situation."

Without waiting on a response, he turned to the young man who had found her and ordered, "Private, escort this young lady to my Humvee, and see to it she is issued food and water."

"Yes, sir."

Pat turned to issue orders to the waiting soldiers, never giving Helen another glance.

A few moments later, Helen found herself sitting in what she would have called a Hummer. Her escort went to the back of the big vehicle and returned with two MREs and two bottles of water. "Do you need anything else before I get back to work?"

Helen was surprised at the generosity, almost embarrassed. "No. Thank you so much for these, but I don't need this much. Don't you guys need this food?"

The man looked down at his boots and said, "I'm just following orders. Keep them, we've got plenty today."

He jogged off, leaving her sitting in the passenger seat. It was warm inside, and the heavy doors and steel frame made her feel safe. She really didn't have much to occupy her mind while she waited. She watched Pat as he commanded the men...listened, observed, and worked. She couldn't help herself – checking to see if a wedding ring were on his finger. There wasn't one.

Twenty minutes later, the lieutenant strolled over and began asking her questions about the incident. Helen did her best to recount what she had seen. The officer seemed especially concerned over who initiated or escalated various phases of the clash. He asked for clarification on several points, meticulously noting her exact words. Helen felt like she was being interrogated at times, but appreciated his need for the details.

When he had finished writing, he looked up with an expression displaying a more human-like quality. "Helen, I'm going to have two of my men escort you back to your apartment. They will help you upstairs with whatever you need to carry."

Helen smiled, but felt a sense of disappointment. It took her a moment to admit why. She realized her time with him was over, and she probably wouldn't see him again. That tugged at her insides, but she pushed it away. "Thank you, Pat," was all she could say.

Turning to two soldiers standing nearby, he said, "Sergeant, please take one man and escort this young lady back to her apartment. Use my Humvee. See to it that she makes it safely to her door and assist her as gentlemen."

"Yes, sir," came the immediate response.

Before she knew it, Helen was riding in a motor vehicle for the first time in weeks. The driver pulled up in front of her building and before going inside, opened the back hatch. The other soldier and he pulled out a case of MREs and two large bundles of bottled water. Helen carried her empty buckets.

The electricity wasn't on yet, and she tried to persuade the soldiers to leave the supplies next to the elevator door, but they would have none of it. The sergeant made it clear that he was going to follow his commander's order to the letter. It was 3:48 in the afternoon, twelve minutes before the electricity was to be turned on, so the military escort opted to wait rather than, as one of them put it, "Hump the stairs."

Helen thought it odd that both men completely ignored her while they waited. Not accustomed to being shunned by men, she finally worked up enough courage to broach the subject. She decided to be clever, "Sergeant, have I done something wrong or offended you in some way?"

It took the older man a moment to figure out what she was talking about. In a fatherly tone, he responded. "No ma'am, not at all. I've just been around long enough to know *that* look on my lieutenant's face. I think he's a wee bit smitten with you, and I'm glad. He's a good man, but a lonely one."

Helen blushed despite her best attempts to keep a straight face. Her heart racing in her chest didn't help the effort. She decided to play it coy. "He seemed like a nice person. Perhaps our paths will cross again sometime."

"Ma'am, when I get back, I'll bet my next payday I get quizzed in a proper and thoroughly military manner. I can relay the information such that it encourages or discourages the lieutenant. I'll leave that decision up to you."

Helen was taken aback with the bluntness of the man. Not only was he forward, the whole thing was just plain weird. Here was a professional soldier, a man with a gun, offering to be a matchmaker. *What strange times we live in*, she thought.

"Sergeant, do you want to know if I'm interested in going out with the lieutenant? Do people still date in these times? It's not like we can go see a movie or have dinner out or anything."

The man smiled at her, shaking his head ever so slightly. "Young lady, I've been married for 16 years. My experience has been that two people will make the best of it – regardless if the sky is falling or not. Again, your call, ma'am."

Helen was thinking about how she wanted to answer when the lights in the lobby flickered on. A few moments later, a humming noise came from the elevator's shaft. Right on cue, the building supervisor appeared, ready to check the elevator before letting anyone else in. Helen had seen this routine before; it wasn't a complete diagnostic test, but still better than nothing.

The super entered the car where Helen knew he would ride to the top floor. He had told the residents that he checked the elevator's controls located in the building's primary mechanical room, trying to be as careful as possible. Ten minutes later, the doors opened again, and he announced the all clear. The line of tenants began entering the car, all of them carrying miscellaneous buckets, bags and other containers holding the necessities of life.

The soldiers accompanied Helen to her door, making sure everything was secure. As they were leaving, she turned to the sergeant and smiled. "I hope you'll say good things about me."

The solider looked at Helen and winked, speaking with a reassuring tone. "My pleasure, ma'am."

Crusoe, Texas
March 10, 2017

Anyone trying to access the island didn't have a lot of options. Three sides of the sandy strip were surrounded by open ocean with no place to dock or tie off a boat. The west side was guarded by extremely shallow water. Wyatt and several of the men on the dock discussed the previous night's events and shared a good laugh about the invading killer bears. The conversation inevitably came around to security, and the tone became serious.

"We can't be the only people along the Texas coast with operating boats. What's to stop someone from sneaking in here and stealing or worse," asked one of the men.

Wyatt agreed, surveying their faces for the hint of an idea. When none was offered, he volunteered, "We can keep watch at night. That's probably smart. But during the day, there are times where everyone is scattered around working on whatever. I don't think we can keep a watch 24-7. There are even less of us now than at the marina, and we have more work to do."

"We need some kind of early warning system," suggested someone. "If we know they're coming, it gives us time to get ready. We need some sort of alarm or tripwire, booby trap kind of thing."

Again, there was no dissent among the group, but no one had any experience with setting trip wires on the water.

A long conversation ensued, finally ending with a half-baked concept of using fishing line and a flare gun to build a burglar alarm. Sage's use of a similar technique to defend against the pirates at Redfish had seeded the idea.

David and Todd were recruited to use the water jets and find out if the concept were feasible.

Wyatt watched the two small boats idle across the bay while he checked the tidal charts. Everyone thought the perfect solution would be to string a line just an inch or so under the surface of the water. When a boat came across, it would trip the line and send up the warning flare. The problem was the tide. A line that was one inch under the water could be several inches deep at high tide. It could be exposed when the water was low.

Not every location had the same rise and fall of tide, but the charts would tell all.

He finally determined that Matagorda Bay had an eight-inch tide. That was too much for their plan. If they set the trip wire deep enough to keep it hidden, a small boat could go right over the top of it without springing the warning. He had to think of something else.

As Wyatt sat on the back of Boxer, his neighbor was preparing to go fishing. Everyone took turns at the now-mundane task with varying degrees of success. Some of the guys were beginning to experiment with nets, trotlines and other methods. Wyatt watched as the man gathered his gear, a string of bobbers dangling from his belt. The little pieces of floating Styrofoam caught his attention. *That might just work*, he thought.

Wyatt headed into Boxer's cabin in search of paper and pencil. Morgan and Sage were below, trying to determine a better way to prepare kelp. The aroma rising from the pan wasn't encouraging. *It's constantly about food*, thought Wyatt.

A few quick sketches combined with longer periods of thinking allowed Wyatt to finally arrive at a design that might work. David and Todd were just tying off the water bikes when he finished his drawing.

David reported first, "Dad, it looks like the only place for anything other than an airboat to get through is about 30 feet wide. It's the same cut you plowed through the silt with Boxer. I saw other openings, but I almost got the jet-ski stuck trying to explore them. Even a rowboat couldn't pass through those."

That was good news. Wyatt smiled at the two guys and motioned them to examine his drawing. Morgan and Sage came up from below and joined everyone, spying over Wyatt's shoulder at the contraption he had sketched.

"We'll need two sturdy rods, maybe one of the broken fishing poles. We'll drive them into the bottom as deep as we can. We'll string the line between them, secured to fishing bobbers. As the tide goes in and out, the bobbers will keep the line a constant inch or so below the surface."

Wyatt tried to gauge the reaction to his invention. David looked at Todd, who nodded agreement – it just might work. "How do we hook the line to the flare gun?"

Wyatt flipped to a clean sheet and began to draw his thoughts. An hour later, David and Todd were again on the jet-skis, headed back to lay Crusoe's first early warning tripwire.

Everyone was going to sleep just a little better tonight.

March 15, 2017

Fort Meade, Maryland

Reed was suffering from butt fatigue, the result of sitting in the hard plastic seat far longer than either the chair or his backside was designed to accommodate. The speaker at the front of the makeshift conference room wasn't helping the situation at all. The non-descript man droned on and on about the progress FEMA and Homeland Security were making in the major metropolitan areas.

A quick check of his watch informed the congressman that the stodgy fellow was already 20 minutes over on the presentation, and they hadn't even gotten to the question and answer segment. Don't get frustrated, he told himself, we're all trying to do our best.

Reed casually glanced at his fellow lawmakers to see if he were the only one growing tired of the whole affair. If they were, they didn't show it – poker faces all around.

Finally, the mid-level analyst from FEMA said the magic words, "And that concludes my presentation. Are there any questions?"

Way too quickly, Reed's hand shot up. The Speaker acknowledged him with a nod. "Yes, Representative Wallace, you have a question?"

Reed cleared his throat, "Thank you for the presentation, sir. I appreciate the hard work you folks down at FEMA are accomplishing. I do have a few questions, or clarifications, on my mind though. First of all, what percentage of our 20 largest cities has electricity as of this morning?"

The man at the front of the room shuffled his feet, his expression reminding Reed of someone who had just been caught cheating on his girlfriend. "Well, Congressman, all of them have electrical power."

The Texan tilted his head slightly. "All of them? Full time electrical power has been restored to all of the major cities?"

The man at the front of the room shook his head, "No, Congressman, I didn't mean it that way. All of the 20 largest cities have partial electrical service restored."

"Could you define the term 'partial' for me, sir? I'm not sure what that means."

The FEMA man stuttered, "Well, ummm, ahhhhh…New York City, for example, has electrical power to about 20% of the city about 10% of the time. That would be an example of partial service, Congressman."

"I see. What about Chicago?"

"We are not doing as well in Chicago, sir. We still have about 5 million citizens who have no service. We have another million who receive electrical power about 5% of the time."

"And Houston?"

The man relaxed a bit, "Things are going quite well in Houston. The last numbers I have indicate that 40% of the population receives electrical service at least 4 hours per day!"

232

Reed looked around the room, wondering if he were the only one appalled by these statistics. The expressions returned by his peers seemed to indicate they were waiting on him to continue his line of inquiry. The presenter's face showed clear frustration.

"Sir, is it safe for me to assume that the restoration of running, potable water is reaching about the same number of citizens?"

"No, Mr. Wallace, that wouldn't be a safe assumption. We still have sterilization protocols in affect for every city except Portland. The Portland water system, when available, is safe to drink."

Reed couldn't let it go. "How, if I may, does FEMA recommend people sterilize their water if they don't have electricity to boil it?"

A loud voice from the back of the room sounded, "They can't, and that's why I'm here."

Everyone turned around to see a young woman dressed in a white lab coat stepping toward the front of the room. She strode with purpose, carrying a folder full of papers tangled in the security badge hanging from her neck. She paid no attention to the man she had just preempted, who gladly stepped aside.

"I'm sorry to interrupt this meeting, ladies and gentlemen. I'm Dr. Linda Mitchel, Assistant Director of the Center for Disease Control in Atlanta. I just flew in, and with all due respect to my colleagues at FEMA, I don't have time to wait in line to brief all of you."

All of the senators and representatives sat up in their chairs, intrigued by the urgency and brashness of the new arrival.

The doctor from the CDC set her folder on the podium and withdrew a stack of papers. Reed snorted when she handed the pile to the senior senator from Florida, and without ceremony told the man to "Take one and pass it around."

She returned to the lectern and announced, "We have a nationwide outbreak of typhoid. The CDC confirmed several cases in 13 American cities, and it is in the process of verifying suspected cases in another 9 metropolitan areas. For those of you who aren't familiar with this disease, the anticipated fatality rate without Cipro class antibiotics is over 40%. With said medications, the fatality rate is less than 1%. I'm here, at the request of the director and the president to brief everyone on the situation."

A murmur hummed throughout the room, the legislators opening the report as soon as they received copies. Reed was handed the dwindling stack and hurriedly opened the short report.

Dr. Mitchel continued, "So far, the outbreak is not classified as an epidemic, but my gut feeling is that will change in the next 24 hours. The early cases are the very elderly and the very young – segments of the populations who are traditionally the most susceptible and show symptoms first. As of six hours ago, we had 416 confirmed cases. We estimate at least 200,000 more people are in the early stages and haven't sought medical attention yet. So far, there have been 103 fatalities."

The senator from Idaho glanced up from his report and interrupted. "Do we know where it's coming from?"

"Yes," replied the doctor immediately, "We have identified the source as toxic particulates. In layman's terms, the concentration of people in the refugee camps has led to massive amounts of untreated human waste. This waste eventually dries, forming a paste like layer on land or wherever it is disposed of. Wind, passing vehicles, foot traffic, and other disturbances allow the particulates to become airborne, basically infiltrating and coating everything from food to drinking water. At one camp outside of Nashville, practically every surface we tested was contaminated."

Reed and several others had been talking about the water supply for days. It had been the primary health concern, with everyone from the Army Corps of Engineers to Homeland Security being questioned on the subject. Reed needed to clarify. "Doctor, isn't typhoid normally due to tainted drinking water?"

The woman at the front of the room shook her head. "Yes, but not only drinking water. It can be spread by mosquitos and other insects. What we are seeing is different, something new. We finally isolated the source yesterday. Vast amounts of human waste has dried out and turned into a crust in many areas. This material is now becoming airborne and spreading the disease. It is also a strain that we've never encountered, and it's spreading quickly. As of right now, we're seeing an abnormally high rate of infection in the southern states. The primary concentration seems to be Miami, Tampa Bay, Mobile, and New Orleans. We believe we are actually seeing two different strains of typhoid – one caused by polluted drinking water, the other being airborne. The sewage systems in these areas are all but inoperable, drainage is poor, and potable water is in short supply. Rainfall has been far less than normal in these regions as well."

"Great...just what we needed," commented one congressman sitting next to Reed.

The doctor paused to let her words sink in and then pressed on. "We have to distribute antibiotic treatment in mass quantities immediately or this is going to continue to spread quickly. We could be looking at over 10 million casualties in less than two months."

"What do you need from us, doctor?" asked Reed.

The question seemed to surprise her. After a long pause, she said, "The president has already diverted military and government resources for the manufacture and distribution of the medications. I'm only here to brief you, not request anything."

Martial law, thought Reed. Well at least the dictator-in-chief is taking the time to let us know what's going on. I wonder how long that will last.

The meeting adjourned. As the doctor gathered her materials and prepared to leave, Reed approached her smiling, "Mind if I walk with you, doctor? I've got a couple of simple questions."

"No, not at all. How can I help you?"

"I'm just curious what resources the president is diverting. What's going to happen?"

The woman stepped quickly toward the door, Reed hustling to keep up. She met his gaze and responded, "The plants that can manufacture the quantities of meds we need are in New Jersey. Electrical power is being diverted from New York, as well as the engineers, linemen and other skilled personnel required to get those facilities up and running. The president hated to do it. This outbreak means a lot of people are going to do without for a little longer, but we've really no choice."

Reed had figured as much - another step backwards. "Thank you, doctor. Have a safe flight."

Crusoe, Texas
June 1, 2017

One of the biggest problems facing the citizens of Crusoe was salt. Most of the vessels had small supplies of the mineral, intended to fill table shakers. It seemed like every food gathering, curing or preservation process required large quantities of salt.

It was a retired oil field engineer who dreamed up a potential solution. A shallow, wide hole was excavated on the beach and lined with a plastic tarp. The roughly ten-foot square pit was less than a foot deep in the middle, its bottom sloping gently upwards toward the edges. Someone remarked it looked like a homemade kiddie pool.

A bucket brigade was formed to haul ocean water across the sand and fill the pit. Five gallons at a time, the water was poured in until the depth reached about six inches. The concept was simple: the sun would evaporate the water leaving the sea salt. The work crew had finished two days before.

Wyatt, David and two other men slogged across the hot sand, hoping it had all worked. Digging the pit had been a lot of backbreaking, sweaty work. No one had a shovel. It wasn't a tool common on boats – something no one had thought of before leaving. Plastic buckets scooped pounds of beach by hand resulting in sore muscles and exhausted men. Filling the pool had been worse.

The first thing Wyatt noticed as they approached the tarp was all of the water had indeed evaporated. A thin coating of yellow grit covered the tarp, not the anticipated sparkling white powder. As the men stood around their makeshift desalination project, it became clear that their end product smelled like rotting fish.

"Wow! That really stinks," commented David, pinching his nose to diminish the effect of the offensive odor.

Wyatt knelt down on one knee and gingerly stuck a finger into the grime. A quick sniff curled his face, but he licked the powder anyway. Smacking his lips, Wyatt reported the results of his taste test. "Yup. It's salt all right. To be more accurate, I would say it's more like one of those salt blends – a mixture of salt, seasoned with fish poop, rotting clam guts, and clay."

"Not only is there not much here, the girls are going to have a fit over the stench. There's got to be a better way."

Wyatt gazed at the sun and shook his head. "We need to be getting back," he announced. "Let's scrape this stuff off and take it back. Maybe the smell will motivate someone to come up with a better idea."

Chapter 11

June 10, 2017

The US military began to move west. The actions weren't overt, publicized, or even detectable at first. To the casual observer, the pattern wasn't overly unusual - a new fighter wing landing in Guam, another detachment of Marines on Okinawa, another combat team in South Korea.

At first, only the Chinese high command took notice. It was their profession to keep tabs on the forces arrayed around them, and in addition, they had been warned to expect such movements of men and material. MOSS had briefed the Red Army's general staff to expect saber rattling out of the United States. The intelligence agency also estimated the chances of actual military action were low.

It was the Japanese press that figured it out first, their sphere of influence seeing the most activity. Headlines in Tokyo declared America was forward deploying for war on the Asian continent. It didn't take a lot of dot connecting to speculate who the target was.

The Nippon paparazzi may have lit the fuse, but it was the European press that exploded the story. It suddenly dawned on the entire planet that the US blamed China for its recent difficulties and was preparing for military action.

American diplomats and officials didn't help calm the reaction. The talking points and position statements, distributed several days before the story broke, began with weak denials that eventually turned into cocky assertiveness. The US could move its military assets anywhere it wanted. It was none of anyone's concern. The concept of a war was unacceptable to a world that was already suffering badly. Every continent besides North America may have had electricity, but civil unrest, spread by economic hardship was widespread and growing.

Once again, the White House misjudged the unintended consequences of its own actions. Not since the Iraqi invasion of Kuwait had a government's anticipation of world reaction been so off base. The regime of Saddam Hussein had truly been shocked at the global response after invading its neighbor, believing no one would seriously care about the tiny nation. In the end, that lack of judgment had cost the people of Iraq dearly in treasure and lives. Now the US had made a similar miscalculation, the dark clouds of a political storm gathering on the horizon. The unavoidable confrontation was destined to occur at the United Nations.

The United Nations had relocated to Belgium due to a lack of electricity in New York City. While most diplomats were too polite to say so in public, the civil unrest in America's largest city played as much of a role in the relocation as any lack of light or heat. The necessity to move out of North America had sent shock waves rolling through the guts of the organization. Some nations cheered the move, happy that the world's only superpower had finally been humbled. Other countries were supportive of the United States, but lacked the resources to help the crippled giant.

America expected outrage as details of the attack on her infrastructure came to light. China parried the initial political thrusts by claiming innocence and then accused the US of having an outdated power grid. When the White House leaked allegations of a deliberate attack, the Chinese spun the headlines into a story of America's tendency to blame everyone else for her massive debt – a problem that prohibited proper maintenance on her infrastructure – action that could have avoided the collapse.

Normally, the US would hold her own in any match on the chessboard of international public relations. Not so any longer. Half of the White House staff was absent, with the Department of State suffering from a similar number missing in action. Communications were spotty, and the best minds were concentrating on holding the country together, not contests of diplomatic finger pointing.

Even if the administration had played its best game, the world wasn't going to have any of it. During normal times, the prospect of war between the two bickering countries was bad enough. With a majority of the planet's economies tilting over the edge already, the concept of WWIII was unacceptable. Add in the potential for the exchange of nuclear weapons, and global reaction to the United States was harsh and direct.

Many experts thought that Europe and other friendly nations would come to the aid of the United States with electrical components, circuit boards, and spare parts. While it would have taken some time to retool EU manufacturing operations over to the US electrical standard of 60 cycles, eventually help would arrive. The public fury over a potential war between China and the US prevented even the friendliest nations from lending a hand. Trade embargos were threatened on the floor of the United Nations. Some governments, barely maintaining control of their own populations, even promised to help the Chinese if the US attacked the Red Nation.

The US reaction to all of this was predictable. An almost neo-classic pattern of isolationism swept through the besieged government. While pride and ego were involved, the inescapable feeling of having been wronged prompted this reaction. America was the victim after all – why was the world ganging up on us? We didn't start this – we didn't make the first move.

Caught up in so many struggles, both domestic and foreign, few of the people in Washington realized the worst aspect of the entire affair. Because the US wouldn't be receiving any outside help, the American people would endure more suffering for a longer period of time.

Matagorda Island, Texas
June 10, 2017

David waited for Todd to maneuver the jet-ski between the breakers, amazed at the young man's skill and timing with the craft. *I'm glad he's a master with that thing*, he thought, *if we beach the waverunner, everybody's going to be really mad.* Todd finally maneuvered close enough and David handed him the baited hook and tackle at the end of his fishing line.

Verifying the bale was open, David flashed thumbs-up, and Todd turned his craft, heading directly offshore. Holding the rod and reel high above his head, David waded back to the beach, keeping an eye on his line as Todd carried it further from shore than he could ever cast.

"This better work," David said to himself, "We're going to get in trouble for wasting gas if it doesn't."

The two had cooked up this scheme after looking at one of the navigation charts and finding a marked shipwreck just offshore. "The Hazards to Boaters" listed the sunken vessel as resting in 32 feet of water. David knew big fish liked shelter, so Todd and he began contemplating how to fish off the relic.

The first problem had been locating the wreck. The water outside of the first sandbar was reasonably clear, but there was no way to perform a visual search from the waverunner. What they needed was a sonar-type fish finder that could scan the bottom, hopefully locating the outline of the old vessel.

Since they were sneaking around without asking permission, taking out a boat that was equipped for such exploration was out of the question. It had been Todd's comment that had sparked the brainstorm. The kid had blurted out, "What we need is a big magnet."

That was it!

David had seen an old, discarded alternator lying in a trash heap by the ranger's station. That piece of junk would have some pretty strong magnets inside. Before long, they were trolling on the jet-ski offshore, 30 feet of fishing line with two big magnets trailing behind in the water.

On the fifth pass, the line became taut, but it wasn't the ship. David, riding passenger, pulled up an old Chevy hubcap that looked like it had been underwater for a long time.

Two more passes later, the line tightened again, and David couldn't pull it up. He donned the snorkeling mask and slid off the edge of the jet-ski. After diving down about 15 feet, he could recognize the outline of something hefty and dark below. There actually didn't appear to be much of the ship left, but they had found it. He also noted several schools of good-sized fish, lazily swimming around the submerged hulk.

Todd marked the location on their handheld GPS, and the first step of their caper was complete.

Secretly, they studied the GPS location and the charts the next night. The ship was actually about 400 yards off of the beach. That presented a problem because most of the heavy reels didn't have enough 20-pound test to reach that far from the shore. If they hooked something big, there wasn't going to be much line left to play the fish.

They decided to chance it, more from boredom than anything else.

Todd's waving arm brought David back to the task at hand. The sun was beginning to dry his suit and legs, the morning already growing warm. David readied the fishing pole as Todd dropped the line and then motored away from the area.

David waited, knowing it would take the rig a while to sink 30 feet. They had selected a larger than normal piece of bait, not wanting to go to all this trouble for a small catch. He felt that sense of excitement and mystery that comes with deep-water fishing. *You never know what you'll hook into down there*, he thought.

There was also a hope of easy food. While the boaters weren't starving, gathering food was a constant source of time and labor. Todd and he had spent many days fishing, often sporting quite the catch. It took a lot of protein to nourish the people of Crusoe. More than once Todd and he had returned from hours of fishing with their stringers full. After the cleaning and cooking was done, there still wasn't enough to go around. Other days resulted in nothing – the fish simply weren't biting. David and his father had both thought they would never see the day when angling would become work. "What happened to that old saying about the worst day fishing was better than the best day working?"

Quite a bit of time passed, and David was beginning to think all their effort was for naught. The bait had been down for several minutes, and he hadn't even had a nibble, let alone a bite. He was just raising his arm to bring Todd back in when the pole was practically jerked out of his hand.

David snapped back with all of his strength to set the hook. Another strong tug told him he had a fish. Whatever it was on the other end, it was powerful and fast. The reel started screaming as more and more line was taken by the running fish. *This isn't good*, thought David. *I don't have much left*. He tightened the drag just a bit, hoping to wear the animal out without snapping his line. The fish still pulled hard; David scooped water onto the reel so it kept cool.

Another adjustment slowed the hooked swimmer, and then suddenly the line went slack. David started reeling, hoping the beast had turned back toward him as opposed to breaking his line.

As fast as his hand would spin, David reeled in line. The fight suddenly began again, and the pole was pulled downward hard, the reel whining as its drag worked against the fighting beast. Todd let out a whoop of amazement when the beautiful rainbow-colored Mahi-mahi broke the surface, launching several feet into the air. As the fish fell back to the surface, its head shook angrily from side to side, trying to clear the hook.

The battle lasted 20 minutes. The fish would tire, allowing David to pull it slightly closer to shore. Something would motivate the catch again, and back into the deeper water the animal would race. While this ballet went back and forth several times, David was slowly winning. The beast only had so much energy, and the fight was wearing it down. David felt the effect as well, having to use his shirtsleeve to clear the sweat stinging his eyes, but vowing not to give in first.

The brut finally ran out of gas, the last 100 yards to the beach nothing more than pulling in dead weight. Todd rode close to shore to get a better look at the catch while David reached for the steel leader attached to the heavy nylon strand.

The fish was a trophy. Almost four feet long with a solid girth, there was probably close to 20 pounds of mouth-watering fillet in just this single catch. For a moment, David thought about returning the animal to the sea. It was such a beautiful creature. He shook his head, comfortable with the fact that his kind needed the food.

As David unhooked his rig, another problem entered his mind. It was over a mile back to the boats and the day was getting hot. There was no way to ride the jet-ski carrying the poles, tackle and 40 pounds of scale-covered delicacy. "I'll meet you back at the boats," David yelled to his partner.

Hefting the prize over his shoulder, David started the long trek back to Crusoe.

Kemah Bay, Texas
June 11, 2017

Rose stared out the window at Charlie's grave, absentmindedly noting the weeds fully covered what had been a hump of fresh dirt. Thinking of her husband's death added little to the already deep despair she suffered.

The children and she hadn't had anything to eat in over 10 days. The youngest had started coughing two, or was it three days ago? Rose couldn't remember for sure. A while ago, she had gone to comfort the hacking child and found blood on the dishrag she was using as a handkerchief.

She consoled herself that the worst had passed for the children some days ago. They no longer played, or romped – neither having the energy to even complain - the older one claiming he was Superman and didn't need food anymore. His younger sister went along with the act, claiming with honest eyes that she just wasn't hungry.

The rain had provided some water, but now only a little was left, and there were no clouds on the horizon. The realization that their lives depended on something as uncontrollable as the weather added another layer to the crushing avalanche of despair. How had it come to this?

She had to sit down again, her weakened body only able to stand for a few minutes at a time. Just walking from one end of the house to the other fatigued her like a five-mile run. Rose rested in the kitchen chair, and for the thousandth time went through it all again. At least she tried to. Everything seemed like a blur, and she struggled to think clearly – another sign her body was failing.

She had tried everything she could think of. Neighbors were no help – many in worse shape than she was. Several didn't answer the door - the smell coming from inside of the home making it easy to guess why no one responded.

She had tried to walk down to the water and fish for food, but she didn't know how. Digging Charlie's fishing pole out of the garage and finding some plastic bait had given her hope, but she hadn't come home with any bragging rights. The effort had exhausted her already weakened body even further.

A few days ago, she had gotten in the car, determined to drive until she found someone, anyone, who could help. Charlie had evidently drained the cars for generator gas, and the sedan had sputtered to a stop before a single mile had passed by. Rose started crying again, thinking about the walk back to the house that day. Normally, the kids and she would have traveled that distance without even breaking a sweat. All of them had to stop to recover several times on the trip home, the lack of nutrition hampering even basic function.

The next day she had managed to hike to the marina, intent on breaking into one of the boats and foraging for food. Every single vessel that remained had been looted, and she couldn't find a single crumb of nourishment. She had waited too long.

The sound of her littlest one coughing pulled her back to the here and now, the deep racking from the child's lungs telling Rose the girl was suffering. The medicine cupboard was bare – she couldn't comfort her baby.

While cough syrup wasn't in the medicine cabinet, there was something else.

Rose closed her eyes, saying another prayer. She had been asking for guidance, begging for inspiration. The thought of the bottle of sleeping pills again entering her head.

She gathered her strength and stood, wandering past the children who were lying on the floor, blankly staring at ignored toys. The kids didn't even acknowledge her passing, completely innocent of her thoughts.

The bottle was still there – up on a high shelf where curious hands couldn't reach. Rose paused, thinking there had to be another way, but no solution came to her. She reached for the container and shook the contents. It was almost full – a prescription filled for Charlie after he had lost his job and couldn't sleep.

This was the answer. She had to do it now, while she still had the strength. She had to end the suffering.

Slowly, she made her way to the kitchen where the last of their water remained. She divided the liquid into three glasses, the cartoon characters on the kid's cups bringing a tear to her cheek. *That had been a great trip to the water park*, she thought. *I'm glad the kids got to experience those days.*

Carefully, she ground up several of the pills into a fine white powder. She measured each, adding a little extra to be sure. Stirring the mixture took a bit, the water not wanting to absorb all of the powder.

She carried the three glasses into her bedroom and set them on the nightstand. Going to the closet, she reached high and pulled down a new storybook – one that was being saved for a surprise.

The kids were easy to lure into her room, following mommy and the new book. They didn't have the energy to be distracted anymore. Onto the bed they climbed, mom in the middle, with a precious child's head resting on each arm.

"Kids, mommy found some medicine that will help us all. It's not going to taste very good, but it's not a pill. You each need to drink all of it though. Every last drop, please."

There wasn't enough left in them to protest, not enough strength to complain about the bitter taste. A few moments later, the empty cups were returned to the nightstand.

Rose began reading the book. She noticed both children yawning soon afterwards. A few pages later, neither would respond. She pulled her loved ones close, one hand resting on each chest so she could feel the rhythm of both hearts through their tiny frames.

Rest well, she said to her children. *It'll all be over soon. No more pain. No more hunger. We'll join daddy in a better place.*

The little girl's breathing stopped first. A few moments went by, and her lungs tried to expand one last time. Less than a minute later, her heart stopped. The larger boy took longer, and for a little bit, Rose felt a sense of panic that she hadn't mixed enough of the drug in his cup. Soon afterwards, he stopped breathing.

Rose reached for the third cup and didn't hesitate. She didn't want her children anywhere without her – she wanted to be with them. She gulped the bitter liquid down and pulled the two lifeless bodies in a tight embrace.

The White House
June 12, 2017

Having army tanks parked on Pennsylvania Avenue was a sight the secretary thought he would never adjust to. Being shuttled to the White House every morning in a military vehicle, complete with a machine gun mounted on the roof, hadn't been part of the job description either. The day of his confirmation as the head of FEMA was one of the highlights of his career. It ranked right up there with receiving a post-graduate degree from Harvard, getting married, and the birth of his children. As he motored through the streets of Washington, Scott Fisher wondered if he would ever feel such a sense of success again.

Every morning he had breakfast with the president's chief of staff. At one point in his government service career, that statement would have been a boast. Exposure to prominence was something that moved you up the ladder.

Now, he dreaded those meetings almost as much as the actual briefings with the boss himself. These days, exposure was something one tried to avoid.

Scott was working on tomorrow's presentation, and like so many others over the last month, it wasn't good news. Were it not for the food, shelter and security that came along with the job, he would've resigned weeks ago.

Declaring martial law required the White House to manage the entire country. The effort had proven to be problematic at best. One staffer had compared the situation to the old communist regimes of the cold war era and their central planning committees. The executive branch would issue numerous goals and objectives, but they were rarely met. The various departments, agencies and bureaus could order, demand, belittle and stomp their feet all they wanted, there were just some aspects of the recovery that couldn't be accomplished quickly. In so many ways, the process of enlightenment was extremely difficult for a great number of federal officials. The almighty, all-powerful, never-been-denied US federal government had limitations! There were just some things it couldn't handle, couldn't fix, or was unable to manage. The whole thing was sad, really. Watching the federal government grasp that even it had boundaries was like observing a young child in the process of comprehending he really wasn't a superhero. Until accepting reality, a whole lot of imagination was in play.

Secretary Fisher had observed the men reporting to the president using their imaginations. Perhaps creativity was a more polite word. Like the dictatorial leadership of the old Soviet bloc, governing had become a game of numbers, and the numbers were often 'tweaked' by the time they got to the boss - the net effect being a mirage of progress being presented to the Commander-in-chief. Scott had initially tried to push back on his regional supervisors and other federal agencies. He wanted to know the cold, hard truth, unable to tolerate any imaginings or creativeness.

That effort not only exhausted him, but also damaged his ability to manage FEMA. Sullen bureaucrats began to avoid him – thinking he was on a witch hunt. Cooperation from sister departments dried up, his requests seemingly lost or pushed to the bottom of the priority stack. FEMA's headman knew the president was getting glass-half-full information at best – outright exaggerations and falsehoods were not uncommon. Secretary Fisher, during one of his more cynical moments, had whispered to himself, "Yes, Mien Fuhrer – you still have 100 divisions on the Eastern front." Scott eventually determined it was best for the country to play along and not contradict his fellow cabinet members. Even if the boss were being misled, some help *was* reaching the people.

Secretary Fisher scrolled through the reports on his laptop. There were three critical measurements the president wanted to monitor closely. The first was the percentage of the country that enjoyed electrical power. For all of its financial, military, and political power, restoring the infrastructure to generate and deliver electricity was the most elusive of the administration's goals.

Fortunately for FEMA, the Department of Energy was tasked with that seemingly impossible effort.

Scott's mind drifted to the last briefing, remembering the secretary of energy's voice. "Mr. President, we continue to increase the number of kilowatt hours being generated. As of this morning, another coal-fired plant in eastern Kentucky was brought on line. This plant will provide service to Cincinnati and Louisville for several hours per day."

The president had nodded at the good news, a weak smile crossing his lips. The energy expert continued, "We can now report that 20% of the population receives at least limited electrical power every day."

The chief executive's eyes seemed to glaze over. When he finally spoke, his voice was distant. "One in five Americans, Mr. Secretary? That's all we've been able to turn on - one in five?"

The man delivering the report squirmed in his chair. Scott could understand – he'd been in the hot seat more than his fair share lately. It wasn't the boss' wrath - that wasn't the bad part. What they all dreaded was the inevitable direction these meetings headed - trying to come up with a workable plan to improve the situation. It just couldn't be done. There was no good answer.

Secretary Fisher leaned back in his chair and rubbed his temples. He caught a glimpse of himself in the mirror hanging across from his desk. The gray hair was taking over, and he didn't think for a second it was hereditary. The crow's feet around his eyes grew deeper each day; it seemed almost as if they were having a race with his follicles to see which could make him look old first. At least he wasn't the only one. All of the cabinet heads looked like warmed-over zombies. This crisis had aged all of them and was no doubt taking years off of their lives.

After a brief moment of feeling sorry for himself, responsibility kicked back in, and Scott returned to his paperwork. He was looking for background information to justify his next report to the chief. Even though he knew the scope of the nation's problems as well as anyone, uncovering the facts still made him shudder.

The results of over-cycled electrical energy surging through the US grid were beyond imagination. When generators started spinning faster and faster, bearings failed, wires melted, and transformers blew. One of the initial reports after the attack concentrated on Hoover Dam and its massive electrical generators. Weighing 400 tons each, the overcharged revolutions had caused an epic failure of three of the turbines. No spares were available, but that really wasn't the biggest problem. Hoover was out of business because the Nevada transformer farm that cleaned, regulated, and distributed the dam's energy had burned to the ground. It would take months to acquire the parts to rebuild the facility.

Nuclear power plants hadn't fared much better. The attack had fried millions upon millions of computer circuit boards all over the nation. Multimillion dollar machines were rendered inoperable by a $1.00 electric component buried somewhere inside. The safety systems, cooling pumps and controls panels of the nation's power plants were severely damaged. No matter how desperate the country was for energy, no one was stupid enough to fire up a nuclear plant without a completely functional safety and monitoring system in place.

Just like Hoover, even if they could generate electrical power, the distribution system was badly damaged as well. Up-voltage and down-voltage control systems were wrecked. Transformers and regulators were fried. Spare parts couldn't be manufactured without electric juice, and the few components that were in stock hardly mattered when compared to the scale of the damage.

Depending on the position within the grid, some homes had their circuit breakers melted, while other folks simply suffered blown televisions, fried computers, or busted light bulbs. When electricity was restored to these residences, it was common for fires to ignite – sometimes causing entire neighborhoods to burn to the ground.

Factories and other consumers of high voltage current suffered the worst. The higher megahertz electricity unleashed by the Chinese attack delivered more bite at 460 VAC than the normal household's 115 VAC. Production lines, refineries, distribution systems and communications facilities were all severely damaged.

As one expert described it to the president, "It wasn't as bad as an EMP attack, but resulting damage was in the same vicinity."

The Secretaries of State and Commerce had been tasked with securing spare parts offshore, but that had been a worthless effort. Most of the European equipment wouldn't work in North America - it was of a different design. Additionally, when the US stopped all payments, Europe had been catapulted over the edge into crisis. While their riots and general social upheaval weren't even close to what the US experienced, the leaders of the Old World weren't too happy with the United States. When it became known that the US blamed China for its woes, the situation worsened. Furthermore, when military forces were ordered to Japan, Guam, and South Korea, the entire world thought the two nuclear powers were going to duke it out. Tensions had been high ever since.

Most of the failed circuitry was of Chinese manufacture and no one at the White House would even think of suggesting approaching "the Reds" for help. Japan, Singapore, and Taiwan all had manufacturing capabilities, but after the downfall of the US, those countries were unsure of America's military commitment to the region. The governments ringing the Pacific suddenly became very cozy with China.

Publically, China ranted and raved over the financial hardship caused by the collapse of the dollar and the $1.5 trillion worth of US Treasury notes it held. When the US started moving military assets toward the Red border, China had really put the pressure on her neighbors.

Everyone already knew all of this, even the Commander-in-chief.

On the rare occasion when a generating plant was repaired and juice flowed through the distribution system, there were still problems. Fire was the single biggest issue. Water couldn't be pumped, and gasoline couldn't be refined, so the fire departments were handicapped at best, unresponsive at worst.

It was late winter in the northern region of the United States, and ordinarily many homes and buildings were heated with electrical power. If a city or town were lucky enough to have water pressure restored, the pipes froze and burst in tens of thousands of structures and neighborhoods.

The second primary report delivered to the president focused on the nation's gross domestic product. The secretary of commerce was tasked with this part of the recovery. Efforts to replenish the food, medical and water supplies were compared to consumption. Without consistent electrical power, the output of the nation's farms and factories was less than most third world countries. The mighty economic machine that was America was broken.

Secretary Scott returned to his keyboard and began outlining his section of the briefing. He grimaced at what his assistants had secretly taken to calling his report – The Body Count News. The name fit, he supposed. Massive numbers of causalities from starvation, disease, lack of medical care and violence still racked the nation daily. The east and west coasts were the worst - their high population densities and less affluent neighborhoods suffering complete anarchy in some locales.

The numbers had been so astonishing, for so many days, it had become difficult to associate a human factor with the reports. Recording the deaths and burying the bodies had been an almost unmanageable undertaking without computers. State parks had been converted to burial grounds – mass graves the norm in many places.

FEMA tried to evacuate as many of the residents as possible from the worst areas. Fires ravaged entire neighborhoods, soon followed by looters and gangs, like vultures scavenging the remains. The resources of the federal government had been completely absorbed in less than a week. Secretary Scott shook his head at the memories of those first few days. The 3,000 camper-style trailers the agency kept for temporary housing were less than .00001 percent of what was required. Gasoline and diesel fuel dried up before even a third of the housing units could be pulled out of storage and moved to where they were needed.

For all of their planning, budget and training, Scott had to admit his hardworking employees had been overwhelmed by the sheer scope of events. Even with the military's assets coming on line, it was as if the government was an ant trying to eat an elephant. The analogy caused him to smirk, remembering the solution to the problem – an ant eats an elephant one bite at a time. The reality was people were dying by the thousands between bites.

Scott hit the key to tabulate to totals on his spreadsheet. He couldn't help but stare at the number, wanting to double-check the tally but knowing deep down inside it was accurate. His throat constricted, and soon his eyes began to water. He covered his face in both hands and let it go, wondering if he would ever stop crying.

The computer screen didn't react to the number. Its algorithms and binary code simply sat and waited on the next command. The screen calmly displayed the number - 45,000,000 estimated causalities.

Section III

From the Deep

Chapter 12

Crusoe, Texas
June 14, 2017

Morgan took the plastic trash bag from Todd as he pulled the water bike close to the bulkhead. "How did it go?"

Todd was upbeat about the results, "We got about five different types this time. I know where to look now."

Morgan peered inside the bag, noting it was chockfull of assorted seaweed, all varying by texture and hue. It had been agreed that Todd and David should explore the huge rocks that lined the ship channel and determine what could be harvested. Now it was time to test them all to see what was palatable, and experiment with grounding, boiling, drying, frying, and sautéing. The colonists had already identified uses for three different varieties, some of which didn't taste half-bad. While stationed in Okinawa during his stint in the Marine Corps, one of the men had become quite the connoisseur of the local delicacies, including countless preparations of seaweed. He wasn't Chef Emeril, but he did bring a certain culinary expertise to the table.

After the harvest came the taste testing. The settlers agreed that several of the algae could only appeal to a starving man whose taste buds had perished. Other types projected such a robust flavor; they seemed best used sparingly for seasoning only. The wild greens found on the island were fairly bland, and all of the community's store-bought salad dressing was consumed in the first few weeks. The thin, brownish-red stalks were called dulse and had proven a great spice. Other types were boiled down to make broth, while some species were dried in the sun and eaten whole as a salad or side dish.

Morgan was always worried about toxins and allergic reactions, so a process was developed to ensure no one got sick from eating something disagreeable. The first step was to rub a small portion on the skin and wait a few hours. If a rash didn't occur, then the next test involved rubbing just a tiny bit on the tester's lip. If that didn't produce any bad reaction, then the tongue was the next experiment. If the specimen didn't cause any negative results, then just a mere fragment was ingested.

So far, they had been lucky. Only one variety had been found to disagree with human consumption, and samples of the variety were shown to all of the food preparers so it would never be used.

Being a nurse, Morgan ran the testing process with the documentation and attention to detail of a professional lab. First, she separated the samples and compared them to known varieties. Next, she labeled, photographed, and described each species in detail. Morgan meticulously catalogued the results and stored the document on her smart phone. It wasn't just the seaweed that had to pass Morgan's scrutiny, but every unidentified food source. She smiled to herself, thinking about the knowledge she had acquired. Another few years and she might be able to rival the wisdom of the typical Native American, indigenous to this area thousands of years ago.

The island had several small brackish lakes along its western shore, and these had proven to be Crusoe's breadbasket. The shores were lined with common cattails, those plants proving to be a wonderful source of nourishment. Stalks, roots and pollen had all contributed greatly to the diet of the islanders.

A lack of yeast was initially a big problem. Boats weren't exactly equipped for baking, and no one had any of the substance on board. It was the cattails that saved the day, their pollen used as flour that was mixed with water and covered with cheesecloth. After a week of sitting in the open, wild yeast had been captured from the air.

Soap was another ancillary product of the cattails and seaweed. Kelp was burned to a fine ash and then mixed with the milky substance from the shoots of the more mature shafts. Several of the women thought it made a better shampoo than any they had ever purchased from a drugstore.

While the small island was devoid of larger trees, several acorn-producing varieties were identified at the far south end of the island, and the meaty seeds had been collected, blanched, and salted.

Frogs, shrimp, crab, fish, birds, rabbit, rattlesnake, and occasionally bird eggs provided a healthy diet of protein. The men built traps and snares with scrap wire and wood.

The seeds of fruits and vegetables, salvaged from items stocked in the fleet's refrigerators and pantries and repurposed for propagation, were being carefully nurtured in Crusoe's gardens. Tomatoes, potatoes, corn, and even squash were babied along in makeshift flowerpots on the back of practically every vessel. Because of the felonious habits of the local raccoon and rabbit populations, shore side planting was avoided. Black tie galas prior to the collapse were replaced with a kind of "Horticultural Expo," a popular social event to compare the growth of these non-native plants. One of the pre-teens suggested that a Crusoe 4-H Fair might be in order by late summer.

As Morgan began sorting the new colors of seaweed, she wondered if any of the new samples would mimic the taste of pepper. She missed the bite of the fresh ground black spice on her meals.

Plymouth, Ohio
June 20, 2017

Rusty heard it first. The red lab's head rose off the rug and spun toward the road, something unusual attracting his attention. Grover Peterson lowered the book he was reading and stared at his pet. "What's the matter boy?"

Grover sat the book on the end table and pushed himself out of his favorite chair. Rusty didn't point unless there was something worth checking out.

Before he reached the front door, Grover recognized the car engine. The sound of gravel against rubber tires reached his ears well before the sedan came into view. The otherwise non-descript Ford wouldn't normally have attracted any attention were it not for the fact that it was the first car to rattle down the road in weeks.

The 12-gauge double barrel next to the front door was reassuring, but Grover didn't sense ill intent from the vehicle as it slowly drove past his mailbox. When the car stopped and backed up, he moved his hand to the barrel. When the driver turned into his driveway, he picked up the scattergun and Rusty barked, his fur bristling on the back of his spine. "It's okay, boy. I see it."

Grover lived in a rural, country cabin that had originally been built by his grandfather. His father had expanded both the home and the acreage of the northern Ohio farm. Grover had remodeled and modernized the place after his dad passed away some years ago. The homestead was still called the Peterson Farm by everyone in the area, even though Grover had broken the tradition of living off the land after his graduation from college. He didn't want to be a farmer like his father – he wanted to make things with his hands.

As he watched the car approach down the long driveway, he noticed there were at least three men inside. This wasn't good news because the shotgun only held two shells. Still, why would troublemakers be so stupid as to drive right up to the main house in broad daylight?

As the sedan drew closer, the license plate disclosed it was a government vehicle. That didn't mean as much now as it would have before the collapse. It would buy the interlopers a little more time to explain why they were here – but not much.

All four doors opened when the automobile stopped. Grover reached into the hall table's drawer and put a handful of shells in his pocket. Three of the uninvited callers wisely remained adjacent to the car while the fourth strode across the sidewalk and up the wide, wooden steps leading to the front porch. Rusty growled right before the three knocks sounded on the door frame.

"Who is it?" Grover yelled from beside the threshold.

"Mr. Peterson? My name is Dan Somerton. I'm with the Department of Homeland Security. I'd like to speak with you about Sugarhill Machine and Tool, sir."

Grover's eyebrows arched at the response. He phrased his answer carefully. "No offense, Mr. Somerton, but times have been a little strange lately. How would a body know you are who you say you are?"

While he couldn't be sure, he thought the man on his front porch actually chuckled. "Mr. Peterson, I have my federal identification. The other men with me are from the Department of Commerce and the Department of Defense. We want to speak to you about getting Sugarhill back up and running again."

"Please show your identification, sir."

The man on the porch reached inside of his jacket pocket and produced an official-looking ID card. Grover couldn't read it, but it seemed legitimate enough. He'd have to take the chance.

Cradling the shotgun in his arms, Grover unlatched the deadbolt and opened the front door. The hooked screen door stood between them, not much of a barrier if his instinct were wrong. The young man waiting on the other side smiled and pretended not to notice the 12-gauge. He probed, "Would you like to talk out here or inside Mr. Peterson?"

"I think we'd all be more comfortable inside. It's a little cold out there for these old bones, if you know what I mean."

"Fine with me, sir. I need to invite my colleagues to join in our conversation - if that's okay with you?"

Grover nodded, hoping deep down inside he hadn't made a big mistake.

The young man motioned to his friends, and soon everyone was shaking hands in the living room. Rusty transformed from guard dog to tail wagging, attention seeker, rubbing the legs of the strangers like he'd never had company before. Grover propped the shotgun against the arm of his chair and rested.

Grover had sipped the last of his South American roasted coffee beans four days ago. Warm tea would have to do, as there hadn't been any ice for weeks. The older gentleman's offer was politely declined; everyone taking a seat after the social amenities were exchanged. Rusty returned to his reserved spot at Grover's feet, head on front paws but eyes keen for any indication of someone interested in petting his head.

Somerton got right to business. "Mr. Peterson, we have identified Sugarhill as a key component supplier for several different critical path manufacturing facilities. We are trying to jumpstart these plants...get them going again. We drove by your facility a short time ago, and the building seemed intact. Do you know of any reason why you couldn't start machining product again?"

Grover didn't answer immediately. The young man had said a mouthful, and he was working through it bit by bit. Finally he glanced around at his visitors and responded. "Sugarhill...critical? Our business has been down...way down...for the last five years, young man. I find it hard to believe we're 'critical' for anything."

Peterson's statement met with understanding nods all around. One of the suits replied, "We understand, sir. Still, your firm is listed as a supplier of several key components in the Government Services Administration's database. Is that information incorrect?"

"Yes, we still can make everything, or at least we could. Most of my business went to China, young man. The only reason I kept the place open was to provide jobs for a dozen locals who've been with me for a long time. Sugarhill has lost money the last few years."

Somerton expanded, "We can't import from China any longer, Mr. Peterson. The parts Sugarhill can make are very important if we are going to get the country moving again. Can you provide us with a list of whom and what you would need to start making these items?"

One of the other visitors handed Grover a single sheet of paper listing several different SKU numbers and descriptions. The items were all familiar, having been manufactured at his company over the years. Grover surveyed the list, making mental notes. "Nothing special or difficult here. You'll have to round up my machinists and provide the raw materials. We'll need electricity and water. A couple tons of quality bar stock and probably a few machine tool parts. Provide those items and a few things I've probably forgotten about, and we can produce these products." Grover's confidence seemed to make his visitors happy.

The business owner still didn't understand how resurrecting his flailing enterprise would fit into the grand scheme these bureaucrats were hatching. Even before the collapse, having three federal agencies send representatives to invite him to contract with the US government would have been odd; these days it was truly bizarre. "Gentlemen, I'm still a little puzzled. Sugarhill is a small, dilapidated, old country machine shop. Nothing more - nothing less. If we didn't make parts for the local farmers, I would've closed the business years ago. I know there are dozens of bigger, more modern shops in Toledo and Cleveland. Why us? Why now?"

Somerton smiled as the mixed lab curled up at Grover's feet shifted his weight to find his sweet spot. "Mr. Peterson, according to our information, Sugarhill never upgraded to modern, computer-driven lathes and presses. Our understanding is that all of your equipment setup is manually configured. The surge through the power gird destroyed millions of circuit boards in those modern machines, and we can't replace them. Those hi-tech shops can't even make paperclips right now."

Grover nodded his understanding, signaling the man to continue. "Another factor is Sugarhill's location. Some of the urban areas are...um...shall we say 'unsettled' at the moment. Plymouth, Ohio seems to have weathered the storm pretty well."

The last remark caused Grover to snort. "The county sheriff suffered a heart attack, and we've barely kept up with burying the dead. We've had more suicides in the last four weeks than the last 50 years. The elderly can't get their prescriptions, most folks are hungry, and even a bout of the flu can turn deadly.

We've had two women die during childbirth since this whole mess started. I wouldn't exactly call that 'weathering the storm pretty well.'"

Much to Grover's surprise, the young government man didn't back down from his observation. "Mr. Peterson, I'm sorry the people around Plymouth have suffered, but what you've described can't compare to the pain and suffering the larger cities are experiencing."

Everyone decided to change the subject. Much to Rusty's dismay, the four men soon left after agreeing to meet Grover at Sugarhill first thing in the morning.

~  ~

Just after dawn, Dan Somerton was sitting outside Sugarhill's facility when Grover and Rusty arrived. A high chain-link fence surrounded the 20,000-square foot metal building. After unlocking and opening the gate, both men parked on the gravel lot at the front of the building.

Grover hadn't been inside for a few weeks, having seen no need to waste what gas he had left in his truck. The last visit had been to empty out the vending machines of every candy bar, bag of chips and roll of breath mints. He donated the two sacks of goodies to a local church to shore up the empty food bank coffers.

Grover retrieved the coffee, sugar, and creamer from the break room for his own use.

As the two men approached the entrance, Somerton snorted. Someone, probably Grover, had nailed a hand-painted sign on the entrance: "No food inside – already picked clean."

Grover noticed the young man's reaction and shrugged, "I think it was worth a try. Seems like it worked."

A quick tour of the shop revealed everything was as he had left it. Grover wouldn't have been shocked if vandals broke into the property despite his brief, but succinct note on the door. After the past few months, nothing would surprise him again.

Grover cleared a desktop for Dan in the front office, before pulling out various bills of material, drawings and machine instructions from the myriad of file cabinets lining the walls.

The two men worked for almost five hours straight before determining how many of the government's wish list Sugarhill could create - if raw materials were provided. Grover watched, fascinated as the young government employee removed a large, cell phone-looking device from his bag and dialed a number.

Almost immediately, a voicemail system answered the satellite phone. Grover thought it was funny as he listened to Dan leave a message asking for a call back.

After disconnecting the call, Dan shrugged his shoulders. "They are so busy. They have over 500 threads going all at the same time."

"Threads?"

The government's man nodded. "Yes, that's what they call them. When all of the agencies finally got their act together, they established a set of priorities. Here, let me show you."

Dan rummaged around in his briefcase and pulled out a sheet of paper, handing it to Grover.

The document carried the seal of the president of the United States, and outlined the official priorities for all government agencies for the recovery. Grover scanned the list:

1. **Energy** – Electrical power, refined fuels, nuclear, oil, natural gas, solar and wind
2. **Communications** – Cell, internet, land-line, radio and television broadcasting
3. **Transportation** – As per #1 above, delivery of non-electrical power for heating, manufacturing and industrial usage
4. **Medical** – Hospitals, pharmaceutical, equipment
5. **Manufacturing** – Critical items required by #1 are deemed top priority
6. **Agriculture** – Spring planting, delivery of feed and other necessities for livestock, fertilizer and fuel for operations

Dan paused while Grover read, then added, "Without electrical energy, nothing gets done. It has amazed a lot of people how critical that link in the supply chain is."

Grover's expression reflected his understanding, "That's why you want us to make these specific parts. They're used in electric turbines. You need them to repair the power plants."

Dan nodded. "You're correct, sir. We can provide mobile electrical power, but it's very limited. We started at the beginning and are working our way through each step. In your case, Sugarhill needs steel. We knew that before we came here, so a small mill outside of Flint has been operating for three days now. We drove two of the US Army's big generator trucks to the mill, parked them outside, and hooked up the cables. We'll do the same for Sugarhill in a few days. The steel from Flint will come here. After you make the parts, we'll take them to the next step. That's what we are calling a thread. There are over 500 of these threads in progress right now."

Grover was impressed, but also awed by the complexity and scale of the undertaking. "Where did the mill get the raw materials it needed? Did you start at the mine?"

Dan shook his head, "No, we got lucky there. The mill had enough stock onsite to make what we needed. It's rare for any manufacturing plant to keep much inventory. It's expensive to store on the shelves, and with modern computer systems, they could order and receive delivery right before they need it. That's a great system during normal times, but it has made it very difficult to get the country jumpstarted again."

Grover started to comment, but Dan's phone rang. The conversation conducted over the high-tech gadget sounded like any other materials planning meeting. Sugarhill needed A, B and C – when can those items be expected?

"We'll have all of this stuff here in four days," Dan continued. "I think we need to start gathering your machinists together and preparing to restart the shop."

Grover agreed. "I don't think that will be a problem. I do have one question though – how are we going to pay my people? Money isn't much good right now, and while some of them would see the big picture, others are struggling with day-to-day living. To ask them to leave their families right now? Well, there would need to be some sort of an incentive."

Dan smiled knowingly. "Do you think food would be proper compensation?"

"No doubt about it. You have access to that much food?"

Dan grinned and answered, "If food will do the trick, I'll deliver the groceries. Let's start going door to door tomorrow and make sure we can get everyone in here."

"We'd better take my truck. People are a little edgy these days, and your government car might not be welcome."

"I understand…. Believe me, I understand."

Matagorda Island, Texas
June 21, 2017

Wyatt lounged on Boxer's bridge and inspected the community of Crusoe. Like a favorite lounge chair in the living room, he had taken to the captain's chair as his favorite perch to enjoy the day's first cup of coffee. The coffee was almost gone, and he dreaded when he could no longer relish one of the few luxuries this life afforded.

Just like Wyatt and his favorite chair, the residents of Crusoe settled into a routine not unlike any small town. Each morning, Wyatt and the others busied themselves with the small maintenance items required to keep their boats functional as a home. After those tasks were completed, the boaters tended to gather around the dock to discuss community needs as a whole.

Energy was always the single biggest concern. Gasoline or diesel was required to generate 95% of Crusoe's electrical power, and there weren't any gas stations open for refilling the fuel tanks. As the weather progressed from warm to hot, it grew more difficult to sleep or find comfort during the day without running the air conditioners. Everyone suffered, unwilling to waste the fuel consumed by running the gensets.

There were three boats in the fleet that had substantial wind or solar power. Even with the fairly constant onshore breeze, the wind turbines wouldn't produce enough juice to run air conditioners. Batteries could be recharged, but climate control required more power than any of the renewable systems could provide.

Not all of the boats had arrived at Crusoe with the same amount of fuel. This had been a major challenge for the community, as some people believed everyone should share equally while others thought each family unit should stand on its own. Eventually, a system of barter was instituted, with the fuel-rich boaters trading for other necessities. One of the most valuable commodities turned out to be toilet paper.

Wyatt worked the calculations a dozen times. The gasoline-powered boats would empty their reserves first, probably in the next 20 days. The diesel boats would fare better, lasting another 30-45 days. After that, the community would be limited to what was provided by the sun and wind.

Because fuel was a finite resource, every possible method of conservation was implemented. Firewood was scavenged from the rubble of the old base, as well as from the beach. Patrols gathered what washed ashore twice weekly. Food was cooked, water heated, and fish smoked using dockside pits. While every boat in the fleet was outfitted with microwaves, or ovens of some sort, the outside kitchens required little precious fuel and thus replaced their technologically advanced cousins.

Making fresh water was another energy draw, as water makers ran off electricity. The pioneers determined that water usage should be divided into two categories, public and private. Each boat maintained water in its private storage tank, while public water facilities were established onshore.

One of the industrious residents created a series of shower stalls that utilized the sun to heat the water. Hanging overhead in clear plastic bags, the Crusoe Public Bathhouse even sported its own handmade sign. Wyatt smirked when he laid eyes on the facility, thinking how much the rustic structure reminded him of "Gilligan's Island."

Dishwashing, food processing, and laundry were all deemed public uses of water. The diesel boats typically were equipped with the largest capacity systems and the most fuel, so they became known as the Crusoe Water Company. Wyatt sat and watched the morning bucket brigade filling their containers at the back of a diesel boat. Each morning, several residents carried that water ashore to be used for public consumption. It was a lot of work. Wyatt snorted when he overheard one of the residents complaining, "I never thought about how heavy water was until I moved to Crusoe."

When they had first arrived, such a remark would have gone unnoticed. Now, Wyatt paid attention to those things, always trying to gauge attitude, morale and sense of community. Governing what was essentially a small town appeared easy at first. Everyone seemed to pull together, given that ultimately their survival was always in question. After the newness of the island wore off, small quarrels began to pop up here and there. Initially, these minor disagreements typically involved policies or systems that impacted the entire community. Some residents, for example, tired of fish as the main source of protein. They began to lobby for investing more time in gathering alternative sources of nourishment.

Wyatt realized early on that some organized form of decision-making was going to be necessary to keep the peace. Every boater couldn't vote on every issue that arose, so a town council of sorts was formed.

The boats were rafted together in three rows, with each row electing its own representative. A row could have an election anytime it wanted. Issues, disputes and grievances were aired before the council meetings, which were always open to the public. So far, everyone had abided by the decisions made at these morning assemblies. Wyatt had pondered more than once what would happen when someone decided they didn't want to follow the determination of the council. To date, the rule of law had held.

Some disputes focused on the division of labor. The vast majority of the boaters were over 50 years old, and several nursed minor health issues. Todd, David, and Sage were the youngest members of the community and were initially treated like everyone's grandchildren. After arriving at Army Hole, these younger, more energetic residents were inundated with requests to help with this, fetch that, or carry those. Happy to help at first, their generosity quickly wore off as each was assigned a normal workload on top of the friendly, informal requests. The situation eventually degraded to the point where Sage spoke up at one council meeting, asking the gathered crowd if slavery had been reinstituted while she had been sleeping.

A few personality conflicts arose as well. Essentially, everyone's house was practically on top of the neighbors' – a cramped experience for some. The close proximity of the boats resulted in occasional spats ranging from accusations of eavesdropping to neighbors playing loud music late into the night. One solution was the discovery that the parks department had constructed a bunkhouse next to the ranger station. This small cabin could accommodate up to eight people and had survived the years relatively intact. It was a couple from one of the smaller cabin cruisers who announced one afternoon that they were going on vacation. Tired of the small, cramped space their vessel provided, they packed up blankets, air mattresses and a picnic basket and headed to the bunkhouse for an overnighter. The Crusoe Holiday Six quickly became popular, as did camping on the beach.

As the weather grew hot, so did tempers. There was so much physical, sweaty labor involved to just provide the basics, people became easily irritated.

It was Morgan who came up with the idea to reschedule as many chores as possible at night. Lights were rigged high on the boats with solar recharging. Dishes, laundry, cooking and other preparations were migrated to the cooler air of the evening.

The single biggest problem was morale. It had been almost five months since the world had fallen apart, and there wasn't any sign of a recovery. It was the younger members of the community that worried Wyatt the most. Sage had asked her father if he thought she would ever have a date again. David had joked about how he should have married his high school sweetheart, teasing his mother over the fading hope of having grandchildren. Morgan smiled and laughed at the jest, but Wyatt knew the entire affair bothered her.

The older members of the community seemed to deal with the lack of television, internet and cell phones in stride. The "under 30" crowd struggled with the change. For a while, DVD movies were a popular recreational activity, the young and able-bodied congregating at night to share the event. After a month or so, attendance began to drop off, and Wyatt heard mumblings about how watching the visual images of the past were depressing.

Visits to the beach for swimming, picnics and throwing Frisbees were popular for a while, but that activity began to decline in popularity as the temperate spring air turned to the blistering hot, Texas summer. Morgan commented on how the newness of sand and surf quickly wore off. It was a good thing too, as the last squirt of sunblock coincided with a sweltering day, adding to the avoidance of outdoor recreation.

There were positive aspects to life in Crusoe. Most everyone lost weight given the diet of fresh foods, increase in daily exercise, and the unavailability of quarter pounder combo meals. Several of the middle-aged residents reported having more energy than before, with colds and sniffles being almost non-existent.

Alcohol consumption was no longer an option - the last few bottles of hard liquor being designated as emergency medical supplies and locked away with Morgan's other first aid equipment. Wyatt chuckled out loud, thinking about how several of the men had threatened to build a still. The project had never materialized because no one knew how to ferment spirits without sugar.

Wyatt stretched his legs, his gaze wandering ashore where Todd and David were cleaning the salt from two fishing reels. He was proud of how David had become the younger boy's friend and helped eased Crusoe's youngest member through the problems associated with their new life. Wyatt could see how David had benefited from the relationship as well. He made a mental note to try and reward the two young men somehow.

Plymouth, Ohio
June 25, 2017

Grover gazed at what amounted to the most unusual parade Plymouth, Ohio had ever seen. In the lead was a plain-looking government sedan, complete with flashing blue lights mounted on the roof. Nothing out of the ordinary there, he mused. Most parades started with a police escort of some sort.

It was what rolled by afterwards that was so out of place. Two military Humvees with machine guns mounted on the roof were next in line. Helmeted soldiers manned the ominous-looking weapons, moving the heavy barrels right and left as they rolled by. Grover noted the shiny brass belts of ammunition hanging beneath the black guns. *Those aren't just for show*, he thought.

Behind those armed attendants were two huge military trucks painted in forest green camouflage, accented with black stenciled numbers all over the sides. Grover guessed those were the generator trucks, but couldn't be sure. He'd never seen anything quite like them.

Another armed Humvee was followed by two private tractor-trailers. The common over-the-road trucks were commandeered by soldiers, each cab outfitted with a rider managing the barrel of an M16 as it protruded from the window.

A bright yellow school bus followed the semis. Reflecting sunlight blocked Grover's line of sight inside the windows, but he knew there were no schoolchildren inside. He realized that the food, electrical generators, and other equipment on its way to Sugarhill were extremely valuable. The bus transported dozens of soldiers – designated sentries for his small machine shop.

Grover's truck was the first vehicle of what would become Plymouth's second parade of the day. Dan and he had dedicated days to canvassing the community; personally contacting Sugarhill's machinists and other employees to make sure enough staff would be available to manufacture the desperately needed parts.

The campaign had yielded some tragic results. So many people were dead or too sick to work. The surviving population of Plymouth, Ohio suffered from lack of nutrition and the diseases that naturally followed, as well as lack of access to maintenance medications, ordinarily taken daily to control the symptoms of hypertension or diabetes or clinical depression. Regardless of the cause, Sugarhill would barely have enough staff reporting to restart the company. Grover was determined to roll up his sleeves and contribute.

Providing transportation for those healthy enough to report for work proved problematic. As automobile tanks had been drained to provide fuel for generators, no one had any gasoline left. It was the FEMA representative who managed to deliver three five-gallon plastic cans of gas to mobilize the workforce.

Grover drove from duplex to cottage to farmhouse, pouring a gallon or two in his employee's cars and trucks so they could make it to Sugarhill. Those personnel were now lined up behind him, ready to follow the military convoy to the plant. Everyone switched off their motors to conserve every last drop of the precious liquid.

Due to security concerns, Grover was instructed to hold until the last escort vehicle passed, wait for a few minutes, and then follow. The small, once friendly town of Plymouth was an abstract backdrop for the military hardware slowly snaking its way down Main Street. Grover couldn't help but consider the surreal picture the situation had created. The brick and clapboard storefronts broadcasted a message of welcoming, rural America. The locally owned businesses that lined Main were inviting, honest places to fill a prescription, shop for second-hand goods or share a sandwich for lunch. Watching an armed, ready-to-engage military force passing by windows that advertised fresh pie and a sale on paper towels was disturbing, almost bizarre.

Grover waited the prerequisite amount of time before pulling onto Main and following the government procession. He glanced in his rearview mirror to verify everyone was part of the convoy. A few miles outside of town, they encountered one of the military Humvees blocking the road. Grover was identified and waived by, as were the six civilian cars and trucks following behind him. Presumably, folks who didn't have business at the machine shop wouldn't be allowed to pass.

The once-abandoned business became a beehive of activity. Soldiers scampered here and there, distributing power cables, boxes of supplies, and other equipment. As soon as the employees had collected in the front office, a man wearing the uniform of a major greeted everyone and explained that the Army Corp of Engineers would have the power turned on shortly.

Before long, duties and tasks were assigned to all of Grover's staff, and everyone began to work, trying to reboot Sugarhill.

Within two hours, electrical power was flowing through the shop, provided by the rumbling generators parked outside. That milestone caused the men working inside to pause, many of them staring up at the florescent bulbs like they had never seen electric lights before. Grover let it go, intrigued by the reaction. A few moments passed before the boss cleared his throat rather loudly, a signal it was time to get back at it.

By late that evening, the first lathe was turning. Sugarhill was in business again.

Plano, Texas
June 28, 2017

The small U. S. Air Force shuttle landed quite smoothly, the pilot braking hard to slow the rolling plane before it reached the end of the short runway. Even in normal times, the Plano, Texas Regional Airport didn't see that many jet aircraft. In reality, the plane could have skidded sideways and spun in circles and Reed probably wouldn't have cared. He was going to see his family.

The congressman also failed to observe several damaged aircraft parked outside the hangars. The charred rubble of a nearby maintenance facility went completely unnoticed as well. Reed just wanted to hold his wife and children.

Six Texas National Guardsmen were waiting for the aircraft. Two would remain behind to protect his plane while the pilots were escorted to a nearby facility for food and rest. A pair of the reservists would accompany Reed to his father-in-law's remote ranch. Texas was still a dangerous place for travelers – or anyone else for that matter. Five other government vehicles from various agencies and authorities waited on Reed's traveling companions. The representative's head came out of the clouds long enough to realize all of the drivers were armed.

In a way, Reed felt guilty. He was using resources that no doubt could have been utilized doing other things. The remorse wasn't overwhelming, just a small tugging that slightly tainted what would have otherwise been the perfect homecoming.

A small, unfolding staircase allowed everyone to depart the aircraft. Reed had talked little with the other passengers during the flight. A combination of FEMA, DOD and Homeland Security personnel were aboard. Their conversations had held little interest for Reed. His mind filled with visions of his family, curiosity over how much the children had grown and a longing to hold his wife. Right now, nothing else was going to hold his attention.

"Congressman," approached an older man wearing captain's bars, "If you'll please accompany me, we'll be on our way."

Reed nodded, glad there wasn't going to be another delay. In minutes, his overnight bag was loaded into the back of the Humvee, and they were moving.

The military version of the Hummer wasn't very comfortable – lacking the amenities normally associated with the high-end civilian model. The dash wasn't padded, the seats were quite hard, and there wasn't a stereo in the console. Reed barely noticed and didn't care. He was going to see his family.

The two guardsmen were very quiet, and that suited Reed just fine. No doubt they had their own problems, missed their own families or were worried about their own homes. Reed couldn't fix that, and had learned several weeks ago not to dwell on things he couldn't fix. There were simply too many objects-beyond-repair in his current life.

The drive through suburban Dallas didn't shock him. Piles of ashes where there had been thriving businesses, gas stations boarded up, people standing in line for handouts or medical care...the scene reminded him of Washington – probably the same as any major American city.

As they passed, Reed couldn't help but notice the faces of the people. Words kept popping into his mind, words like hollow, sunken, forlorn - zombies. Children didn't move with the energy of youth as they should have. Reed watched a mother with two pre-teen kids walking down the sidewalk, all of them stirred with the lethargic gait of the elderly, the infirm or the weak.

Dirty faces and stringy hair were the norm. Many of the people appeared to just be standing or sitting – no place to go or nothing to do. The passing Hummer was a curiosity, but a minor one. The military vehicle wasn't even worthy of the energy required to move one's neck so as to follow its progress.

Reed had played sports in high school. While his athletic ability wasn't worthy of note, he had developed a keen eye toward judging momentum. He could always tell how the game was going to end by watching the body language and expressions of the players. Momentum was so important. The winners knew how to turn it around. The better teams seemed to sense how to manage it.

"We're losing," he muttered quietly. "We've lost momentum, and the world is kicking out butts. We're beaten, and the game's not even over yet."

Reed forced himself to direct his vision ahead, determined not to allow anything or anybody dampen his mood. He only had one day, a short 24 hours to visit. He wanted to make the most of it.

Before long, they were out of the urban area and into the countryside. It was a relief. The open spaces of northern Texas rewarmed Reed's soul, recharging his mood. It was if they had driven out from under a giant dome of gloom and despair. The air was different out here - the fog of suffering was diluted. *These people are doing better,* he thought. *They're better off, if for no other reason than not having to witness so much pain in their fellow man.*

The two-hour drive seemed to pass quickly, despite the rock-hard seat and jarring ride. Reed pointed to the lane leading to the ranch where his father-in-law was waiting by the gate. Climbing out of the older, faded pickup, the tall man moved to unlock the heavy chain. Dressed in worn jeans and button-collar plaid shirt, the old cowboy looked distinguished in a western sort-of-way. His rugged demeanor, worn boots and dirty Stetson gave Reed a sense of peace. Who better to have looking after his family in a world that resembled the Old West than a son born of those times?

At the end of the long, winding driveway waited his wife and children. Reed almost didn't wait for the driver to come to a complete stop. He threw the door open and rushed to the reunion, not having enough arms to deliver the embraces so mightily needed.

~  ~

Cob McCormick gingerly perched in the old lawn chair on the back porch. "There's a front moving in, boy; I feel it in my bones," he said to the old hound at his feet. Bluto's answer was a short wag of his tail and nothing more.

Cob knew it was the broken leg he'd suffered years ago. It was more accurate than any of these high-tech weathermen on television. The old rancher couldn't suppress a chuckle. The notion that not only was his old injury capable of forecasting, his bone-barometer had outlasted all those high-tech

Doppler thing-ah-mah-jiggers and electronic climate voodoo machines. He knew it was going to rain tonight, and those television weathermen weren't saying much these days. *Another victory for the old ways*, he thought.

For the hundredth time, he concluded the broken leg had been punishment – the Lord's wrath. A warning from God directed at an out-of-control youth to mend his unbridled ways. Cob shook his head at the memory, a slight color warming his leathery face. It was as close as Cob got to shame.

"No," he commented to Bluto, "it was that ornery cuss Slang Adams. It was his fault we all went down to Mexico to drink and carouse. It was sinful, boy. Nothing more and nothing less."

Bluto's soulful eyes gazed at his master with an expression that seemed to say, "I've heard this story a million times before." And in fact, he had.

"How was I supposed to know that pretty senorita had a jealous boyfriend? How was I to know he was skilled with a shovel handle?" Cob reached down and scratched the old hound's ear, the act initiating a rapid sweeping motion of Bluto's tail. "No, old boy, a man's past deeds come back on him later in life. I can remember all of us piling into the back of Slang's worn-out, Oldsmobile convertible after that last football game. Full of ourselves, we were. All young and invincible - heading to Mexico to sample beer and pretty girls."

Cob shook his head at the memory and wondered why he dwelled on that injury so much. Maybe it was because it was the only time in his life another man had bested him. Maybe it was because of his father's reaction.

Cob's mom had gone off like a rocket when she found out the truth, clutching her Bible to her chest and ranting for hours. Cob's daddy just shook his head, pretending disgust for his wife's sake. Later, when they were alone, he'd only had one question for his wayward son – "You didn't run into a pretty gal down there by the name of Katrina, did ya?"

His old man hadn't waited on an answer, and the incident was never spoken of again. Cob realized his father was sending a message – I can't throw the first stone because I'm not without sin.

"Bluto, I've been shot by a rustler, suffered broken ribs, been thrown from a horse, and lost count of the number of fistfights with ranch hands. Why do I keep coming back to Mexico?"

Again, Bluto wasn't any help.

Cob waved off his companion's silence. The dog was beginning to act like his wife, BeaGwen - both of them evidently bored with his reminiscing. The rancher changed his gaze to the backyard. While he would never admit it, the old gruff loved having his grandkids here at the ranch. Having his only daughter back home during these troubling times was a bonus. Cob casually observed the kids run around the ancient rusty swing set, yelping and laughing with their parents.

Cob had to admit Reed had turned out okay. He hadn't been happy when his baby girl had run off to college so far away. When she had returned home with this Wallace fella, well, Cob just couldn't seem to warm to the kid. Despite

BeaGwen's being partial to Reed, the announcement of their marriage had almost put him in his grave. Bluto had always judged Reed acceptable as well, so the wedding had proceeded without strong protest.

Cob looked down at Bluto and raised his eyebrows. "I guess he wasn't a big city lawyer for so long. Being a state representative is honorable, I suppose. Service to your country is never a bad thing."

Cob glanced up in time to see Reed hobbling toward him, out of breath from playing tag with the kids. The congressman took a nearby chair. "Cob, I can't tell you how thankful I am that my family has your place as a retreat. I would've gone insane with worry over the last few months if they hadn't been here."

Cob nodded and spoke without turning to acknowledge Reed. "No problem, son. She may be your wife, but she's still my baby girl in a way. I wouldn't have had her and the kids anyplace else. They'll be just fine right here until things settle down. How's that going, if I may ask?"

Reed paused for a moment, unsure of how to answer. He decided the tough, old rancher could handle more than most people. "It's not good, Cob. The government is broke, there's no money coming in, and other countries won't do business with us. The military is fed up, the federal employees are at the end of their ropes, and most people have lost hope."

The lack of reaction didn't surprise Reed. He had gotten to know his father-in-law well over the years. He was a rugged individual and had seen his share of hard times. Cob rubbed his chin, clearly in thought. The rancher bent down and scratched Bluto's head, finally ready to speak. "You know, they asked for it. Ever since FDR, they've been asking for this. In a way, I'm surprised it took this long. The whole premise of how the government was working just didn't make sense."

"What do you mean by 'premise,' Cob?"

The old gentleman scanned the horizon with his hand. "You know, we raise cattle here. The land isn't naturally blessed with enough vegetation to feed more than a single longhorn or two per acre. A man can't make a living off of a couple head per acre, so we plant our own feed. We had to grow our own in order to expand the herd. Now, back in the day, there were some old fools who thought growing crops was a better way to make money. They raised grain, no cattle, and tried to sell it every year. They all failed."

Cob paused for a moment, his protective gaze focused on one of the children who had just fallen down. When laughter confirmed the child was okay, he continued. "There were others who were strictly cattlemen. Planting crops was considered radical, not the business of a true rancher. They tried to buy their feed from others, but it was always too expensive, and eventually, they all failed as well."

Reed didn't get it. When Cob looked up, the congressman's expression said as much. "The federal government has vacillated between being "cattle only" to "crops only," depending on who's in power. The Republicans want to be cattle only. They think the cattle should be more robust, be able to survive without store-bought feed. Their answer was always to buy more land in order to grow the herd and stay in business. The Democrats, on the other hand, think it should be crops only. They want to borrow money to plant the crop and pay it back after harvest. Neither system works on its own. Both of them kept borrowing money to cover the failure. They kept going into debt, thinking next year's crop or beef prices would cover the loss. It never did."

Reed was beginning to catch on, curious over the analogy. "So Cob, how did you do it?"

The old man shook his head at the remembrances raised by the question. "Son, it wasn't easy. There's a balance between the herd size and the amount of debt you're willing to risk on planting and harvesting. I was lucky and found the key years ago."

Reed's vision was on the backyard, but his mind was on Cob's words. He knew the basics of ranching economics, but had never thought of it the way it was being described.

Cob wasn't finished. "Didn't you tell me a while ago that the government didn't print its own money?"

Reed nodded, "Yes, that's right. The Federal Reserve controls that function. The government borrows from them."

"Reed, isn't that the same as the rancher who won't plant his own crops? He has to go buy feed from someone else? During a drought, feed is everything."

The congressman shook his head and pushed back. "It's not that simple Cob, but I'll play along. The government has tried the other way, too. A long time ago, the government was like the rancher who only planted crops. They printed their own money, and it didn't work. It was too easy, and it got out of control. Anything they wanted to do, they just printed money. Pretty soon, the currency wasn't worth anything."

Cob's gaze focused on Reed, and his voice became monotone. "How much land you have is the key Reed. Some of the land has to be reserved for grazing while the crops grow. Another portion has to be set aside for planting. You can't plant on land you don't control. You can't let your herd graze on your neighbor's place."

Reed realized Cob was trying to tell him something, but it just wasn't registering. "I'm still not getting it, Cob. I'm sorry, but my brain is a little foggy. Let's say for a minute that the government printed its own money. How do you keep politicians from going wild? How do you establish control? It's been tried before, and the results were disastrous."

Cob didn't hesitate. "Our founding fathers believed in checks and balances. The government should set up the exact same system on both the creation of money and how much they spend. Just like the rancher having good years of harvest and bad years for livestock, the government should have the same restrictions on printing and spending. The rancher is limited on both by how much land he has. Land is everything; it imposes its own set of checks and balances."

Reed shook his head, internally dismissing the concept. "Cob, I hear ya, and I can't disagree, but it'll never work. The country is down and almost out. It's not the time to make major changes."

The old gent looked at Reed with clear eyes and a soft voice. "I wonder how many people told FDR the same thing back in the 30s. You and I may not agree with what he did, but he got in front and led the people. Sometimes leadership is all that folks need."

Cob stood and stretched. The children raced to the porch, tired of their game. "Grandpa! Can we ride the horses?"

Cob turned back to Reed, his expression clearly indicating the conversation was over. He leaned close to the little ones' faces and announced, "Sure enough, kids. I'll go saddle up Thunder and Lightning for ya."

Reed leaned back in his chair, his mind cycling Cob's words.

Fort Meade, Maryland
July 1, 2017

Reed's smile was genuine for the first time in weeks. The government was moving back to Washington, and martial law was being rescinded! The news had been announced yesterday at a joint session.

Before the official word, rumors had spread around Fort Meade like wildfire. Excitement filled the hall as rows of folding chairs had been assembled, and all of the elected officials and their staff had gathered together. When the Speaker of the House and President of the Senate delivered the word, the entire building had erupted in unbridled celebration.

As congressmen from both sides of the aisle hugged, shook hands and patted backs, no one bothered to ask what the condition of the country really was. Truth be told, seeing the nation move forward, even by baby steps, was all they could think about right now. The mood was jubilant; the nation was returning to democracy, and the details could wait.

If anyone had bothered to ask, the news would've been mostly positive. America was slowly returning to a country of services, capabilities and in a few isolated areas - conveniences.

Electrical service was re-established incrementally. Some cities and towns delivered power a few hours per day, while others had fulltime service as soon as the lights blinked on the first time.

The internet was only a few days behind. In some locations, digital modems surprised owners, or at least those who were paying attention, with green lights indicating connection. On one street in San Francisco, a wild street party had broken out when it was discovered that the World Wide Web was truly worldwide again. Initially, the net was slow. What few web pages were active took several minutes to load. While it would take months before the majority of internet sites were functional again, it was a major relief for many people just to feel connected in some way to the outside world.

Email was one of the most utilized web applications in those first few days. Millions of families had spent months without any communication with distant relatives or loved ones. Sometimes the news was good – everyone was okay. Often, the inbox bore heartbreaking messages of lost friends and kin. After grieving, most people agreed that the "not knowing" had been the worst of it.

Texting was available before actual cell phone calls or landlines. Those who managed to charge their cell phones were surprised to receive messages before any other type of service registered on most devices.

The first cable television systems broadcasted from New York, Miami, and Boston. No one knew how many customers were receiving the transmissions, but limited news and information was finally flowing to the public.

The agencies of the federal government were the primary sources of radio and television programming, and most people didn't seem to mind. A citizen viewing a broadcast could receive valuable information regarding the current situation both locally and nationally. The daily transmission of "public information" programming addressed topics ranging from where to receive medical care to which companies were requesting employees to report for work.

Church groups, synagogues, and other non-government organizations began to contribute a great deal to the recovery. The problematic role of providing meals and basic medical care changed as things improved. Job fairs, volunteer coordination, day care and other social services were in high demand, with thousands of private organizations stepping up to provide these acute needs.

While petroleum refineries and other critical infrastructure were given the absolute top priority, the American entrepreneurial spirit awakened, and businesses of all types made a go at reopening their doors. Bistros, cafes, and sandwich shops alike asked employees to report as soon as possible, even though they had no idea when food deliveries would begin. Post-collapse clean up in the food service industry was daunting - many eateries had freezers full of spoiled and decaying food to be disposed of. Some restaurants had been looted and needed repair in order to serve paying customers.

For most of the country, the frustration levels were high. It seemed that the supply chain couldn't get itself sorted out fast enough for anyone. Some cities had an abundance of gasoline, but no diesel fuel. The restarting of the American machine sputtered and spurted, but never died. Despite a constant bombardment of obstacles and barriers, no one even considered giving up.

Chapter 13

New York, New York
July 4, 2017

Helen perched at the bar in her kitchen, picking at the government-issued meal consisting of what was supposed to be meatloaf and mashed potatoes. She was reminiscing about the fresh salads once served at the corner deli when a knock at the door startled her. It took her a moment to compose herself because visitors were such a rare occurrence these days. *It's probably nothing,* she thought. *I bet Mrs. Winston wants me to watch the kids again while she takes the trash downstairs.*

Helen brushed non-existent crumbs from her slacks, smoothed the wrinkles from her blouse, and swiped her bangs. She balanced on her tippy toes and peered through the peephole, barely recognizing the uniformed man in the hall.

It's him! Her heart's pace quickened as she scanned the living area in panic, completely unprepared for guests. It suddenly dawned on her that he might leave, and she didn't want that. She called out, "Just a minute!"

Helen didn't know what to do. There was so much wrong, and she didn't know where to start. Her head pivoted, seeing an apartment that was messy, her clothes that were plain, and thinking about her slightly askew appearance. *Oh well,* she thought. *Not a thing I can do about it now.*

She smoothed her hair one last time as she opened the deadbolt and other locks, hoping he wouldn't think her paranoid for taking what she judged as prudent precautions for a single girl in New York. When she pulled the door open, his eyes met hers, and he flashed a ready smile. "Hi. Hope I'm not coming by at a bad time?"

Helen just stood there for a moment, unsure of how to respond. She finally pulled it together and answered. "No...no...please come in. I'm just embarrassed; my place is such a mess."

"Oh, no – I don't want to intrude. I was in the area for a commander's meeting, and we finished early. I thought I would check in on you, and, well, invite you to a movie. It is Independence Day, after all. I thought you might show kindness to a soldier."

"A movie?"

Pat looked down, unsure if her response were due to surprise at being asked out or the fact that there was actually a film playing somewhere. "They show a movie once a week now for officers and their spouses...or dates. I'm not sure what's showing tomorrow, but I thought you might like to get out and do something different."

Two hundred things flooded Helen's mind at once. A myriad of consternations arose, ranging from apprehension over having enough water to bathe, to questioning which of her clothes were clean. In the end, none of that mattered. "I'd love to see a movie, and I don't care which one it is. It's very kind of you to ask."

The young officer seemed pleased at her response. He glanced over her shoulder into the apartment and asked, "Do you need anything? Have enough food and stuff?"

"I'm fine, and thank you for asking. Since the electricity has been on more lately, it's been easier to get around. I've even had air conditioning through the night twice this week!"

He nodded, "Things are slowly getting better. I heard that electricity will be restored to this area full time in two weeks or less. They are even gathering up the NYPD officers so they can take over for the military sometime soon. Before you know it, this city will be back to normal again."

It dawned on Helen that they were still standing in the doorway. Again she offered, "Would you like to come in? My place is a mess, but you're welcome to come in and sit down."

"No, no thank you. I can't stay long. Gotta get back to the unit. What about if I pick you up at 1900 hours tomorrow night?"

Helen's brow wrinkled, not understanding. "What time? I don't under..."

Pat interrupted her, "I'm sorry...I've been doing this for too long. Let me try again. Can I pick you up at 7 tomorrow evening?"

Helen smiled, "You bet. Do I need a formal gown?"

"No," Pat said shaking his head. "Jeans will be just fine. There'll be food as well. I'll have you home by 11."

After a quick goodbye, Pat pivoted and was gone. Helen closed and relocked her door, lost in a torrent of emotions. *Things **really** are looking up*, she thought.

Matagorda Island
July 4, 2017

Sage had been in a funk all day. It was her turn for dishwashing and fire patrol – random luck of the draw that she'd been assigned her two least favorite jobs on the same day. With the way things were going, laundry would be on tomorrow's list.

"I'll post about my crappy day on Faceb..." she started to mumble to herself. The realization social networks no longer existed stopped her cold. *We've been here four months, and I'm still thinking about Facebook?*

As she meandered back toward Boxer, she overheard two of the men talking about it being Independence Day. *Maybe that's why I'm in such a down mood*, she thought.

Sage's mind wandered back to last year's Fourth of July holiday. She had met up with Karen and Teresa for a trip downtown to see the big fireworks display. The trio had run into some boys and shared their blanket at the park, oohing and ahhing at the colorful display.

The trip down memory lane led to concern over her friends. She knew Karen was probably okay – her folks had a country place outside of town. Teresa was a different story. Her folks were divorced, and her mom had to work two jobs just to pay the rent on their little apartment. She wished there was some way to talk to Teresa, just to see how her friend was doing.

Sage stopped walking and absentmindedly gazed at a flock of birds banking in formation. "I wish I had your freedom," she whispered quietly to herself. That statement caused another wave of depression to roll through her mind. Her nineteenth birthday was coming soon. *Who would have thought my life would be over after only 19 years?*

She realized that was the crux of the problem. She had no life. Gone was her hope of becoming a nurse like her mother. Her social activities had vanished into thin air. She couldn't watch a new movie, go to the mall to flirt with the guys, or even chat with her friends on the phone.

The more she thought about it, the more her feelings felt like a heavy weight on her chest. Sage's eyes watered up, thinking about everything that was no more – all that she had lost and could never recover. There was no future here, nothing to look forward to.

Standing alone at the dock with her shoulders slumped, arms hanging loosely from her sides, Sage began to weep. At first, her eyes felt wet, and she had the sniffles. Then her throat felt tight, and her lungs needed breath. When her mind found the memories of the stuffed animals still lying on her bed back at the apartment, her body was racked with sobs.

Sage didn't hear the footsteps behind her. Despite the near hysterical tears, she jumped a little as a strong pair of arms pulled her into a gentle embrace. She knew from the smell and touch that it was her father. She glanced up, realizing some minor comfort from the concerned look on his face.

For a brief moment, embarrassment flashed across her face, but it faded instantly. Her father didn't say anything – he held her tight in a loving embrace and slowly petted the back of her head. Sage let it go. The emotional floodgates opened, and her body shuddered with the release. For several minutes it all poured out, and she felt like a little girl again.

When she was empty, she pulled back from Wyatt and rubbed the tears from her cheek. Wyatt produced a familiar handkerchief – one he had carried for years. That small square of cloth almost made her start again – it had been used to dry her eyes for as long as she could remember. The worn cotton carried a heritage of comforting skinned knees, healing broken hearts, and mending fences with her brother.

"It's alright, baby...it'll all be okay," were her father's first words.

Sage dried her face and cleared her nose, folding the hanky to find a dry spot. "Daddy, I'm sorry...I don't know why I'm so..."

Wyatt pulled her close again, expecting another barrage of tears. Sage controlled it this time, pushing it back down inside. "I just miss my friends…and school…and life."

"Come on baby, let's go for a walk."

Sage nodded, and the two turned to stroll down one of the many paths leading away from Army Hole. After they were out of sight of the dock, Sage gave voice to her fears. "It's just not fair. Everything's been taken away from us. I'm nothing now – just a dishwashing blob that gets up every morning and repeats the same routine…like a zombie."

Wyatt nodded his understanding. "Sage, there are positive things about this life. I know it's difficult to find them sometimes, but they exist."

Sage wasn't buying it. "Name one positive thing."

Wyatt thought for a moment and then smiled. "Okay. Right before we left, you thought you weren't going to be able to come with us to the boat. You had a final coming up, and your boss wanted you to work extra hours. As I recall, your mother said you were very stressed out."

Sage remembered, "Yes, It was pretty hectic that day."

Wyatt stopped walking and faced his daughter. "Now, we don't have those stressors. There are few outside deadlines, no bills to pay and no grades to worry about. You didn't even have to file your taxes this year."

Sage thought about her father's words for a bit. Frowning, she responded, "I understand what you're trying to say, but I had a purpose then – a goal. Most of my problems before were because I was working for something; money, a degree, a relationship - something to make me better."

"Sage, there's plenty here to work for – lots to improve. I'm sorry our old way of life disappeared. I wish I could fix that, but I can't. We have to make the best of what's been handed to us."

The two turned back down the path and continued their journey. The ocean breeze carried the sound of seabirds and the smell of saltwater. The worn path yielded into soft sand, and Sage stopped. Using her father to keep her balance, she pulled off her shoes and continued barefoot.

"The sand feels good between my toes."

Wyatt smiled at his daughter's ability to recover. "Before everything fell apart, if I called you and said we were taking a long vacation at the beach, you would've wanted to go. Even if I told you there wasn't any cell phone or internet connection, you would've still wanted to go. Am I right?"

Sage nodded, "Yes, but I would've known we were coming back at some point in time. I wouldn't be worried about my friends or future. Escapes are great – exiles suck."

Wyatt laughed at his daughter's phrasing. "Yes, I know what you're saying. I feel it too, Sage. I think about people I've known…friends…family…and wonder how they're doing. There's no way to escape it."

"So how do you deal with it? You seem so calm and collected, always in a good mood. How do you and mom…and all the others do that?"

It was Wyatt's turn to stop and ponder before answering. "It's all in here," he said pointing to his temple. "It's all a state of mind. You've met people before who always seem positive. They don't let anything get them down. They always are looking forward and only use the past to count lessons learned. That's what it takes, Sage – that's what all of us are doing."

Sage rolled her father's words over and over in her mind. She knew he was right. "I can't seem to get there, Dad. I can't figure it out. Maybe you're right – maybe I'm too immature to handle this."

"Sage, I don't think you're immature. I think you're 18 years old, very bright, and one of the most rounded people I've ever met. Let me help you. Open your mind just a little bit and give me just a bit of space, and you'll see I'm not completely off base here."

"Okay, father-of-mine," Sage said, "I am officially putting out the welcome mat to my brain. Come on in. I just have to warn you – it's a little confused in here from time to time."

Wyatt laughed again. "First things first, you're 18, and people at that age need to have some fun, blow off some steam. When was the last time you sketched?"

Sage's head tilted back, her eyes searching the sky, having to think about the answer. "Oh my goodness, it's been over a year."

Wyatt continued, "I remember a young lady who had talent. I remember a girl who thought about pursuing a career as a professional artist. Why don't you release all of this isolation and frustration through art? Why not draw or paint or sculpt? I bet you'll find relief – maybe even help some of the others here on the island."

Sage didn't know what to say.

Wyatt continued, "You know those survival shows we used to laugh at on TV? You remember those handsome, muscular, ex-Special Forces guys who went crazy places with camera crews?"

Sage nodded, grinning at the description.

"Well, I don't remember very many of the tricks they taught, but they always repeated the same basic message – 'Survival is often more mental than physical.'" Wyatt pointed at his temple, "Survival is mostly up here. Our brain is our greatest tool. Use your brain, Sage. Use it to survive...no...thrive, regardless of the circumstances."

After briefly mulling her father's words, she balanced on her toes and kissed his cheek. "Thank you. I think I'll give your idea a try."

Plymouth, Ohio
July 7, 2017

There were over 30 soldiers, machinists, and government officials standing in Sugarhill's gravel parking lot. All of their attentions were focused on the

274

firm's small forklift as it struggled to raise a pallet full of freshly machined parts onto the back of a semi-trailer.

Grover turned to Dan and observed, "You'd think none of us had ever seen a shipment of parts before. It's not like these are for the space shuttle."

Dan surveyed the gathered onlookers and nodded his agreement. After a bit, he leaned closer and said, "I think the end-use of these components is more essential than any space exploration right now. If the other projects are as successful as we've been, a lot of people will have electricity soon."

Grover had come to appreciate the civil servant. Dan delivered everything as promised and rolled up his sleeves to do whatever was required. *If we had more like him, we probably wouldn't have gotten into this mess in the first place*, thought Grover.

There were actually three different shipments of parts going to different locations. The army had sent additional escorts while the soldiers onsite were unhooking the huge generators that had been providing the electrical power for the shop.

Dan noticed Grover inspecting the activity. "We're on our way to southern Indiana next. There's a small circuit board manufacturer near Columbus that is going to produce a few thousand replacement parts for us."

Grover nodded, wondering if it required less or more effort for electrical components than machined steel.

Before long, all three trucks were loaded and ready to roll. Grover was proud of his people and wished he could provide some sort of reward or compensation for the crew. They had worked 14-hour shifts for four days to make the deadline for shipment. Grover inspected every single part himself to ensure tolerances were met despite the harried circumstances. The men had produced some of the best quality he'd ever seen.

Much to everyone's surprise, the army major who had been supervising the project asked everyone to stay put. The man climbed aboard the bed of the trailer and proceeded to thank the hard-working people of Plymouth and Sugarhill.

When everyone finished clapping, the officer nodded to a group of soldiers standing nearby. These bystanders began to carry out cases of military meals and setting them on the ground in front of the Sugarhill workers. It was a lot of food – more than any of them had seen in months.

Dan pulled Grover aside, out of sight from the main body. He offered his hand, "Grover, you've been a pleasure to work with, sir. If I get a chance, I'll try to stop by after things get going again. Until then, I have a surprise for you." Grover looked down to see Dan holding out a small paper bag. With a puzzled expression on his face, he opened the bag to find a one-pound can of ground coffee and a box of dog biscuits. The old man showed one of the most genuine smiles Dan had ever seen. "Rusty will love these!"

Washington, D.C.

275

Everyone stood when the president entered the conference room. He moved with purpose to the head of the table, scanning each face in the room as if taking mental roll call, all the while smiling and nodding. "Please, everyone be seated."

The collection of senators, congressmen and cabinet members took a few moments to get settled. In front of each was a clean white note pad, two sharp No. 2 pencils and a glass of water.

The purpose of the meeting was a mystery. Normally when someone called such a high-level powwow, an agenda was provided – or at least a description. This assembly had merely been described as a "matter of national security."

The chief executive wasted no time. "Thank you, everyone for coming. As you all know, we have definitive Intel that China was directly responsible for the recent hardships experienced by our country. Over 55 million of our countrymen died as a result of their actions. I've read some projections that estimate it will take 30 years for our nation to heal the economic wounds inflicted by their actions."

The president paused, scrutinizing the expressions of the men and women before him. Reed detected anger in the man's eyes, a boiling hatred that had been brewing for months. After the visual tour of the room, the commander-in-chief continued. "We, the governing officials of the United States of America, *cannot* let this act of war pass by unaddressed. To do so would endanger our recovery, our future, and place the citizens of our great nation in further jeopardy. To let such an act go unanswered would embolden our enemies, both present and future. It is for this reason that I've asked all of you to come today. It is for this reason that I've called this council of war."

Reed's mind erupted in protest. Had he not been cowed by respect for the man's office, he would have loudly objected to such thinking. *The country wasn't ready yet*, he wanted to shout. *We're barely on our feet, and you want to start a war?*

The chief executive seemed to read his thoughts. "I know many of you are sitting there...thinking I'm 'off the reservation.' I *know* we've just started the healing process. I'm sure Roosevelt's staff felt the same way. The country was just recovering from the Great Depression, and suddenly a war was thrust upon them."

The president paused to let his words sink in. "Our people pulled together then, and I trust they will now. There are some who believe a war drives economic expansion. Many historians opine that America's growth during the 1950s was due to the engine-of-commerce developed to fight World War II. Let me be clear, that is not my motivation. That is not the purpose of this meeting. China has benefited from our suffering. China is stronger now than before they attacked us. I believe it is necessary to right this injustice and using our still-significant military power is the right tool for the job. If we don't, I fear that

China will soon establish itself as a formidable, communist-led superpower in a very short time. The world has already rushed to their doorstep to do business. Our very assailants are filling the economic vacuum left by our decline."

Reed's outrage was dulled by the president's words. He had to admit the man was good – very good.

"Ladies and gentlemen, I don't want war. I have no desire to order thousands of young Americans to their death. We've already lost so very, very many. On the other hand, it is a reasonable possibility that China will continue to interfere with our recovery. They are in an even stronger position now to thwart our efforts from an economic, political and military perspective. Does anyone here really believe they won't press their advantage? Can anyone here honestly look me in the eye and argue that Beijing won't accelerate their efforts to dominate globally?"

No one volunteered to take up for the Chinese or challenge the president's premise.

"So, with that said," the president continued, "I believe we must respond is a measured, calculated way. Everyone at this table has done exemplary work helping our nation recover. All of you have proven to be the core leadership of the recovery. I'm afraid I must add to your workload. With the strictest confidence, a matter of national security, I would like recommendations, suggestions and options for how we respond to China. We will reconvene in three days and begin the formation of a plan. Thank you one and all."

The president stood, smiled around the table, and promptly exited. The room he left behind was forlorn. Reed knew the man was right about China. The congressman guessed similar meetings were being held in Beijing but for the opposite reason. Waiting his turn to exit the room, it dawned on Reed that a part of him really wanted to make the Chinese pay. He wanted revenge. He wanted to see them suffer like his fellow Americans. He wanted to test *their* endurance.

But war? Death, destruction and possible escalation to a nuclear exchange made Reed shudder. This couldn't be the right answer.

As his driver maneuvered through the ever-increasing traffic reappearing on the streets of the nation's capital, Reed focused on the scenes passing by his window. The heaps of debris reminded him of bombed cities; the ever-present lines of haggard, depressed people reminiscent of the refugee camps – foreboding images of humanity normally associated with a war-torn region. The children could have been pictured in late night television commercials asking for donations to assist starving orphans in a distant land. The patriot inside of him wanted revenge. His spirit wanted the people who did this to his neighbors and friends to feel the wrath of unchecked vengeance. Reed took a deep breath and tried to clear his thoughts.

And yet not a shot had been fired, not a single bomb had been dropped. The Chinese had accomplished all of this death and destruction using a new kind of weapon. Reed wondered if the old style tools of war could do as much damage. If the full conventional military might of the US were deployed against China, would the damage be this extensive? Would the number of dead and dying be so high? Even if the destruction were equal, thousands of US service members would perish in the effort. The Chinese had accomplished their victory without a single causality.

Reed's mind continued to play it out. The attack against the United States had cost practically nothing. How much treasure would it cost the US to wage war using the traditional methods? Reed remembered the forecasts of the Second Gulf War's ultimate price tag. Destroying things wasn't cheap.

There had to be a better way. Reed agreed with the premise that China couldn't be allowed to get away with their actions, but a hot war wasn't the answer. The US had to come up with a way to leapfrog this new weapon that had been used. *Maybe the ultimate revenge involves crippling them without firing a shot either.*

After being dropped off, Reed couldn't focus on anything else – he had to find a solution to the problem. The ring of his cell phone caused him to jump. While some limited service had been restored, it was rare to receive a call. It was his wife, which was even more of a pleasant surprise, given her remote location.

"Hello."

"Reed," her voice twinkled, "I can't believe I got through! Dad took the kids and me for a horseback ride up to the ridge, and I had the phone in my saddlebag. It beeped, and all of a sudden I had bars!"

"Oh, honey, it's great to hear your voice. This is such good news. I hope we can talk more often now…" An annoying tone filled Reed's ear, signaling a lost call.

He looked at the phone, tempted to try and call her back, but the display indicated, "No service." Still, it had been good to hear her voice. He could just imagine the look on Cob's face, justified yet again in his dislike of technology. The call made him think of their last conversation on the porch, the old man trying to relate government to ranching.

Wait a minute, thought Reed. "That's it!"

Chapter 14

Matagorda Island
July 8, 2017

Wyatt watched his children from Boxer's swim platform while rinsing the sand from his feet. He had learned the hard way that Morgan didn't appreciate having beach sand tracked through the cabin. Midway through the footbath, animated body language had drawn his attention to the shore where Sage and David were clearly involved in a sibling disturbance. He'd observed such activity for over 15 years and considered himself an expert. *I could make book on the outcome*, he mused.

What was so riveting about this exchange was trying to predict who would come out on top. For years David had carried the league's best winning percentage, the contests often determined by simple physical strength. As the two had grown older, Commissioner Morgan had outlawed physical contact. His son quickly learned that he would no longer be allowed to dominate with pure muscle – mom and dad would throw a penalty flag.

At an early age, Sage surged to become the league leader in flops, fakes and feints. The post-toddler girl quickly realized that the mere accusation of brother-bullying was enough to ensure her victory. The older, larger boy often found the penalty box disquieting.

David, not to be outdone, became a crafty opponent and took advantage of the new rules. His scouting report listed a growing repartee of diversions, misinformation, and frame jobs. Without slow-motion replays, there was no way to tell how many broken vases, kitchen messes, and unkempt toys were actually Sage's fault.

Throughout adolescence these contests raged, each contender improving upon the other's tactics in a never-ending cycle of "one-ups-manship." Mom and dad refereed to make sure no one was seriously hurt. A strict off-season was enforced – lest the two combatants focus more on fighting than being team players for the family franchise. Any consideration of the two eventually loving each other was often in question.

Wyatt smiled as he watched the contest taking place a few dozen yards away. Despite the two being out of earshot, he could have done a remarkably accurate job of portraying who was saying what – what cards were being played, and who was bluffing.

Sage obviously wanted something from her brother. The "ask nicely" approach had failed early, but that had probably been expected. Wyatt watched as the athletes changed tactics, each trying to capture the momentum and coast to final victory. Before long, David was on defense, Sage surging into the lead with a late rally. Wyatt had to grin at the girl's tenacity – whatever she wanted today, she wanted it bad.

With a critical eye worthy of a sports commentator, Wyatt immediately detected the change in David's body language. The clock was running out, and his son had lost momentum. It was a precarious position. Admitting it was too late to salvage a play-off spot; his son resorted to vying for future draft picks. Before long, a deal was struck and the contest decided. The contestants hugged - a half-hearted display of sportsmanship ending the fray.

David headed off toward the ranger station. His head was low, and Wyatt was pretty sure he was giving himself a good talking to. The agony of defeat was always a bitter pill to swallow. Sage, on the other hand, strode with her head high and a slight grin on her lips. Wyatt could picture his daughter running around the stadium waving her celebration to the crowd. As she stepped onto Boxer's deck, Wyatt asked, "Everything all right?"

"Sure is. David's going to be a little late for super – he's on his way to the airfield to get me some planks of old, weathered lumber I picked out. They were too heavy for me to carry back."

"Wood?"

"It was your idea, Dad. I'm going to use the boards as a canvas. I've got some ideas on how to make a combination painting and sculpture out of the planks."

Wyatt now understood the earlier contest. "And what did you have to trade David to get him to act like a beast of burden for your project?"

"Oh, he felt sorry for me. I've got to take his shift doing the dishes on Tuesday."

"That's it?"

"Yup. He's really turning into a nice guy, Dad. I was shocked at how easy it was."

Wyatt was skeptical, but didn't say anything. He figured David had sensed the same restlessness and depression in Sage. David was pretty perceptive most of the time.

"So, Sage, what are you going to paint?"

"I don't know, Dad. I probably won't decide until I get started. Maybe I'll just open up and let everything I feel bleed all over the canvas."

Wyatt winched at her description, the concept of his daughter's blood a negative image. Still, he was glad she was doing something to help herself.

Washington D.C.
July 9, 2017

An informal, secret committee was unofficially formed. The members of the House and Senate who had attended the president's briefing were all included.

Reed hadn't slept all night. He'd run the numbers over and over again, looking for any reason why his idea wouldn't work. There was no hole, nothing he could find.

He'd been in his office on Capitol Hill first thing, surprising the Capitol Police with his pre-dawn entrance. Brenda had been dispatched to the Library of Congress four times. The intermittent web service had received its share of curses, but the two had gotten the job done despite the computer glitches. All of the time spent researching, refining, and verifying assumptions made from memory indicated his plan was sound. He was ready now – ready to go out on a limb and present his solution.

The senior senator from North Carolina cleared his throat and called the meeting to order. The distinguished gentleman from the Tar Heel State skimmed a piece of paper in front of him and announced, "Ladies and Gentleman, Representative Wallace from Texas has passed along a strongly worded request to make a presentation to our esteemed committee. Barring any urgent protest, I see no reason why we shouldn't begin there." After a quick glance around the room, the senator nodded at Reed, "Congressman."

Tempering the combination of nerves and excitement, Reed strode to the podium at the front of the room. Behind him was a large flat panel monitor being driven by a laptop under Brenda's control. His assistant's reassuring smile from the back of the room helped Reed relax. The screen flashed, displaying the first image of what was a hastily prepared slideshow.

Reed began, "Thank you, Senator - I'll be brief. Our meeting with the president two days ago troubled me, as I'm sure it did most of you. I just couldn't get over the feeling that waging a war at this time wasn't in the best interest of our country. While I agree with the president's position that we as a nation can't let this attack go unanswered, I also feel strongly that we aren't ready to trade blows with anyone, let alone a nation of several billion people."

Reed scanned the crowd, reassured to see several people apparently agreed with his reservations. He continued, "I've had one of those eureka moments - a brainstorm born of desperation to save our nation and avoid the deaths of thousands of our military. We have an opportunity before us, ladies and gentlemen – a chance to turn a horrible situation into a positive one. I believe we can rebuild our great republic while at the same time addressing our enemies. I believe we can accomplish both of these prerogatives with a very simple change in our national policy, and without firing a single bullet from an American weapon."

The congressman had their attention now and was ready for the "shock and awe" portion of the presentation.

Brenda manipulated the computer and the image behind Reed changed:

(Editor Note: *Reed's slide presentation can be found in Appendix A*)

The congressman half turned and casually pointed to the glowing monitor behind him. "What you see here is a simple chart showing the sources of the federal government's revenue – or where we collected the money spent in 2016."

Everyone was given a few moments to digest the numbers before Reed continued.

"Imagine how strong our economy would be without any federal taxation. No personal income tax. No corporate income tax or burden on small businesses. The frustration and cost of tax preparation, legal wrangling over the interpretation of our tax code would be eliminated. Trillions of dollars, normally paid in taxes by corporations large and small could be repurposed to invest in our nation. Every working American would receive an instant increase in their take-home pay. Disposable income would soar."

Reed signaled to Brenda for the next slide.

"Not only would our people benefit from such a system, but every corporation in the world would want to do business in the United States of America. Such a tax-free environment would create a drain on the talent, investment and educational resources of every other country on the planet. Corporations, researchers, doctors, scientists, and entrepreneurs would be beating down our door to live and work here...here in the tax-free United States."

Reed pointed to the display behind him and continued. "The amount of US dollars in circulation has been controlled by the Federal Reserve System since the 1920s. I don't want to change that, but I do propose we alter how the new money is distributed and used."

Reed paused to sip from the glass of water on the podium, giving his listeners a chance to digest the introduction to his revolutionary idea. "I propose to substitute our existing income tax revenue from three different sources."

Reed quickly stole a glance around the room to gauge his audience's reaction, realizing he needed to make this idea as understandable and simple as possible.

"For over 80 years, the new money released into our economy has simply been *given* to private banks. The federal government, as we all know, has borrowed and taxed for its income. For years, our leaders have fought pitched political battles over spending versus taxation. Spending has always won out, and the interest on the money we have borrowed is a significant portion of our national debt. This growing debt is also one of the main reasons the Chinese so easily inflicted such punishment on our nation."

Reed paused for a moment, his voice softening. "I propose that the government print its own money and spend it rather than collecting taxes."

The senator from Nevada jumped in at Reed's pause. "Minting money in amounts dictated by politicians always leads to ruin. This has been tried dozens of times, with the same result - disaster. Hitler came to power because of such policy and what it did to the German people. The British almost destroyed the early American economy by dumping counterfeit bills during the Revolutionary War. I could go on and on."

Reed shook his head, "No, Senator. I want to back the money with the land holdings of the United States, as our government owns more than a trillion acres of land. I also believe we need to implement strict controls over how much money we can print – eventually a constitutional amendment."

The senator wasn't done. "So what you are proposing is some hybrid of neo-chartalism and a gold standard. But instead of gold, the currency is backed by dirt?"

Reed nodded, "Yes, I suppose that is as good of a description as any, Senator. There is one more caveat to my proposal. The government can only create the same amount of money as there is real growth in the size of the economy, with a limited amount built in for a controlled inflation. This will avoid the pitfalls experienced with this method in the past."

A murmur spread through the gathered officials. Reed nodded to Brenda who advanced the slides. He raised his voice to bring everyone back to his presentation. "Economic growth isn't enough. Even with an average annual increase of 6% of the GDP, that won't equal the tax revenue we utilized before the collapse. There are two other sources required for my plan to work."

Reed gestured to the monitor behind him. "As all of you know, we have suffered millions of causalities. This fact, combined with a tax-free environment, leads to a serious discussion about immigration. In reality, our projections indicate that we will have to address two separate immigration issues. The first being the same problem that has plagued our nation for years. We've been unable to agree on a compromise between controlling our borders and allowing America to be the melting pot of the free world. A solution has eluded us for a long time. My proposal is simple – allow anyone who wants to come here a quick, efficient access to legal status within the country. For a period of time, collect income taxes from them until they have reached a certain level of contribution and then grant them citizenship."

Again, the room burst into several different conversations at once. Reed held up both hands to calm everyone down. He nodded to the closest man. "Congressman Wallace, you mean to say you want to sell American citizenship? Has our great nation deteriorated to the point where we will sell a passport like a blue-light special at Kmart?"

Reed nodded, "Yes, Senator, that's exactly what I'm saying. Canada has been doing it for years. Several EU countries have similar programs. Some of these nations even have a 'cash up front' policy. My plan would allow each immigrant the chance to prove, over time, that they are capable of pulling their own weight. Once proven, they receive their citizenship and can stop paying taxes."

Looking around the room, Reed realized he was making progress with some members of the committee, while others were extremely skeptical. From the back of the meeting, a voice sounded, raising a concern. "Congressman, I applaud your creativity, but the banking and finance lobby is extremely powerful. They are the engine of our economic train. The banks aren't going to accept this."

Reed stared back at the New York congressman and simply stated, "What banks? As of right now, there isn't a solvent financial institution in the country."

This time, Reed let the sub-conversations ride. His harsh statement was reality, and everyone in the room knew it. After a reasonable time, he again overrode the background noise. "I am, however, glad you raised that question, Congressman. Banks, when running again, need capital to expand. Our previous fractional polices wouldn't have to change."

Reed shook his head no. "Ladies and gentlemen, I have no grudge against banking. I understand the role it has played in the growth of our nation. In a tax-free economy, I believe that industry will have plenty of opportunity to grow and prosper. This is the basis for the third leg of my tax revenue stool."

The Texan paused for a moment, ready to launch the most controversial portion of his plan. He swallowed and inhaled deeply. Brenda held her breath and changed to the next slide.

"All of the methods I've described so far aren't enough to equal what we now collect in taxes. There is one more piece to the puzzle. My plan includes a modest, 1% tax on all debt payments. Regardless of mortgage loan, credit card, or money borrowed to buy a new automobile, I believe it is fair to tax that debt."

The attendees were shaking their heads, some murmuring under their breath. Reed didn't give them a chance to sidetrack the meeting, continuing with the sales pitch as if his dinner that night depended on closing the deal.

"Our system has always been one of progressive taxation – the more wage-earners make, the higher the percentage they pay in taxes. Collecting a small percentage of everyone's debt will continue this tradition. On average, wealthier individuals borrow more money than those with lower earnings. One other important aspect of this tax is to reinforce the importance of personal savings and investment. The one percent I propose should not adversely impact the level of borrowing in our economy."

Congressman Wallace nodded to Brenda, who advanced to the final slide.

"In summary, my plan provides for the same level of income that our nation collected before the collapse. Those monies will come from the growth of our Gross Domestic Product, a fair taxation of immigrants, and interest collected from all private debt. It will become our primary responsibility to improve the standard of living for every American. This motivation will become a natural part of our political system. As we all know, politicians love to spend money on their constituents. The only way we, in Washington, will have more money to spend is if the economy is expanding. No more raising taxes for public or social programs. The failsafe of borrowing money will no longer be an option. The only way we, and future elected officials, can spend more is if the United States is thriving. The enforcement of this budgetary restraint, I believe, should be accomplished via Constitutional Amendment."

Reed stepped closer to the conference table and leaned on its edge with both fists balled tight. His expression changed to one of anger, and his voice became low and serious. Gone was the salesman. Absent was the politician. He spoke as an angry man, "The best part of this proposal, my esteemed colleagues – the aspect that is the most important to me personally, well, it has nothing to do with economics or money. What moves me *personally* is the impact to the Chinese if our nation adopts this plan. They attacked us using electronic trickery. They manipulated the weakness of our debt and financial position of our government. This plan will crush their communist system, which cannot survive without taxation. They cannot continue to grow without siphoning off of the top of their people. They will not be able to compete with us, and their engine of commerce will crumble."

Reed looked around the room, trying to judge the acceptance of his proposal. He exhaled when the Speaker of the House broke his silence for the first time since the meeting had begun. "Mr. Wallace, would you be so kind as to bring up that slide showing sources of revenue again? I would like to ask a few questions about your numbers."

Internally, Reed flushed with joy. The Speaker wouldn't have bothered if he didn't see his plan as having possibilities. The Texas Congressman knew his little slide show was only the beginning – merely a seed planted. A lot of work would be required for the concept to survive and bear fruit.

The meeting lasted four hours longer than scheduled, Reed's presentation being the only topic of a long agenda that received any attention. Finally, fatigue began to set in, and several members made it known enough was enough.

As the members made for the door, several congratulated Reed on his initiative and creativity. The Speaker and President of the Senate lingered to the last. "Reed," began the top man in the senate, "you've done well, young man. I want to warn you that this will take a while if it is to become the law of the land. There will be a seemingly endless parade of experts, economists, professors, lobbyists and others who will demand their voices be heard. Don't become discouraged. The Speaker and I have already agreed that we need to put this on the fast track. The time is right; the solution is right. We will contact the president in the morning. At minimum, you've put his war on hold for a while."

Matagorda Island, Texas
July 30, 2017

"Morgan, have you seen Sage?"

"I think she's up at her studio giving Laura Owens a painting lesson."

Wyatt scratched his head at the term "studio." He had been vaguely aware of Sage's renewed interest in painting, but had been so occupied with chores he hadn't had the time to follow her progress.

"Do you know if she has my toolbox up at the *studio*?"

A voice full of playful frustration sounded from the cabin, "Now how would I know where your toolbox is? I'm worried about you, Wyatt. You're getting to the age where the symptoms of Alzheimer's begin to show. You can't find your daughter, and now you've lost your toolbox."

Wyatt snorted at the retort – his wife was obviously busy with something and sending the message of "You're on your own."

Grumbling over having failed in his parental duties of teaching children to put things back where they found them, Wyatt began the trek to Sage's studio.

With the intent of scolding Sage for taking his tools and not returning them, Wyatt strode toward the runways where he knew she had found a shady spot to sit and paint. He cut off the path and quickly found the small strand of trees where she had been hanging out lately.

Approaching the spot, Wyatt stopped mid-stride, absolutely stunned at what he saw. There, mounted onto the trunks of several trees, was a virtual art gallery of scrap lumber that had been painted and carved. Sage was standing in front of three lawn chairs, demonstrating some technique to three of Crusoe's citizens, their rapt attention focused on her instruction.

It wasn't Professor Sage that captured Wyatt's eye – it was the artwork. Several boards of grey, weathered lumber were adorned with some of the most detailed painting he'd ever seen. The wood had been carved and then adorned with a mosaic pattern of embedded seashells, shiny rocks and other raw materials from the island. Beautiful brush strokes complemented the works, with colors of homemade pigment that accented the style.

His missing tools forgotten, Wyatt ventured closer to his daughter's work and examined it with his mouth hanging open.

"Hi, Daddy."

Wyatt snapped out of his daze, "Hi, baby. Sage, this is unbelievable work. I don't think I've ever seen anything like it."

Sage blushed and looked down. "Really? You really like it?"

"Oh, Sage, this is…well…this is just enthralling to look at."

The students agreed, comments like, "I couldn't believe it the first time I saw what she was doing," and "I was so very impressed, I just had to know how it was done."

Wyatt slowly walked around looking at each example. He could tell his daughter had refined her methods as she progressed. Feeling everyone's eyes on his back, Wyatt realized he was interrupting the class and turned to apologize. "I'm sorry to barge in like this. I'll come back later."

After hugging Sage, Wyatt was halfway back to the boat before remembering his tools. *Maybe Morgan is right – maybe I should be worried about Alzheimer's,* he thought.

Matagorda Island, Texas
August 4, 2017

Wyatt climbed the ladder to Boxer's bridge carrying a plate of fried oysters, complete with a side of kelp salad. He had been hoping a postcard-worthy sunset would perk up the bland meal, but cleaning the filters on the water maker had taken longer than anticipated.

He glanced down at the plate of food, and for what must have been the hundredth time wished for a bottle of Tabasco sauce to go with his meal. A little oil and vinegar would've helped the kelp approach the threshold of having taste.

Stop it, he chided himself. *You have food, and there are probably millions of people out there right now who will kill for this meal.*

Munching the first bite of oyster, Wyatt glanced to the west and stopped mid-chew. He stared for a full second, not believing his eyes. There, off in the distance was a red blinking light – the kind used to warn aircraft of a high tower.

Almost choking on the food in his mouth, Wyatt finished his bite without his eyes ever leaving the flashing red strobe. He was sure it hadn't been there before. He was positive he would've noticed it. Afraid to look away, fearing the signal would disappear, Wyatt called out for David.

It was a few moments before his son joined him on the bridge. "What's up, Dad?"

"Son, tell me if you see anything unusual in the western sky."

David's scan was brief before he zeroed in on the flashing light. "Well, I'll be. How long has that been there?"

"Morgan!"

It took his wife just a little longer to arrive. As she climbed to the bridge, she noted the distraction of both men. "What are you two staring at?"

Neither answered, and in a moment the response became unnecessary. "Wyatt, if that means what I think it means, I would say that's about the prettiest light I've ever seen."

David spoke up, "I'd have to agree with you there, mom. I don't think I've seen anything that pretty in a very long time."

Wyatt finally broke his trance, "Amen to that."

Sage's voice sounded from the cabin below, "Hey, what's everyone doing up there?"

David replied, "C'mere, sis – this will make your heart sing."

Sage grunted as her head appeared at the top of the ladder. Soon, there were four sets of eyes staring at the solitary, blinking, red light.

Washington D.C.
August 4, 2017

Reed adjusted his tie one last time. He chuckled at his fussiness but then excused himself – after all, it wasn't every day a freshman representative was invited to stand behind the president of the United States as the chief executive signed landmark legislation into law. Rarer still was the fact that Reed was personally receiving credit as one of the authors of the new tax code.

It hadn't been easy. After his presentation recommending a tax-free America, the secret committee hadn't remained secret much longer. News of Reed's concept had spread faster than the fires that had plagued US cities just a few months before.

As the word spread, every special interest group and political organization in the country prepared for war. While eliminating the entire tax code caused concern, collecting money from banks and immigrants resulted in outright panic. The ensuing political battle reached epic proportions. Endless meetings with lobbyists were conducted. A seemingly infinite parade of experts, economists, professors and businessmen gave thousands of hours of testimony. Arguments raged while party affiliates attempted to influence virtually every aspect of the process. Countless hours of speeches were orated on the House and Senate floors, some speakers delivering into the wee hours of the morning.

Reed checked the shine on his shoes, realizing all of the hoopla seemed so frivolous now. At first, he had embraced the friction as the necessary process of a democracy creating new law. Initially, he had consoled himself that all of the bickering and in-fighting was necessary and wise. As time wore on, his attitude began to change.

His proposal was so radical most of Washington didn't know quite how to react. The concept was so politically neutral, the power base was unsure of how to respond. Since it wasn't from the left, it was assumed to somehow benefit the right. Since it wasn't from the right, the left believed there had to be a hidden advantage for the other side. As time wore on, it dawned on both the right and the left that his plan would eliminate most of what the two sides had been fighting over for decades. Having nothing to disagree about was initially deemed unacceptable by the establishment.

At one point he had given up, resigned to the fact that the two parties were fighting over the potential of having nothing to fight over. Reed couldn't believe his fellow elected officials thought so little of their service to the people. He couldn't comprehend anyone would find value in the deadlock that had plagued the US government for years.

It was the president who understood Washington better than anyone. When it all started spiraling out of control, Reed judged the commander-in-chief disinterested and unsupportive. The chief executive came across like a parent watching young children settle a dispute. Short of anyone being injured, he was going to let the kids battle it out, keeping himself above the fray.

Reflecting back, Representative Wallace now understood the president's methods. With impeccable timing, the executive branch swooped in and played a powerful political card – patriotism. Like an ace topping a royal flush in poker, the White House used national pride to win the hand. It had been well done.

Once the two parties were in sync, it was all over for the outside influences. Labor, banking, finance, insurance, military contractors and even the NRA had all tried to waggle their pet projects into the new law. Their efforts were wasted. When it was finally through committee, the new tax code of the United States of America was 11 pages long. Over half of its rhetoric addressed the taxes to be paid by those seeking US citizenship.

Other bills were required, and those were making their way through the obstacle course as well. Immigration, Treasury, the role of the Federal Reserve Board and the Security and Exchange Commission were all going to play different roles in the future.

For today, Reed pushed all of that aside. Today, the new tax code would be signed into law. It had passed with unanimous votes in both the House and Senate.

Reed slipped on his jacket and headed for the door. *I wonder if the president will give me one of the pens he uses to sign the new legislation.*

Matagorda Island, Texas
August 15, 2017

Word of the tower light spread quickly around Crusoe. Over the next few evenings, Wyatt noticed a tendency for the colonists to glance in that direction occasionally as if to reassure themselves that it was still there. Despite the positive sign of civilization, the distant beacon initially raised more questions than it provided answers. Had order been restored? Was the country coming back online?

Radio waves eventually answered most of the questions. The first non-Crusoe voices were picked up on the handheld units carried around the island. An excited neighbor rushed to Boxer, the woman holding her radio in the air like a torch. "Wyatt! Wyatt! I hear people talking, and it's not any of us!"

As they offered a longer reach, bridge-mounted units were flipped on, eager ears tilted toward the speakers. Sure enough, distant ship-based traffic was detected on a few frequencies.

Less than a week later, AM radio started broadcasting. Static frustrated the boaters at first, as they could only make out small blurts of information. Stations transmitting FM signals came online two days later.

The news that martial law had been lifted initiated an impromptu beach party complete with loud music, grilled fish and limbo contest. A follow-on report detailing the limited restoration of electrical power resulted in more smiles than Wyatt had seen in months. Still, there were lots and lots of questions. Was there food? Gas? Water?

Some of the boaters wanted to head back immediately, others unsure if it were safe to return. The news reports seemed to center on the larger cities. How far into the suburbs had the recovery spread? Another issue that dominated the conversation was fuel. A few of the larger diesel boats had enough left to make it back to Southland, while none of the gas boats did. Should they consolidate passengers? Shuttle? Carpool?

The residents of Crusoe decided to commission a scout. Sage owned the newest model cell phone, kept fully charged so she could listen to music. Despite questioning looks from Morgan, Wyatt would always remember the day Sage and David motored off on one of the jet-skis, her phone in a waterproof plastic bag.

Two hours later they returned, smiling broadly. They had picked up cell service strong enough to make phone calls at the north end of Matagorda Bay. The cell company actually had 411 service working. Someone answered at Southland and verified that indeed, water and electrical service was restored. "The city still recommends you boil the water before drinking it, but it's flowing," was the response.

Food was evidently still in short supply, as was fuel. Sage tried to call two different marine fuel piers, and neither had answered. Still, it was clear that progress was being made back in the world.

Debate flowed on when to leave the island. The group finally decided that everyone would stay together until it was known that fuel was available. They had left as a community, survived as a community, and would return the same.

Three days later, Todd came back from a seaweed-gathering trip with news that he had encountered another boat on Matagorda Bay. The fisherman claimed a fuel pier in a nearby costal town had just received electrical power, and its tanks hadn't been looted. They would even accept credit cards.

One of the gas-powered boats was dispatched and returned with enough go-juice to make it home. The owners were rationing the valuable commodity. One by one, the boats untied from the giant raft that made up Crusoe and voyaged to the nearby burg for fuel.

~  ~

"Are we ready?"

David's voice was filled with excitement as he stood on the dock, holding Boxer's last line, ready to cast off. Wyatt scanned from one end of the island to the other, partially making sure his path was clear, partly solidifying the memory of what had been their home.

"Let's go," he shouted back.

Boxer backed away from her mooring as Wyatt was joined by the entire family on the bridge. The mood was an odd mix of apprehension and excitement.

Morgan leaned over and kissed the captain for good luck.

As the flotilla exited the Matagorda Ship Channel into the open waters of the gulf, Wyatt wondered if they had left too early. As the fleet moved north toward the Galveston Jetties, he relaxed somewhat as more and more radio traffic came through Boxer's speakers.

When they came within radar range of the Galveston Ship Channel, the first thing Wyatt noticed was the lack of the huge cargo ships they had encountered on the trip down. The Estes Marie and several others had evidently made it to port.

Entering Galveston Bay proper cheered everyone up. The busy intersection of the Bolivar Roads had traffic – two large freighters steaming south from the Port of Houston.

The joy pulsing through the group diminished somewhat as they passed Redfish Island, the memory of two deaths occupying everyone's mind. Wyatt looked over at David, doubting his son would ever want to visit the place again. He wouldn't blame either of his children for the sentiment.

Entering the Clearlake Channel that late afternoon showed the flotilla just how much things had improved. Workers swarmed the restaurants with brooms, hammers and a buzz of recovery. The Vietnamese shrimpers actually waved, and there were no armed guards.

There was no sign of the ghost boat they had towed out of the channel. Gone were the refugees from the channel's shoreline.

It was another positive sign when Morgan nudged him and pointed out two pleasure boats cruising the north side of the lake. Many more were sighted before they reached the entrance to Southland.

As the returning boats entered Southland one at a time, a sense of melancholy crept in. At least three vessels had sunk, probably from damage caused by looters. Every boat they had left behind had been ravished in some way. Broken glass, life preservers, rope and other non-edible contents were scattered all over the piers.

Boxer's slip was clear and Wyatt spun the big vessel perfectly, backing her into the tight space. David and Sage wasted no time in tying her off and then stood, mesmerized by the mess strewn around the marina.

Wyatt shut down Boxer's engines and remained seated at the helm. With his hands resting in his lap, Morgan watched as her husband began weeping. Her first thought was that something was wrong. Placing her hands on his shoulders, she asked, "Wyatt, what's wrong? Are you okay?"

Taking a deep breath, her husband looked up with watery, red eyes and smiled. "We made it, baby. We did it. We're back home."

Chapter 15

New York, New York
September 9, 2017

Helen and Pat walked in stride, enjoying the coolness of the early fall day. While the leaves weren't turning just yet, the air carried a warning that winter wasn't so distant.

Helen's heart felt like it was spring. She normally dreaded the snow and wind, but not today. Part of her high spirit was because of Pat. Over the last few months, she had developed such strong feelings for the man. Her first clue was how badly she missed him when they weren't together. Later, she began counting down the hours to when they had a chance to go on what he called, "pseudo dates." Before long, she found herself wondering what he was doing while they were apart.

A few weeks ago, he had uttered the magic words. The date had ended early, Pat needing to report for duty before the sun would rise. After a gentle kiss, he had stayed close to her and whispered, "Helen, I love you." Since then, she had become an anxious, clock-watching school girl – time moving at a painfully slow pace between their rendezvous.

She wasn't sure what it was about Pat that made her feel so warm and safe. Anyone who could maintain such a positive attitude while the world was falling apart had to be a good person. He not only treated her well, but everyone else around him received equal grace. Even the other soldiers who followed his orders seemed to like and respect the man.

Having a relationship that was going the right direction would've been enough to warm Helen's soul, but there was more to it than that. The world was going in the right direction as well. Everywhere she looked, there were signs that New York was coming back. It was as if the calendar was completely backwards. Spring was preparing to bloom in the city – not the grey of winter.

Electricity was now on all of the time. *Such a simple thing*, she thought. The first of a long list of amenities that she had taken for granted her entire life. Yesterday, trucks from Florida had arrived with crates of oranges and apples. It was the first fresh fruit she had tasted in months. The flavor was unbelievable. The water was now safe to drink and flowed every time she engaged a faucet. At first, everyone had been warned to boil the liquid coming out of the tap, but Brenda hadn't cared. To take a hot, bubbly bath had been paradise.

Today, they noticed workers posting a sign on a subway entrance. Pat stopped their progress and both of them just stared for several minutes. The sign was big news – the subway would start limited service in two days.

Private cars still weren't allowed. It would take several weeks before traffic signals would be functioning again. Taxis were becoming more common. The city's leaders had decided to gradually allow more and more of the iconic yellow transports to enter service.

Everywhere there were signs of a thawing city trying to regain its feet. Delis were offering limited menus, and the big department stores were decorated with banners promising to reopen soon.

People scurried along the sidewalks with briefcases and computer bags again, their body language indicating work was waiting for them. Helen's firm hadn't reopened yet. She was volunteering for the FEMA relocation services - four hours per day.

A policeman directing traffic at a busy intersection drew the pair's attention. More and more law enforcement were replacing the soldiers who once controlled the streets. Yet another sign of normalcy returning to Gotham City.

That's the only bad part, she thought. *Patrick isn't going to be here much longer.*

As the couple headed toward Helen's apartment, they passed a movie theater displaying a large banner which advertised a "Grand Re-Opening," complete with a free movie next Tuesday. The smaller print warned that management was doing everything in its power to obtain popcorn, but no promises.

"Helen," the lieutenant began, "I have something I need to talk to you about." He paused, gazing at her with the most serious eyes, taking both of her hands into his.

Oh no, she thought. *Here it comes. I've been dreading this – he's going to tell me his unit is leaving.*

"What's the matter, Pat?"

"Helen, my unit is going to be pulling out soon. We're being reassigned to Syracuse."

Her eyes moved to his chest. She worried if he could feel her hands trembling as he held them. Sighing, she finally managed to swallow the lump in her throat so that she could once again talk. "Oh no, Patrick. I knew this was coming, but I was hoping it would be a bit longer. Do you know exactly when yet?"

The solider shook his head, "No, we don't know the exact date, but it will be soon." He paused and looked around, "Do you know what this place is?"

Helen didn't want to be distracted. Unsure of where he was going with the question, she glanced over her shoulder and then back into his eyes. "Yes, this is where all of those people were killed."

Pat squeezed her hands. "You're right, but there was something else more important about this place. This is where I first met you. I think I knew right then."

She didn't understand what he meant, "Knew what, Patrick?"

"I think I knew I loved you the first time we talked. I know it sounds silly, but it's really true."

He reached into his pocket, pulling something out. She hardly noticed the motion, still trying to cope with the thought of being without him. And that is when it happened. He took a knee right there on the sidewalk and opened a small box containing a plain gold band.

"Will you marry me, Helen?"

Kemah Bay, Texas
September 30, 2017

The fresh Texas sun dawned on a most unusual sight. Breaching the entrance to Rose and Charlie's neighborhood was a convoy of men and machines that could easily have been mistaken for either a military maneuver or an alien invasion.

Alerted by the hum of the engines, survivors peered around their curtains or through their blinds. Outside, the procession began with two police cars, complete with blue flashing lights. Immediately behind the law enforcement escort was an entourage of human-shaped figures donned in bright white, full-bodied latex suits. The creatures were crowned with shield-like masks and black hoses that flowed to large breathing tanks strapped on their backs.

Following the platoon of masked men was a parade of vehicles that included delivery vans, fire trucks and ambulances. Two military Humvees brought up the rear of the motorcade.

In reality, the apparent intruders from outer space were medical personnel and other volunteers, shielded with hazardous material suits. The grim purpose of their visit required protection from exposure to all sorts of dangerous elements. Bacteria and viruses weren't the only threats. The armed escort provided by the police was deemed necessary after numerous incidents had occurred. As thousands of such units spread throughout the nation, some residents hadn't welcomed the intrusion. Reports of bullets, arrows and other projectiles welcoming the crews had spread quickly, so an armed presence was added to the columns.

As the procession entered the neighborhood, the men in white began spreading out and knocking on doors. Rarely did they receive any response - in which case portable drills were used to overcome door locks. Announcements were made before entering the private homes. Most times, the odor from inside served as an accurate predictor of the outcome. Now and then, living occupants were found, often too weak to answer.

Two of the men entered Rose and Charlie's bungalow. After receiving no response, they began searching the house, eventually locating the decomposed bodies of Rose and her two children. "This one's a clean one," said one to the other. The second nodded his understanding of the phrase...a weapon hadn't been the cause of death, and no animals had gained access to the bodies.

Plastic body bags were fetched from one of the delivery vans while a search of the house was conducted. Pictures were removed from frames and any identification found in the residence was included in a thin file of documentation. Black, permanent ink markers scribbled the same serial number on bags of the victims' personal effects and bags of the victims themselves.

It was all over in 15 minutes. The remains were gently stacked in one truck while the file was stored in another, joining a grim collection that numbered in the hundreds. As the crew left Charlie and Rose's home, a streak of bright orange spray paint was used to mark the door. One of the searchers turned to another and asked, "Have you heard if they are going to build any sort of monuments over the gravesites? I've heard rumors it will be like the Vietnam Wall in Washington."

"No, I haven't," was the cold response. The guy asking the question shrugged, accustomed to moody co-workers. This was depressing work.

Over the next few weeks, thousands of similar convoys performed their gruesome tasks all over the United States. Some homes were found completely empty and put on a list to be rechecked later. Survivors were discovered in others, often rushed to the now-functioning hospitals by the trailing ambulances.

Eventually, either the government or a bank would take possession of empty properties. Already, mayors and councilmen were thinking of incentives to repopulate their cities. Inexpensive housing might be a popular benefit.

Homes weren't the only structures searched. Every office building, farm, store and school could be sheltering displaced or desperate people. One shopping mall was found to be occupied by over 100 people. Warehouses, especially those filled with foodstuffs, had become home to entire settlements. Shanty towns had sprung up along remote interstate exits, populated by stranded motorists with no place to go.

The final task for the government team was the restoration of electrical power. After Rose and Charlie's neighborhood had been searched, the utility crews checked gas lines, transformers, water mains and wiring. With the fire department standing by, the suburbs began the transition from darkness to light.

Washington, D.C.
November 20, 2017

Reed wasn't greeted with Brenda's usual smile. Normally, the girl was way too cheery, but the look on her face indicated something was wrong.

"Congressman, there's an FBI agent, along with another man, in your office. They were, ummm, rather insistent."

Reed's expression relayed the puzzlement he felt. "Thanks, Brenda."

As he entered his office, the two men stood and introduced themselves. "Congressman, I'm Federal Agent Dayton, and this is Chief Investigator Myers from the Federal Reserve. We're sorry to drop in unexpectedly like this, but something has come to light that we felt you deserved to know."

Reed nodded and moved behind his desk. After taking a seat, he responded, "No problem, gentlemen. What can I do for you?"

Investigator Myers took the lead. "Congressman, this morning at 6:00 a.m., a convicted murderer was put to death via lethal injection in Huntsville, Texas. His name was Roger James Swan. Have you ever heard of him?"

Reed shook his head, "No, sir, can't say that I have."

The man from the Fed continued, "I spent most of the night with Mr. Swan. He is an ex-employee of the Federal Reserve, and actually worked for a short period in my section. I guess Mr. Swan decided not to share his retirement with his wife and murdered her."

Reed couldn't connect the dots. "I'm sorry Mr. Myers, but I can't see what this has to do with me?"

The FBI agent took over. "Congressman, Roger Swan confessed to murdering your father, along with four other people. He wasn't caught until the demise of his spouse, but we have strong evidence to believe his confession was factual."

Reed sat straight up in his chair, the FBI agent's statement resurfacing the memory of Mr. Agile's meeting from what seemed like a lifetime ago. "Evidence, Agent Dayton? What evidence?"

It was Myer's turn, "Last night, while he was having his last meal, Mr. Swan told me where to find your father's wallet. I called the Dallas police, and they found it exactly where Swan said it would be."

Reed was stunned. Mr. Agile had been so convincing...so sure. Reed's follow-up had made it even more certain. Now this? Without thinking, the representative stood and wandered to his window. After a moment, he turned and asked, "Why? Did he say why?"

Myers nodded. "Swan said he had been working on a scheme to sneak insider information out of the Fed and sell it. He said your father caught on to the plan. Swan claimed to have almost blown the whole caper because he entered the wrong date in a computer system of some sort. We're still looking into that, but the wallet was pretty specific proof."

Reed agreed. "Gentlemen, I'm at a loss for words. I have believed for some time now that my father was murdered by someone within the Fed, and I wondered if there were some conspiracy or cover up there."

The FBI agent's voice softened. "Mr. Wallace, we know you've been checking into the Fed for some time. Not very many people file a Freedom of Information request like you did. We kept an eye on your activities for a short time. You never did anything illegal, so the surveillance was dropped long ago. The reason why the FBI is involved now is to provide a measure of confidence. I want to give you my personal pledge that this matter will be followed up on properly. I believe you and your family need this entire situation laid to rest and without doubt."

Reed nodded his agreement.

After shaking hands with both men and seeing them to the door, Reed replayed the meeting in his head. He decided to accept the two men's position. He had to let the conspiracy theory go. He took solace in the fact that Mr. Agile was right; his father's death was not a simple robbery. But more importantly, his father had died for a purpose beyond simple robbery – protecting the US from some ne'er-do-well.

Reed sat at his desk for a few moments, letting it all sink in. As his mind reconciled everything that had happened, he finally came to the conclusion it was all for a purpose. This year, his family would have the most meaningful Thanksgiving holiday ever.

That resolution cheered him up, and he called out to Brenda. "Hey, I hear that Red's Café is open for business again. Want to get some lunch? I'm buying."

Beijing, China
January 13, 2018

Minister Hong's chauffeur was using the car's horn like a panic button. "Stop," the minister commanded from the back seat. "See what they want."

"Yes, sir."

The driver opened the door and briskly approached the cluster of soldiers blocking their path. After examining the driver's identification papers, a choppy conversation began. From the back seat, Hong watched closely, fascinated with the lack of reaction displayed by the soldiers after they realized who was in the car. Something was seriously wrong if his chauffer's credentials didn't invoke more of a response.

A few moments later, the driver returned to his seat behind the wheel. Without looking back, he reported. "Sir, the soldiers are stubborn. They claim to have direct orders from their commanding officer threatening their execution if anyone is allowed to pass this checkpoint. They did, however, inform me of an alternative route that is clear."

Hong nodded. "That is acceptable, driver. Proceed along the alternative. This is why we always leave early when important appointments are involved." After a brief pause, he added, "There is no doubt a serious traffic accident ahead."

The minister was lying about the accident. He knew exactly what the problem was but saw no reason to fuel his chauffeur's already considerable level of nervousness. After a few maneuvers, they were on their way again.

Hong watched the streets of Beijing through the heavily tinted windows of the large sedan. As they passed hundreds of people riding bicycles and walking along the road, he detected a difference in the citizens' demeanor. Heads were slightly bowed, and eyes avoided contact. People walked at a slower pace, and fewer citizens carried parcels or bags.

Dismissing the observation almost as soon as it registered, MOSS' minister refocused his attention out the front windshield. *Yes,* he thought, *the economy is a little more difficult as of late. This is nothing the Chinese people haven't survived before.*

As they approached Tiananmen Square, Hong experienced a mental flashback to 1989. Today, just like so long ago, Red Army tanks blocked the intersection and smoke filled the air. Hundreds of policemen with riot shields and helmets lined the streets. But today, the broad expanse of Tiananmen was devoid of even a single soul. The minister craned his neck and could see a sizable crowd only a few blocks distant. Rows of soldiers blocked the throng's access to the square – desperately trying to deny the protesters the street. Hong knew why the military had drawn the line far from the square. The crowds would no doubt be emboldened if they reached the now legendary location.

The driver had to turn several times before reaching their destination. Hong decided he would make a positive remark on the man's service record for negotiating the treacherous route without comment or panic.

Arriving at the Zhongnanhai complex late, Hong had to step at an impolite, hurried pace in order to make the scheduled start of the council meeting. After the security guard outside the conference room opened the door, Hong entered the room and momentarily froze. Instead of the anticipated six members of the council, only the president and the Minister of Finance were present at the table. Along the opposite wall, two men he didn't know stood with their hands behind their backs.

"Greetings, Minister Hong," stated the president, his tone unusually cool. "I'm delighted to see you have arrived promptly as usual."

Hong ignored the criticism and moved to take his normal seat. The president held up his hand to stop his progress. "That won't be necessary, Minister."

"Sir?"

Reaching for the single sheet of paper resting on the table in front of him, the president looked up at Hong with eyes that reminded him of a snake ready to strike and consume a rodent. The cold, hard, emotionless state of the president's gaze sent a chill down Hong's spine. Something was wrong – badly wrong.

"Minister Hong," the president began, "As I'm sure you are well aware, our people are suffering badly. The momentum is gone from our economic growth. Millions find themselves unemployed. Our collected tax revenues are at a ten-year low. Relationships we have nurtured, both political and economic, have disappeared."

The president paused, but only for a moment.

"Social unrest, labor strikes, and general bedlam have broken out all over the country. You, no doubt, witnessed evidence of these facts on your way here."

Hong, unsure of where this was all going, simply nodded his agreement.

China's leader continued, "A polarization of the international community has occurred, resulting in an alignment against China. The Golden Mountain project, initiated by *your* ministry and managed by *you* personally, has resulted in economic hostilities against our country on an unprecedented scale. To make matters worse, the people are widely aware of why their jobs have disappeared. The general population knows why such hard times have befallen the Middle Kingdom. They demand justice."

The president pushed the single piece of paper across the table at Hong. With hesitation, he picked it up and began reading. Before he had finished, he looked up and hissed, "This is a confession! You expect me to take all of the blame for what has transpired?"

The president pretended to be busy with other papers. Without looking up, he simply stated, "Sign the confession, Minister."

Hong slammed the paper down on the table. "I will not sign such a lie! What treachery is this? Both of you approved this operation, and it succeeded. My plan disabled the single biggest threat to our future. The actions of my ministry brought America to its knees. It isn't my problem that the rest of our government couldn't take advantage of the situation. Why am I to be dishonored when I've done nothing but succeed?"

The president continued to work on the stack of papers in front of him. He didn't acknowledge Hong's words in any way. "Sign the confession, Minister."

Hong's head snapped from the president to the Minister of Finance and back. Now, understanding how the game was going to be played, he made an instant decision not to participate. He turned toward the door, reaching for the handle.

One of the men standing along the wall calmly brought his hand from behind his back. In his grasp was a brightly colored handgun that appeared to be made of plastic. Before Hong's hand could turn the door knob, the stranger pulled the trigger.

A two-pronged projectile exited the pistol-device trailing two wires. The man was an excellent marksman, and his aim was square in Minister Hong's back. The sharp, pointed edge of the projectile penetrated Hong's clothing and embedded itself in his skin. Almost instantly, 15,000 volts of electrical energy flowed through the wire and into the minister's body.

Unlike the US version of the Taser, which is designed to disable the target's nervous system, the Chinese weapon was built to disable with pain. Using a lower voltage and higher amperage achieved the desired effect.

Hong felt as though his entire body was on fire. Every nerve ending seemed to be burning, even his bones. The shock of the pain caused his field of vision to momentarily flash white and then completely black. Within a second, the muscle control of his legs gave out, and he fell to the floor with an audible thump.

The president waited a few seconds before glancing down at Hong. China's leader turned to the two strangers and nodded, prompting them to quickly set the barely conscious minister in his chair.

Hong's upper body swirled, barely staying upright in the high-backed seat. The president said, "Sign the confession, Minister."

Despite the pain and lack of muscle control, Hong managed a single motion from his head - no. His eyes focused on the president, and his mouth moved to say the word, but no sound came out.

The president looked up at the strangers and nodded.

The second man produced his own version of the plastic pistol, this one a different color and of a slightly different shape. Without hesitation, he smoothly pointed the weapon at Hong and pulled the trigger.

Another metal pitchfork flew at the minister, this time striking him in the arm. Before his brain could acknowledge the sting, 8,000 volts raced down the leads and entered his already weakened body.

This time the current lasted longer than before. Hong's mouth opened wide, and his eyes rolled to the back of his head while his entire body bounced up and down in the chair. After two seconds, the electricity ceased its attack, and Hong fell forward, his forehead banging into the table. A small whiff of smoke rose from the cloth of his shirt, and the smell of urine filled the room.

It took almost a minute before Hong showed any sign of life. The four other men in the room detected an unusual, high pitched sound that they soon recognized as Hong's weeping. For the fourth time, the president said, "Sign the confession, Minister."

Hong managed to lean back in the chair, his complexion ash white and skin covered in sweat. The head of MOSS seemed to be having trouble focusing his eyes, but the intent of his head's motion was clear. "No."

The president sat back in his chair and sighed. "Hong, I've known you for a long time. You should place your trust in my words. These two men have dozens of reloads for their little electric toys. They've not progressed to the stage where permanent brain and heart damage occur - yet. You and I, we both know you are going to sign that paper. Why not do so now and avoid all of this unpleasantness?"

Hong managed to turn his head toward the strangers. Without any facial expression, one of the men took a single step toward the conference table and sat a handful of orange and red tubes on the mahogany surface. He then broke open the pistol-device and reloaded the weapon. His ice cold, emotionless gaze settled back on Hong.

The president calmly said, "Hong?"

The Minister of MOSS nodded at the paper. The president placed a pen in Hong's shaky hand.

AP Press Release –Tokyo, Japan 08:00 GMT January, 18, 2017

The Chinese Central News Agency today reported that the minister of China's super-secretive Ministry of State Security had been arrested on charges of treason, embezzlement and sedition.

According to Chinese news reports, the powerful member of the ruling council is directly to blame for recent cyber-attacks on the United States.

A spokesman for the president is quoted as saying, "Minister Hong has been arrested and is awaiting trial. The Chinese government is conducting a full investigation into the matter. The evidence uncovered so far indicates unauthorized, covert actions were taken against the US, but to date all indications are that the results were negligible and have been greatly exaggerated by Washington."

Another source within the Chinese Ministry of Information added, "The United States is using China through the unlawful actions of this one man as a scapegoat. China is and will always be a nation of law. The president condemns these acts and promises to take measures to ensure no such event occurs in the future."

Anonymous sources inside of the State Department expressed skepticism that the Chinese cyber-attack was the result of a single man's actions.

Shanghai, China
March 9, 2018

Huang Fu rose from behind his desk and verified his office door was locked. *Now would be an unfortunate time for an interruption*, he thought. Moving to a wooden bookshelf in the corner of the spacious office, he removed a specific volume and carried it back to his desk. He glanced again at the door, fighting an urge to check the locks again. He chided himself for the thought and whispered under his breath, "You are a small fish and unworthy of attention. Quit acting like a man cheating on his lover and get on with it."

Huang opened the book. Inside the hardbound cover, several pages had been neatly carved out, resulting in a small rectangular storage compartment. Lying flush within the paper-container was a thumb drive that could be plugged into the computer residing on his desk. He had imitated the clandestine storage method after seeing an old western spy movie some years ago. It made him feel stealthy and calmed his nerves - somewhat.

Mr. Fu's shaking hands fumbled with the small object, having to make two attempts to remove it from its paper hiding place. Throwing one more nervous look at the door, he inserted the drive into the computer and began typing in the three levels of password security required to access the data.

His computer monitor changed to display a neatly organized spreadsheet containing rows and columns of numbers. He had named the file "Future," because that's what was stored inside – his future.

Fu Machine and Tool had been in business for 17 years. Mr. Fu had started the firm in a small shack-like structure on the outskirts of Shanghai after graduating from university. A second-hand drill press and small lathe were the first equipment, purchased with a government grant from a British-owned facility in Hong Kong.

Huang still had those original machines, now sitting clean and freshly painted in the lobby of his 11,000 square meter factory. Practically museum pieces when initially acquired, those two simple devices had been the beginning of a new chapter in his life. He would miss walking by them every morning on his way to the office.

While he waited for the numbers to update on his screen, Huang thought about what would happen if his actions were discovered by the authorities. Technically, what he was doing was illegal in so many ways, yet by the strict code of the law, building Fu Machine and Tool had been a violation as well. It was all so confusing.

His primary education was strictly communist. The state owned all industry, and the people worked to contribute to the common good of everyone. By the time he entered secondary school, the lines became blurred. When China regained control of Hong Kong in 1997, everything started changing rapidly.

At first the authorities had looked the other way when a few, daring, young entrepreneurs had started cottage businesses to supplement their income. Inspired by their cousins to the south, the tsunami of privatization rolling north from the former British colony had been unstoppable.

Huang shook his head thinking about those early days. The apprehension he felt over his secret data store was nothing compared to what those early adaptors had endured. He still marveled at the change he had witnessed during his lifetime.

Mr. Fu understood timing was important in all matters of life, and his business timing had been perfect. His endeavor had ridden a wave of new freedoms fueled by economic growth and his country's determination to play a role on the global stage. At first, other Chinese firms had been his customers. Machining simple bicycle parts had led to more complex work for the military. His quality and timely delivery resulted in additional orders – large orders.

A trade fair in Shanghai was the first time he'd met an American. The odd man fit several of the stereotypes he had heard about westerners, but was also different in many ways. The American wanted to place an order for tractor parts. A lot of tractor parts.

The permits, paperwork and general bureaucracy had been a struggle, but he waded through, determined to grow his business. In four months, Mr. Fu received an export license and never looked back.

In two years, America was his biggest customer. After four years, he exported more than what he sold domestically. After ten years, he didn't even bother with domestic orders. The profit margin realized by selling goods to other Chinese firms just wasn't worth it.

FM&T grew to over 200 employees in just 10 years, reaching a peak of 380 just a year ago. The Fu family remained humble with their newfound wealth. Their flat was more expansive than many, but not enough to flaunt their success. Fu registered on the list to acquire an automobile just like millions of other citizens. He waited months before his name came to the top of the list, only then to be offered a substandard product. Mr. Fu graciously accepted delivery of the unreliable, featureless automobile even though he could easily afford to purchase the most expensive German model and have it imported.

Over time, the frustration with the vacillating direction of the government began to set in. He was part of a growing upper class of successful individuals who were responsible with improving the lives of their fellow citizens, yet he couldn't relax and enjoy the fruits of his labor. The communist leadership was always a dark cloud looming on the horizon. No one could predict how strong the storm would be...how much wind, lightening and rain it would generate. Some thought it would simply blow over without harm. Others hunkered down and waited for intense destruction. The Communist Party was always the shadowy figure looming in the background - a stifling presence at best; a deadly threat at worst.

The new upper class of China began to network. They initially banded together in a brotherhood of growth, always communicating under the premise of trying to improve the lives of their employees – and the communist system. Over time, it became a complete façade. The deep undercurrent of their cult-like activity became prosperity. Emails, social networks and face-to-face meetings may have appeared innocent enough to any authority peering in, but in truth there was an embedded secret code that could only be deciphered by those who had tasted success.

Huang orbited around the core of this new society. He wasn't a brave man – definitely not a political risk-taker. His primary motivation was to build things and expand the lifestyle of his family. He had no interest in political or social change. Over the years, he justified the eavesdropping and fringe involvement as a means to grow his company. Any inquiry by the authorities could be answered with the plausible justification of making new contacts to increase business and help the people. In many ways, it was truthful. All of that gradually changed as FM&T continued to grow.

There had been a few watershed events leading to his ultimate corruption. His first trip to Europe had been one of the early experiences. A wide-eyed, young factory owner, the five-day trade expo in Belgium had exposed Huang to the power and capabilities of the West. His first trip to America had almost blown his mind. He realized that his fellow business owners were telling more truth than the government. The West was already where his countrymen wanted to be, in fact, the evil democracies were light years ahead. If capitalism and free enterprise were so terrible, why had these forms of government enabled such advancement? This question troubled him, leading into the deep analysis necessary to reconcile his empirical evidence of the success of western culture and the evil image communism gave it. Mr. Fu was uncomfortable with the results of that examination. He didn't know what to do – couldn't come up with any plan. The internal struggle was pushed deep below the surface of his psyche and hidden in the innermost compartments of his being. That was the only thing more secure in his life than the data appearing on his screen.

Eight months ago, everything had been flipped upside down. His biggest customer, America, had collapsed in just a few days. His accounts receivable, almost 100% owed from US customers, was wiped out in less than a week. The newscasts made it clear that he had little hope of ever getting paid.

Then the Americans pointed their military toward China. Like most other citizens of the Red Nation, patriotism and pride had overridden any business concerns. That initial swell of nationalism soon dissipated, however. The Americans never attacked, and business dried up.

Mr. Fu removed the thumb drive and inserted it back into its hiding place. After returning the book to the shelf, he leaned back in his chair and recalled those troubled days.

The strongest image in his mental playback was of the hundreds of employees at FMT, standing around with nothing to do. Each day they would clock in, greeting each other as they streamed into the plant. There were no orders, nothing to be made. Any maintenance, cleaning or other make-work had been completed days ago. The plant was as spotless as it had ever been. Having nothing to do, the workers had simply reported to their assigned work area and waited, silently watching the clock. The supervisors and low-level managers had joined them in the ghost-like ritual.

After a few days of this inactivity, Huang started sending people home. No orders meant no work and no pay. That was just how a business worked...or so he thought. The following day, an official from the Ministry of Commence arrived to speak with Huang. Why had he sent his workers home? Why weren't they going to receive any wages?

"There are no orders, sir. My customers were in America and have stopped purchasing from us." Huang had replied.

The government representative glared at Huang like he was from Mars. "I do not understand, Mr. Fu. Why don't you just make what you make for someone else?"

"Who?"

"Well, I'm not sure. How did you find the American customers?"

"It took years to develop those customers, sir. I can't just magically make new ones appear."

"This is of no consequence. You will not be allowed to terminate your employees. This is a violation. I suggest you begin replacing your customers as soon as possible. In the meantime, your workers are to return to the job, and they will be paid."

Huang had held his tongue, wanting to lambast the idiot. In his most polite tone he asked, "Sir, where will I get the money to pay my employees? Our firm doesn't have those types of deposits on hand. We will run out of cash within days."

The official had dismissed the business owner, clearly frustrated with the conversation. "That is not my problem, Mr. Fu. Find a way, or my next visit will be more serious."

Huang had secured a loan from the Central Bank having to put his state-of-the-art machine tools up as collateral. He had been tempted at one point to use his personal finances to keep the business open, but even his considerable wealth wouldn't pay 350 people for an extended period of time.

What followed was a whirlwind series of trips to India, Japan, South Korea and Australia. For an entire month, Huang had traveled the globe looking for new customers, but none were found. The downfall of America and the overhanging threat of nuclear war had practically crushed every potential market. Most countries were focused on keeping their own labor force working, not importing goods from China.

Despite all of his hard work, very few orders trickled in to FMT. Those that came in were low profit, modest projects - insulting to the advanced capabilities of his operation. Eventually he was granted permission to gradually reduce his labor force. It was his banker who spoke to the Ministry of Commerce and provided an out.

Three months ago, the Americans finally attacked, but not with bullets or bombs. Business completely withered, and the fledgling foreign customers he had been nurturing simply vanished. It was an Australian shipbuilder who broke the bad news. "I'm sorry, Mr. Fu, but I've received quotes from an American facility that are 20% lower than your proposal."

At first Huang had thought the man was simply being racist - giving other white men an unfair advantage. Then his network of colleagues began reporting similar competition from America. Huang found out that that without having to pay taxes, the US firms could undercut practically anyone. America was back, and with no taxation, the world was rushing to her doorstep.

Following the pack wasn't always a bad thing, he mused. Many times, people joined what was better or provided a superior solution for all the right reasons. He had to admit, doing business without government interference or the looming threat of being imprisoned at any time was appealing. Not having to give the wasteful bureaucracy its annual stipend of his income was even a stronger draw.

Huang had begun the clandestine process of relocation. The first challenge had been to get his money out of China without drawing attention to the effort. His personal wealth had always been diversified into several different assets, gold being one of them. His reserves of bullion had been shipped to Japan a few days ago, hidden inside of a fake order of parts and now residing in a bonded warehouse.

Gradually, slowly, he had shifted his investments. Several visits to the American Express office in Shanghai had resulted in a handful of pre-paid debit cards – each worth almost $100,000 in US dollars. Banks in Canada, New Zealand, and Panama had all received large deposits - the transfer of funds being disguised as payment for raw material or spare parts purchases.

Two days ago, his wife and children flew to Japan to attend a trade show. He would meet them there tomorrow and never return to China. A new home in Houston had already been purchased. It was five kilometers from the new plant where crews were already installing the latest machining technology available. There was even the promise of a proper automobile.

FMT was going to be resurrected, this time in the United States. Huang believed his experience, drive and skill could rebuild his company. He also believed the US was the best place to do so.

Mr. Fu sighed and reached for his computer's keyboard for the last time. He queued a program purchased over the internet a few weeks ago - the new software promising to erase and scramble the machine's memory beyond recovery.

His finger hovered over the key for only a moment. He pressed the button and barely glanced at the screen as the destruction of a lifetime of achievement was initiated.

Three minutes later, he strolled by the display of his original machine tools in the lobby. Mr. Fu stopped and touched each one and said his goodbyes. He wished he could take them with him, but that simply wasn't possible.

Ten minutes later, Mr. Fu was in the back of a taxi headed for the international airport.

Forty minutes later, the wheels thumped the bottom of the Japan Airlines 767 aircraft after takeoff. The flight was only two hours and ten minutes. His family was going to meet him at the Tokyo airport. After waving off the steward's offer of a drink, Huang reclined the first class seat as far as it would go. For the first time in weeks, he fell into a proper sleep.

Southland Marina, Texas
July 20, 2018

Wyatt stepped out of Boxer's head, brushing the front of his jacket and fussing with his hair. Looking up at Morgan, he asked, "Well, how do I look?"

Morgan finished her sip of coffee and flashed him a bright smile. "I'd hire you, but then again, I'm a little partial."

Her husband wasn't convinced. "Are you sure? I mean, you don't think the tie is too old fashioned or anything, do ya?"

Morgan set her cup on the counter and walked to him, pulling on the jacket sleeves and giving him a serious once over. "The jacket looks great on you, babe. You've lost a little weight and look fit and tan. I think you'll do fine."

Wyatt shook his head, not so sure. "It's been so long since I've had an interview. I feel like a college kid going for my first one."

"You'll do fine," she replied, and then decided to distract him. "Tell me about this company again? Fu Machine and what?"

"Machine and Tool. They are a high-tech machine shop from what I read."

"I've never heard of the company before. Do you know how big they are?"

"No, I get the impression they're new here in the states. The owner, Mr. Fu, seemed uncomfortable with English. I should settle down – there are dozens of jobs on the internet sites. I even read one article that predicted a labor shortage for the next three years."

Morgan nodded her agreement. "The hospital is hiring like crazy as well. It's kind of sad in a way – how many people perished. There are over 200 photographs on our wall now."

Wyatt sighed, "I wonder how long we'll morn. The grocery store still has hundreds of posters on their bulletin board. It's so sad – all those people looking for lost relatives or family members. We're lucky."

"It's about time we had some luck Wyatt, but I know what you mean. Our memorial wall at the hospital is depressing if you look at it that way. It's also a reminder to everyone to never let that happen again. I just wish we had been able to learn our lesson without all those people having to die."

Morgan's cell phone began ringing, causing her to pause. She looked at the caller-id and mouthed the word "Sage" to Wyatt. She tapped the screen and said, "Morning sweeties, how are ya?"

Wyatt paused for a bit, fatherly instinct wanting to verify Sage was all right. After listening for a few moments, Morgan broke out in a huge smile and said, "Oh, Sage, that's fantastic news!"

Wyatt caught his wife's eye and mouthed the word, "What?"

After listening for a few more moments, Morgan covered the mouthpiece and said, "The Houston Museum of Modern Art is going to display Sage's art work from the island. She just got the call."

"Wow, that's outstanding news! Tell her I love her, and I'm proud of her. Also, let her know I want the first tickets!"

Wyatt glanced at his watch and knew it was time to go. He didn't want to be late and needed plenty of time to find the place. A lot of traffic signals weren't working yet, so it was prudent to leave a little early.

Morgan said, "Hold on," into the phone and kissed Wyatt goodbye. "You'll knock 'em dead, babe. Best of luck."

The End

Epilogue

AP Press Release – Washington, D.C. – U.S.A. 08:00 December 1, 2019
The US Bureau of Labor Statistics today announced weekly claims for unemployment reached the lowest level since the bureau began tracking the bellwether indicator over 100 years ago.
Only 12,700 people filed new claims for unemployment benefits, dropping the nation's overall unemployment rate to 0.3%.
Most analysts credit the unprecedented growth of the United States economy for the historic low number of people looking for work, citing the 11.4% expansion in 2018 and the anticipated 12.4% growth in 2019.
Economists predict a slight cooling of the US economy in 2020 as more and more nations mimic the US policy of zero taxation, thus negating the competitive advantage currently enjoyed by American firms.
In related news, the US trade surplus grew to 1.3 trillion dollars in November. Experts believe resurgence in manufacturing in North America will continue to fuel the trade surplus for another 18-24 months until the remaining industrialized nations catch up with the boom in US output.

Appendix

Reed's slides used in the presentation (Chapter 14).

SOURCES OF REVENUE

LAST ACTUAL YEAR

2016 Federal Revenue	$ (in Billions)
Income Taxes	1,165
Social Security	837
Fines/Other	138
Excise Taxes	78
Corporate Taxes	196
Total	2,414

SOURCES OF REVENUE (Expansion)

5 %   Average increase in Gross Domestic Product (last 50 years) with 1.7% inflation factor

$16 Trillion   Size of the U.S. Economy in 2016

———————

$800 Billion   Amount usable as revenue with controlled inflation

SOURCES OF REVENUE (Immigration Tax)

20 million   Total number of documented non-U.S. workers

$40,000   Average Income

———————

$161 Billion   Income Taxes Collected at 2013 rates

SOURCES OF REVENUE (Interest Taxes)

40 trillion Total amount of U.S. private debt

1% Proposed Tax Rate on Interest

$400 Billion Taxes Collected on U.S. debt

SOURCES OF REVENUE

LAST ACTUAL YEAR

2016 Federal Revenue	$ (in Billions)
Income Taxes	1,165
Social Security	837
Fines/Other	138
Excise Taxes	78
Corporate Taxes	196
Total	2,414

PROPOSED

2018 Federal Revenue	$ (in Billions)
Expansion	800
Social Security	837
Fines/Other	138
Excise Taxes	78
Interest Taxes	400
Immigration Tax	161
Total	2,414

Made in the USA
San Bernardino, CA
28 July 2013